MAN-KZIN
WARS
IX

THE MAN-KZIN WARS SERIES
Created by Larry Niven

MAN-KZIN WARS IX

CREATED BY
LARRY NIVEN

BAEN

MAN-KZIN WARS IX

This is a work of fiction. All the characters and events portrayed in this book are fictional, and any resemblance to real people or incidents is purely coincidental.

A Baen Books Original

Baen Publishing Enterprises
P.O. Box 1403
Riverdale, NY 10471
www.baen.com

ISBN: 0-671-31838-1

Cover art by Stephen Hickman

First printing, January 2002

Library of Congress Cataloging-in-Publication Data

Niven, Larry.
    Man-Kzin wars IX / created by Larry Niven.
        p. cm.
    ISBN 0-671-31838-1
    1. Life on other planets—Fiction. 2. Space warefare—Fiction. 3. Animals—Fiction. I. Title: Man-Kzin wars 9. II. Man-Kzin wars Nine.

PS3564.I9 M36 2002
813'.54—dc21   2001043635

Distributed by Simon & Schuster
1230 Avenue of the Americas
New York, NY 10020

Production by Windhaven Press, Auburn, NH
Printed in the United States of America

10 9 8 7 6 5 4 3 2 1

CONTENTS

MAN-KZIN
WARS
IX

PELE

Poul Anderson

1

Close to noon, the Father Sun baked pungencies out of turf and turned the forest that walled the northern horizon into a wind-whispery surf of leaves and shadow. Closer by, a field of *hsakh* stood golden. Kdatlyno slaves were hand-cultivating it in the ancient way, growing fiber that would be handwoven into cloaks for the mighty to wear at Midwinter Bloodfeast and then burn. Scattered elsewhere were the dwellings of the Heroes attendant upon this household. Though stately enough, they were dwarfed by the manor looming ahead of Ghrul-Captain.

These lands were a minor holding of Grand Lord Narr-Souwa's and the building was fairly new, in a modern style. Mosaic of red-and-black thunderbolt pattern decorated walls that sheered up to steep roofs of copper kept blindingly polished, whose beam ends gaped in the forms of carnivores. Tradition had made the lower windows mere gun slits, but those on upper floors were arrogantly broad. Saw-toothed spires at the four cardinal points flew ancestral banners.

As was fitting, Ghrul-Captain had come afoot, unaccompanied, from a landing field now out of sight. But he loped like a warrior to battle and passed the gate with head high. A display of fearlessness also behooved him, showing him not unworthy to enter the presence of the one who waited here.

His hopes heightened when he received due courtesy in return. A pair of armed Heroes met him, gave greeting, and escorted him down a granite corridor to an elevator, and thence to a flamewood door that recognized them and slid aside. There they left him. Ghrul-Captain stepped through. The door silently slid shut at his back.

The chamber was austere, paneled with various metals, its floor turf-like and sound-absorbent. Two open windows let in daylight and summer air. He glimpsed a hookbeak at hover outside. Furnishings were scant, mostly a minimum of communications equipment. He was alone with Narr-Souwa.

That Grand Lord half-reclined on a couch, like a slashtooth at its ease between hunts. He bore no weapons other than his teeth and claws. His only ornament was a scarf loosely draped across a frame whose black-striped orange fur was getting grizzled, but the scarf was of genuine silk, somehow brought from Earth itself. His eyes smoldered yellow, undimmed by the years.

Ghrul-Captain did not simply come to attention and salute, as he would before an ordinary superior. First he lowered his head and knees, tail between thighs. That galled him. It was meant to, he knew. He should think of it as a test. The sword blade, bent, will spring back to keen-edged straightness and ring as it does, if the steel be true.

"Ghrul-Captain of the Navy begs leave to present himself." The request sounded flat in his ears.

Narr-Souwa peered at him for a while that grew long.

"You may relax," he answered at last. "This interview is at your plea. Justify yourself."

Ghrul-Captain had rehearsed in his mind. "As my lord knows, I advanced my *proposal*"—he laid a measured weight on that word—"through proper channels. I never looked for response at this exalted level, and still less the glory of a flesh-meeting." Which might, he thought, be the prelude to a death sentence. If so, may I be turned loose in yonder forest for him and his hunters to chase down as they would any other brave, dangerous animal. Maybe I can take one or two to the Darkness with me.

"I want to get the actual scent of you and the sense of how your blood runs," explained Narr-Souwa. "Yours is an unusual suggestion . . . especially from a member of your house."

I have nothing to gain, much to lose, by self-abasement, Ghrul-Captain knew. "Noble One, my wish is to redeem the honor of that house."

Narr-Souwa stroked his chin. "Honor has been satisfied. High Admiral Ress-Chiuu made a decision and issued orders that proved disastrous. It cost us a warship's whole complement. Worse, it let that ship fall into the hands of the humans. Their naval intelligence has surely been dissecting it ever since. When condemned, Ress-Chiuu went boldly into the Patriarchal Arena and acquitted himself well against the beasts. It was good sport."

Ghrul-Captain drew breath. "So their spokesmales have graciously informed his kin. But, sire—my lord will understand that we want to make full redemption."

Narr-Souwa's eyes narrowed a bit. "And thus regain his holdings, as well as the prestige," he said shrewdly. "The database has told me that you would inherit his estate in the Hrungn Valley."

For an instant the memory and the yearning stabbed

Ghrul-Captain, lands broad beneath the Mooncatcher Mountains, castle raised in olden days when kzin fought kzin hand-to-hand, graves of his forebears, a wilderness to rove in freedom. He curbed himself. "My lord is wise. But I wish yet more to win back the trust, the favor, that raises to leadership."

He had kept the title to his half-name, but been relieved of command over the *Venomous Fang* that had been his. Small she was, but swift, agile, deadly. Ahhai, the beautiful guns and missiles, the standing among his peers and over his crew, the tautness of close maneuver, and space, space, the stars for a hunting ground! "More than life do I want to take a real part in the next war," and gain repute, a whole name, the right to breed.

Narr-Souwa folded his ears a bit, unfolded them again and murmured, "So you expect a second war with the humans?"

"Doesn't everyone, sire?"

Contempt spat. "*They* hope otherwise. Most of them."

Ghrul-Captain deemed it best to wait.

The Grand Lord sighed. "We need time to make ready, time. The more so after that major setback at the ancient red sun. This later affair at the black hole was less catastrophic, but—it has doubtless changed the minds of still more monkeys about us. Certainly they now have important data on our Raptor-class ships."

"With deepest respect, sire," Ghrul-Captain ventured, "I submit that we should not let them gather information we do not even possess."

"Hr-r-r, yes. That expedition they are planning, to the young sun and its doomed planet. Well, but what intelligence we have on it inclines me to believe it will be what they claim, *purely scientific*." Perforce Narr-Souwa spoke that phrase in the closest rough, snarling approximation to English the kzin voice could manage, for nothing quite like it existed in any language of his race.

Here was a moment to show initiative and thoughtfulness. "Monkey curiosity, sire. I took this into account. They are—no, not so much flighty as . . . playful. The most playful breed in known space. The oldest of them are like kittens."

"Kittens that never grow up to realism or dignity. Vermin of the universe . . . But how does this little new game of theirs concern us?"

"Sire, I tried to make that clear in my petition. They suppose they may learn something they do not yet know. What that might be, they do not know either. It may well prove of no practical value. Nevertheless, my lord, those monkeys have a way of turning anything into a weapon if they feel the need. Anything."

And thus they beat back our invasion, Ghrul-Captain recalled, and were the first to acquire the hyperdrive, and stuffed what they snivel is peace down our throats. He nearly gagged.

"Granted." Narr-Souwa's eyes seemed to kindle. His whiskers lifted, his voice dropped to a purr. "Do you imply the Supreme Councillors have not studied the enemy's history?"

"Of course not, Grand Lord," Ghrul-Captain protested. "Never!" Boldness was advisable, within bounds. "Still, sire, they have much to think upon, many spoor to trace. I merely offer them an idea."

Narr-Souwa mildened and nodded. "That we should dispatch an expedition of our own there to observe what happens."

Ghrul-Captain knew better than to reply, "Yes, sire," as though expressing agreement with a near-equal.

"It is not a bad thought," Narr-Souwa went on, quite softly. "No, not at all bad in itself. And—I have personally reviewed your record—you are in fact well qualified to lead such a faring. You have had experience with technical teams. In two situations that could have become troublesome you exercised sound judgment. Such restraint does not come easily. Well do I know."

Rapture flowed into Ghrul-Captain, that a great one would speak personally and at such length to him, *him.* "May I always hunt well and bring home a pleasing quarry, sire!"

The tone went businesslike. "Perhaps you do not quite grasp the difficulties. Time is short until the event. Likewise are our resources for space operations."

Encouraged, Ghrul-Captain said, "The lord will remember that my proposal goes somewhat into specifics."

"To the extent of your knowledge when you composed it. Hr-r, the details can quickly be settled—and must be, if we are to act. There is also another matter, to which we must reluctantly accord importance."

"Will my lord enlighten me?" If he does, blazed through Ghrul-Captain, I'm in!

"We shall not spare a warcraft for a mission as dubious of profit as this," Narr-Souwa said methodically. "Besides, that would be a mistake in any event. As I indicated earlier, because of the incidents I mentioned, those humans who credit us with hostile intent have gained a certain advantage over those who wish it were not so and"—sardonically—"to borrow a monkey saying I have heard, let the wish become the father to the thought. We would be unwise to make any fresh overt move that could strengthen those who call themselves the advocates of preparedness. To send a combat vessel to a star they have announced they will be visiting and will have a presence at for a long time to come—that would probably be such a move."

"Sire, I have admitted that the Council would likely

order economy of means. Indeed, I respectfully advised it," bearing in mind the needs of a navy, still rebuilding after its shattering defeat, which must meanwhile keep control over the remaining kzin empire.

"We can assign a transport, no more." Yes, clearly Narr-Souwa had pulled in all available information and tracked out all its implications beforehand. "It will carry what auxiliary vessels may be needed, but nothing adequate for a serious engagement. This being the case, our psychologically best gambit is to let the humans know that we do intend to send such a scientific group. Do you seize my meaning?"

"Yes, sire. An earnest of peacefulness, of desire to cooperate— Aargh!" Ghrul-Captain could not hold the growl back.

Narr-Souwa took it understandingly. "Beware of otherwise natural emotions," he warned. "Quite possibly, once they hear from us, the monkeys will provide their ship with an armed escort. That crystallizes the necessity of quiescence. Think of a male, spear-hunting slashtooth, who must withdraw and bide his time if a whole pride of them comes down the trail. Later he will find one alone."

Ghrul-Captain gulped. "My lord speaks wisdom. I will not forget."

"I trust not. Your record gives reason to expect you can hold yourself and your crew on a tight leash. It will be a test of your fitness for a new and higher command."

Ghrul-Captain quivered. "Yes, lord, but—but we won't only make our observations from afar, like the monkeys. We'll try—discreetly, yes, of course, lord—try to learn what they do discover and what they infer. I think we can beat them at their own game too, and show them what Heroes are."

"Do not take risks merely for the sake of that."

"No, lord, certainly not." It might be harder to curb his personnel than himself, but Ghrul-Captain felt confident. "However, as my proposal notes, we have a special craft available to us, the prototype of *Sun Defier*. My lord doubtless knows that that was the tug designed and built for Werlith-Commandant's mission to the ancient star, able to operate closer to it while keeping the crew alive than any other vessel in known space. It was lost in the debacle, but the engineering works has kept the preliminary model that tested the concept. This is much smaller, of course, less powerful, but unique. The humans have nothing like it. They prefer to orbit afar, send in robotic probes, and not hazard their own precious pelts. Lord, a live pilot might well observe and experience things that it would not occur to a stupid robot to try for. We may win a prize the monkeys never realize existed."

"Yes-s, that will be good, if feasible. You must decide on the spot." Narr-Souwa paused. "Return with whatever accomplishments are yours and give them to our judgment. Then we shall see what further you have proven yourself worthy of. We shall see."

2

"This has changed everything," said Peter Nordbo.
"Yah. Obviously," answered Robert Saxtorph. "Damn. *God* damn."

He had jumped from his chair on hearing the news. Now he sat back down, heavily in spite of the light gravity. For a moment his gaze went from the man behind the desk, outward, as if in search of help.

He found no more than beauty. The main office of Saxtorph & Nordbo lay near the top of a building which, although on the edge of town, rose tall. One window held sight of the roofs, towers, steeples, and traffic of Munchen. The other gave on green countryside, scattered homes and groves, a distant range of hills blue against a blue sky. Alpha Centauri A spilled morning radiance across it. B was not yet visible and, currently close to maximum separation, would shine only as the brightest of the stars. A flight of rosewings passed across a snowy cloud. Kind of like wild geese, he thought vaguely, but sunrise-colored. Not that I've ever seen wild geese, except on a screen. Yes, Wunderland's still a lovely world, as alive as Earth used to be before people screwed her up.

"It would not have been a particularly profitable charter for us," said Nordbo.

Saxtorph's burly frame swung around to confront the gray-bearded face. "No," he admitted harshly, "but Dorcas and me, how we lusted to go! What a bodacious spectacle! And the publicity would've been worth more than the money," to the single privately owned hyperdrive craft in known space, competing with the lines of half a dozen governments.

"That has become worse than worthless."

"How?"

"I've had time to think this over, you know." Saxtorph and his crew had been en route from Jinx with a load of organics cheaper to grow there and haul here than to synthesize. Centaurian industry hadn't fully recovered from the long kzin occupation. Maybe—his mind wandered again for a second—it never would, but concentrate instead on whole new kinds of enterprise. Which ought to leave room for *Rover* to ply her trade.

But he didn't want her always to be just a tramp freighter. She'd been more. He'd left with his head full of the wonderful discovery the astronomers had made, the fact that an expedition to go for a close look was being organized as fast as possible, and the near-promise that his ship would carry it. She'd proven she could survive pretty terrible surprises, she'd have no other commitments, and Nordbo was closing the deal. It helped that the headquarters of the Interworld Space Commission was handy, right in this same system; he'd gotten on friendly terms with key bureaucrats.

If only the engineers had miniaturized hyperwave transmitters enough that a ship could hold one, Saxtorph thought, not for the first time. Then: What'd have been the use? I'd've gotten the bad news sooner, that's all.

"*In der Tat,*" Nordbo went on, briefly reverting to Wunderland's chief language, "I saw at once that the ISC would forbid you to go, and forestalled them by offering to cancel the contract myself. It was the responsible thing to do, anyway."

"Are you sure?" Saxtorph challenged almost involuntarily.

"Yes. You will be too, once you've swallowed your disappointment." Nordbo sighed. "Robert, we agreed when I became your partner, *Rover* will steer clear of any volume of space where there's a significant chance of your encountering kzinti. You destroyed their base at the ancient star and uncovered the secret that they now have the hyperdrive. You killed a naval crew of theirs at the black hole—"

"Self-defense," Saxtorph snapped. "Both times, it was them or us, and we didn't start the fracas. The second time, it was Tyra also."

"You needn't tell me."

Saxtorph's massive shoulders slumped a bit. "Sorry. I got carried away. . . . Yah. Aside from the few of them amongst us, probably every kzin alive would cheerfully die to collect my scalp." He straightened. "But, hey, do they have to know it's *Rover*? Change the ID code, disguise the body lines, give her a new paint job."

Nordbo smiled wryly. "Forever the optimist, aren't you? No, much too risky. We'd certainly lose our insurance."

"Uh-huh," Saxtorph must agree. "Seeing as how they'd be in a tiny danger of having to pay up."

"The danger would not be tiny, and it would be to you and yours, Robert."

Dorcas, Saxtorph thought. Her, and everything we've shared all these years, and the kids we still hope to have someday. Not to mention Kam, Carita, and Buck. And any passengers.

"The kzinti say their expedition will be strictly scientific, like ours, employing simply a transport and a few auxiliaries," Nordbo continued. "But everybody knows that will be a naval transport with at least some armament. If they learned *Rover* had come, as they might very well— No, it would be too much to expect of kzinti, not to attack."

Saxtorph surrendered. "Okay. Okay. You've gotten through this thick skull of mine. You're right." He rallied his spirit. "What'll we do instead?"

Nordbo smiled afresh, warmly. "The coin has a bright side. Because I saved the ISC embarrassment, I was able to drive a bargain. They naturally prefer our names never be associated with this. So . . . we keep silence. In return, we have a commission to bring several special cargoes to the puppeteers' tradepoint and distribute the exchange goods to four different human planets."

Joy flared. "Holy Christ! Clear to there!"

"And well paid. With a clause that will allow us to develop the route further for ourselves if we choose and the puppeteers are willing."

"Pete," Saxtorph declared, "I take every hard thought about you back. I apologize, I heap *sthondat* dung on my head, I adore. You're flat-out a genius."

A parallel gladness: How grandly this guy's gotten over his decades of exile, a kzin prisoner, and the death of his son. Even though I got the reasons for it made an official secret, he knew, he knows. He threw himself into our partnership to escape. Oh, he did a lot more than furnish some capital we badly needed, he hadn't lost his skill at handling people either, but it was an escape. In the three years since, however— He and his new wife seem like being about as happy as Dorcas and me. And now he's wangled this for us.

"Aw, shucks," said Nordbo. "Isn't that your American expression?"

"Your triumph calls for a drink, followed by unbridled celebration." And, Saxtorph thought, what happens at the cannibal star will be fun to watch when the databases arrive home. We'll've been having real-time adventures just as much fun, or maybe more.

He took forth his pipe and tobacco pouch. "First, though, fill me in, will you? Who's going to carry the mission?"

"I helped arrange that too," Nordbo told him. "A little reshifting of schedules made the *Freuchen* available."

"Oh, fine. She *is* mainly for exploration—done good work in the past . . . A tad crowded, maybe, for an expedition like this, with the tonne of gear I imagine they'll want to take."

"They'll have ample extra room. A naval vessel will escort them."

Saxtorph grinned. "Well, well. The ISC's being smart for a change. Nothing 'provocative,' no, never; but the kitty-cats won't be tempted to touch off an 'incident' and claim afterward it was our side's fault."

Nordbo nodded. "That's the unspoken idea. Nobody wants a fight, myself least."

"The *Freuchen* . . . Yah, the establishment, scientists and politicians both, owe us one, over and above the puppeteer contract. They owe you, rather."

Nordbo gave his friend a steady look. "I cashed in that part of it. Which is why I'm especially relieved by their having an escort."

"Hey?"

"Tyra's going along."

"Huh?"

"She was after me about it from the first. A writer by trade, and what a story to tell! I managed to make her assignment part of the bargain, and didn't suppose you would object. Not but what they won't get their money's worth. She'll make the public love that science."

"Well, yes, she always was a venturesome sort. Not strange, seeing she's your daughter." And can wind you around her finger, Saxtorph said silently. As she damn near did me, till she decided not to finish the job. I've never said anything to you or anybody. Nor did I stay regretful. Dorcas and me do belong together.

He knew how suddenly seriousness could grab hold of the other man. Nordbo generally kept his deepest feelings to himself. But he and Saxtorph had grown close, and from time to time everybody needs somebody who will listen.

"Robert, she's been unhappy. She doesn't let on, she wouldn't, but I can tell. I don't know why. Yes, she's grieved for Ib, side by side with me, but—but that's past and done with. It isn't like her to brood. Is it?" He had missed out on the years when she grew up.

Did our not-quite-affair really hurt her so badly? wondered Saxtorph. I sure never thought that, seeing how she behaved. Afterward—well, friendly when we've met, of course, but in the nature of the case that hasn't been often.

What can I do except wish her everything good?

"No, her style is to get on with her life."

Nordbo steadied. "She's been doing so. It's simply that I felt her heart wasn't altogether in it. Now, I do believe, this prospect, this amazement to see and take part in, I think it's healing her."

3

Having climbed high enough up the complex and changeable Alpha Centaurian gravity well, the lancer *Samurai* slipped into hyperspace. *Freuchen* followed seventy-two hours later. The naval ship was to reach destination first and make sure of security before the civilians appeared.

Although no passenger liner, *Freuchen* often made long voyages, and long stays at the far ends of them, which might well involve hardship and danger. Facilities for privacy, recreation, and exercise were not a luxury but a necessity. A couple of watchcycles after leaving 3-space, Tyra Nordbo and Craig Raden were in the gymnasium playing recoil ball.

That game takes strength and wind as well as speed and agility. This being a Wunderland vessel crewed mostly by Wunderlanders, her gravity polarizers maintained the interior weight to which they were accustomed. Nevertheless the Earthman found himself hard challenged. The match ended with score tied and both breathing from the bottoms of their lungs, sweat agleam and animal-odorous on their skins.

"Whoof!" Raden laughed. "Congratulations and thanks. You gave me a good one."

"The same to you," Tyra answered. Her tone was warmer toward him than hitherto. It had been fun. And, she must admit to herself, the sight of him was fun too—medium-tall, slim and supple but well-muscled, features Roman-nosed and regular, with bright hazel eyes, beneath wavy brown hair. That doesn't mean I have to fall over you—or under you, said defensiveness.

"Frankly, I didn't expect it from a person of your origins."

Then why did you invite me to play? she flared inwardly. An approach? Likely. They say you're quite a tomcat. "We're healthy," she snapped.

"Oh, absolutely. Normal adaptation to a lower gravity. No offense intended, please believe." Raden shook his head and clicked his tongue. "Foolish of me. I should have given more thought to what I saw, besides enjoying the view."

He made no pretense of doing otherwise. Tyra's height equaled his, which was not surprising in a Wunderlander woman, but damp T-shirt and shorts clung to a figure as full and robust as that of any Earthling female in good condition. Flaxen hair in a pageboy cut framed a face strong-boned and blunt, where little save a few fine lines at the blue eyes hinted at an age of about forty terrestrial years, perhaps three more than his. "You'd be unusually athletic on any planet," he added.

She shrugged. "I'm not obsessed with aerobics. I just enjoy some activities."

"Which especially, if I may ask?"

"Swimming, wingsailing, hiking, mountaineering, that sort of thing."

"Tastes we share, then. The results do come in useful occasionally, don't you agree? I understand you too have spent a fair amount of time on different worlds, and not merely in their tourist resorts."

"My work. Gathering material, getting ideas." He's pushing familiarity pretty fast, isn't he? "You're an astrophysicist." Put him in his place. Imply that his travels were a gadding about.

Raden's smile faded, his voice went amicably earnest. "Look here, Fräulein Nordbo, may I suggest we become better acquainted? We've a rather long haul before us, and then a time about which we can predict nothing other than that it will be busy, till we've done whatever we can. Let's go as friends."

"Have I seemed unfriendly?" she asked with caution.

"No, no. A bit aloof, perhaps."

"We're barely into the voyage."

"Why not start it on the right foot? Suppose after we've washed and changed clothes, we meet in the wardroom. I'd be honored to stand you a drink or two before dinner."

"Honored? You?" She spoke coldly, to make clear that she didn't like being patronized.

He caught on at once. "I'm sorry. I truly am. What I wanted to say was 'delighted,' but I was afraid of seeming too forward. You're known as a formidable sort."

That's hard to resist, Tyra confessed. Damn him, he can turn on the charm like a light. Anyhow, it's true, we need to become comrades, all of us on board. There's unknownness waiting yonder, and kzinti.

"Not intentionally." She didn't have to force her smile. "Thank you, I'd be delighted myself. In half an hour?"

Command and competence were as vital as in any spacecraft, but an explorer did best without social distinctions between ranks off duty. The wardroom was open to anyone who wanted sociability. Nobody chanced to be present but steward Marcus Hauptmann and planetologist Kees Verwoort, pushing chessmen. Already at ease with Tyra, they nodded as she came in. Nattily attired, Raden jumped from a chair and strode to meet her. "Ah, jolly good," he said. "What would you like?"

"Draft Solborg." She sat down at the little table where he had been. Several more were spaced around the room with their chairs, plus a few loungers. Underneath each was the magnetic inductor that would secure it to the deck in case of untoward acceleration or free fall.

"Forthcoming. Hm, not too early in the daywatch for a glass of wine. They've shipped a reasonably decent dry Riesling." Raden got them from the dispenser, which debited his personal ration, and brought them over. He took his place opposite her and lifted his goblet. *"Skaal."*

So he's remembered, Tyra thought, or he's taken the trouble to find out, things about me like my hailing from Skogarna, and that this is our toast there instead of *"Prosit."*

She didn't know how to feel about that. Well, pay him in kind. "Here's how," she responded.

Glasyl clinked against stein. The beer was a welcome tartness in mouth and throat.

"Ah-ha. Then you know I'm American, Fräulein Nordbo?" Raden said genially. "Most people off Earth seem under the impression I'm a Brit."

"Next time I'll say 'Cheers' if you prefer." Was she parrying something?

He laughed. *"Touché!* Yes, I admit to certain affectations. And I did study for a while at Cambridge." He sipped and went on in a philosophical tone. "Such details are apt to look vanishingly small across a few

light-years, aren't they? Consider how societies diverged
when only subluminal transit was available. They've
not had much time or opportunity thus far to catch
up, have they? Rather amazing, how knowledgeable you
are."

Is he showing off his serious, intellectual side? wondered Tyra. Or do quantum jumps come naturally to
him? "No surprise, Dr. Raden. Writers collect oddments
like glitterfowl. You know that."

"Well, yes, I am a writer too, of sorts. But second-
arily. Not a rival of yours on this mission or, I hope,
ever."

"I've seen your popular science works, those of them
that have reached us, and your 'Multiverse' show." Be
honest, she told herself. "I've enjoyed them, in fact
admired them."

"Thank you. I look forward to seeing what you've
done."

"Nothing like yours. Mainly travel pieces, some assorted
journalism, some fiction, a couple of things for children."

"I'll doubtless write up this expedition and its findings
myself, elsewhere than in the scientific databases. But
I don't imagine I'll overlap what you do in the least."

And my audience won't be ten percent of yours,
even if my accounts get distribution on Earth, Tyra
realized. The famous young scientist, popularizer,
lecturer, sportsman, yes, licensed spaceboat pilot and
bronze medalist in the Saturnian Ring Run—all very
well publicized—showman— Unfair? Am I being nasty
and jealous? Or just shy? I'm not sure. I'm not used
to either of those feelings.

"I have in mind telling about the people with us and
what happens to them personally," she said. "But you
will do that too, along with explaining the discoveries, same as always, won't you?"

"Mostly incidentally, trying to get across that science isn't a revelation handed down from on high, it's something that intelligent creatures do. You'll concentrate on the human story. We are not in competition. We may well prove to be in cooperation."

"M-m, maybe. You're kind to say so, Dr. Raden."

"Please," he replied gently, "must we continue formal? I'm Craig to my friends."

Impulse grabbed Tyra. "And I'm not properly 'Fräulein.' I've resumed my family name, but I was married twice."

His gaze searched her. "To what kind of man, that they'd give up one like you?"

She flushed, but stiffened less than she probably should have. "Things simply didn't work out. If I'm not mistaken, you've had similar experiences."

"True. And I'm not self-righteous about them, either . . . Tyra." Quickly: "Yes, I'm trying to cultivate your acquaintance, not entirely for its own sake. I hope we can talk about your adventures at the black hole."

"That was Captain Saxtorph's department," she demurred. "I was hardly more than a passenger."

"Forgive me, but according to what I've gathered, you're overly modest. You had a great deal to do with what went on." Again quickly: "Although you've wanted your part in it de-emphasized as much as possible. Aristocratic reserve?"

As little as possible about Ib— She put down the pain. "Wunderland doesn't have aristocrats any longer."

"Still, the heritage, the pride . . . This very ship bears the name of your clan. . . . Well, I certainly don't mean to intrude. If ever I ask anything, or say anything, you don't like, please let me know. I swear to respect your privacy."

Disarmed, she blurted, "What'll be left to talk about, then, that you can't have retrieved from public databases?"

"Endlessly much. You and your companions met something unique in our knowledge—a mini black hole, and the artifact the tnuctipun built around it, billions of years ago. . . . Gone, now, gone. Surely you see what this means to me and every astrophysicist, cosmologist, archeologist, anybody who's ever looked at the stars and wondered."

"I only had glimpses and heard others rattle off numbers they'd taken from their instruments."

"I think you observed more, perhaps more than you know. At any rate, I'll wager your story of it is vivid."

Tyra could not but smile. It was as if his enthusiasm smoothed away every lingering hurt and reopened her eyes to wonder. "You flatter me."

He turned playful. "I'm good at that. Especially when it's sincere."

She laughed. "We'll have time enough under way."

"Yes, indeed. I won't be champing at the bit as impatiently as I expected. Thank you, Tyra."

He led the conversation on to undisturbing reminiscences, anecdotes, jokes, a cheerful hour.

4

An alert yowled. Ghrul-Captain sprang from his lair, down a passage and up a companionway to the main control chamber. He shoved aside the watchkeeper, a kzin currently known as Sub-officer. "Sire," the underling told him, "the optics and nucleonics register a spacecraft approaching."

"What else would it be?" Ghrul-Captain snarled. "Do you take me for a *sthondat?*"

"No, sire, of course not—"

"Silence till you have something worth saying, if ever." Ghrul-Captain crouched into the central command seat.

The other drew back, submissive but poised. Bristling whiskers, broadened pupils, and half-folded ears showed anger. It was purely reflexive, not directed at his superior. This was what happened to one of his standing, like harsh weather on a planet. He may have counted himself lucky not to be punished.

Actually, while Ghrul-Captain had needed to vent

some wrath, he could not afford to disable personnel
for anything less than outright insubordination. The
Strong Runner was undercrewed, underweaponed, alone.
And his instruments were identifying the stranger as
a human warship.

For a heartbeat he glared at the scene in the viewscreen. The target sun was a small disc, its luminance
selectively dulled till an extravagant corona was eye-
visible. Undimmed, a big world much farther out shone
brighter than the true stars. They sprawled in strange
constellations—seen at more than thirty light-years from
the Father Sun and well off the galactic plane. The Ice
River itself looked slightly different, against the background blackness of space.

His gaze focused on the meters and readouts before
him, and then on the image a computer program was
constructing. He had been taught to know that lean
shape, those rakish lines of gun turrets and launch
tubes. A lancer, a light naval vessel but easily able to
annihilate this wretched carrier. It was about five million
kilometers off, adjusting its vectors with an acceleration he could merely envy. A proper warcraft would
have spotted it immediately when it emerged from
hyperspace, wherever in this system that had been.
Surely it had picked him up then, and set about reduc-
ing the gap between.

Ghrul-Captain forced steadiness on himself, as he
might have donned a pressure suit too tight for him.
He would have to communicate with the monkeys and
offer them no threat. The necessity was foul in his
mouth. He could have voice-ordered a beam in the
standard band to lock on; instead, his claw stabbed
the manual board.

They were obviously awaiting it yonder. In some
thirty interminable seconds, the time for electromagnetic waves to go back and forth, his comboard lighted

up. He sent a "Ready" signal—make *them* introduce themselves to *him*—and activated the translator program.

The screen came to life with a human face. Those always suggested to him the faces of flayed corpses. "United Nations Navy unit *Samurai* calling kzin vessel," it gabbled, while the translator gave forth decent growls and hisses. "Request conference with your commanding officer."

"I am he," Ghrul-Captain answered. "I will speak to none but your own master." They could kill him, but they could not make him lower himself.

In the time lag he felt a ventilator breeze stir his hair. It bore a sharp tinge of ozone. But no cleansing thunderstorm was going to break. Not now. Not yet.

The scan switched to another den and another face, dark brown. From its delicate lines and glabrous cheeks he decided it belonged to a female. *Ruch!* Still, human females were supposed to have as much consciousness as the males, and often held important positions. He must accept the perverted fact and cope with it.

"Captain Indira Lal Bihari, commanding UNN *Samurai*," she was saying. "Our intentions are peaceful. We trust they can remain so."

"Ghrul-Captain, master of *Strong Runner*." He would volunteer no more. If that piqued her, and if he could know it did, he would have won a tiny satisfaction.

Full lips drew back, upward. Ghrul-Captain had studied many views of human faces but never learned to tell whether a baring of teeth meant amusement, conciliation, or anger. "Apparently you prefer that I take the initiative. Very well. Your people announced they would send an expedition here like us. We were not quite certain of its nature or its timing. I am not much surprised that you arrived first. Kzinti are . . . quick to act; and our preparations have doubtless been more elaborate.

"We have ascertained that you have one large vessel carrying boats and probes. Our basic arrangements are similar. However, this ship has gone in advance of the civilian to make sure all is well, and will remain in her vicinity after rendezvous. I assume you agree it's wise to take precautions against possible contingencies." That smile again. "Do you wish to respond now, or shall I proceed?"

"We will not tolerate interference with our undertakings. That includes too close an approach to any unit or work of ours."

While the time lag hummed, Ghrul-Captain considered what else to say. He had better not antagonize her, for he did need information. Fortunately, humans were devoid of true pride.

"None is intended, Ghrul-Captain. Should any of you be in distress, we will gladly give assistance." He lashed his bare pink tail but held his ears up under the insult, realizing it was unwitting. "Otherwise we will keep as separated as feasible. Let us establish a few rules between us to this end. We can begin by spelling out our plans to each other."

"What are yours, then?"

She must have prepared the speech that followed the silence:

"While at hyperspacing distance, our civilian mother ship will unload a disassembled hyperwave transceiver, with radio relays to the inner system, and leave a gang to make it ready. The job should not take long, given their robots. They'll have a boat and rejoin the rest of us when they are done.

"Subject to change as circumstances warrant, the mother ship and escort will take ecliptic orbit around the sun at approximately three-fourths of an astronomical unit. The scientists will make observations from there, but naturally will also dispatch probes and boats on appropriate courses. These will include visits to the stable planets and their satellites, for survey, and landings if closer investigation seems warranted. We propose to notify you in advance of these, as well as any important maneuvers of the ships themselves.

"Early on, the scientists will put three small robotic observatories in polar orbit around the sun, at about the same radius, 120 degrees apart, to keep the inmost planet under constant study from that angle.

"We . . . request . . . noninterference, too. We will always be open to communication with you. Let neither party judge hastily. Correct, Ghrul-Captain?

"This is our basic plan. May I ask what yours is?"

Ghrul-Captain did not answer for a minute or two. First he must overcome his rage. He wanted to scream and leap. But he had nothing to kill, only this phantom of a monkey five million kilometers out of reach. Useless, anyway, for anything but one instant of release, which would bring down his mission and his dreams.

The humiliation, though! Her words had come like one whip flick after the next. Not that the she-monkey intended it. She was totally insensitive. It never occurred to her how she flaunted those capabilities—a hyperwave station brought along, a swarm of lesser craft, three solar watchposts—before his poor little expedition—wealth and power such as belonged to the race of Heroes, before her rabble overran and robbed them.

There would be a day of justice, a night of revenge.

Not for years.

Meanwhile, he remembered, and helped congeal his feelings thereby, *meanwhile I may do a deed they cannot and dare not match, to shame them whether they know it or not—we will know, at home—and, possibly, bring back a prize they are also unaware of, which may possibly hold within it the making of* some mighty weapon for their destruction. Yes, possibly I will.

First he must reach an accommodation with them, at least for immediate purposes. Grand Lord Narr-Souwa and he had developed some ideas about that back on Kzin.

"You may ask," he said, as the stranglehold on his throat slackened. "For the present, I deem it best that my ship take the same orbit as yours, 90 degrees ahead. That should be a safe distance, while leaving you able to communicate with me on short notice when necessary." And for us to keep an eye on you. "You understand that we will dispatch our own lesser craft as we see fit."

He cooled further during the time lag.

Bihari didn't seem to notice how she had been disdained. He didn't want to believe that she had noticed and simply didn't care. "A question, if you please. We have detected activity of yours at a certain satellite of an outer planet. May I inquire what the purpose is?"

"Supply operations," Ghrul-Captain snapped. He would give her no more. Let the monkeys discover the rest as it happened.

She didn't push the matter. Evidently she had been briefed on kzin ways. Or did she have direct experience? Had she fought in the war? Ghrul-Captain almost hoped so. One prefers an enemy for whom one can feel a trifle of respect. "I see. If you don't wish to speak further for the time being, shall we close?"

He replied by cutting off transmission.

5

Tyra had more and more enjoyed her voyage, until near the end. Everyone aboard was an interesting person. While not yet ready to do formal interviews, she took pleasure in cultivating their acquaintance, from Captain Worning on down. She had met some of the half-dozen crew before, but not all, and none of the scientists except Jens Lillebro, a physical chemist at the University of Munchen; the rest were from Earth. Not that the distinction was absolute. Anybody serving on an explorer was necessarily a technician of wide-ranging skills and scientific turn of mind. Thus, the work gang who would assemble the hyperwave unit, engineer Reiner Koch and boat pilots-cum-rockjacks Birgit Eisenberg and Josef Brandt, would be much in demand after they rejoined the ship. Tyra heard many good stories and found ample cause for admiration.

She was oftenest in Craig Raden's company. She preferred to believe there was more on both sides than physical attraction. Of course, that played its part.

Among other factors, she was the only woman out of the six with whom anything but the mildest flirtation was possible. Biologist Louise Dalmady made a team with her husband, Emil. Stellar astronomer Maria Kivi, middle-aged, kept quiet faith with her husband at home. Planetologist Toyo Takata was young and pretty but, in spite of being as shy as her colleague Verwoort was bluff, made plain that this was her great career opportunity and she wanted no distractions. Matronly mate Lili Deutsch had her own family back on Wunderland and seldom missed a chance to speak of the new grandchild. Pilots Eisenberg and Brandt had for years been a pair in every sense of the word. Once Tyra spied Raden and physicist Ernesto Padilla exchange a wry glance and a rueful grin. Had the first staked his claim on her? Whether or no, he was never offensive, merely fun and fascinating. They played games physical, intellectual, and childish; they listened to music and watched drama and quoted favorite poetry, they explored the ship's wine stock, they joked, they talked.

And talked and talked. He was a magnificent conversationalist, who always made it a two-way thing.

His account of the finding of their destination fascinated her. She knew about spaceborne interferometry—Wunderland had lately embarked on a project to build a set of such instruments and orbit it around Alpha Centauri C—but why had Earth's matchless facilities not identified this situation long ago? He explained in some detail how many other, more obviously exciting ventures were absorbing funds and attention, notably though not exclusively visits to the sites themselves, while the search for additional high-tech civilizations, beyond known space, grew ever more tantalizing. The star they were seeking had of course been catalogued in early times, but nothing further. It appeared completely ordinary, obscure in its remote location. Finally a slight spectral flutter, noticed in the course of a systematic survey of that region, betrayed it.

How had this given data enough to show not only what was happening, but when the climax would come? Raden had a gift for making analytical techniques clear to a non-mathematician. The precision awed her.

"Well, there's a significant probable error," he admitted. "We'll be getting there none too soon, possibly a little too late for the actual event. Let's hope not! Sheer luck, making this discovery just when we did. True, it isn't unique, but to have one within our own lifetimes, at an accessible distance—" He laughed. "We live right, I suppose."

The last weekly dance of the trip became an especially gleeful occasion. The gym was festooned with homemade decorations. Champagne sparkled on a sideboard. Every woman joined in, with no lack of partners, while music lilted from the speakers. Best for Tyra was when she and Craig were together. She was a good dancer; he was superb.

The hour was late when he saw her to the compartment known as her stateroom. They paused at the door, alone in the passageway. He took both her hands. "It's been wonderful," he murmured. "Throughout."

"Yes." She felt the blood in her face and her pulse.

"It needn't end immediately, you know."

"We have three daycycles left."

"Once I'd have thought that was three too many. Now it's far too few." He stepped close and laid arms around her waist. "Tyra, we do have them. Beginning this nightwatch."

Not altogether surprised, she slipped free with a motion learned in a dojo and drew back a pace. Though her heart thudded, she was able to look into his eyes and say quite steadily, "I'm sorry, Craig. I like you very much, but I don't do casual."

Robert Saxtorph thinks I do, wrenched within her. I had to make him think that, didn't I? After I saw I had no right to ruin his marriage. The kindest way— make it not too hard for him to let go—wasn't it? Wasn't it?

"We don't have to stay casual, Tyra," Raden said. "I'm hoping we don't."

He could be lying. She recalled his reputation. Or he could be sincere . . . temporarily. Or if he really meant it, or if there was a chance he might come to mean it, still, the gulf between them was interstellar. Not easily or surely bridged. Nevertheless— "Let me think, Craig. We'll have time, also at the star and on the voyage back. We'll stay friends at least. Won't we?"

He nodded. "At least," he answered low, with a smile. "Goodnight, then, dear." He leaned across, kissed her gently on the lips, and departed.

She stood for a moment staring after him. He knew better than to insist, tumbled through her. A gentleman, as well as everything else. Suppose he had kept trying—

Memory stabbed her again. Perhaps that was why she went to her bunk bewildered.

She slept poorly and awoke feeling on edge. At breakfast in the saloon she ate skimpily, said nothing, and when she was done returned to her room and screened book after book. None could hold her. When she went to the gym, it lay hollow and forlorn. Just the same, a workout followed by a shower was refreshing. She came to lunch with an appetite.

Raden was on hand, chatting easily with others. He gave her a smile as if nothing had happened, and brought her into the conversation. Afterward, however, as they were going out, he came alongside and asked, "Can we talk a bit?"

"What about?" Her voice sounded ragged in her ears.

He shrugged. "Anything you like. If I upset you, I'm terribly sorry and want to make amends."

So he had read her mood in spite of her effort to seem her usual self. "No, I'm not upset, not offended." She managed to give him back his smile. "A compliment, really, and if I couldn't accept, I did appreciate." How honest was she? She didn't know.

He took her elbow. "Look, it's early in the watch for a drink, but on that account we should have the wardroom to ourselves. No harm in nursing a beer. Can we sit down and simply talk? I promise not to go importunate on you."

It wasn't possible to refuse, was it? She liked the idea, didn't she?

Yet she must work to keep from showing her tension. To gaze across the table into his handsomeness reawakened the old pain and whetted it. She'd laid it aside, she'd actually been happy, now she must start over.

Self-pity wasn't in her nature. Resentment took its place. Oh, she had more sense than to blame him. He'd had no way of knowing what a nerve he touched. For that matter, she hadn't known it was still so raw. To rail at dice that fell wrong was idiotic. However, the anger had to strike at something.

"Yes, we'll be busier than a one-armed octopus," he was saying. "Perhaps with the kzinti too."

"God, I hope not!" burst from her.

"I'm hoping for it, actually. I'll see what I can do toward bringing it about, in whatever degree."

Startled, she asked, "What?"

"We might manage some scientific collaboration. You know how fruitful, how inspiring and stimulating, our exchanges with other races have been," he said earnestly. "We're overdue for an interaction with the kzinti that isn't hostile."

"How?" demanded scorn.

He raised his brows. "How not? They're intelligent, sentient beings. Their civilization surely has its own riches. What might we learn from them?"

"New ways of murder and torture, maybe," she sneered.

"You can't be serious, Tyra. Yes, they've been aggressors, they've committed atrocities, but that's been true of humans in the past. Read your history. Nor have we lost the potential, I'm afraid." He gulped from his stein. "Blood guilt is one of the most vile and dangerous concepts our race ever came up with. We've got to put it behind us, for decency's sake, for survival's sake."

She unclenched her teeth. "I'm not talking about inherited guilt. I'm talking about inherited drives and instincts. The kzinti are what they are. You can no more deal with them in good faith than you can with a— a disease germ."

"They live among us, Tyra!" he protested.

"A few. In their enclaves. Eccentrics, misfits, atypical—abnormal, for kzinti. But don't ever turn your back on one."

His whisper sounded aghast. "I didn't imagine you were a racist."

"I didn't imagine you were an utter fool." The flare damped down. "Craig, I *know* them. I grew up under their occupation. I saw what they did to my people. I *felt* what they did to—my father, my family—" The tears stung. She blinked them away. "And then I myself—but that doesn't matter. They tried their best to kill my friends and me, that's all. What does matter is how often they've succeeded with others."

"Culture— Ethnic character is mutable. It can grow in the right directions."

"When enough of their most murderous are dead,

out of their gene pool, maybe then," she said. "You and I won't live to see the day, if it ever comes. And first the weeding has to be done."

"This is appalling." Raden sighed. "Well, evidently the attitude is a common one. We'd better drop the subject."

"Yes," she said coldly. She knocked back her beer and rose. "Thank you for the drink." She left him.

The relationship continued amicably, but warmth had gone out of it.

6

While *Freuchen* accelerated sunward, the first observer probes shot forth from her and began transmitting their readings and images. When a synthesis of the sights was ready, everyone aboard crowded into the wardroom to see it on the big screen. Excitement swiftly became awe.

In itself the star was nothing unusual, a type G dwarf. It had formed from the primordial cloud only about a billion years ago, and as yet shone with only about 65% the luminosity of Sol or half that of Alpha Centauri A—fierce enough! Though not naked-eye visible, material was still raining into it in vast quantities. Optical programs, selectively and suitably taming fieriness, showed it wildly turbulent. Spots swirled in flocks, flares and prominences fountained, corona shimmered as far as a million kilometers outward.

Six planets went about it in eccentric orbits. The inmost would not survive much longer.

It had formed at a distance where the growth of a gas giant was possible, and it became one in truth, a mass of ten Jupiters. But already the unbalanced gravitational forces of an irregularly distributed proto-system had been spiraling it inward. Its pull on itself remained so strong that it lost little or nothing as it neared the sun and temperatures soared. The atmosphere distended, though, until now an ovoid 280,000 kilometers long glowed furnace hot, chaotic with storms that could have swallowed Earth or Wunderland whole. Friction with the thick interplanetary medium had almost circularized its path, and worked together with resonances to make this ever shorter. Stripped of moons, it raced through the coronal fringes a million kilometers from the stellar photosphere, around in eleven and a half hours, each time faster and faster. Rotation had been slowed by the huge tidal bulges until cloud whorls needed fifteen hours to face out to the dark again.

Such were the facts and figures. The reality was roiling, seething, terrible magnificence. It was as if the bloodbeat in the ears of humans struck dumb by the sight faintly echoed those surfs, eruptions, hurricanes, and violences.

After many minutes of silence, Raden said very quietly, "Yes, our luck has held, barely. I got the latest computation earlier this watch. The planet's practically at the Roche limit. It's due to start breaking up."

"When?" asked Captain Worning.

"Not quite certain. Maybe as soon as two weeks, maybe as much as five or six. What will happen then and how—we don't have an adequate model to predict. We need more data, endless data."

"What we also need is names for those . . . bodies," said Lili Deutsch. "Catalogue numbers are too unhandy and hard to remember."

"Yes," agreed Toyo Takata. "And they are a mockery of this." She shivered. "It is not well to mock the elemental powers."

She's not superstitious, thought Tyra. She's right.

"Some of us have been talking about that," put in
Ernesto Padilla. "What of Hell for the star and Lucifer for the planet?"

"No," replied Maria Kivi. "Lucifer brought his fate
on himself."

Words, words, a shield against the overwhelming
mightiness yonder. Tyra raised a hand. Eyes turned
toward her; she seemed to feel the touch of Raden's.
"I have been thinking too," she ventured. "I—I suggest Pele and Kumukahi."

"Who the devil would they be?" barked Marcus
Hauptmann.

"From Hawaii on Earth," Tyra told them. "A myth
they remember there. Pele was the volcano goddess.
Kumukahi was a young chief who unwittingly insulted
her. She destroyed him."

Kamehameha Ryan had related it, back in Saxtorph's
Rover. She had tried to keep him out of her mind.
Through no fault of his own, memories of him hurt.
Maybe that was why this came back to her in a sleep-
less nightwatch two daycycles ago.

"Splendid!" Raden exclaimed. "Perfect! You'll know
names for the other planets too, won't you? Thanks
a thousandfold."

"I don't remember much more. Not enough to go
around, certainly."

Takata said, "But I can supply some. I have family
in Hawaii, and works on folklore they sent me are in
my personal database."

"M-m, well, all right by me, but not official," Worning
rumbled.

"Leave that to the officials. I'll undertake to over-
bear them if they get stuffy." Raden carried the rest
along on the tide of his enthusiasm.

As if this really mattered, Tyra thought. Oh, it does,
in a way, but that much? To him?

Because it came from me?

Congratulations surrounded her. Raden beamed and waved above the heads. "We'll have a drink on that, Tyra, as soon as may be," he called.

I'm forgiven, she thought. Not that I suppose he was ever angry with me, just with my attitude. . . . The anger was mainly mine, and unreasonable.

He's not going to let me stand aside from him if he can help it.

The knowledge was at once a gladness and an alarm signal.

Raden turned to the captain. "I'll take the boat out for a closer, personal look tomorrow."

"What?" protested Worning. "We won't be in our orbit yet."

"She has delta vee to burn. Not that I'll waste any."

"She's our one auxiliary until the hyperwave gang rejoin us."

"*Samurai* will be close, with several, in case of emergency. Which is ridiculously improbable. And you know I'm a qualified pilot."

"Why, however, when our probes are not even all deployed?" the captain asked.

"Precisely for that reason. A live brain, a trained eye, alert for the unforeseeable. Which, at present, is virtually everything in and around Kumukahi. I'll wager you a month's pay we'll be rewriting the robots' programs immediately after my first excursion."

Worning scowled. "I do not take the bet, because I will not allow this. It is reckless."

Affability and persuasiveness flooded over him. "Captain, with due and considerable respect, I beg leave to prove to you that it isn't. Instead, it's the best investment we can make. Time is short. We can't afford to miss a single chance of learning something. It'll never come again."

He'll win, Tyra knew, and go cometing off, laughing for sheer joy. He will return like a knight of old from a joust with giants.

She could well-nigh see plume and pennon flying in the wind of his gallop.

7

She had planned to conduct some interviews aboard *Samurai*, but it was an astonishment to be invited, virtually bidden, over there just four days after *Freuchen* took orbit. A naval auxiliary with a tight-lipped pilot flitted her quickly across the few hundred klicks between, and she was conducted directly to a communications-outfitted cabin. Captain Bihari sat alone at a desk, confronting a screen live but blank. The door slid shut behind her.

"Be seated," was the brusque greeting. However, when Tyra had taken a chair opposite, the officer said with a grim smile, "This should give you quite an interesting story." The tone was serious. "For my part, I want a responsible outside observer, to report the truth afterward. Already we're having a crisis with the kzin. Please stay where you are and keep silence while I am transmitting. You will note that you can see what goes on but are not in the scanner field. I don't suppose these ones would recognize you and recall the part you played against their kind, but if any of them did, matters could get entirely out of hand. The situation is bad enough without taking the slightest added risk."

"I could have stayed aboard the *Freuchen*, patched in," Tyra said.

Bihari frowned. "Too many others could eavesdrop. I don't call them untrustworthy, but—different people interpret things in different ways, and soon rumors run wild." She sighed. "The political balance on Earth is such that we have to—we have orders to avoid any unnecessary word or action that might conceivably be taken as 'aggressive' or 'provocative.'"

Tyra stiffened. "Really? Well, ma'am, you must decide what is necessary, mustn't you?"

"Yes, and justify it, here and at home. I wouldn't put it past certain parties to claim we falsified our databases. Easy to do, after all."

No, Tyra thought, Craig would never be so paranoid. He simply, genuinely wants peace—what decent human being doesn't?—and believes we can have it if we try. "I see, ma'am. I'm your impartial witness." Is that possible for me? . . . I'll have my opinions, but I won't write lies.

"You've come barely in time. I have commenced conversation"—again the wolf's grin—"as the diplomats say, with Ghrul-Captain aboard their mother ship. His response to my complaint, as the diplomats would also say, should arrive shortly." Eight or nine minutes either way for radio to travel between the vessels circling Pele.

Dismay: "It's about Birgit and the Dalmadys, isn't it?"

"Who or what else would it be?"

The fact jabbed through Tyra. Eisenberg had piloted a boat carrying the biological team to the third planet, Kama-pua'a. The second was less favorably positioned at present; though the third orbited farther out, it wasn't much more than thirty hours off, at one gee with midpoint turnover. If something unexpected began happening to Kumukahi, which it might at any moment, the boat would be wanted back straightaway. Meanwhile, husband and wife could do science yonder.

"But—they weren't going to land where the kzinti are," Tyra protested.

More remembrance. Kama-pua'a was another giant, with a swarm of moons. The two biggest had thin atmospheres. They were close enough that tidal flexion, as well as whatever internal heat remained, kept them warm enough that life was perhaps, barely, germinating on either or both. Its origins were so various, probably many of the possibilities still unknown. . . . The boat had sent images back, a great spheroid banded with clouds and storms, the craggy surface of Moku-ola ahead, the joyful expectations inboard. . . .

The kzinti had established their bases on the small outer satellite the humans called Poliahu, obviously mostly ice.

"You know and the kzinti know what sensitive instruments can do, especially at short ranges like that," Bihari said. "Frankly, I would have liked very much to send some of ours along, but my orders— Hold."

The screen filled with a tigerish countenance. The voice rumbled with a menace and—glee?—that the flat English of the translator had no need to convey. "Your words are insolent. No Hero can tolerate such. You will make amends for the intrusion, amends which I will specify, or your spies will suffer the consequences that they have earned."

Bihari kept her tone level, steeliness only in the dark face. "I deny again that they are spies and that your gang had any right whatsoever to seize them. They will be returned promptly, unharmed, or there will indeed be consequences. However, as a point of information, what demands have you in mind?"

She ceased transmission pending the reply, turned to Tyra, and said, "This is preposterous, as I think even a kzin must realize. They can scarcely be carrying on military work there."

"No," Tyra answered. "Not exactly. I can guess what it is."

"Tell me."

"They used a special kind of tug at the old red sun where Captain Saxtorph surprised them. It could fly close, to nudge ferriferous objects into trajectories for collection. The crew survived those passages because the craft, besides having big reflecting surfaces, was heavily loaded with water. Vented to space, the water cooled it during the time of exposure. I think these kzinti have one like it along, though it must be smaller."

Bihari nodded. "Yes, of course I remember the reports, but thank you for reminding me." She stroked her chin. "Our own long-range observations do show large excavations, and structures that may well be prefabricated facilities for purification and transfer. . . . Yes, I feel sure you are right. Thank you again. You have done us a service."

Our instruments are all directed at Pele and Kumukahi, Tyra thought. "They can't claim that's military."

"Not logically. If it were, it would be a violation of the peace treaty. But—proprietary processes— I can't predict how an Earthside court would rule. I suspect dear Ghrul-Captain was rather well briefed before he left home. The kzin may be mad, but they are not stupid; and . . . there have been humans eager to inform them. There doubtless still are."

"Civilian, military, no difference to them anyway," said Tyra with a bitterness that the memory of her brother redoubled.

"You understand."

"He's been on the lurk for an excuse, any excuse, to make trouble for us. What can we do?"

"That will be seen," said Bihari.

They spoke little more but sat each with her thoughts until the kzin face came back.

"Your two ships will move to hyperspacing distance," stated Ghrul-Captain. "When they have done so, we will allow the three creatures we hold to rendezvous with you. You will then depart."

"And leave further discoveries to you," Bihari retorted. "Sir, you know how underequipped you are. Priceless knowledge will be lost, which it is our mission to obtain." She paused. "Very well, you have made your—initial offer, shall we say? Mine is that you release our people and their boat immediately, unconditionally, and unharmed. In return, we will consider this a misunderstanding which, fortunately, was resolved by mutual reasonableness. I expect your decision as quickly as transmission lag allows."

The screen blanked.

"What next, ma'am?" Tyra whispered.

"We have about a quarter of an hour. Ample time." Bihari activated an intercom and ordered battle stations. Tyra heard running feet and clashing metal. In minutes, a monitor screen showed assault boats leaping from their bays, spearlike athwart the stars.

It thrilled in her. Yet what would Craig think?

When Ghrul-Captain's image reappeared, he must have known what his radars and other detectors were revealing. Tyra wondered whether that smoothed his arrogance a little. It certainly did not quell him. "If you do not wish me to send the command for the execution of your agents, you will not try my patience further. I make this much concession in the interests of peace. You will turn your hyperwave transmitter over to us, with complete instructions for its use. I am prepared to consider that a barely sufficient atonement."

Yes, Tyra thought at him, and after that you can do anything you think you might get away with. You aren't armed like us, but—Robert wiped out your red-sun base by crashing an asteroid on it. Your ice tug? I don't know. But I can hear that you don't gag on words like "peace." Was this what you were after all along?

"Ghrul-Captain," said Bihari glacially, "what I will consider barely sufficient atonement is the liberty of our people. My command is in attack mode, as I trust your instruments have verified for you. If we do not hear from those people in minimum transmission time that they are coming safely back to us, we will destroy you. Yes, they will die too, but a Hero understands what honor demands. I require your immediate response."

Blankness.

"Whew!" gasped Tyra.

"Now the burden falls on you," Bihari told her gravely.

"What? How?"

"To make them see at home that this has been the only way."

"But, but you may lose your whole career—"

"Much worse, the movement for preparedness and a firm stance will suffer. And so a new war will become all the more likely. I think you can help make that clear to the human race. Will you?"

"I'll t-try my damnedest," Tyra promised. Whatever it may cause between Craig and me.

Bihari smiled. "I haven't misjudged you. Nor do I think I have underestimated you."

They waited in silence, together.

Ghrul-Captain snarled while the translator gave: "So be it, then. To treat with your hysteria would be unworthy of Heroes. Your wretched slinkers may return to you, and good riddance. But beware of coming near that planet again."

Bihari nodded. "We grant you that. The third planet will be off limits for us, within a ten-million-kilometer radius. Please note that nothing else in the system, except your vessels, will be. Let this agreement be made in full honor, and our original terms of relationship continue in force. As soon as I learn that our people are bound back unharmed, I will take my command off battle footing. Please acknowledge."

The screen blanked anew.

Tyra felt and smelled that she had been sweating. A chill passed through her. Fire followed. "That was wonderful!" she cried.

Bihari smiled as if unperturbed. "Thank you. They'll be nearly out of their skins with rage, driven to do something or other showing they actually are superior to the monkeys. Let us hope it won't be too dangerous—to us, at any rate." She leaned forward. "I also hope, and I believe you can, when you tell the story, you will soften it, make it seem as minor an incident as possible."

"Yes," Tyra murmured, "that would be best, wouldn't it?"

8

Every deployed robot and observatory, every probe, each of the boats when sent forth, transmitted continuously back to *Freuchen*. The computers printed ever-changing displays and images. Aboard, Tyra could follow moment by moment.

"Yes," opined planetologist Verwoort. "The catastrophe will begin any day now."

Kumukahi writhed, distorted and in torment. The night side flickered with enormous lightnings, shimmered with their glare cast back from roiling clouds the size of Earth or greater, flashed with the red sparks of explosions, or whatever it was going on in the upper atmosphere, all above a dull glow of sheer heat. The day side seemed afire. Bursts of incandescent gas leaped from it like flames. Some broke free and whirled off, vanishing as they dissipated, toward the sun. Storms mightier than Jupiter's Red Spot, and perhaps of greater age, fought to keep their structure as they poured along the steepening slope of the inner tidal bulge. A segment of Pele's disc, dimmed by the imagers to seething purple, filled the right edge of the big screen.

"The spectrum grows more and more strange," said his colleague Takata. "In the past few hours I have been finding an increase of iron, largely hydrides . . ." Her voice trailed off.

"Spewed up from below, I suppose," suggested the physicist Padilla. "Should heavy elements not have sunk to form a core?"

"No," answered Verwoort. "They exist, yes, and they would be more plentiful in lower layers, but with as vast a mass of hydrogen and helium as this, the percentage is so small that it must always have been diffused. The core is metallic hydrogen, maybe pressed into a still denser form than in Jupiter. This upwelling should tell us much about the gaseous atmosphere."

"It is not the only peculiar chemistry," Takata said. "Jens will have plenty to consider when he gets back."

"What will we see when the whole thing breaks apart, before it falls into the sun?" asked the steward Hauptmann. While he was intelligent enough, science was not his forte, and with as many people to look after as there were on this voyage, he had been too busy to keep track.

Kivi shook her head. "It won't break like a melon," she explained. "The planet's self-gravity will hold it together as it fills its Roche lobe. We can't predict events with any precision, and no doubt we will be surprised. However, we can say that turbulence within may well eject great gouts of material, forming a spiral that streams into the star. The magnetic effects—but that goes too far into speculation. Eventually the planet will take a teardrop shape, filling its Roche lobe, and pouring its substance down that spiral until it becomes an accretion disk. This will go on at an accelerating rate for some undetermined time. Decades at least, possibly centuries." She sighed. "How I wish we had probes that could observe from sunside!"

A goodly number were aflight, but those that had gone between planet and star were suicides, sending only bare glimpses before heat and radiation killed their electronics. Tyra's mind strayed for a moment to an image she had seen two daywatches ago. *Samurai*'s long-range observations had, earlier, picked up a craft that emerged from *Strong Runner* and went out to the ice moon of Three. Now it had returned, presumably loaded. Spheroidal, with broad fins, blinding-bright reflective, it was of a size to account for the mother ship apparently having only three other boats along in spite of being designed as a carrier. The view that *Samurai*'s computer reconstructed and shared with *Freuchen* showed it maneuvering about, a test run. Spectroscopy revealed it venting some water vapor from widely over its surface.

Craig Raden had been with her then, gazing as intently. "A sundiver for certain," she had said. "Not nearly as big as the one Captain Saxtorph encountered, and probably not as well outfitted. It can't have life support for more than one or two. A prototype, pressed into service."

"You seem to have studied the subject rather thoroughly," he drawled.

She felt how she flushed. "Naturally, after I'd been with *Rover*'s people, I was interested in their past experiences and went back to the database entries."

Was he watching her? She didn't look toward him. "For an opportunity like this, they'll take the risk. A bold venture, ingeniously thought out, and very possibly scientifically invaluable. We *must* find our way to cooperation with them."

She made no reply. Worse than useless, reviving that quarrel. He had likewise been careful after the crisis to say merely that Bihari could have shown more restraint.

After all, Emil, Louise, and Birgit were back among them, uninjured albeit shaken. Once again, though, the relationship between Tyra and Craig was not quite cordial. That hurt worse than she cared to admit.

Kumukahi's image was slipping close to Pele's in its headlong rush around the sun.

"The polar orbiters are doing fine work," Takata was saying.

"At a distance," Kivi answered. "If we had had time to design and build a sundiver of our own—"

"We didn't," snorted Verwoort. "We can recommend the making and dispatching of several when we report home."

"Robots," said mate Deutsch a bit sadly. "Nothing but robots to keep watch after us."

"Well," replied Captain Worning, "decades or centuries would be a long and expensive time to maintain humans on station. They might grow bored."

Padilla laughed. "Besides," he put in, "when enough atmosphere is gone that the core drops below a critical threshold, it will explode. *I* would not want to be any closer than hyperspace escape distance."

"Yes," agreed engineer Koch, "better we live to see the images."

Kumukahi dropped below yonder restless horizon.

"Let us check with the boat," proposed Worning, and entered a command. Tyra's heart stumbled.

Josef Brandt was piloting for physical chemist Jens Lillebro. Raden had invited himself along. "Not my cup of tea, strictly speaking," he had said with his irresistible smile. "But one never knows what sort of clue lies where, does one? At least I can take a few observations of Pele from that angle. Those spots on her are acting downright eerily," as the planet's gravitational force swept through the photosphere.

The screen in *Freuchen* awoke again, to a view of

Henrietta Leavitt's cabin. Brandt sat intent at his controls, Lillebro at his spectroscopic readouts. Raden saw that they were in communication and responded. "All's well," he proclaimed. "We're closing in on the asteroid, and will have velocities matched quite shortly, at about five klicks' distance. Behold."

No time lag was noticeable. They were only some 15,000 kilometers away. Kivi had identified the body among the data pouring in from the continuous automatic sky-scan and, retrieving earlier information, computed an orbit. Now they saw a rough gray lump, about three kilometers long and one at maximum thickness, slowly tumbling.

"Apparently chondritic," commented Raden. "You'll notice the remarkable sparsity of craters. You're right, Maria, it must be from the outer belt, lately perturbed into an eccentric path."

Pristine, Tyra knew, formed hardly more than a billion years ago, in a thinly bestrewn region where there had been scant occasion or time for collisions. Probes were to examine such rocks later. But who knew how much later? Composition and structure might well give unique insights into the early life of every planetary system. This chance was too good to pass up. Should Kumukahi make sudden call on *Henrietta*, she could boost back to *Freuchen* in well under an hour.

"Backing down on it, essentially," continued Raden's voice. The asteroid swelled fast in sight. "As you recall, we'll run parallel and let Jens stare while we send minisamplers—"

The thing erupted. A white cloud burst raggedly forth. Gravel and boulders sleeted outward.

Tyra heard herself scream.

The view swung wildly. The barrage became glints across a whirl of stars. Somebody in the boat yelled, "*Almächtige Gott!*" Somebody else ripped an oath.

The view returned to the cabin and steadied on Rader. Sweat studded his brow, but he grinned, well-nigh laughed. "Whoop, that was close! Thank Josef here. The autopilot isn't programmed for— He yanked us free. Barely, but he did it."

Brandt looked around, his own expression grim. "Barely is correct," he grated. "Some of those stones could have holed us, or even been bouncers."

Tyra shuddered. She knew what he meant. The boat lacked a protective screen-field. The hull was self-sealing. But a small object that punched through could lose too much energy thereby to make an exit, not too much to ricochet back and forth and quite likely hit a man.

"Was für den Teufel—what happened?" roared Worning.

Lillebro spoke almost calmly. "I can guess. The chondrules surrounded a mixture of ices, which also mortared them together. The agglomerate was metastable, and the impulses from our polarizer drive as we neared touched off volatilization and—it will be fascinating to learn what reactions."

"A bomb," added Raden. "I daresay they're not uncommon in young systems, but all of them are disrupted—solar input, impact energy, perhaps cumulative cosmic ray effects—long before intelligence evolves locally to notice them. What a discovery!"

"It has just begun," said Lillebro with rising excitement. "The gas spectrum, and we'll collect specimens—"

"No," decreed Worning. "You will return here. At once."

"What? But, sir, now that we're aware—"

"Of what are we still unaware? I will not risk one of our two boats and three of our lives for something that robots can examine at leisure. Return. That is an order."

"Yes, sir." Brandt did not sound unwilling. Lillebro sighed. Raden gave a wry grin and a rueful shrug.

When he cycled aboard, Tyra was waiting at the lock. She reached for his hands. "You might have been killed," she stammered, and could not altogether hold back the tears. "You might have been killed."

He drew her to him. "Do you care that much?" he whispered. "I dared not hope."

9

A bunk could be folded out to double width, though it then filled most of the deck space in a so-called stateroom. Lights could be turned down to softness. Music could be commanded, *Là cì daremm' la mano, Liebestod,* afterward the lilt and gentleness of *Fynsk Foraar,* though likewise softened to a background.

"That was amazing," he said as low. "I didn't quite expect a supernova."

"Thank you," she answered, snuggling, refusing to wonder if he'd used those words before or how often. "Same order of magnitude to you, sir. But let's settle for ordinary novas. They can repeat."

He chuckled. His lips brushed her cheek. "Shameless hussy."

"I'd better be. You too. How many bets will be paid off tomorrow?"

He looked away. She heard the sudden seriousness. "You told me you . . . don't do casual."

She confronted her own spirit. "I don't."

"It's far too early to make promises. On either side."

"I realize that. But I decided, nothing ventured, nothing gained." And, if this didn't last—certainly the obstacles were many—she would at least have a profit of memories. As he would; she'd see to that. And she had the strength to pay the price. Which maybe wouldn't be required of her.

His eyes met hers. "I'm being as honest as I'm able," he said, "because in fact I am in love with you."

"All right, it's mutual."

"I wish I could, well, give you more. Now, I mean, before we go . . . home. We have so little here."

Through the eased-off happiness she felt her mind sharpen. She had given thought to this too. She did not believe the idea had snapped the leash she kept on herself. His escape did that. Nor was it a price she set, a bargain she struck.

Nevertheless—

"You can," she said.

His head lifted off the pillow. "What?"

She moved slightly aside from his warmth and male odor to lean on an elbow and keep hold of his gaze. "When Kumukahi begins breaking up, you'll be out there to watch, won't you?"

"Of course. We haven't that many free machines, and we don't know enough to write adequate programs for any. Who can tell what human observers might catch?"

"Take me along."

"Eh?" he exclaimed, and sat straight. After a moment, he leaned back. "No, really, darling, it's not feasible. If the event begins in the next few days, and it probably will, Birgit won't yet be fit to pilot. That leaves Josef for one boat, crammed with scientists and their gear."

Tyra nodded. "I know," from what *Rover*'s crew had told her. Neither they nor Eisenberg were weaklings, but kzinti captivity was at best unnerving. Given a stiff enough emergency, you could force yourself to carry on for a while. Thereafter medications merely helped time and nature. Eisenberg was absolutely right to disqualify herself for another week or two.

"And autopilot won't do for the other, not when we are bound to be surprised and must react fast if we are to collect the data," Raden went on. "I shall have to steer." Even now, she heard the relish.

"Exactly," Tyra said. "In that case, you can pick who comes with you, can't you? If you make a point of it."

"Well, I see where it could give you a spectacular story. But no, the hazard—no."

"What hazard?" she challenged. "You're skilled, you're not a fool, you won't take unnecessary risks."

"Not knowingly. Still, who can foresee what happens?"

"Who can foresee what will happen anywhere?" She moved back to his side and laid an arm around his neck. "Yes, I may get quite an eyewitness account, but that doesn't matter, Craig, truly it doesn't. This," she crooned, "is something you can give me, because it's something splendid we can share."

She was entirely wholehearted and honest. Well, almost.

Her free hand roved. She knew she could persuade him.

10

The three ranking kzinti met for their last time in the command lair of *Strong Runner.*

"Once more, master, I ask that you reconsider, and take me with you," said Rach-Scientist.

Ghrul-Captain growled negation. "And once more I tell you that you are wanted to oversee what other data collection this expedition can do, and bring the booty safely home, whatever may become of me. You have been less than enthusiastic about my plan. Do you challenge my decision?"

Rach-Scientist slipped his tail briefly between his hocks. "No, master, assuredly not."

Ghrul-Captain relented. "Bear in mind, this is a trial run, the first severe one. Yes, the instruments will peer and snuff, but foremost is to prove that the vessel can run such a course. That ride is for me alone." And for me alone the glory, and the triumph that it will be over the monkeys, he thought; it was as if he tasted fresh blood. "On later flights, yes, perhaps I will let you come too."

"Master, I have not questioned your wisdom, nor do I now," said Shayin-Mate. "However, I venture to ask that you record a summary of your intent. Should anything go awry, against my wishes—"

Then you will be acting captain, who takes the ship back, makes trophy of the prestige that that confers, and contrives to lay the full blame for the debacle with the monkeys on me, thought Ghrul-Captain sardonically. Not altogether against your wishes.

He did not resent it. In the mate's position, he would have done the same.

His rage at the humans flared. Because of their contumely, the exploit ahead of him would merely win back the standing Ress-Chiuu had lost for him. No net advancement. Unless, of course, he could do the foe a real injury. . . .

"The lords at Kzin will want a quick overview of events," Shayin-Mate went on. "The technical reports can be digested for them later."

Ghrul-Captain's fury smoldered back down. He expanded the ears he had folded and gibed, "Since you feel yourself incapable, I will pace the track for you."

"Master, it is simply that your own words will have the most force. I hope with all my entrails you will be on hand to deliver them personally."

"So be it." Ghrul-Captain set the intercom scanner to record. Having curtly stated the purpose, he declared:

"I am about to take the sundiver *Firehunter* on a swing around the sunward side of the giant planet we have come to spy out. The planet has just commenced its death struggle, so this is urgent. How things will go is unpredictable; they may become too violent for another such flight, although I am ready to dare whatever looks possible. For the same reason, unforeseeability, I make the flight piloted rather than robotic." As well as there being no honor in risking a few machines. "I will accelerate inward, cut the drive at a suitable point, and have the planet itself take me around. I will then be moving at high velocity on a hyperbolic orbit which, if allowed to continue, would carry me nearer the human ships than is . . . desirable. However, well before then, I will reduce the vector and start acceleration on a quartering path to rendezvous with *Strong Runner*. Available delta vee is ample.

"Perhaps observation of these extreme conditions at that close range will yield data of military value. It is sure that nothing like my mission has ever been attempted before.

"Glory to the race!"

He switched off and looked straight at Shayin-Mate. "Will that do?" he asked: a sarcasm, for it had better.

The other dropped his gaze. "Thanks and honor to our captain."

Rach-Scientist said nothing. En route he had expressed doubts about the utility of the scheme. The passage between star and planet would take less than four hours. What few instruments could endure the environment must be rugged, heavily shielded, basically simple, and therefore of very limited capabilities. His class was necessarily allowed a certain latitude, and Ghrul-Captain had been content to override his objections. But to pursue them, especially now, would be insolence meriting punishment.

And, yes, in the end he wanted to fare along. He too was a kzin.

"I go, then," said Ghrul-Captain. To linger when the game was afoot did not become a Hero.

He strode down passageways and sprang down

companionways to the portside boat lock. *Firehunter* waited alongside. A guard made obeisance as he reached the gang tube between. He passed on.

The control den, the only section of the vessel with life support, was a hemispherical space less than five meters across, crammed with equipment and storage lockers, just enough room free for a kzin to curl up on a pad and get a little sleep—hardly a fit prison cell. The air hung chill and stale-smelling. Yet in the viewscreen above the main control panel blazed his goal. He exulted while he settled into the command seat, activated the systems, heard the purr of power and felt the slight tug on him when his craft cast free.

Heavily burdened with her surrounding shell of water, she could not accelerate as fiercely as he would have wished. But her speed did mount, second by second, sunward bound. Ghrul-Captain hissed his satisfaction.

11

Tyra and Craig would be alone aboard *Caroline Herschel*. They could take several days, perhaps as much as a week, depending on what they found. "Not long enough," he grumbled, "not by half. Well, I'll come back, make better arrangements, and set forth again."

"I don't thnk this arrangement is a bad one," Tyra purred.

He laughed. "Nor do I. But the idea *is* to do science."

"Don't worry, dear, I won't get in the way. Not of the science, at least. Remember, I'm supposed to report it. We won't be tied down twenty-four hours per daycycle, though, will we?"

"M-m, no. The instruments will generally operate themselves. I'm basically to oversee, and make decisions when the inevitable surprises jump at us. Otherwise . . . we'll often sit goggle-eyed, I'm sure. But no, not the whole time."

"Don't worry," she said demurely. "Some happenings won't be reported."

She could not have been accommodated in *Henrietta Leavitt*, in any case. That boat would be crowded with scientists and their equipment. The Dalmadys did best to stay aboard *Freuchen*, working up what results they had obtained so far. Likewise, Padilla was fully occupied with the data flooding in from probes and observatories. Verwoort remained also, having lost a coin toss with Takata; it was unwise to send both planetologists together, and he'd have more than enough to keep him busy.

Henrietta departed in the prograde direction, boosting to a path that would take her as far sunward as was deemed safe. A boat from *Samurai* went along, just in case, and to keep a better eye on the kzin mother ship, orbiting ninety degrees ahead of her. Mainly, Bihari wanted her to follow the progress of the sundiver lately detected on a course for Pele itself. Furthermore, the navy craft had capabilities that would be substantially helpful to the scientists.

None accompanied *Caroline*. She was going retrograde, to study from a different angle what happened in the star rather than to the planet. The only kzin vessel she would see, and that from a considerable distance, was the sundiver when it swung half around Kumukahi and came out of the glare on a hurtling hyperbolic trajectory. Carrying two people, the boat could readily hold everything Raden needed for his work.

She even offered some extra space. He came upon Tyra when she was stowing a portable cooker-washer, kitchenware, tableware, and assorted things to eat. "What the deuce?" he asked.

She grinned. "I'll have more leisure to spare than you," she explained. "I want to show you I can cook too. I wheedled Marcus out of this—yes, the chill cabinet has room for it—and we'll have beer and wine as well. No need for us to pig it on dry rations and recycled water." She sighed. "Alas, no candles available."

"Well, we can turn the lighting way low—"

"Or block off the sun. Simply the stars . . . No, maybe that's best for later."

He cocked his head at her. "D'you know, you're the damnedest combination of the romantic and the practical."

"We women have to be."

"And we men get to enjoy it. How I pity the kzinti!"

Thus they took off merrily. The last thing they heard before the airlock closed behind them was Verwoort's bawdy farewell.

The next few days were sheer wonder. Personal joys became not separate, but integral with the whole. Tyra had an educated person's knowledge of science. Fascinated by what Raden told, especially about what was being newly revealed to him, she found that talking with her stimulated his thinking; she actually made a few suggestions that he called excellent. It was happiness merely to see and feel his glee; she could watch him in his preoccupation for hours, as she used to watch the sea at her childhood home or could lose herself in the splendor of open space. However, she seldom indulged idleness. Besides her cuisine and a few other minor things, there was her writing. How to find words for what she beheld, how to tell it? Personal impressions, text for a documentary, background for a novel, a cycle of poems—nothing could ever really capture truth, but the thrill of the quest was upon her.

A hundredth of Pele's mass skimmed around it and had begun to rain down into it. Incandescent tides raged, brewing maelstroms that crashed together and spouted monstrous plasmas; blaze scudded like spin-drift; invisibly, magnetic lines twisted around each other till they snapped and energies exploded that dwarfed whatever mortals knew to touch off; the deeper lay-ers roiled, and maybe certain atomic nuclei were fus-ing in strange ways: mystery, mystery, unfolding in fury.

The sun was not shaken to the core, Raden said. These were transient effects. In the course of the next century or two, they would die down, leaving little other than a slightly changed chemical composition and thereby, perhaps, a main-sequence evolution slightly hastened. Nor was this present chaos quite akin to a storm such as humans knew. However mighty it appeared from afar, it was gases in a soft vacuum. The deadliness lay in the radiation, charged particles, searing infrared, blinding light, lethal X-rays. Heavily protected, a spacecraft *might* still pass quickly through unscathed.

Might. Nobody knew. Nobody before them had been this close to this kind of catastrophe.

Tyra's mind dwelt more on Kumukahi. A planet, no matter how huge and alien, was closer kin to home than any star. Whenever it swung into view and she had the use of the screens, she strained at the mag-nified image, gripped, half terrified.

Pele had drawn the spheroid into a teardrop, but a living and throbbing one. The extended tip seethed and surged like a monstrous, fluid volcano. Hydrogen-helium smoke poured as from a nozzle, redly and restlessly aglow with fluorescence. It rushed ahead, girdling the planet's slayer with a ring that wound into a spiral whirling ever inward. Sparks and gouts flew free, knots of momentary concentration, like lava bombs. The titanic outpouring shuddered, shifted, ever changeable, spurted lesser eruptions of moon size, wrapped itself in clouds that then boiled away to give sight anew of the cata-ract streaming upward. Everywhere else churned chaos.

All was red, a thousand shades never the same for two instants, from murky roan through carmine to blood damasked with blue-white.

Kumukahi's dying in style! thought Tyra once; and then: That's how Robert would put it.

She dismissed the pain, which had become small, and went back to what she had gained.

12

The rage toward which Ghrul-Captain rushed filled heaven. The air in which he crouched recalled to him an equatorial desert on Kzin. An overloaded cooling system gusted and whined. It was time to go into sundiver mode.

Firehunter could have done so automatically. This, though, was his flight. Whether or not any other Hero ever knew, each thing he did raised his honor, was a blow he himself struck at the enemy. He stabbed the manual override. "Hro-o-o!" His roar echoed through his cave.

Steam vented from a thousand pores in the metal shell that enclosed the hull. The optics did not show it to his eyes, but the instruments did. The craft must take care of this for him, sensors gauging moment by moment how much to release. Calculation had shown that, given close control, there should be enough, just enough, to see him through the danger zone—if the calculations and the data upon which they drew were nearly enough correct. He had to trust them as he trusted his weapons. A Hero did.

And he was still the master of the wild hunt ahead. Again the control displays showed him what they would do of themselves and when. He heeded them as he would have heeded the scent of a quarry. But again it was he who cut off the drive.

Now let the planet sling him halfway around itself and cast him forth at more than cometary speed. For those three and a half hours, while the instruments drank down what knowledge they could, he must watch and wait—only that, if all went well. If not, he must choose what to do and do it. Nobody could have programmed for every unforeseeable violence. The fact brought no sense of helplessness. He had the heat to fight, with copious drinks and his own endurance. Meanwhile, he lurked watchful, as if in ambush.

Nevertheless awe came upon him. Under these conditions, optics were altogether inadequate, yet he saw, however partially and blurrily, he felt, he defied.

Firehunter flew between two walls that towered and reached beyond sight, one red-hot, geysering in mountainous lightning-shot clouds, shuddering beneath them until he imagined he could feel the thunders in his bones, the other a white-hot furnace out of which licked crimson tongues of flame. A thin opal haze shimmered everywhere around the spacecraft, fantastically writhing, where long livid arcs leaped and knots exploded into bursts of gigantic sparks. Ghrul-Captain sailed amidst a wreck of the gods.

Over and over again he roared at it, his challenge, his triumph.

A crash smote his hearing. *Firehunter* reeled. The noise became a hailstorm that dashed against metal and rang in his cave.

That smote through!

Ghrul-Captain saw the brief cloud gush out. Immensity swallowed it. An alarm keened. Readouts raced crazily over the pilot panel. Ghrul-Captain knew himself for a warrior suddenly stabbed.

Something had riddled the outer hull. It had not pierced the inner, but the water cells were ruptured and the fluid of life boiling away.

The bombardment ceased. He had passed whatever it was, or it had ended. No matter. It had slain him.

"No!" he bellowed, and snatched for the override. Start the drive. At full boost, he might break free before he baked.

Weightlessness took him, like a falling off an infinite cliff. Lights still shone, ventilation whispered. But nothing responded to his claws. He glared at the panel. The gravity polarizers were dead. He had no thrust.

How? flashed through him. An integrated system, well armored— But the damage to the massive water circulators and everything that regulated them, the escape of those tonnes, vibrations, resonances, yes, the plunge in temperature—he was breathing air gone wintry—yes, that could have disrupted critical circuitry. Then safety locks cut in and the fusion generator shut down. Nothing was left but the energy reserve in the accumulators.

That's as well, he thought starkly. Radiation from reactions running free would have killed me in minutes.

Which would have been better. Easier.

"No!" he snarled. A Hero did not surrender.

He was on trajectory, outward bound. The chilling gave him a short respite before temperature mounted. It might level off, as he receded, before he was cooked dead.

If he survived, it would be an exploit unmatched in

history. None could then deny him his birthright, and more, much more.

If not, this remained his deed, wholly and entirely his, which nothing could ever take from him.

13

"Oh-oh," said Raden very softly. "I don't like this *at* all."

Tyra's pulse jumped. "What is it?" Her voice sounded shrill in her ears. It must involve the kzin sundiver. *Freuchen* and *Samurai* were peering with high-tuned instruments, as the thing came out of Pele's blinding glare and deafening plasma. But they were almost two light-minutes farther away than *Caroline* had ventured. They had sent their request that the boat likewise keep watch. Orbiting ahead of them, the kzin mother ship currently had the sun between it and its explorer. Whoever was in command there had not deigned to respond to the human offer to relay information as soon as it was received.

Raden gestured. "Look."

Tyra peered over his shoulder at the viewscreen before which he sat. Magnified, chosen wavelengths dimmed or amplified, the image was hardly more than a schematic. To her eyes, a small segment of Pele was a

purple rectangle filling a slice along the left side of
the screen. Prominences were tendrils, the corona a
ghost-shimmer. A starlike speck gleamed nearby. That
must be the best that the boat's sensors could do at
this remove, lacking interferometry, she thought almost
mechanically. Raden's finger pointed at the displays and
readouts beneath the video.

"The spectroscope gives no hint of water molecules
or OH," he said starkly. "She ought to be venting yet,
to maintain an endurable temperature till she gets clear
of the peristellar zone. Instead, the infrared emission
is like an oven's, or worse. And doppler shows she
isn't boosting to escape. Hyperbolic trajectory, slung
off by the planet at terrific speed but not fast enough.
Something's gone terribly wrong."

It would be obscene to rejoice. However, Tyra could
not find pity in her heart. "What may have happened?"
she inquired.

"God knows, at this stage. Close examination ought
to give an idea or two." Raden turned his head to stare
at her. "Meanwhile, though, the crew are being baked
alive!"

"If they haven't already. Or he. Whichever. What do
you want to do?"

"Try saving them. Nobody else possibly can."

"How can we?" The figures he had mentioned to her
spun through her head. If the sundiver's periapsis
grazed through the significant fringe of Kumukahi's
distended atmosphere—and what other course would
a kzin plot?—the planet had hurled it forth at more
than a hundred KPS, far over stellar escape velocity,
bound for the stars. . . . But the plan must have been
to decelerate till the craft could swing around to rendezvous with its mother.

Raden swiveled about in his seat. His fingers danced
across a keyboard. Meanwhile he voice-activated

transmission. "*Caroline* to *Freuchen* and *Samurai*. By now you'll have seen that sundiver's in trouble. The other kzinti can't match velocities and lay to till long after the ones aboard are dead. I propose to make rendezvous and rescue them if they aren't, yet. If this craft has the capability. That's being checked. Assuming a positive answer, we'll need to skite off immediately. I'll await your response."

Three or four minutes— "Have you gone crazy?" Tyra protested.

He gave her a lopsided grin. "No, in my opinion I'm being more sane than most. If the computations tell me what I hope they will . . . Ah!" He swung his chair again to stare at the readouts. She stood above him, behind him, helpless, listening to his monotone. "Yes. Just barely feasible. Killing our present vector, boosting to match while approaching, yes, it calls for accelerations up to ten gee. Within stress limits for our craft, though an engineer would probably shake his head a bit. The thermostatic system will be overloaded too, but not overwhelmed if we're quick. And we'll squander energy. We should have enough delta vee left afterward to make it home. If not, the difference by then will be slight, and *Samurai* has a tug plenty well able to meet us and haul us back. We can do it."

Abruptly his tone rang. "Therefore we must."

The comscreen lightened, view split to show two faces. "This is lunacy," growled Worning. "No!" and Bihari, quietly, with her ironic smile: "The kzinti aren't noted for gratitude. My recommendation is a decided negative."

"Ma'am and sir," Raden replied, "let me respectfully remind you that while this vessel is in free space, I'm in command, with discretionary authority. If I'm mistaken, a board of inquiry will pass judgment later. Now I've no time to lose. We're on our way."

He rapped his piloting instructions. In a moment or two the boat left free trajectory. The interior gravity polarizer field kept weight steady under Tyra's feet, but she saw the stars whirl into a new configuration and felt a brief surge of power fully aroused, a shiver in the deck and through her bones.

"Well, you are within your legal rights," Bihari said. "I am not so sure about the moral ones. You understand, do you not, that we can do nothing to help you until much later in this game."

"And the devil knows how the kzinti will react," added Worning.

"Contact them, of course," Raden answered. "Explain the situation. That I—we—have no intention of more than a rescue attempt, and we'll lay no salvage claims or anything like that. In fact, I promise to leave whatever kind of black box they have, the data this flight gathered, alone, for them to retrieve. Let me suggest you offer them any other help you can give. That's traditional, after all."

He laughed. "Don't worry about us. We're within our safety factors. Quite an adventure!"

He cut off transmission, pending further reception, rose, looked into Tyra's eyes, and reached for her hands. She withheld them.

His smile was gone. "There will be hazards," he said low. "Aren't there always? I rejoiced to have you along, darling, but now I'd sell my chance of having an immortal soul—no, that's too cheap a price—I'd give everything I own for you to be safely back aboard *Freuchen.*"

Every material thing, maybe, she thought. The bank accounts, the royalties, the vacation home, the sailboat, whatever. But how could you divest yourself of your reputation, your fame? This deed can only add to them.

Her bitterness shocked her. It wasn't reasonable. Was it? "Well, I'm not there," she said, "nor sorry."

As if to reinforce her, the comscreen brought Worning and Bihari back. "Playing the noble knight may be very well, Raden," Worning snapped. "But you're spending the resources of our expedition, and putting critical assets at risk, for no other gain."

"Oh, God, can't you see?" Raden exclaimed. "That's a living, sentient being yonder, maybe two, with a ghastly death ahead of them. Could you stay idle in my circumstances and still call yourself a man? I don't believe that, Captain Worning. I don't believe you would."

This time he left transmission going while he appealed to Tyra. "Nor would you." With a quick, wry grin: "And call yourself a woman. Which you are, incredibly much."

"I think you're confused about the issue," she told him out of the ice within her. "A human being, or a— a dog, yes. Kzinti, no. They're something else."

He seemed appalled. "You can't be serious!"

"Yes, they're as intelligent as we are, in their fashion. Maybe they can feel pain as much, in their fashion. But it doesn't mean the same to them. They have nothing like sympathy, compassion, anything we humans have had such a struggle to keep alive in ourselves. Craig, I've seen what they do. I've *lived* with it."

Dada-man, snatched away from everyone he loved and who loved him. Mother, dying of grief, unjustly disgraced. Ib, betrayed into dishonor. The endless years of the occupation, friends killed, crushed, hunted down like game animals, eaten. The murderous assault at the black hole . . . And those were merely things she had witnessed or heard of at firsthand. She knew of too many more.

She heard the shock: "But this is racism. The old horror. Jews made booty of, Amerindians massacred,

Africans enslaved . . . I grant you, it's a horrible culture, but they can learn better. The Mongols were once
the terror of half a world. They became one of the
most peaceful people on Earth—"

"If you please," interrupted Bihari, answering Raden's
reply to Worning, "I daresay you suppose you're making
a goodwill gesture, which will go toward improving
relationships. I have my doubts, but since you are on
your way and not open to argument, we will communicate with the kzinti, fully and frankly, and stand by
to render any assistance we can that they will accept.
We will keep you informed. Meanwhile, we shall be
on alert status."

"*Ja,*" rumbled Worning. "Good luck. You'll need it."

The images blanked. Neither captain meant to nag,
nor would they allow anyone else to stammer best
wishes.

"We've got a couple of hours to make ready," Raden
said. "First aid, for openers. A very near thing at best.
Prepare for unpleasantness, Tyra. A cooked corpse
or . . . worse."

"I've known worse."

His expression, stance, voice pleaded. "Do you really
feel we're altogether wrong to do this?"

It was not simply that she happened to be with him
and got no choice, it was that she *was* with him, for
as long as might be. Maybe for life. "No," she made
herself say, and confessed inwardly that he did have
a certain logic, that without some forthcomingness—
which could only begin on the human side—the hatred
and slaughter might well go on until one race or the
other went extinct. "I'm with you," and now she took
his hands and presently returned his kiss before they
got busy.

She refrained from wishing aloud that they had a
firearm along.

14

"We have still received no response from the kzinti," Bihari reported. "Among other things, that means we don't have the code for opening any of their airlocks. Since you are closing in, I have ordered a naval 'key' program sent to you. I suppose you know it directs phased currents through your contact module and analyzes the reaction to each set of pulses. A search pattern conducted at electronic speed. It ought to determine the unlocking sequence within a few minutes. The program is classified information, but merely at 'confidential' level, and may be shared in emergency. Instructions will accompany it. Prepare to download."

Raden nodded. "I rather expected this," he told Tyra. "I didn't think the captain would leave us to cut our way in with laser torches. Dangerous, as well as slow. No doubt she'll order the program wiped from our database after we return, but actually, one relies more on interstellar distances and infrequent contacts to keep such things from spreading. All colony worlds have similar tools, civilian as well as military, and many spacecraft carry them. You might need to get into a friendly ship, too—a Crashlander, say—when for some reason the crew couldn't just let you in. Or any of all the other unpredictable situations."

He spoke rapidly, dryly, as if he were lecturing to a class. Tyra listened, though she already knew most of it. This must be a way for him to release some tension. Mainly he directed himself toward the keyboard.

Sweat gleamed on his brow. Tyra felt it on her own face and soaking her armpits. She wondered how much of it was due to excitement—fear?—and how much was the body trying to maintain temperature. The compartment, the whole interior had gotten unpleasantly warm, and still the temperature crept upward.

The thermostatics weren't failing; they struggled as best they could against an input for which they weren't intended. *Caroline* had unfolded her extra radiation surfaces, like huge wings, their thinness tilted normal to the swollen sun-disc. Unless you have vapor to release, as the kzin venturer had had, radiation is the single way to shed excess heat in space, and it does not work very fast.

The wings of an angel, speeding on an errand of mercy— Memories arose of themselves in Tyra, childhood, church, the steel steeple of St. Joachim's shining above Munchen . . . during the kzinti occupation, it stood in more human minds than hers as a symbol of freedom, eventual liberation, but you seldom said such things aloud, never where kzinti might hear, because then they would likely tear it down. . . .

Caroline was closing in, sensors at maximum, autopilot adjusting vectors like a high-wire walker. . . . Yes, Wunderlanders had revived quite a few such acts during the war, more often performed for live audiences than cameras, another silent declaration that humans were not cattle. . . .

Optics gave a clear view of the sundiver, massive, ungainly against the stars, but—she must admit—its own sign of indomitability. She could magnify until a single section filled the screen for close study. She saw the holes strewn over the outer hull, small, not really very many, but sufficient to let the water seethe unchecked away. And forward she identified a damaged outercom dish. That explained why there had been no contact on any band. The damage didn't look great to her. Crew could readily have fixed it and regained communication, except that none could venture outside and live to do the work. Could a robot? Kzinti technology seemed to lag others when it came to robotics. Nevertheless— But maybe there was no robot, or maybe no person left who was able to dispatch one.

Minute by minute, the image expanded. *Caroline* was closing swiftly in on the reality.

Raden finished at the keyboard, rose, and stretched, seeking to limber muscles too long tautened. "Is the medical care station ready?" he asked. Laying everything out for that had been her job.

"Yes," she snapped.

"I'm sorry. Stupid of me to ask. You're always competent." He sighed. "Not long now. I damn near wish it were. Then we could perhaps— But we'd better prepare ourselves."

She gave him a smile.

He did pause to frown at the spacecraft's image. "Quite a bombardment," he muttered. "I doubt it holed the inner hull. I'd expect somewhat different spectroscopic readings in that case, and sheer off right away. As is, all we know is that it's an oven inside there."

They started aft. "Have you any idea what did it?" she asked. "Does Pele have a ring of meteoroids?"

"No, Maria would have identified one, even a thin strewing of gravel, and told us. Implausible anyway, on general principles. I have been speculating, though, whenever I got a chance. A notion has occurred to me. It may be utterly wrong."

An eagerness flickered amidst the forebodings. "What is it? I promise not to laugh."

"Thanks. I badly needed a grin." Raden spoke on as they made their way to the space gear lockers and busied themselves there. "Do you remember the anomalous iron content Maria found in the high Kumukahi atmosphere?" She nodded. "We don't yet know what spews it out. I'd say the best guess is convulsions in the planetary body; then rising air currents—what storms those must be!—bring it aloft. Pele isn't an ultraviolet emitter on the scale of Sol or Alpha A, but that close, Kumukahi surely gets plenty to split molecules or radicals into atoms—ionized atoms—once they're up where the air is thin. Then—here's my guess—tremendous magnetic fields are interacting, the star's and the planet's, changeably, chaotically. It may result in vortices that pull ferromagnetic atoms together over an enormous range. They join into macroscopic clumps, pellets, perhaps still carrying some charge. Then a surge in the fields accelerates them to escape velocity, or nearly. They're thrown out of the atmosphere, probably in bursts, like shotgun fire. The sundiver ran into a cluster. The planet had given her such a velocity of her own that the encounter riddled her.

"Whether I'm right or wrong, the notion suggests precautions for the future, doesn't it? We need data, data, data, observations, missions, year after year before we can hope to make a halfway decent computer model." His tone and eyes came ablaze. "Unique in our experience. What a wild fluke of luck! What a chance to *learn*!"

For a moment the enthusiasm caught her too. She had always been fascinated by science, but none of her men before now had been scientists. To see, to be a part, of truly doing it— If nothing else, life with Craig would never be dull.

The mood chilled and hardened in them both. They had work on hand.

Elementary prudence dictated wearing space gear. It needn't be cumbersome full armor, simply protection against possible hot spots, noxious gases, or the like. They stripped off their clothes—gazes flying up and down, and a pulse in the throat—and took skintights from the suit locker. Those were easy to pull on. The molecules flowed to make a dermis from neck to ankles, shinily reflective, leather-tough, silk-flexible, veined with electronics and tiny capillaries for exuding sweat vapor or other unwanted fluids but sealing the body off from the outside. Boots snuggled similarly to feet and ankles. A backrack went on nearly as readily, for powerpack, airtank, regulators, water supply. The collars of the clear, hard helmets made themselves fast to shoulders and coupled to the rack. The wearers could talk by radio or, with sound amplification, directly; they likewise had good hearing, while sensors woven into the integument provided tactility.

His smile quirked at her through the barriers between. "All set for the dance, Tyra?"

"Well, I'll take a promissory note for my corsage," she forced herself to reply in kind.

Sternly: "To repeat the doctrine one last time. I go first. You stay behind at the entrance till I call for you. If I call, 'Get away!' instead, or you realize that something's gone seriously wrong, close our airlock and release the gang tube. Worning will instruct you how to bring *Caroline* back. This isn't heroics, it's plain

common sense, and you know how and why to follow orders."

Softly: "Not that I expect danger. Horror, perhaps.
You may well be tougher than me, dealing with that.
You're a remarkable lady, Tyra, and I'm an incredibly
lucky man."

"I love you," she whispered, and knew she meant
it. Whatever happened in the future, she had been set
free of regrets from the past.

They waited for a span that felt endless, although
clocks showed little change. Then she felt a thud go
through metal and knew that the vessels had made
contact.

She stood trying to visualize events. *Caroline* nudged
the sundiver. Both recoiled the least bit. The autopilot had gauged nicely; airlocks were nearly aligned.
Caroline's gang tube need only extrude two or three
meters to enclose the lock opposite and grip with molec-
ular forces. The search program got busy as directed,
stimulating crystals into vibrations that it detected and
analyzed. It found the combination that would activate
the mechanisms. Quantum levels fluctuated, utterances
of command. Engines in the outer and inner portals
of the kzin hull swung the valves aside. Gas billowed
into the tube. Instruments verified that, while not in
any normal state, it was not potentially destructive.
Caroline's lock opened.

Heat rushed over Tyra in a flood. Protected, she felt
it only slightly. The suit could maintain her in the oven
for several minutes at least. She was flashingly, self-
ishly glad she could not smell whatever stenches the
inflow bore.

Raden sprang forward. She followed as far as the
airlock chamber and halted. Raden spun upward. His
heels kicked ridiculously as he went out of her sight.
The gravity polarizers inside the sundiver had failed

too, she understood. Well, he knew how to handle himself in microgravity.

After a few hundred heartbeats his voice reached her. "Come on through, Tyra. There's just one of them. He's in bad shape, but alive. Come help me bring him over to us."

15

Heroes scream when they leap to do battle. They bear pain in silence.

That was a battle of its own. Ghrul-Captain had never dreamed how long and lonely it could be. Often he wanted to make an end. If necessary, he could claw his throat across.

But his folk might yet regain the spacecraft. Finding his body, they would see how he died. If he had endured to the end, always watchful for the chance to somehow strike back, they would bring home his praise. His kin would gain pride, and renewed standing. He would live on in memory, song, fame. If what he had done turned out to be to the good of the Race, he might be given a shrine and yearly blood sacrifices.

If nothing else, they would remember how he had dared. Something no kzin had ever done before. Something no monkey ever would.

Yes, let him keep this before him, that he was not a monkey who whimpered and fled, but a Hero.

He bobbed about randomly. Now and then he bumped into a side of the cabin. Though the lining was a soft insulator, every touch seared, and he jerked free with the breath hissing between his fangs. His fur was singed, his whiskers scorched, his tail one blister from end to end. Each shallow breath filled his breast with pain. His ears were clenched tight. He seldom opened his eyes to the parching, baking air. Dreams had begun to weave distortedly through the darkness behind the lids. He tried to fight them off.

If only death would come, the cool, kindly night— No, he must not think so, the wish was unworthy of a Hero. Let him rather hold that fact to his bosom, and the victory over the monkeys he had achieved.

It was what meant most, he thought whenever the tide of delirium ebbed back for a while. If only within his own spirit, he had struck a blow at them. Someday they would find out how deeply the blade had gone in. One stab, true, one out of the millions it would take to bring them down and avenge the Race, but his.

Something stirred, something made noise. He hauled himself to full awareness. A shape, not a vision, a real thing that touched him—anguish lanced; he almost cried out—and gabbled. Behind its helmet was a face like the face of a flayed corpse.

Monkey.

Another soared in. He snatched for recollections. *Strong Runner* swung afar. The monkeys, the rich, battening monkeys had sent boats out. One had laid alongside his.

What did they want? To take him captive, maybe try to sell him back to his folk—to seize the knowledge his vessel had won from the wreck of a world—or hand him over freely and gloat?

It hardly mattered. They were monkeys, victorious. They were pulling and shoving him with them.

No, never. A kind of joy gleamed through the pain that had become Ghrul-Captain's universe.

Monkeys crawled around in their tree. They jeered at the hunter below and pelted him with dung. But all the while, their bough was bending under their weight, until they were in reach of him.

To kill these would be his vengeance for the Race and himself. What happened afterward mattered little. He might or might not be able to pilot their craft back to *Strong Runner* in time for the medic to save him. Certainly their fellow monkeys would shriek and jabber; but they'd do nothing decently warlike. Certainly, too, his achievement would go far toward inspiring the Race, would help hasten the day of reckoning.

His warrior skills returned to him. He should bide his time, let them carry him off to where he'd have weight under his feet, where he'd draw some lungfuls of air like the air of home. Then he'd be ready. Enough strength would flow back for long enough. Later he could rest in the blessed cool, rest and rest, sleep and sleep.

To loosen his muscles was the start of his preparing. He shut his eyes again and tried not to wince or gasp when the monkeys touched a burnt spot. They didn't mean to. There drifted through him a recollection of a teacher at his academy, discussing the monkeys, saying, "What they call conscience makes cowards of them all."

16

"Easy, now, easy," Raden said. "The poor devil. You or I wouldn't have survived this long, or wanted to. We can't let him crash on the deck when we enter our gravity field."

"No," Tyra agreed, "but we can't drag him to the first aid station either. He *weighs*," that huge body.

"Yes. I think probably we'd do best to turn off the polarizer while we convey him. First, though, for God's sake, we have got to get him out of this damned kiln."

They maneuvered the kzin through the gang tube. Straining, they eased his sudden ponderousness to the deck beyond. He lay sprawled, seemingly barely conscious. The eyelids weren't quite shut, a yellow slit gleamed between. Raden straightened and tapped instructions for airlock closure. Ventilators whirred, sucking away the hot air. Tyra imagined that, through her suit, she felt the freshness gusting in. She stepped a pace aside to catch her breath. Her glance flitted across scorch marks, blisters, raw fire wounds. I suppose this was our duty, she thought. Do we have any analgesics that work on kzinti? Maybe they can tell me on our ship or maybe we can only make haste there.

The giant stirred. He struggled up. For half a minute he stood unsteadily, breath harsh in his throat. Bloodshot eyes glared.

"What the hell?" Raden exclaimed. "Don't be afraid. You're with friends now."

Silly, flashed through Tyra. The kzin probably doesn't know English. And if he did, would he listen?

He didn't quite scream and leap. He uttered a hoarse, broken cry and lurched toward the man. Claws slid forth. He swiped a mighty arm. The spacesuit fabric ripped.

"No! Don't! Are you crazy?" Raden stumbled backward. The kzin followed. Again he slashed. Raden barely dodged, into a corner.

And we have no weapon, Tyra silently shrieked.

Maybe I do! She wheeled about and fled. Growls, snarls, and human yells pursued.

Up the companionway. Down the passageway. A remote part of her knew how fast she bounded and ran, but it felt nightmarishly slow. Swivel through a doorway into the tiny galley. The largest knife she had brought gleamed in a rack. Her father had taught her always to keep cutting tools sharp. She snatched it and sped back.

She half expected to find Craig disemboweled. But he knew his martial arts, sidestepped, ducked, weaved, dropped to the deck and bounced up again. The kzin was slow and clumsy. Though red flowed from half a dozen shallow gashes, the dance of death went on.

The kzin didn't see her, or reckon her for anything if he did. She got behind him and sprang. Her legs clamped around his great barrel of a body, her free hand dug into an ear and hauled. The knife struck.

The kzin coughed a roar and reached back. She clung

while she worked the blade across his throat. Blood spouted. She felt claws rake through her own suit. She clung and cut.

The kzin buckled. She let go and jumped clear. The kzin went to his knees, to all fours, onto his belly. He struggled for a while as the life pumped out of him.

Tyra had left the knife in his neck. She and Raden fell into each other's arms. "Are you all right?" she choked.

"N-nothing serious, I think. You?"

"Same."

They stood thus, shuddering, until the body slumped and lay quiet. Blood reddened the chamber; excrement befouled the deck. So much for a heroic death, thought Tyra vaguely.

"What shall we do?" Raden mumbled.

She rallied a little. "Take care of our injuries. Disengage the spacecraft. Call our own. And . . . and send this corpse out the airlock." Unwillingly, she thought: Let him go on to the stars. "Set the pilot for rendezvous with *Freuchen*, and go to sleep. Sleep and sleep. Later, we can clean up this place. And think."

They trembled for an hour or more. A kzin wouldn't have. But they were merely human.

17

The captains met with them in Bihari's cabin aboard *Samurai*. She wanted complete privacy.

"You were wise not to report more than the bare minimum on your way back," she said. After they arrived and gave her the whole story, the medical program ordered them to sickbay for two daycycles under sedation. Released, calmed, they would need a while more to feel entirely fit. However, a flit across to the lancer was, if anything, refreshing—a sight of stars, Milky Way, majesty and immensity.

Worning nodded. "*Ja*, we can't be quite sure the ratcats don't keep a few little receivers orbiting about; and you didn't have the equipment to encrypt."

Raden winced. "I, at least, didn't trust my judgment in this case either," he confessed. "How might the kzinti react to a . . . a terrible incident?"

"I could have told you that," Tyra said. "I'm damned glad we have a better warship than they do."

"They don't have the news to react to in any case,"

Bihari stated. "When they discovered that you'd made a short contact with the sundiver, they finally replied to my messages, demanding to know the details. I put them off until you came. Then I informed them that you found the pilot dead. Ghrul-Captain, he was. The master himself."

"Daft," snorted Worning. "You don't send a skipper off like that. They're maniacs, the whole lot of them."

"They're different from us," protested Raden.

"Which makes them deadly dangerous," Tyra retorted.

He sighed. "I've admitted to you, darling, I've been shocked out of, of what seemed like realism. Yes, we do need to keep on guard. Although negotiations— Well, I was afraid the blunt truth might antagonize them. So I left it to you professionals, Captain Bihari, to explain things tactfully."

Tyra shook her head and clicked her tongue. He was honest, he'd change an opinion when the facts convinced him it was wrong, but down underneath he'd always be an idealist. Which probably was part of his being lovable.

"What did you say to them?" she asked.

"That you'd made a gesture," Bihari answered. "Because his vessel wouldn't cool down before he was roasted like a food animal, you gave him space burial. A mark of respect and honor. Shayin-Mate, the present master, seemed pleased, perhaps a bit relieved. I added that you did nothing else aboard, never touched the databases, which they could verify as soon as a mission of theirs overhauled the derelict."

Raden's haggardness lighted up. "Excellent, ma'am! Tyra and I won't let the secret out either, will we, darling?"

"I'd like to," Tyra replied. "You were so brave and—"

"Scarcely like you." His hand reached for hers.

She shrugged. "Needs must. The story wouldn't give them a pretext for starting the next war. They aren't ready yet."

He frowned slightly but kept silence.

"Maybe it could complicate diplomacy a little, though," Tyra went on. "And surely it'd complicate relationships here at Pele. All right, ma'am and sir, it won't go beyond the four of us." I'll keep the glory to myself, and wish he'd share it with me, but he never will, she thought.

He relaxed and laughed. "I couldn't have robbed that database anyhow," he said. "Couldn't have endured the heat and wasn't acquainted with their systems."

"I wish you had been," growled Worning. "I'll hate seeing that knowledge fall into their claws."

"It cannot be critically important," Raden reassured him. "Once we've established a permanent scientific presence—robotic, no doubt, but permanent—we'll soon have all of it and much more. Meanwhile, we've gotten the truly invaluable piece of information. Not just that there's a hazard we must protect future probes against, but that there's an extraordinary phenomenon. Whether or not my hypothesis about the iron proves out, we hold a clue to understandings we never even knew we lacked." His voice dropped. "Tragic, that a sentient being died for it. If only we could commemorate him somehow—"

Jesu Kristi, thought Tyra, after he did his best to kill us? Then, ruefully: That's my Craig.

"But we *have* learned," Raden said, with a lilt in his voice that she also knew. "This alone justifies our expedition. Let the kzinti take what he earned for them."

"As a matter of fact," answered Bihari, "they aren't going to." Startled gazes sought her. "Shayin-Mate told me he would launch a missile—he told me exactly when, giving us plenty of time to track and stand alert—that will overhaul and destroy the sundiver. It started off about half an hour ago. He also said, um-m, 'The Heroes have accomplished everything they intended, and will return home very shortly.' The latest indications are that preparations for departure are already in train."

"Kzinti—simply giving up?" asked Tyra.

"Well, perhaps they have no boat capable of rendezvous with one on such a trajectory. _Caroline_ barely was, and the parameters were more favorable than they are by now. Under no circumstances would the kzinti make us a free gift of anything the mission gained. On the other hand—I can't prove this, it's an intuition, but rising from experience. I strongly suspect Ghrul-Captain was the driving force behind their entire venture. The acting master may well be seizing an opportunity to minimize his role, or actually make him out to have been a fool. Thereafter Shayin-Mate becomes the paragon who frustrated the humans, salvaged everything that could be salvaged, and brought his ship home to fight another day. He can hope to be made Shayin-Captain. Kzinti have their own internal politics."

Tyra grinned. "Not altogether unlike ours, hm? You're right about that much, Craig."

Her look upon him remained soft. He returned it. The humans wouldn't be here much longer either. She'd insist he take several weeks' leave of absence, or vacation or whatever they called it in Earthside academe, to spend with her. She wanted him to meet her father. She wanted to show him the merry old inns of Munchen, the ancestral house and sea cliffs at Korsness, the scenery and geysers of Gelbstein Park, the tremendous overlook from the peak of the Lucknerberg, the dancers in Anholt, all the wonders of

Wunderland. Maybe later he could take her likewise
around Earth. Maybe then they could think about
making a home.

HIS
SERGEANT'S
HONOR

Hal Colebatch

Chapter 1

"There is a 'cease-fire.' "

The word was not new to kzin military terminology, though used rarely. The kzintis' forebears had offered a cease-fire to the remnant of human resistance on Wunderland once.

The smoke stung Raargh-Sergeant's eye and nose but he held himself rigidly alert.

There were black commas with dangling limbs drifting high in the air with the smoke, he saw: a group of dead kzin and human fighters still held aloft by lift-belts, debris of the previous weeks of fighting. The wind brought the sound of bells pealing from the monkey temple as well as drifting smoke from the burning city and from the straggle of huts beyond the monastery gates. A gust of wind drove two of the floating bodies together. A side arm that one of them still clasped fired a few random bolts into air and ground, throwing up rock and flame. Neither kzin moved.

"We have our orders," Hroarh-Captain said again. "You

are not permitted to die heroically. Go to barracks and remain there until you hear further, either from me or another proper authority. I go to seek Hroth-Staff Officer.

"You are, as you know, the senior surviving Sergeant," he added. "I look to you to help preserve what order and discipline there may be in the Patriarch's armed forces . . . all that is left of them. We are Regulars. We are professionals, not wild outland barbarians, and our Honor is in that. We have taken oaths and our Honor is in obedience. Remember that a dead Hero is useless to the Patriarch."

He moved to the half-repaired battle car which Raargh-Sergeant had been loading with weapons for the last attack and killed the engine. It sank to the ground, a visibly dead, defeated thing. Junk.

"You have kits, Raargh Sergeant?"

"No longer, Hroarh-Captain." *At least I know mine is dead. I need not tear my liver wondering if he somehow escaped.*

A kzin of the old type would have affected indifference to the fate of his male kits once they reached some maturity and did not dishonor him, but times had changed with the extinction of so many bloodlines. Heroes and indeed bloodlines had perished wholesale as one fleet after another attacked Sol System and limped back with its dead and its wreckage. More recently the UNSN's raids had devastated much of the system's infrastructure. Then, like lightning falling from a clear sky, had come the bizarre, unexpected war of kzin against kzin, between the followers of Traat-Admiral and Ktrodni-Stkaa, and finally, with much of the kzin fleet destroyed in space in fratricidal combat and the ground war beginning to escalate beyond the nuclear threshold, the UNSN's Hyperdrive Armada had swept in with its bombardment from the skies and then infantry landings, coupled with widespread—in fact almost universal—

uprisings among the human population of both Wunderland and the Serpent Swarm. There would be many lost kits . . .

"Nor I," said Hroarh-Captain. He looked as if he was in no shape to get more offspring even if chance permitted, but obviously Raargh-Sergeant could hardly broach that topic.

"A dead Hero is also useless to all others who look to him for protection."

A ball of orange fire was rising into the sky from the old human ruins on the plains a few miles away. Some band of Heroes had made a stand there, to be blasted to the Fanged God by attack from the skies which the humans now ruled. The kzintis' sensitive hearing filtered out a chaos of distant explosions and the supersonic booms of aircraft.

"There are moments," said Hroarh-Captain, "when self-control is the only weapon a warrior has. There is no shame . . ." He twitched convulsively; the ground-effect cart that took the place of his legs lurched, spitting pebbles from the dirt. He had no tail to signal his emotions and the torn remnants of his ears were held steady but his mane was flat as Raargh-Sergeant's. Both felt shame beyond measure.

"I have been summoned," Hroarh-Captain went on. "I will return as soon as possible. Maintain discipline and await further orders. Remember that the situation may change quickly.

"Remember always, a warrior has a duty to all those under his care." He gestured with his remaining arm to the Speaker-for-Humans who, with its female deputy, stood between them. Moisture was running down its pale face and it was shaking. The deputy's expression was hard to read.

"This human has been loyal to the Patriarchy and will remain in charge of human affairs here," the officer went on. "It—*he*—and those under him are under the Patriarchy's protection still. You will exert that protection. But humans in general are no longer slaves or prey. . . ." He folded and unfolded what were left of his ears thoughtfully, almost as if he were groping for words.

"You are old, Raargh-Sergeant. You are a good soldier, and it was my pleasure to recommend that you be honored with a partial name for your valor and bloodlust in the Hohe Kalkstein. . . ."

The name called up memories for both of them. "There was good hunting in the forest and the caves there. I can smell the limestone now. War in the great caves has pleasures all its own. . . ." Raargh-Sergeant tried to cheer his captain. He remembered the great caves of the high limestone, and the strange, three-sided war a few lucky Heroes had fought in the depths with the feral humans and the brainless but savage creatures the humans called Morlocks. Happy days. Once they had placed Morlock skins over their heads and waded through a cold shallow underground stream to come upon a human position . . .

"So I recall. But I recommended you too because I know you have the cunning of a lurker in tall grass, and are no fool who is burnt to death by the passion for glory in his over-hot liver. There are few old and foolish soldiers. You are a survivor and more than ever do we need our survivors of guile now. Continue to survive. That also is an order."

The wind brought a renewed sound of fighting. The sergeant flicked his own torn ears. "The cease-fire does not seem to be very effective, Hroarh-Captain," he said.

"The humans are also fighting among themselves. That is no business of ours now . . . unless the Patriarchy's honor is involved."

Raargh-Sergeant brought his own remaining natural arm up in a claws-across-the-face salute as Hroarh-

Captain headed away, holding up a white cloth. *Hroarh-Captain was a good officer,* he thought, *although he is still alive. Or because he is still alive?* Then he turned to the human.

"Do I give you a name now?" he asked.

He spoke in the slaves' patois. His was the third generation on the planet and though his sire had been but a sergeant also he had been raised by human house-slaves. He understood Wunderlander well but it was still difficult to pronounce.

Raargh-Sergeant had dealt with this human frequently before when it had been in charge of maintaining order and discipline among the local slaves and taxpayers, and it had been in charge of a force of armed human auxiliaries for some time, but its rank description seemed inappropriate now.

It—*he,* as Hroarh-Captain had said—replied in a sort of Wunderlander in which the slaves' patois and a few Kzinti or Kzinti-derived words were making encroachments. A Hero could certainly use such a language to a slave since matters of dealing with slaves were beneath most considerations of dignity.

"I am called Jorg, Raargh-Sergeant Noble Hero," the human told him. "My deputy is called Jocelyn. If you will give us leave, I will go and try to keep order as I may. I am leaving a guard of twelve of my men at the gate under my orders. They are armed and are instructed to keep other humans out."

Raargh-Sergeant did not know if it was competent for him to give the humans leave now, but it hardly mattered. He made a dismissive sign with his tail, and the humans withdrew, Jorg with many an uneasy glance over its—*his*—shoulder. *It is easier if you think of it as "him."* Raargh-Sergeant watched the human out of sight, and the human "guard" deploy, then he turned and limped stiffly across the parade ground to the barracks.

Circle Bay Monastery had been taken over by the kzin forces in the last days of the war. Most of its humans had fled and though a few "monks" lurked in cellars and remote rooms, it would have been a rash human who without authorization had shown himself before a kzin there in the last few days.

But few remained of the kzin garrison now, and all of these were more or less seriously wounded or disabled, clustered into what had been the Sergeants' Mess. He reviewed them as he entered.

Lesser-Sergeant, the closest thing to a friend that one in his position could allow himself; First and Second Section-Corporals, both badly shot up; Trainer-of-Strong-Muscles; Guardian-of-Stores/Fixer-of-Small-Weapons; a junior doctor, almost helpless without either his equipment or his natural forelimbs; an orderly; and two infantry troopers—one of them his personal servant and groom, an old sweat whose reflexes had long ago slowed too much for front-fighting—the other half-conscious, leaking blood and serum and twitching from some head wound that would be fatal soon if he could not be taken to a fully-equipped military doc.

The place resembled a hospital save that in normal times a hospital would have had proper medicines, treatment facilities and better prostheses as well as regeneration tanks and machine-doctors. As it was, it looked like a first-time soldier's bad dream of what might happen to him. As well as what were mainly crude and temporary field prostheses, meant to be fitted in actual battle conditions to keep Heroes in action, Junior Doctor had a few primitive salves and dressings, some commandeered from the human monks' "infirmary." Presumably the salves were effective for Heroes. Perhaps Junior Doctor had tried them on himself. His eyes were violet with pain.

The nine fully-conscious military kzin had fourteen

eyes and twenty-five natural limbs remaining between them. But they stood like Heroes, as poised for action as might be. Whiskers were keen and quivering and some even managed to hold their tails jauntily.

There were also a pawful of kzinti civilians: a trainer of kzinretts, a couple of Computer Experts, a Trader with an annoying cough, a very young and evidently orphaned kitten, still spotted and milk-feeding, that Junior Doctor had managed to sedate and was now sleeping on a nest of cushions, the ancient, near-blind Bursar of the Order of Conservors—flotsam of war. The place had been designated an assembly area for civilians as things had fallen apart elsewhere but few had made it: kzin fighting spirit and poor administrative ability had seen to that between them.

In no kzinti eye was there a trace of fear, and every one of them, soldier and civilian, still had his *wtsai*. All looked mature enough to preserve self-control, though all, he knew, would fling themselves against the humans at his order. *But the battle car would not have taken us far into the monkey lines if we had ridden it into a last attack,* Raargh-Sergeant thought, looking at them.

The insurgent humans were no longer fighting, as the ferals had in the old hill campaigns, with an assortment of makeshift and captured weapons. Though the Wunderlanders were increasingly running riot, and Markham and other feral leaders were said to have landed from space, more and more of the human infantry were regular UNSN troops with heavy battlefield weapons, armored vehicles and plentiful air support.

In its last major battle, their own regiment had gone in almost entirely on foot, its transport destroyed by air attacks. These few had survived by chance, and by Hroarh-Captain's decision, when command had recently devolved upon him, to keep a small garrison of the least battle-fit at the monastery to protect what civilians and loyal humans they might. Hroarh-Captain was probably the regiment's last surviving officer: kzinti officers always led their Heroes into attack, and the UNSN had been pouring in supplies of precision-guided weapons.

A few traces of the room's brief service as a Mess were still to be seen. There were the accumulated battle trophies of years—rings of dried kzinti and human ears donated by famous Heroes, stuffed humans and pieces of humans who had put up memorable fights, and bits of armor and weapons, various skins, the *wtsai* of old Krawth-Sergeant mounted in a translucent block, a silver-inlaid jar of Chuut-Riit's urine, presented after the second battle of the Hohe Kalkstein, the drum. Dried Morlock heads from the great caves like fanged brainless parodies of men. A mural on one wall showed a Hero rampant, locked in battle with a troop of humanoid monsters, hind claws dug into a heap of simian corpses.

There were even two live humans—the Mess-slaves, shivering and terrified.

There were still distant sounds of bells and battle here. *No business of ours,* Hroarh-Captain had said. The ancient walls of the monastery were thick, but pierced as they were by many doors and windows, and damaged further in the recent fighting, they made a poor defensive position. There was no point in thinking about that. *There was,* Raargh-Sergeant thought, *little point in thinking about anything.* Thought might too easily lead to despair, madness and the neglect of Duty.

He signaled a slave—a *servant*—to bring him his usual bourbon-and-tuna ice cream, but knew he must resist the temptation to drink himself into oblivion.

There was no power for the Mess television—not that many had wanted electronic entertainment there anyway—and the official communications channels seemed to be blocked or disabled, but he felt he should see what was happening.

He crossed the courtyard, signing to the human guards that they need not prostrate, and headed down the crooked alley running between the straggle of huts outside, one of which advertised itself as an internet cafe.

The monastery was situated in rolling meadowland, high on the lip of an ancient meteor crater. Once the humans had raised herbivorous animals on its pastures and vegetables in its gardens, but in recent years, until the Patriarchy had commandeered it, a great straggle of refugee huts had grown up about its walls and fences. These were burning in several places now, and with the heaps of wreckage and refuse and with the smoke of their burning mingling with the smoke drifting from the burning city it was hard to see far.

Any live humans around kept well out of sight. A pair of dead ones lay by a stoop, fluffy white Beam's Beasts already cuddling into them. The blue-eyed, poisoned-fanged vermin had been multiplying in and under the maze of human shanties. Greasy patches nearby littered with acid-corroded bone fragments showed they had been busy for more time.

The internet cafe itself was an older, more substantial and cleaner building, one of the original monastery out-buildings, standing on a slight rise of ground.

As he entered the cafe he was glad, not for the first time, that the mealy smell of humans was odd rather than repulsive, for it was strong here, but in any case he took it for granted now.

The cafe, he noticed with some surprise, for he had not entered it before, had both human and kzin-sized chairs and keyboards which combined human letters and the claw-mark-derived Kzinti alphabet, with lay-outs for either five small thin or four short massive fingers, though several of the chairs were overturned and the building itself was empty.

Kzin warriors and Heroes would never deign to mix with monkeys on such terms, even if they made pets of certain individuals, but not all kzinti were warriors and Heroes, especially not some of those who cared for thinking machines. Perhaps, he realized, some kzin *Nirrrds* had come here and mixed with monkeys to escape the casual persecution (which could be lethal) of fighting Kzin.

The Net itself could not be knocked out by any single blow and there were evidently either cables or some satellites left operating, for some screens still displayed. He sniffed warily for booby traps, and used the basic energy and poison detectors from his belt, but could find nothing. Even a one-eyed kzin's sight was sharp for monkey tricks, but who could tell how a computer was wired? *Live in fear of booby traps and you'll do nothing now*, he thought. Danger could never be allowed to deter a Hero.

He took a kzin chair, positioning himself to face the door, and keyed in "News."

It was slow and there were few television channels functioning. One showed a ruined kzin security headquarters. Humans in the headdresses of their "police" were dancing before the camera. No, not dancing, he saw. The heads had been removed from the bodies and other humans were waving them on poles.

Another site showed humans, pink-naked, some leaking red circulatory fluid, cast by other humans into a cage at the Munchen Zoological Gardens. Then a vehicle drove up, doors were opened, and panic-stricken, yammering kzinretts were pushed in amongst them, slashing to left and right. Otherwise there was fire, death, buildings falling. On one television channel a short column of wounded kzin, some carrying others, shuffled away under a guard of human armored vehicles and troopers. On another were charred creatures of indeterminate species that had been too near a flash, laid out in a silent row. Other official sites and television channels simply showed the last official word, beneath a hologram of Hroth-Staff Officer and the sigil of the Patriarch: for troops, to rally and fight; for humans (programmed by loyal humans) to be calm, await instructions and do nothing to hamper the movements of defending Heroes. Cameras in the Serpent Swarm and on Tiamat told much the same story.

Some other netcams filmed gaping vacuum, one a room opening to space where Heroes floated dead, branching trachea of their lungs protruding from gaping mouths. Monkey had a term for that, he remembered: they called it *eeeting a Krisstmus-trreee*. There was a scene of the wreckage of what had once been a spaceship's bridge, evidently a major warship, with more dead and decompressed Heroes drifting and tumbling. Was one in the ceremonial garb of Traat-Admiral? Another in that of the Chief Conservator? A monkey trick?

He keyed in various other sites: most were inoperable, or cameras showed signs of desolation, carnage or monkey celebrations. Another camera was transmitting from the bridge of a UNSN warship, clean, well-lit and fitted out, with uniformly-clad humans and bulging weapon pods visible beyond the ports.

More monkey clamor outside. He rose and advanced to the door, his hand not on his *wtsai* but not too far from it. If the monkeys were hostile and had guns, the *wtsai* would make little difference. He flexed his claws, natural and artificial. If they were hostile and did not have guns, it would make little difference either.

The Jorg-human and the chief of the monkey priests were backing slowly up the alley. Jorg had a gun in his hands. A crowd of feral humans was advancing upon them. They appeared to have no modern weapons but were carrying clubs and stone missiles, some in a half-crouching position that suggested to him how their ancestors might have looked when they hunted on Earth's plains before some demon gave them lasers and reaction drives.

They set up a howling at the sight of him. He wondered if they might throw missiles. If so, anything other than a claw-swinging charge into them would be unthinkable. Nor, he thought, looking at them, would it necessarily be suicidal. One Hero, even knocked about, could take on more humans than this. Then he saw two or three humans in the first and second ranks of the troop were carrying half-concealed strakakkers. So it *would* be suicidal. Well, that made little difference where honour was concerned.

He dug his hind claws into the dirt, ready to scream and leap. They sensed his poise—humans of the third generation of the occupation of Wunderland tended to be able to read kzin body language—and became still. One human at the rear, who had been holding up *something* on a pole, lowered it very quickly, too quickly even for Raargh-Sergeant to be *quite* sure what it was in the smoke-filled air. Then Jorg moved and the human growling began again.

The monkey priest ("abbot" was the human word though like many human words easier to visualize than pronounce), whom he knew and had played games with, was speaking to them, ordering them to disperse. As far as Raargh-Sergeant could gather, he was telling them to let things take their course, and not let violence now imperil the cease-fire or cause more humans to be killed.

"Do you think *I* am a collaborator?" he was shouting. He had thrown back his dusty cloak to reveal some sort of ceremonial costume beneath, hung with monkey

ornaments. "No! And well you should not! But I place
these under my protection now!"

"You have no power!" shouted one human.

"I do not believe your memory is so short, your gratitude so small, that you do not remember what the monastery and my brothers did for you so recently. You
took its protection for yourselves willingly enough a
little while ago. I extend its protection, and mine, to
these, I say!"

That evidently had some effect. Two other humans began
to jabber urgently with the one who had shouted. He
finally made a head-nodding gesture. There was silence
again for a few moments. Then the troop began to disperse. "We'll be back!" shouted one. Raargh-Sergeant
felt his dignity demanded he ignore the whole event.
He walked to the abbot and Jorg as casually as the state
of his legs would allow, aware of human eyes watching them from the shanties and alleyways. His spine
crawled as he waited for the blast of a strakakker. But
"Cease-fire," Hroarh-Captain had said. Where was
Hroarh-Captain now?

"Things are getting uglier," said Jorg. It seemed an
odd statement to Raargh-Sergeant, to whom no humans
were beautiful. "Things are starting to break up fast."

"Time," said the abbot, "time may let tempers cool.
It would hardly help to lose either of you now."

"They could have gone for you, too," said Jorg.
"Whatever you did for them in the past—and I think
I know more of that than I should!"

"I was aware of that," said the abbot. He turned to
Raargh-Sergeant and made a gesture that was somehow an acknowledgement of respect without being a
prostration, not good enough for a few days ago.
"Neither of you may know," he went on, "but my
predecessor enacted a scene very much like that in
reverse, many years ago. Perhaps I had the easier part.

But we might do well to get you behind some high walls. The next mob may not be refugees whom the monastery sheltered."

Jorg spoke urgently into his wristcomp as they walked. As they reached the monastery gates, a dun-painted groundcar with the insignia of the human police daubed on it appeared out of the smoke. The human driver got out, handed Jorg the keys and, before anything could be said to him, was gone, pelting off and disappearing down the alley.

"Another loyal servant of the Patriarchy and government," Jorg said, though it seemed to Raargh-Sergeant that his behavior could bear the opposite interpretation. "I'll do a patrol, round up those I can and bring them here. Thanks to you it's probably safer than anywhere else."

"You should be careful," said the abbot.

"I think it's a little too late for that," said Jorg, "and even a collaborator can have a sense of duty."

Three of the twelve humans who had been posted at the gate appeared to have gone, Raargh-Sergeant saw as they approached, but the remainder were still fallen in with weapons. They made the stiff, unnatural movements with them as the three approached which he realized were meant to be salutes. At least some of them did.

"Will you join us?" he asked the abbot. "We could play *chesss*."

"Thank you, Raargh-Sergeant, but I think I would do better doing what I can to calm things here, while I still have a little credit."

Raargh-Sergeant lashed his tail in puzzlement. He thought he more or less understood the abbot's position in the human hierarchy—the kzin had their own priests although the military tended to respect the old warriors of the Conservor caste rather more. But he did not fully understand the ebb and flow of human authority. The abbot looked too old and frail, even by human standards, to make his authority stick, and he had no weapons, especially now when the human government seemed to be melting away. And how many loyal humans remained at the gatehouse? Nine? Or had another slipped away even in the last few moments?

He reentered the Mess and turned on the strategic tank-display. A specialized idiot savant, it was little more informative than the internet: a few orange patches of kzinti units surrounded by the green of human. But the human-kzin fighting seemed to be almost over.

Tail twitching, he paced and waited, watching the last of the orange lights die one by one, trying to remain coolly alert while closing his ears to the more distant sounds. He erased the Mess records, though they held little in the way of military secrets, and smashed the Mess computer, the only possible military asset in the place.

He passed out the last meat from the refrigeration unit, telling the others to make sure that the larger bones went into the excrement turbines. *A last luxury,* he thought, *and better disposed of before the monkeys see it.*

He heard a vehicle in the parade ground and wondered if it was Hroarh-Captain back already. But it was Jorg, the human. He brought the car to a stop near the Mess door and scurried in, going down in a quick reflex prostration under the eyes of the kzin. A kzinrett and a male kit, a little older than the one already in his care, were squalling in the armored rear section of the car.

"Raargh-Sergeant Noble Hero, I have brought two who may be sheltered here. I think the humans will kill them otherwise. I found them wandering. You have seen that there are gangs of feral humans . . ."

There was little to be done with the terrified female until she could be settled down. The kit was evidently not hers, since she let it be taken without much protest. Raargh-Sergeant's prosthetic arm allowed him to extract the youngster without mauling, and, held in a familiar grip by the scruff of the neck, it soon quietened to a low mewling sound, arms wrapped round Raargh-Sergeant's chest.

"They came from the direction of Munchen with a wounded Hero. The Hero placed them in the car," Jorg told him, "then a troop of armed feral humans swept down upon us. He placed these in my charge and went to delay the ferals while I got the car away. I did not see what happened to him."

But you can guess, Raargh-Sergeant thought. *As I can.* "Why should the feral humans not follow them here?" he asked.

"I thought they would be safer here than anywhere else. The humans still fear to approach this garrison. And behold!" He pointed to the kit's markings, to the distinctive red-orange blazon showing through the juvenile rosette pattern on the chest and to the ear tattoos.

One of Chuut-Riit's! Raargh-Sergeant realized with a new shock. Not one of those who, so he had heard, had been involved in his terrible death, but one of a younger generation. *Perhaps the last of the Riit blood on the planet!*

And in my care!

"Say nothing of this," he told Jorg. "Get the car indoors and under cover." It was venting a cloud of fumes from a ruptured fuel line and would go no further without repairs. The kzinrett would have to be calmed. The Trainer could do that. Perhaps when she was settled she could be placed with the sleeping suckling. If she did not kill it, her nurturing instinct might take over.

"Courage, my brave one," he told the kit. "The Patriarch is watching you. Have you yet a name?"

The kit hiccuped and whimpered. "Vaemar," it said at last, staring up at him with huge eyes.

A nursery name, given by its mother and pronounced in the Female Tongue.

"Vaemar-*Riit!*" he told it. He had no right to confer even partial names, let alone promote anyone to Royalty. But this reminder of its ancestry seemed to steady the kit.

"I can walk, Honored Soldier," it said, plainly unsure how to address the gaunt, scarred giant who held it.

"Thank the human who saved you," said Raargh-Sergeant. *He had better start getting on good terms with the monkeys quickly.* "He is called Jorg"

"Is that its name? Does the human have a name?"

"That is what he is called." Jorg looked unhappy. A human who insisted it had a name, except for the convenience of telling it apart from other humans, would have had a short life and an unpleasant one a few days before. Raargh-Sergeant realized that in their last few words, Jorg had indeed omitted to address him by his own partial Name, which a few days previously would have been an equally fatal breach of human-to-kzin etiquette.

"Thank you, Jorg, for saving me," said the kitten in its still high, warbling voice. "I shall not forget," it added with some memory of regal manner. Jorg made the prostration again.

Dust particles flashed and fell in a shower of tiny jewels. A bar of green lit a cloud of drifting smoke. A laser blast shattered one of the pinnacles on the chapel tower. The brickwork of the wall erupted as shells struck it. Raargh-Sergeant recognized the coughing of one of the super-Bofors guns that the feral humans had secretly fabricated in the hills.

A section of the wall bulged and collapsed with a roar, burying the two abandoned cars. *No strakakkers yet, and possibly not even aimed at us,* he thought, as chunks of rubble bounced past. "Inside! Quick!" he ordered. As he herded them under the archway and into the building, the kzinti attack car, its molecular-distortion battery's containment field apparently ruptured, went up in white light behind them, scattering stone. He thanked the Fanged God that there had been almost no charge left. The whole monastery might have been levelled otherwise.

And then he realized: *Our weapons were in that!* He was in command. He should have seen to it that they were returned to the Mess, in the absence of an officer. Another thought came to him, distorted by bitterness: *No wonder the monkeys have won this war.*

Above, a formation of human aircraft hurtled by in victory rolls. Nothing remained in the sky to challenge them.

Chapter 2

The others had their *wtsais*, but that was all, apart from some trophy blades on the wall. Now the naked defenselessness of the place, their lack of weapons, hit him like a physical blow.

A normal kzin would take on any number of humans in hand-to-hand fighting and tear them to pieces until his strength gave out, which would normally not be before the last tree-swinger had been dismantled, but these were wounded crocks, and the monkeys had heavy weapons. A long-silent television the humans had kept behind the bar suddenly blared into life. It could only receive human channels and he had forgotten it. Deliberately, he smashed it with a stroke of his claws. He did not want scenes of monkey triumphs to inflame and provoke what for want of better he must call his "garrison." He placed the newcomers at side windows, instructing them to keep watch. *A fine addition to our strength*, he thought. *A kitten and a trained monkey.* Though the temple bells were still ringing in the distance and once he heard the whirr of a strakakker and a scream, it sounded as if things were becoming quieter outside. He could hear human voices gathering.

"What is happening?" asked Bursar in his high, cracked voice.

"Be silent, old fool!" A scream from Orderly, whose nerves had, it seemed, become unequal to the strain. "*Sthondat*-begotten!" (One, and especially if one was Nameless, did not insult *any* Conservor, ever.) "Let us strive to hear!"

"Insolence!" Conservors were awesome in their self-control, but such words from such a being were too much. Bursar reared up as if he had been struck a physical blow.

Orderly screamed and leapt. But if Bursar was ancient and nearly blind, his *wtsai* was swift. The two orange bodies rolled across the floor, slashing and shrieking. The terrified human servants leapt (creditable leaps for humans) onto the top of the refrigeration unit and clung there as the claws and mono-molecular-edged steel blades whirled. One of the kzinti Computer Experts, abstracted and slow of reflex for a kzin, was struck. He grabbed his *wtsai* with a scream and leapt into the fray.

Raargh-Sergeant would not normally have interfered in a duel—kzintosh traded insults knowing the consequences—but this was pointless madness, and triggered by no real injury but by an explosion of unbearable tension. And every Hero was needed at his post. He kicked at the great bulks, knocking them apart. Bleeding from several deep gashes (kzinti arterial and venous blood varied in color between purple and orange), they staggered apart. Computer Expert was down, curled round a belly wound that Raargh-Sergeant saw at once was too deep. Still, as a fighter he was little loss.

Two hard swift blows of his prosthetic arm knocked the *wtsais* from the grips of the other two. He was aware of Lesser-Sergeant and First-Corporal at his side, their own *wtsais* levelled. *Discipline is still holding,* he thought. *Once I would have swum into that fight with a scream and leap of my own. Or am I getting too old on top of everything else?*

"No more. I decree Honor is satisfied. There are enemies enough for us all outside the gate without Heroes killing Heroes today."

They glared at him for a moment and then their eyes seemed to clear. Perhaps the sheer physical weakness and general exhaustion of all those present were what saved the situation. He felt Lesser-Sergeant and Corporal relax at his side as the tension ebbed. They too lowered their *wtsais*. Lesser-Sergeant, with two human bullets and a half-heeled ratchet-knife wound in one knee, still shedding bone, had made a standing leap the entire length of the Mess to attend him. *A useful companion, Lesser-Sergeant,* he thought, *he moves fast and keeps his head. May I call him friend? Corporal too. I need kzintosh like that now, and so do all our kind need them on this God-forsaken day.* He remembered them both in the Battle of the Hohe Kalkstein, and was grateful now, as he had been then, that he had them at his side. He saw too that the youngster was there. He had placed himself before Raargh-Sergeant's right leg, where he would have been a nuisance and hindrance if Raargh-Sergeant had had to leap, but which was also the place a warrior-son traditionally stood to defend an Honored Sire in closed-room combat. *Where my own son would have stood,* he thought. *Had he survived he would have been old enough to be a useful warrior now.*

"Junior Doctor, attend to them."

That would be a challenging task for Junior Doctor in his present condition, but he could contrive something. Computer Expert at least knew enough of Duty to die quietly, without sound effects to further demoralize or inflame the others or appeals for painkillers or medication from their limited stock to be wasted on him. Conservor was chanting the rites over him.

"Humans!" He ordered the shivering slaves, "Clean!" The sooner the smell of kzinti blood was out of the air the better. The air was filled with the frustrated emotions of a duel cut short. He saw that one of Bursar's fangs was snapped, and Orderly's arm hung useless, a tendon cut. *One dead and one less sound limb between us, when we have too few to go around already. At this rate the monkeys need but hold back and let us finish ourselves off. I wonder what they mean to do?*

If I were a monkey, what would I do now? he thought, and the answer came instantly: *Kill us.* It was so obvious as not to need debate. But the monkeys were strange. Even after two generations plus of occupation and after Chuut-Riit had ordered a systematic study of them, late in the war, they had remained full of oddities. The few kzin on Wunderland who had developed relationships with monk—with *humans*, as games partners, as co-investigators of scientific or technological problems, or computer experts, had tended to be oddities themselves. The sort who died young unless some special talent made them worth preserving. Some kzin had complained of the increasing survival and even rudimentary prestige of those whom the monkeys described as *komputerr-nirrrds*, itself yet another monkey loan-phrase which on *Ka'ashi* had entered the Heroes' Tongue.

Now the humans, instead of proceeding to extermination, had offered a cease-fire.

Well, he thought again, *we, or rather our grandfathers, offered them a cease-fire when we conquered this planet. Let a lot of them go, to carry the news of us back to Sol System. We wanted slaves and food, and we didn't want to smash up an industrialized infrastructure. Is that how they think of us now? Slaves and food?*

He remembered that some feral humans had made a point of eating kzin flesh, but when captured and examined had revealed that they had done it as a gesture only and did not really like the taste.

Apparently we mistook things from the first. We wanted Sol to know the terror of our Name and thought the news of us would terrify the human homeworlds. Sire told me of Grandsire's tales, and how as the First Fleet approached Sol System and the monkey ships rose to meet it, it was thought they were bearing tribute. Those First Fleet Heroes were, amid the satisfaction and the anticipation of easy wealth, disappointed to be deprived of a fight. Then came the giant laser beams, the blizzards of slag from the mass-drivers, the bomb-missiles and the reaction-drive cannon . . . There was rejoicing, Grandsire said, when it was realized the monkeys were actually going to give us a fight! . . . Rejoicing, for a long time . . .

He paced to the door, looked out. There were six humans posted at the gate still. They were carrying weapons in stiff, unnatural positions.

The feral humans will probably have those guns off them quickly, he thought, and remembering the monitor screen, *and then the heads off them too.* He wondered how kzin would react to other kzin who had acted as agents of conquering aliens. But the situation was too far outside kzinti experience to imagine. *At least it has been so far,* he thought with bitter pessimism, *it may not be for much longer.* Time to act. There was the human.

"Jorg, those trained monk—human—soldiers are under your command, are they not? H'rr."

"Yes, Raargh-Sergeant, for the moment."

"Do you think their weapons should be inspected?"

"Oh . . . I see. Yes, Raargh-Sergeant! As you think best!"

"Lesser-Sergeant!" He barked in the imperative tense.

Lesser-Sergeant had been badly burnt in a falling aircar. Kzinti military medicine, functioning well until recently, had saved him and though after weeks in a doc his fur has not all regrown and his tail was a twisted stump, apart from his leg wounds more recently acquired, he was now one of the fitter and more complete Heroes present. He was also one of the more impressive-looking.

"Command me, Raargh-Sergeant!"

"Those loyal monk—humans at the gate are under our Jorg-human's command. It is time they were inspected. We may have to show them how to maintain their weapons. Come!"

There were now five loyal humans at the gate. They were trembling as the kzin approached. *We do terrify them*, thought Raargh-Sergeant. He had always known, in a sense, that he terrified humans. That was as it should be, part of the natural order of things. Yet this realization had a novel taste to it.

There had been no non-feral human on Wunderland, whatever its position in the monkey hierarchy, but abased itself before the humblest kzin. He had hunted humans, ferals and criminals in the public hunts, and seen their eyes roll up and their bodies collapse in terror when he had run them down. He had all his life taken human slaves and monkeymeat for granted. But now the thought, so long a taken-for-granted fact of life, was somehow new and uncomfortable. *If we terrify them, what will they do to us?*

"Weapons inspection!" he growled.

They handed over the guns quickly enough. This was still a place where a human would not disobey a kzin, let alone a kzin like Raargh-Sergeant with his size and scars and a large collection of kzinti and human ears dried and hanging at his belt.

Kzinti side arms, heavy for humans. Even with one arm and a basic prosthesis, Raargh-Sergeant could heft one easily. Full charge. Lesser-Sergeant and Jorg collected the others. In the small gatehouse were a pair of heavier squad weapons mounted on tripods and some spare charges.

"Filthy!" He spat, as he had so often spat at kzinti troopers. "Disgracefully neglected! These weapons are the property of the Patriarchy! There should be disciplinary action!"

Jorg stepped forward.

"Your punishment is a severe one," he told the other humans. "You are dismissed from the forces of the Wunderland Government! Get rid of those uniforms! Get away while you can!"

"Perhaps you should join them," said Raargh-Sergeant, as they watched the five humans racing off into the smoke, struggling out of their costumes even as they ran.

"No, my face is too well-known. And besides, I have responsibilities."

"Responsibilities?"

"I am still part of the human government that has tried to hold things together. I speak and understand the Heroes' Tongue well for a human and I know some Heroes. I still might be able to do something to help reduce the chaos and violence."

Somewhere off in the drifting smoke, down the alleyway where the humans had disappeared, came a confused shouting.

"We had better get back under cover, anyway, before the ferals return. I am happier with some strong weapons."

Something flashed across the sky, an arrow-head formation of aircraft in pursuit of a single fugitive. Kzin or loyal human? Whoever it was would have few places to hide, unless they somehow got into space and the dust and planetoids of the Serpent Swarm. A fugitive on the ground would have more chance.

In theory it should be possible for kzin in their turn to carry on a "guerrilla" (or "gorilla"?) war as the humans had done, save that the surviving kzin were so thoroughly shattered in their minds by an almost incomprehensible defeat, and so many of their military units had fought to the death, that on the whole planet there could be few left but civilians and crocks like those here. There were rumors that after the first great UNSN raid Traat-Admiral had begun the planning of a secret redoubt, a fallback position in the event of an attack and invasion backed by relativity weapons, but as far as Raargh-Sergeant knew these remained rumors only.

Most of their last attacks—like the attack he himself had been planning and preparing, he realized—had been no more than thinly-rationalised suicides. But how could you fight an enemy with a faster-than-light space drive? How could you fight an enemy that did not scruple to use relativity weapons to smash whole cities and asteroids with their kzinti and human populations?

The door of the Sergeant's Mess seemed a frail protection as he slammed it behind them and dumped the weapons in a heap, yet the Mess, makeshift and ruinous as it was, was still a world he knew. There was something comforting about the trophies, the hides, even about this small but fearless band of crippled Heroes and their charges.

An eight of eager Heroes fell upon the weapons. Raargh-Sergeant had to snarl to stop them fighting over them. Disposition was simple enough. The two heavier weapons covered the door, a Hero—his groom—with a side arm was dispatched to watch the rear. Raargh-

Sergeant allocated three of the remaining side arms to himself, Lesser-Sergeant and the senior Corporal.

He turned to the civilian Trader, the only unwounded kzintosh. He put out his claw and touched the scars of the civilian's nose that told he had once given military salutes.

"You have served the Patriarch, of course?"

"Indeed, Raargh-Sergeant. Gunner in the Third Fleet."

"Few came back sound from that."

"My ship was fortunate. *Hero's Blood-Soaked Mane.* And blood-soaked we were. We dueled and beat the human dreadnought"—his throat and vocal cords did something very difficult—"*Blloo-Baboon.*"

"I recall the name," said Raargh-Sergeant. He did not wipe away the spit. This one was a Hero too. He was not quite sure he remembered the human ship being classified as a dreadnought, like the great Kzinti Conquest Fang-class. Human dreadnoughts tended to be named after their ancient sea dreadnoughts. Many of them were large and powerful enough for kzinti to give their names a recognition and respect they denied the names of individual humans, and they tended to fight in squadrons. Further, while they could be killed, they were very seldom boardable while their weapons functioned. But Heroes were entitled to a little boasting. It was good to remember old triumphs now, whatever the *Blloo-Baboon* had been.

"We destroyed his drive and weapon turrets and boarded him and took loot. Fought the monkeys cabin by cabin, through ducts and corridors. Cherrg-Captain died beside me. Sections we cut off but they still fought. It went on for days. In one section they had a tank filled with a weak solution of sodium chloride as a habitat for those thinking sea beasts they sometimes carry, and with it they made chlorine gas.

"It was I who first reached the human bridge with

no weapons left but my claws and a sprayer of hydro-
fluoric acid. When we had settled the men and manretts
we leapt into the tank and fought the sea beasts.

"It was good to fight creatures with teeth for once,
though when we got into the deep end of the tank,
some Heroes died. Then the gravity failed and sea
beasts, liquid and Heroes all went into free fall together.
The strangest battle I have ever fought. They had no
ears to take but I took this." From a pouch that hung
from his belt he brought forth the dried, withered half
of a dolphin jaw.

"It was red when we waded out. Good eating, men
and sea beasts both. They had been using the sea
beasts as strategic matrix theorists, so we counted them
as warriors.

"We brought the ship home as a prize. One of the
few that the fleet took. We were well rewarded. There
was much loot to share and few left to share it among
when the *Blloo-Baboon* was dismantled at Tiamat. So
I became Trader."

"What is going to happen?" asked the kit, who had
moved beside them. Its eyes were glowing at this talk,
despite the story's unHeroic end.

"We wait," said Raargh-Sergeant.

"Will there be fighting?"

"I hope not." Then, as he saw the shock on the kit's
face at such a near blasphemy, Raargh-Sergeant added
quickly: "Not yet. We must wait until we are stronger. Heroes must often lurk long in the tall grass. Such
was the wisdom of your Great and Honored Sire." He
bent and gave the kit a quick grooming lick.

Then to Trader: "You came away unwounded?"

"No, Raargh-Sergeant, but the wounds do not show
now." Trader's breath caught suddenly and he began
to cough again.

Raargh-Sergeant could not ask more. That could imply

anything. Some boarding battles had been fought with nerve agents that did strange things. Now that he observed Trader closely for the first time, he saw that he was older than he looked, or looked older than he was. At any rate his age was wrong, and in his spittle was a fleck of purple blood. Yes, beneath regrown fur there were more substantial scars.

"You still have your fighter's reflexes?"

"Command me, Raargh-Sergeant! It is long since I have fought, but if they have become slow, yet I will discipline them once again with the hot needles of Honor and Vengeance!"

To admit so much must mean he was in a bad way. Still, the others were patently worse.

"I will give you this side arm. Stand guard at this window for now. You are Gunner again."

Computer Expert who had fought was dead now. Raargh-Sergeant dragged his body away to an annex and closed the door. A stupid, futile death, though the Fanged God would know that he had at least died in battle. He hoped the air conditioner would clear the odors of battle from the room quickly. There were sounds of human voices without.

There were humans back at the gates now, approaching cautiously, wearing different clothes. A light human vehicle drew up. The female human called Jocelyn, Jorg's deputy, alighted from it. She strode across the rubble-littered courtyard with barely a glance at the now-wrecked kzinti battle-car.

"Do you know what she wants?" He asked Jorg.

"I think I can guess. You notice she is no longer wearing the Government's uniform."

"I saw her decorations were different."

"She is also wearing a trophy belt, I see," said Jorg.

"With kzinti ears on it!" Raargh-Sergeant noticed that his remaining claws had unsheathed. He tried to retract them and found that he could not. But beyond the shock and outrage, he realized that the female human had done this thing deliberately. He strangled a snarl in his throat that would have unleashed the others.

"Also human ears," said Jorg. "Fresh ones. There are also more humans behind her."

Jocelyn knocked with her fist on the door. Since the kzinti had requisitioned the buildings, no human female had entered the Sergeants' Mess except perhaps for dinner. The other kzinti trained their weapons on the doorway. *We could wipe these out quickly enough, but there will be others.* Already humans must be surrounding the monastery. And the UNSN would be arriving with heavy weapons soon. His every instinct screamed to him to order the others to cut loose with everything they had, then fall upon the monkeys beyond in one last, Heroic charge. For Sire and Grandsire there would have been no question. *Which may be why they are dead, and I am alive, for the moment. I would like to see another sunrise, but they must have wished that too . . . and . . . and . . .*

"Shall I let her in?"

"Yes."

Six other humans accompanied Jocelyn as she entered. All were dressed alike and all held weapons. *Knocked up as we are, we could still make short work of them,* thought Raargh-Sergeant. The omnivores were slow-moving and fragile, their muscles, teeth and claws were as much jokes as their vestigial sense of smell. *Such weak, spindly little creatures! What can you say for them?—apart from the fact that they are the only race that has ever met the kzin in war and beaten us.*

"Take off your trophy belt," he said. Then he added: "Or cover it."

The six humans behind did not seem to know the Heroes' Tongue.

"Why?" said Jocelyn. He ignored the insolence of the question, telling himself as rage welled up that a human female was beneath being able to insult him.

"It is the custom of the Mess. This Mess is our club, our dining area. Only Sergeants—Kzin Sergeants—and *Ptrr-Brunurn* may wear trophy belts here. It is a tradition."

"You seek to humiliate me, to establish dominance."

She had answered in the Heroes' Tongue, or as near to it as a human voice could reach. That was almost as much a jolt as the trophy belt had been. A few days previously any human, let alone a female, so speaking to a kzin would have lost its own tongue on the spot for such impudence (the idea of one other than *Ptrr-Brunurn* wearing a trophy belt and standing before a kzin with it would not have existed). The Heroes' Tongue was hard for most humans to understand and far harder for them to speak even badly. Yet if her accent and inflections were weird and alien, the grammar and tense were nearly correct. *So they have been studying our language. Probably for years. I suppose their computers helped them. What fools we were not to attend more to what they did! What else do they know about us? Enough to defeat us, plainly.*

"I do not seek to dominate," he told her. *Though if I do dominate you, so much the better.* "You will show respect for our Mess. This is our place."

The humans were not presenting their arms to the firing position yet. The kzinti were standing by theirs, but Raargh-Sergeant remained sure that even more-or-less wounded as they all were, they could bring them into action faster than the human eye could follow. Then Jocelyn removed the belt and signed for a human to take it.

"There have been some changes in command structure," she said. "The individual formerly known as Captain Jorg von Thoma has been relieved of his duties and all titles of rank. The so-called Wunderland Security Police no longer exists and has been declared a collaborationist organization by the Provisional Free Wunderland Government."

"What is *collaborationist*?" He pronounced the word more or less understandably.

"It is a word that a lot of people will hear soon. Traitors to humanity who will be dealt with."

"Did not the UNSN kill enough humans in its raids? You are quick to kill your own kind when you can."

"Oh? Do you reproach us for that? How many Heroes die in death-duels? Did not the UNSN fleet win its first battles in Wunderland Space because your own forces were in the midst of a civil war when it arrived?"

"If this is a word-duel you have made a good stroke. Yes, we fight among ourselves. Too much, even, I will say who am old and wounded. But we are warriors. Battle is necessary to keep the warriors' claws sharp, to see that only the most Heroic survive and breed. But this . . . killing your own kind in the moment of, of . . . your victory"—that was a hard phrase to get out—"what Honor is there here? And what point in a word-duel now?"

"There is Honor," she said. He had not realized that humans attached large significance to the word before. *Perhaps Honor comes more easily when you are winning*, he thought. *But in that case it is not Honor at all.*

"They are part of the forces of the Patriarchy," he told her. "I am responsible for the forces of the Patriarchy here in the absence of superior officers. Hroarh-Captain has charged me. This human is under the Patriarch's protection, and until I am relieved of the charge, the Patriarch's Honor is on my head."

"I will speak of that in a moment. Those humans"—she pointed to the two Mess-waiters—"are to leave. No harm will come to them. They were constrained and enslaved and have committed no wilful offense."

Raargh-Sergeant nodded. She spoke to the humans in their own language. They edged towards the door, plainly readying themselves to run. Then she halted them.

"They are to take those with them." She gestured to the stuffed human trophies. "They will be disposed of with decorum." Then she pointed: "Why is that one so mounted?"

The figure she indicated stood in a translucent cube, its arms folded and eyes closed. It was a ragged, shabby thing, torn and gaping with innumerable wounds. There was a complication at what had been its waist.

"That one is disposed of with decorum already," said Raargh-Sergeant. That is"—he pronounced the human syllables with care—"*Ptrr-Brunurn.*"

Jocelyn stepped over to the plinth and read the name. "Peter Brennan."

"A great fighter. Once he led a feral band against us in the hills that did much damage. When he was cut off at last, he killed an eight plus one of Heroes though armed with only a ratchet-knife while the others of his troop escaped. We did not eat him but honor him and honor Kzarl-Sergeant who killed him at last. I cannot give you *Ptrr-Brunurn.*"

"You say his full name. I thought kzinti never said the full names of humans."

"We say his. It is a Mess tradition. Before setting out on a hunt for ferals, we have toasted *Ptrr-Brunurn* and Kzarl-Sergeant for many years. Since before I became Raargh-Sergeant."

"I never heard of him."

"It was many years ago. Soon after the first landings, in the time of my GrandSire."

"We have lost so much even of our own history. But

we will find it again! We are not like the wretched
Jotok."

"No. It may have been our mistake to think you were.
Jotok are faithful slaves when they have been trained."

She peered more closely at the trophy.

"He still has kzinti ears on his belt!"

"Yes. We did him Honor. We left him his own trophies."

He smelled or sensed a sort of change in her.

"Perhaps that one may stay. The rest go now!" She
rapped out human orders. The waiters and two of her
guards gathered the human trophies and carried them
away.

"Now," she said, "the traitor. He comes with us."

"You did not call him traitor a few hours ago. He
was your dominant one. Are you not traitor to *him*?"

"It has been said that treason is largely a matter of
timing. But treason it is."

"He is loyal to the Patriarchy."

"And I am loyal to humanity."

"If we had put a Telepath on you a month ago, I
think you would have gone to the public hunting
arena."

"No. I knew it might happen. I have carried the
means of suicide for years." She felt in the pocket of
her garment and produced a white capsule. She spoke
for a moment in a different voice, as though surprised
at a thought.

"Now I can throw it away. We were taught other
techniques—how to make ourselves die of shock quickly
when we were tortured. Now . . . I cannot quite believe
it yet . . . we may forget them. The whole ghastliness is
departing from us. We may live as . . . as humans again."

Suddenly she whirled on him: "Some may say it was
the humiliation and helpless anger of our slave status
that hurt us most. Well, they lie. It is possible, easy

for some, to be a certain kind of slave. No, those things were bad enough but it was not humiliation or anger that we felt worst but naked *terror*, terror of our lives and our people in every waking moment and in our dreams as well! How many humans took to wandering mad—mad from sheer *terror*—before the ratcats or the collabo government tidied them up in their different ways? There is not a human family on Wunderland that has not dead to mourn!"

"Nor a kzin family."

"You started the war. Is war too hard for you?"

She opened her hand and let the thing drop to the floor. He saw liquid run out of her eyes which she quickly wiped away. "And my people, who I, to keep sane, had thought of as having gone away for a time, who I told myself, in the night, that I would meet again when I chose, I can mourn now as dead." He was no Telepath but all kzin had a rudimentary ability to detect emotional emanations at short range if they cared to use it. The terror of prey was a powerful stimulant as well as a guide when hunting in darkness or tall grass. Now he felt this creature's rage and hatred giving way to a greater degree of calm. The liquid ran more freely. Did it discharge emotions with it? *You can learn something new every day*, he thought.

"And now, Raargh-Sergeant, we come to the meat. Hand over Jorg von Thoma and the weapons. I will place you under my personal protection."

"Jocelyn-human, I will not."

"Then you will die. I speak not in challenge. I but state a fact. Kill me on this spot and the result will be the same. You see my people at the gate."

"The Patriarch's Honor is involved. And mine."

The six-foot human female and the scarred eight-foot felinoid carnivore stared at each other. Raargh-Sergeant knew all eyes in the room were upon them.

"The live humans are your people. I see I have no right to detain them now. Also I accept that with the human victory you have a right to the trophies. It comes to my mind that were I the victor I would wish to see what had been the bodies of Heroes disposed of according to the customs of our kind. So be it. But the Jorg-human is under my protection, and so are all these of my kind. I will not give up the Jorg-human and I will not give up the means of protecting my charges."

"I offer you my protection. I . . . I will give you my Name as my word."

"I do not mean to insult you, but I know that humans lie. Honor does not hang on human names. I do not say it to condemn you. You are made so. You yourself have already turned against your profession of loyalty to the Patriarchy."

"We took oaths to you kzin in order to save our lives. A promise made under threat of death does not bind."

"All promises bind. There is no exception, ever, ever! How could it be otherwise when Honor is real? Were I to give my word under threat my word would still be my word though the stars fell and till the Fanged God took me. But I will not leave my folk defenseless. And you do not offer the Jorg-human your protection."

"No, I do not offer it to him. We have waited too long, endured too much. The collaborators will pay for their treachery and for what we have suffered. We hate them even more than we hate you!" She controlled herself with an effort.

"So I have seen."

"In return I offer you and these kzin safe conduct to . . . wherever you wish to go."

"And where would that be?"

"The UNSN has set up holding camps. You can see it is caring for the surrendered kzin—giving them food, medical care even. I . . . I will go further: safe conduct to the hills, if you give me your Name as your word that you will harm no humans. You see I do not believe that *you* lie. You can stay there till things . . . settle down."

You have won one planet. Do you think you have won the war? What when the Patriarch's forces return? No, I must not be too provocative. Yet where else is there for me to go? Perhaps, false arm and wounded legs and all, I could live like a hunter, as Sire once said the Fanged God meant kzintosh to live . . . free in the hills of Ka'ashi, with kzinretts, perhaps, get more kits, ensure my line. Jocelyn watched him as though reading his thoughts.

"I never believed I would say this to a ratcat, but this is your home, too, isn't it?"

"*Rratcat?* What is *rratcat?*"

"The name we always called you kzin out of your hearing."

"You mean to insult me?" His *wtsai* was in his hand, his body in the fighting crouch. Fast for a human, a ratchet-knife was in one of her hands, the outline of its blade extended, its high wailing sound filling the room, a pistol in the other. Humans and kzinti raised their weapons.

There was a sudden cry. A nightmarish parody of a human was moving towards them. A thing long dead, with vast staring eye sockets empty save for fragments of dried matter, and yellow fangs. As Jocelyn turned to it with a cry of her own he struck with the *wtsai*, twice, but to disarm, not to kill, knocking her weapons to the floor. Then they saw what the thing was. A dried Morlock head and hide from the trophy hoard, carried by the kzin kitten. At any instant the situation could have exploded. Then some human of the guard laughed, and others joined in. Quickly Jocelyn laughed as well, though the laughter to human ears would have sounded forced and mechanical. There was even kzin laughter. She picked up the weapons carefully, offering no aggression, switched off the knife and replaced them in her belt. Then she ostentatiously buttoned the flaps that covered them. It had been a very near thing.

"You mean to insult me?" he asked again.

"Not necessarily . . . I don't know." Then: "I apologize. No insult was intended. My words cannot affect your Honor."

"I have never insulted you!"

"Insulted! Insulted! Didn't you ever understand how much we hated you! You terrified us and enslaved us and killed us in tens of thousands. Killed us in *millions*, not only by direct murder but by starvation and by smashing our civilization into chaos!"

"At first, yes. There was much to be done, much trouble for monk—for humans who did not show respect. But things were becoming orderly with time. You learned decorum . . . most of you."

"We learnt not to show our teeth when we smiled, if we ever smiled. We learnt not to hunt in the woods even with sharpened sticks unless you had deigned to tell us you would not be there that day, not to let our children cuddle pet kittens, not to show possessions that a kzin kit or kzinrett might fancy, not to shout or to pass kzin or kzinretts without prostration or with alcohol or tobacco on our breaths. Death could follow all such even if you did not need us or our children for experiments or hunts. To toil in your war factories so other humans might be killed and enslaved. All slaves, and any runaway slave was monkeymeat, fair game for all kzint—" She corrected herself deliberately. "For all ratcats. Our population is half what it was before you came—as far as statistics can be kept to tell us. And we aged and died and saw our loved ones age and died before their time because there were no more modern medicines or geriatric drugs except for the privileged few—for people like him."

"And you."

"Yes. God forgive me! I have a family too . . . I compromised to stay alive . . .

"Oh, a few humans, Jorg was one—damaged goods, that creature—may have dreamed that they or their descendants might somehow rise—the eternal dream of the deluded slave—and some tried to snuggle into your fur like parasites, and some used you for revenge against their own kind, but most of us who worked for you hated you even more than those who fought openly against you. Wasn't that obvious to you?"

"No. Till Chuut-Riit instituted human studies we never cared what monkeys thought so long as they obeyed and were decorous slaves. Why should we? Oh, I look into the sky and see now why we should have cared. . . . But some humans rose to high places. Life for some humans slaves was good and seemly. Look at your Henrietta-human, a female but executive secretary to the great Chuut-Riit himself."

"There is a special price on that one's head! The UNSN will not protect that one! We will have that head if we must cut down our own liberators to get it! We have prayed to the God to spare her life so we may take it!"

"Some of your monkey lawyers then, have made most useful slaves. Your book *Law of Contracts* stopped several death-duels."

"Should I be glad of that? More kzin dead in duels meant less terror for us, less human land taken, fewer fangs and claws on Wunderland or in space."

"But right at the start we offered you amnesty," he replied. "As the war drew on we . . . some of us . . . came to respect your kind in a way . . . The feral leader

Markham . . . I heard an officer say once: 'That one is almost a kzin.'

"A lost human kit, if it or its parents had not offended and it was decorous, could probably walk with safety past a pride of kzintosh. Will a lost kzin kit be able to walk with safety among humans now?"

"Perhaps you do not know all that happened to human children. Certainly many of them were *lost*. But I do not wish to word-duel now."

"And some thought the Fanged God had sent you to teach us various lessons. I am only Raargh-Sergeant but I know there were officers who thought that way . . . as the war went on."

"Strange. Some thought our God had sent you to teach *us* lessons."

"You think that makes a bond between us, Monkey? . . . Ratcats . . . You always called us ratcats? But you say *Ka'ashi* is my home. So it is. I have lived nowhere else."

"We call it Wunderland, remember. Some of us see you kzinti who were born here as a little . . . different . . . to the first Conquest Warriors." Her voice changed and he perceived some other shift in her chemistry since she had made herself laugh at the kit. "We sometimes call you Wunderkzin. You are changed physically. Already in this light gravity you are taller and more lightly built. It has changed us in the same way, but for you the difference is even greater for Kzinhome was heavier than Earth. I think perhaps you are changed mentally more. May I drink? The Heroes' Tongue is not easy for human throats."

"Yes. I concede that life on *Ka'ashi* was changing us. Who could live with you daffy monkeys and not be changed?"

"Chuut-Riit nearly began to understand us. And unlike most of your geniuses—"

"Chuut-Riit was a warrior! A great Hero!"

"For us 'genius' is not an insult . . . Chuut-Riit, and perhaps Traat-Admiral, were the first high-ranking kzintosh to try to understand us . . . and all the more dangerous enemies for it. And yet I have wondered once or twice if it were not possible that . . . a son of Chuut-Riit, brought up on Wunderland with humans, might . . . No! No! And again, no! Have you kzin driven us mad?" There was liquid on her face again. He smelled its salt.

"There could still be a life here for you and yours," she went on. "Sometimes, just lately, when it seemed we would be slaves and prey no longer, I wondered if the children of our two kinds might work together on this world." She gestured at the sleeping youngster and at the kit, who had been watching them with his huge eyes. "Would you not save those at least? Is one of them not as your son might have been, Raargh-Sergeant?"

This monkey is a female and knows female wiles. Does she try to wheedle me? She cannot know my son and his mother died in the UNSN ramscoop raid. But Chuut-Riit's son! How has the God devised it that I am caught in this vise! The life of a monkey or blood of the Riit is spilt and Chuut-Riit's seed is lost! A monkey under my protection. Raargh-Sergeant's eye fell upon the poison pill. He wondered if it would be deadly for kzinti as well as humans. Probably. After all, their biochemistry was patently alike enough for them to eat one another. He picked it up, then threw it with all his strength out the open door. A dead Hero was no use. Responsibility could not be abrogated that way. And if he died, he would die as a kzin should, in battle, on the attack.

"You spoke of terror. You are not so terrified of this old kzintosh now, with one arm and eye gone and holes in his legs?"

"I have the weapons now. Except for those which you are about to hand over along with Jorg the traitor. There is not a kzin formation left fighting on the surface of the planet or a kzin warcraft left in the space of Alpha Centauri! No, ratcat, I am not terrified now! I am offering you life and freedom if you surrender the traitor and the weapons at once. Death for all otherwise. Your deaths will cause me no loss of sleep nor tears."

"I cannot . . . I will not hand over the Jorg-human or the weapons without authority from Hroarh-Captain or higher Patriarchal orders," he said.

"I will return in one hour," she said. "Then there will be no further argument." She spoke the last words in the Heroes' Tongue's tense of ultimatum. She turned and left, her escort following.

Chapter 3

The tank display showed almost no orange lights now, only the green of human, moving and deploying without interruption.

"Those manretts can be trouble," said Trader-Gunner. "It was a manrett that killed Cherrg-Captain."

A last orange light grew into a globe, flashed and disappeared in a sea of green. It appeared that kzin resistance had ceased everywhere. He clicked to erase the tank's memory. Around the room, the kzinti remained crouched behind their scanty collection of weapons.

"What is happening, Raargh-Sergeant?" Lesser-Sergeant asked him.

"I think there is tension between the two human bands. The UNSN dominates the locals, who have all or almost all turned feral, even many of those who swore to serve the Patriarchy."

"They are not attacking because they fear our weapons?"

"I think they are not attacking because the UNSN wants us alive."

"Why?"

"I do not know. If it is a matter of dishonor we may still die heroically. But I have Hroarh-Captain's orders." He dialed some food. There was almost nothing left now but basic infantry rations. He sloshed bourbon-and-prawn ice cream on one of the unappetizing blocks of protein and carbohydrate and passed it to the kit.

"Now you may say you have eaten Sergeant's food, Vaemar-Riit," he told it. "Soon you will make a soldier!" The kit looked dubious but took determined bites at the brick-like material. *Not what you would have got at the palace*, the Sergeant thought. *Still, none could accuse Chuut-Riit of softness, even to his own. You have missed training by the most lethal combat master on the planet, little one.*

Some *had* accused Chuut-Riit of certain other things, of course, though not within his hearing if they wished to live. According to Lord Ktrodni-Stkaa's faction he had been a human-lover, altogether too interested in the behavior of the slave species (the *former* slave species).

Raargh-Sergeant had attended a couple of Chuut-Riit's lectures on the subject of how valuable, with a few more generations of culling, humans might be. *He was on the right track to be interested*, he thought, *even if, to use a human term, he didn't know the half of it*. He remembered something of those lectures now.

Humans, according to Chuut-Riit, had originally hunted in larger groups than had kzin. This both gave them greater social cohesion and meant the greater growth of power diversity. In the Kzinti Empire, power had diversified because, with the slowness of the speed of light, communications took many years. In the Alpha Centauri system humans had diversified more rapidly and spontaneously. Those who lived among the asteroids were in many ways not the same as those on-planet, tending to be descended from space-born stock in the

Man-Sun system, and all the humans in this system were different to those who lived on their home-world.

Humans could be the most valuable slaves ever encountered. And yet, Chuut-Riit had said in his last lecture, there were things beyond this: the new kzinti study of humans was indicating secret spoor.

Until the war had disrupted communications between them, the humans of their homeworld had set out to subtly and secretly control and influence the humans of the *Ka'ashi* System. The *UNSN*, or *Yarooensssn*, the Sol-humans' chief space and military force, the simian equivalent of the Patriarch's Navy (only Chuut-Riit could get away with saying there *was* a simian equivalent to the Patriarch's Navy) was not the ultimate human power.

There was something called *Arrum*, itself apparently the tool of something else that had no name. There was a system known as *konspirruussee*, which, Chuut-Riit has said, subtly sought to control not only the monkeys, but might in some way come to threaten the Heroic Race itself. Its invisible tentacles reached far. Individuals on *Ka'ashi*, kzintosh who had had dealings with humans, had already touched the edges of it . . .

Well, there was meat in all this. It seemed the *Ka'ashi* humans—the *Wunderland* humans now—were not the ultimate masters of the situation on this world. The *Yarooensssn*—it was easier to visualise the symbols UNSN—had some claw upon them. And, it seemed, there might be something else beyond that. . . .

That was, no doubt, what restrained the Jocelyn-human at present and why he and his charges were still alive. The UNSN wanted them.

For what? Slaves? They must know no kzin would live long as a prisoner or live at all as a slave. Interrogation? There were dark stories of monkey tortures and chemicals for any kzin unHeroic enough to be taken alive, but what could sergeants and rankers tell the UNSN that it did not know? Sport in some human Public Hunt? Most of those here were too shot up to run well, though monkeys might like tormenting cripples (well, monkeys who had refused to run in the Hunt had gained nothing from it).

Hostages? The kzin had occasionally taken human hostages when wishing to compel cooperation or the surrender of ferals but for a Hero, a kit of the Fanged God, the fate of a hostage of his own kind would not deflect his feet from the path of Heroism in dealing with an Enemy. A Hero taken hostage would be expected to die like a Hero. . . . *They must not know of Chuut-Riit's son!*

A darker possibility crossed his mind. Earlier in the war a human female had appeared briefly on television screens promising them roomy cages in the Munchen zoo with a diet of carrots and cabbages to pasture on, should they surrender, but this had apparently been a trick to madden senior officers into losing control and had not been seen for some time. He told himself it was not true. Rather, the UNSN and now Jocelyn had been promising honorable treatment. But which was the lie? *Do not think of it. That way leads to madness, to clouded thoughts and inappropriate actions.* That had been the subject of another lecture from the Great One: "They learnt early to make us lose control of our emotions. They exploited this ability in the earliest space battles for this system, almost instinctively, before they had seen us. It is a variation of the old story of the *kz'eerkti* teasing Heroes into frenzy in the forests of Homeworld."

That reminded him of something. He beckoned to the kitten.

"That was a strange thing you did, Vaemar-Riit," he told it.

"I could think of nothing else, Raargh-Sergeant Hero. The man had to be diverted."

Kits of this one's age spent their time chasing their own tails and flutterbys in the meadow grass. "You mean"—he felt stunned for a moment—"that was what you *planned?*"

"Yes, Raargh-Sergeant Hero. I wished to scream and leap when she drew weapons but I knew I was too little."

"There was danger. You know she might have shot you where you stood. Or flung the ratchet-knife into you."

"Yes, Raargh-Sergeant Hero. I knew. But here your life is more important than mine."

"I see . . . You do not need your blazon or your ear tattoos, Vaemar-Riit . . . not for all to see that you are truly Chuut-Riit's son. And here no life is more important than yours. The kzin of *Ka'ashi* will have need of you." He bent and licked the kitten's head.

Jorg came forward: "Raargh-Sergeant, your pardon, may I speak?"

"Yes. Speak on."

"They demand my life, don't they?"

"Yes."

"Perhaps I should go to them. It would save you."

"You would give your life for us?"

"I think I am a dead man one way or another."

"You want your head on a pole like those others?"

"When you are dead, it hardly matters where your head is."

"We think differently. Look at *Ptrr-Brunurn*. He is honored."

"If I or my kind deserve any Honor, history may honor us."

"I do not understand."

"Passions may cool in a generation or so. They will come to see that we collaborators did what we did partly for them. Yes, for them. Without us to intercede between the mass of humans and the Heroes, things would have been worse for them than they were.

"I do not say this to sound heroi—to sound better than I am. But where would they have been without us to run some sort of government, to arrange some system of food and shelter as poverty and breakdown spread, to police our towns, to keep our farms and mines and factories working as well as we might, yes, to control lawless humans who might have attacked their own kind or brought terrible reprisals for attacking Heroes, to remove litter and maintain orphanages and see the dead were buried, to keep at least a few factories manufacturing the geriatric drugs?"

"Is that why you became chief of the monkey police? To be useful to your own kind?"

"This is no time for lying. I did it partly for those reasons but also to protect myself, my mate, my kits. But I am not innocent. I delivered resistance fighters to the Public Hunt. At first with sickness and shame and loathing and because I told myself I was serving a greater good, later more because it was my job and my nerves were deadened—trained monkey indeed. I and my people ate well when each day more starved. We drafted people to your war factories and shipyards and constructions, yes, and to serve in the Kzin fleets that attacked Earth. Later we helped hunt down Earth and UNSN agents and infiltrators. Some of us did a little sabotage of the administration when it was safe, or turned a blind eye to some resistance, at least before the Telepaths' checks began. We walked a tightrope. I am no human hero, like the abbot of this monastery. I am neither innocent nor wicked. I am guilty."

"The abbot? The Head of the Three Monkey-Gods cult? I have played *chesss* with him"—that human word was easy to pronounce. Indeed it had entered the Heroes' Tongue. "Why do you say 'human hero'?"

"He fed and clothed many refugees here. Also, he shel- tered human resistance fighters. I half knew. God help me, perhaps I would have handed him over long ago or pointed a Telepath towards him, for he was helping prolong the whole agony, but he was too popular with humans. And too many monks had been too brave. To send him to the Hunt would have meant more feral activity, more sabotage, more throats cut, more hydro- fluoric acid thrown over Heroes in city alleyways at night, and more humans killed in reprisals, too, more human land expropriated. My lot was not to steer the ship of human destiny to some fair harbor, just to help keep it more or less afloat."

"He lied to me, then. I spoke to him at times. I thought he showed his mind to me at *chesss*, and when we drank bourbon and ice cream together after a long game. Is there no end to monkey trickery?"

"I did not wholly lie to you. Neither, I think, did he. Once when we spoke he—I mean no insult and nor did he—likened you Raargh-Sergeant to a figure in his holy book, a centurion . . .

"There is much about kzinti I admire—your strength, your honor, your courage. Many humans, even your greatest enemies like Markham, admire you, more per- haps than those who merely tried to endure kzinti rule . . . As to an end to monkey trickery, I don't know. You have a low opinion of humans."

"You are omnivores. You are beneath opinion. We acknowledge some monkeys—like your *Ptrr-Brunurn*— may be entitled to fighters' privileges and honors. I suppose you hated us too. Strange, a few weeks ago nothing in the world would have mattered to me less than how a human felt about me."

"Does it matter now? Yes, very nearly all of us hated you. For a very few lucky privileged ones perhaps admiration overcame hatred."

"H'rr. So my Honor is bound up with protecting a monkey who hates me? Will you kill me, monkey?"

"Did you not just say it did not matter how we felt? I will not lie to you now. How could we love the kzinti? As for killing you, until lately I was not one to think of such things much, save as a dream sometimes . . . Still, there were other things which some of us looked to," said Jorg. "We collaborators took them as signs of justification for our lives, of hope. Future generations might have invoked the wisdom and statesmanship of Jorg von Thoma. I am not a Markham who fights for humanity like a steel blade. . . . Sometimes I have felt that Judas also had a necessary part to play and knew exactly what he was doing and the price that he would have to pay. . . .

"Some of the younger generations of both kinds were cooperating more easily. You know that kzinti and human computer nerds would talk together. Some had begun to meet regularly. Each kind shared insights with the other, even unintentionally, and there was talk of forming something that might have developed into a club. Oh, I know kzinti computer nerds are despised by normal kzin as freaks and geniuses, but it might have been a start.

"And some, a very few, human and kzin poets had talked together, too. There was the story of Gunga Din, a dutiful monkey. I know one kzin poet was moved to describe 'The Charge of the Light Brigade' as pedestrian but showing that some monkeys at least had understandable military common sense and could celebrate a demonstration of it."

"If it comforts you," said Raargh-Sergeant, "know we have gradually come to refer to the most useful and obedient of you by your own monkey rank-titles more, and as *sziirrirt-Kz'eerkti* less . . . or some like Markham as *Ya-nar Kzinti* . . ."

"*Sziirrirt-Kz'eerkti* . . . that means 'trained monkeys,' doesn't it? and the other"—he struggled to pronounce it—"the 'defiers of kzin'?'"

"I know some of our kind were interested in humans. But as you say, they tended to be freaks."

"Perhaps they were freaks your people needed. I mean no disrespect, but was there not a little of that feeling in you personally? No, sheath your claws, Raargh-Sergeant—remember, was not the great Chuut-Riit among those who thought humans were worth systematic study?"

"That took mainly the form of dissection of their nervous systems, as far as I know. I do not think that is what you monkeys who looked to 'cooperation' had in mind. But there was some monkey history, too. And that brought back memories for me . . . When I was a kit a house-slave read me a human poem, 'The Ballad of the White Horse.' I like bits of that, though I do not know why:

> *Death blazes bright above the cup,*
> *And high above the Crown*
> *Yet in that Dream of battle*
> *We seem to tread it down . . .*

"There were other lines: '*are slavery and starvation flowers/that you should pluck them so . . .*' Yes, it comes back to me:

> *Short time had shaggy Ogier*
> *to swing his lance in line.*
> *He knew King Alfred's axe on high,*
> *He heard it singing through the sky,*
> *He cowered beneath it with a cry.*
> *It split him to the spine . . .*"

Jorg nodded as the great felinoid's voice trailed off:
"I know that poem too:

> . . . *I know*
> *The spirit with which you blindly band*
> *Has blessed destruction with his hand,*
> *But by God's death the stars still stand,*
> *And the small apples grow.*"

He went on: "We each worship a single all-power-
ful God, a jealous God. Is that not also a bond between us? That we see something of the same truth
behind the universe."

"That is for Priests and Conservors to say. A Priest
of the Dark Pelt once said to me that with your bearded
Jova you may have a little glimmering of the truth.
Your Bearded God and the Fanged God had their own
respective kingdoms, perhaps. Mark you, he was very
old and had been drinking bourbon at the time. He
thought that though you are irritatingly between herd
animals and hunters, yours is a god of the herd animals you partly resemble. You seek this thing *lurve*
instead of Heroes' Respect for you are partial herd
creatures.

"But I know we Heroes are the only pure carnivores
to whom the Fanged God has granted the power to
leap from star to star. We have encountered no others in hundreds of years of the Eternal Hunt, only a
few herbivores or omnivores at best creeping between
their own planets . . . until now. Assuredly the Fanged
God decreed that we dominate you omnivores as you
dominate herbivores and as herbivores dominate vegetables."

"With due respect, Raargh-Sergeant, it has not worked
out like that."

"Who could have foreseen the hyperdrive?"

"Not I. I might have cut my cloak differently otherwise."

"Chuut-Riit thought human inventiveness was valuable: dental floss, blow dryers, toilet paper . . . You are amused?"

"That is what you valued in our culture?"

"We would never have thought of such things for ourselves . . . but many other things: chess, using reaction drives and ramscoop fields as weapons, ice cream, catnip, some of your liquors, h'rr . . ."

"See. Our words have entered the Heroes' Tongue. You pronounce them without thinking. Could we have worked together?"

"I am Raargh-Sergeant. It is not for me to say."

"There may be many things it is for you to say now. Hroarh-Captain has not returned."

"What do you mean, monkey?" Claws to *wtsai*.

"I respectfully ask you to be calm. Perhaps he is not returning. Perhaps misfortune has befallen him. What if there is no one left higher in the chain of command than you?"

"If so, I will be guided by Honor. And that answers your question. You shall not go to the humans. Honor states that you shall continue to be protected by the Patriarchy. A little while ago I thought of this time as forsaken by the Fanged God. But is that not the point of it: is it not Honor to look at a universe in which your God has forsaken you, and still obey as He commands? What good is fair-weather Honor?"

"Very well. If you are content, so am I."

"Raargh-Sergeant!" Lesser-Sergeant's cry took him to the window at a painful bound.

A human groundcar entered the gates and stopped in the courtyard. It had been an ordinary car such as until lately privileged humans had still occasionally been permitted to use: powered by hydrogen fuel rather than the molecular-distortion batteries which were rather too easily adaptable into bombs. More recently a medium field laser cannon had been mounted on it behind a hemispherical shield. It came to a halt with the cannon pointed at the Sergeants' Mess.

Jocelyn crossed the courtyard, alone and on foot as the kzin crouched at their weapons. *She is brave,* thought Raargh-Sergeant. *A worthy enemy. Her head would make an acceptable trophy for the Mess.* And then, in one of those dangerous and distracting tangents in which he found his mind had begun to run: *So long, so eagerly, did our ancestors search space for worthy enemies!*

"Raargh-Sergeant!"

"I hear you."

"You now have twenty minutes. After that time I will use this cannon to destroy this building and every kzin in it as well as the human traitor. I ask you not to force me to do it."

He made no answer. Among kzin infantry gear were antilaser smoke and dust-cloud generators and mirrors that could, in theory, deflect small lasers for a short time until they boiled or burned away. Nothing that would stop a military laser of that size for an eye blink. Jocelyn turned away after a time and walked back across the courtyard. He saw her addressing a gathering of humans at the gates.

With that cannon she can make it all look like a regrettable accident when her UNSN masters arrive, he thought. *It will be easily explained by monkey lies as a beam that went astray in the final stages of the battle. No monkey to bear responsibility or be disciplined. At such a range, the degree of spread of the laser will be so small as to tell them nothing, and in any case would they bother to examine it closely? Without that cannon we could hold them off, or at least put up a fight such as they could not disguise, even we pawful of cripples. She is probably expecting me to lead all these out in a last charge into the laser canon, as many Heroes have done lately. That would solve her problems. And mine.*

Without that cannon!

Think like a monkey.

There was something forcing itself up from deep in his memory, something sparked by his words with Jorg about monkey poetry, and the monkey studies that Chutt-Riit had begun to put on a systematic basis shortly before his murder. In the old monkey libraries of Munchen there had been other records of Earth, fragmentary and disordered after the burnings and bombings of the initial landings, included primitive moving pictures. One had been shown to his group of NCOs, called *Guns at Batasi*, showing the way a monkey sergeant thought. Yes, and the situation of that monkey had not been unlike the one he now found himself in . . .

"Lesser-Sergeant! Kzintosh!" It was spat in the battle imperative tense. They snapped to the attention position.

"Lead us, Raargh-Sergeant!"

"Lesser-Sergeant, we have still the battle drum?"

"Yes, Raargh-Sergeant. The monkeys were so busy with the other trophies they did not take it. In any case, it is in its shrouding."

Puzzlement in the others' eyes for a moment. Quickly he told them his plan.

"Unshroud the drum, and bring it here. All of you! Junior Doctor, Corporals, Old One, kzintosh all! Can you sing?"

"Sing?"

"Our battle songs! You know them!"

"Yes, Raargh-Sergeant!" from every throat.

"Then sing. Strike the drum! Sing and strike loud! First Corporal, you shall lead!"

Their voices rang out as though in triumph, though it was actually a bawdy song about the mating habits of manretts. The *Sthondat*-hide chambers of the drum reverberated as Orderly leapt upon it.

The humans had not thought of Heroes retreating. The rear of the building was unwatched as Raargh-Sergeant, Lesser-Sergeant, Trainer and Trader-Gunner made their hobbling run from it into what had been the Abbot's apartments. They crossed the cloister and chapel. A human, one of their priest kind, saw them and fled with a cry down a narrow flight of stairs. The kzin had no time or inclination to pursue but dragged a door shut behind the human and wedged it roughly shut. Raargh-Sergeant with his wounded legs and prosthetic arm, and carrying the side-arm, could not scale the rear wall at a bound, and Lesser-Sergeant and Trainer were partly crippled also, but they dragged a large piece of fallen rubble to it to make a step.

Then they were over the wall and in the outer ditch that circled the monastery. The roaring song from the Mess and the drum's booming had apparently masked any noise, and distracted the humans. They crawled forward.

"Look!" Lesser-Sergeant gripped his shoulder and hissed.

Two cars were approaching in the smoky sky. One seemed to be gathering the drifting bodies, which the wind was now blowing beyond the monastery and towards Grossgeister Swamp. The other seemed to be heading for the main gate. They were military vehicles, of course, drab-painted and snouted with weapons.

Get into tall grass! Instinct shrieked. There was none. The monastery had been built in meadowland but the human refugees had taken all the vegetation long since to boil or as fuel for their cooking fires. Only hard bare earth and mud remained, almost black, with a scattering of bones and rubbish. Raargh-Sergeant had no time to curse the lack of camouflage gear: against that ground the kzins' orange fur blazed like a flare.

"Run!"

Crouching low, pain driving wounded limbs, in the partial shelter of the ditch. The drum booming. One of the aircars descending towards the monastery gate. The groundcar, its gun still trained on the Mess building, humans still craning at the sounds of revelry within, but a number of humans moving to the pad where the cars would land. Up and aim.

"Fire!"

Converging beams from the four weapons, fast, but not quite fast enough. Whatever human operated the gun car had been alert. Power-operated, the laser cannon had spun towards them even as they raised the weapons. The beams hit not the gun but the armored shielding.

"Down! Down into the ditch!"

Too late for Trainer, a blizzard of glass needles from one of the human strakakker guns turning his chest cavity into an instant skeleton, his weapon spinning away, Trainer standing grotesque for a second like one of his own lecturer's diagram before collapsing in pink bones and disarticulated limbs. There was other firing, presumably the squad weapons in the Mess. There was a high-pitched squalling from the humans. He recognized the words of some human calling for medical assistance. The gun car's driver was probably shaken by the impacts, but after a moment it fired too, the awful blue-green light burning the smoke and dust just above.

The beam from the car lowered, hitting the far lip of the ditch in a line of live steam and melting slag. *Too near and they will boil us. But they have not hit us yet.* Still, such a laser could only have a short firing time. Getting rid of heat at the source without large and elaborate cooling units was a perennial problem.

And someone was still beating the battle drum, in true defiance now. And the Kzinti voices were raised in no bawdy barrack-room ballad but in the cadences of Lord Chmeee's last battle hymn.

Second Corporal, Junior Doctor and Groom bursting out in a diversionary run, whirling to drive straight at the mass of humans. Second Corporal raising the last side arm, a storm of fire cutting them down. The squad weapons firing from the Mess, their beams keeping the humans down, scattered and behind the walls. But it was a short, professional burst. If the Heroes who had fired remembered their training and his orders they were down quickly and under cover. Trader-Gunner was bobbling up and down, firing from the lip of the ditch, though still, as ordered, firing only at the car.

Beside him was Lesser-Sergeant, moving with battle-quickness, exposing himself for an instant to fire and dropping back. Firing again, jerking and falling into the bottom of the ditch. Raargh-Sergeant crawled to him.

Lesser-Sergeant's skull and jaws had been seared by a beam. He was unable to speak but Raargh-Sergeant held his paw and groomed him with his tongue until he could not see his chest rise and fall. He buried Lesser-Sergeant's trophy belt quickly, hoping it would not be found and dishonored. He took Trainer's rifle— there was hardly enough of Trainer left to honor—but left Lesser Sergeant's beside him. He hissed orders to Trader-Gunner.

A few bolts sizzled past over his head but no monkey dared approach yet. His fur, covered with blood and the mud from the ditch's sides and bottom, glowed orange no more. He backed away down the ditch, pausing momentarily only to plaster more mud over himself.

Trader-Gunner ahead of him was equally covered in dark mud and slime. The big laser had passed through a group of the human huts and they were now burning fiercely, more smoke in the air. He crawled on.

A sound of mud on mud behind made him pause and turn. Lesser Sergeant was not quite dead, he saw. He was crawling up to the lip of the ditch, somehow still holding the rifle. He saw him raise it and fire again. He was burnt so that he no longer looked like a kzin, but even as he was, plainly dying, by rights already dead, he had a warrior's quickness still. Humans fired back. Raargh-Sergeant crawled on, round a curve that hid Lesser-Sergeant's stand from sight, and on. He knew that to go to his companion's support now would be the ultimate betrayal of him, though his liver was sickened and his mane flattened itself against his neck. He heard firing from him for a little longer, and then answering fire. Then it stopped.

Now they were up and running, dark shapes almost invisible in rolling clouds of dark smoke, through the burning wreckage of the monkey houses, Trader-Gunner breathing in tearing gasps and spitting blood, the mud that covered them shielding them from the flames as well as camouflaging.

Then into an alley where the houses were not burning. Back into the deserted internet cafe. A Beam's Beast leapt at him from a computer console, fangs dripping venom. Trader-Gunner shot it in mid-spring, and it carried across the room like a small fiery comet to crash against the wall. He stamped on the burning white fur.

"You know the net?" he asked Trader-Gunner. It took the coughing kzin a few moments to reply.

"Yes, Raargh-Sergeant. I use it every day in my craft."

"You are probably more expert than I. Activate it! Hurry!"

Trader-Gunner threw himself into one of the kzin-sized seats, claws to the keyboard. There was an arc of blue fire, and he leapt up screaming, fingers fused to the keys, vomiting sparks and fire, falling forward dead and burning, smoke pouring from mouth, ears and eyes.

So there had been a booby trap after all. *Perhaps his fighter's instincts had atrophied with sickness as he feared. He should have seen it.* Well, Trader-Gunner had at least had the luck to die in battle, of a sort.

Still, there was the computer Raargh-Sergeant had used earlier that day. That had been safe then and perhaps still was. He would soon see.

He keyed in his military code. With that code any kzin could, in theory, dominate human passwords. He hoped that was still the case. He keyed in human government vehicles, and the number of the gun car.

Yes. It was still working. A netcam gave him a view of the car's cabin, and beyond, of humans standing about and hunting cautiously along the ditch. He called up the car's controls. A car in human use was programmed to have the sensor and receptor cells in its brain overridden by several Kzin keywords.

But the cannon was newly installed by the humans and not connected to the car's brain. Could he drive it forward into the ditch? He keyed in a command and spat curses. The humans had, of course, disabled the key motor-response cells, leaving it under purely mechanical control. Only the brainless netcam was not affected. He could start the car and kick it forward in a straight line, but that was all. It would run into the monastery wall.

Better than nothing, if it squashed a monkey or two, he thought. Indeed, a human stood directly in front of it. He moved to kick in its starter, when he recognized that the monkey wore the robes of the abbot.

That one took me under his protection, he thought.

To run the car over that one would be dishonorable now. Could it not have been any other? Fate is playing some bitter tricks today.

No matter. He had got behind the car anyway. Clutching the two beam rifles, he doubled himself into the crouching attack run.

Out of the hut. Straight down the alley, propping the two weapons steady on a wedge of timber, aiming, firing.

Hitting the laser cannon behind its shield. The car suddenly airborne on a wall of roiling fire, the air hammer of the explosion, a ball of fire leaping skywards from a ruptured fuel-tank, the car turning over, the cannon cycling laser bolts skyward, into the walls, into the ground in gouts of flame, the car crashing back upside-down between the shattered gates. Humans dropping, firing.

He dropped and rolled. He thought that if he kept low he could lose himself for quite a time in the huddle of huts and alleys—until they began strafing them from the air, in fact. It would be a bold human who followed him. He raised his head cautiously, fairly sure that he was unseen still in smoke and shadows.

He heard Jocelyn's voice: "Come out, you one-eyed ratcat bastard! Come out and die!"

"*Sun ov a beetch!*" he called back in his best human accent, wondering if the human insult was appropriate. He had several spare charges for the rifles in his belt, and could kill a lot of monkeys yet. Lesser-Sergeant, and Trader too, would be avenged. Let him get his claws on the Jocelyn-human, and she might be sorry she had thrown her suicide pill away!

Then he heard the aircars landing.

It was obvious what would happen next. The monkeys in the cars would be informed of the situation and would saturate the whole area with fire from the air. How much harm could he do them with the two remaining beam rifles? Not enough, not before they used their beams and missiles. Some of the monkey buildings were already on fire, and they would all burn fiercely with the help of beam weapons.

He saw the snouts of the squad weapons reappear at the door and main window of the Mess. But it seemed no human intended to initiate a duel with them yet, and the discipline that he had ordered held: they kept behind the monastery wall, and the humans remained sheltered from them. The gun car and scattered debris flamed and crackled and smoked.

He raised the two side arms, one in his own hand and one in the prosthetic one, and poised himself. There was nothing for it now but a charge into the monkey lines.

He thought of Lord Dragga-Skrull's great final order, Lord Dragga-Skrull who like him had lost arm and eye in battle: "The Patriarch knows every Hero will kill eights of times before dying heroically!" He braced his legs to spring.

"Raargh-Sergeant!" A kzinti voice, not a human, carrying effortlessly across the monkey clamor.

"Stand up and come forward!"

He stood slowly. There was Hroarh-Captain, disembarking with some difficulty from one of the aircars. A male human accompanied him: short, stocky for a human, wearing the UNSN costume.

He advanced, still carrying the beam rifles. The lights on their stocks indicated they were still charged. Humans whom he assumed had a medical function were busy with the human casualties now. Second Corporal and Junior Doctor were obviously dead. Groom was still moving, but as Raargh-Sergeant watched he howled and died. They had died as kzintosh should die, on the attack.

He stopped a few feet from the group and let them

come forward. They were now covered by the cone
of fire of the squad weapons held by the remaining
kzin in the Mess.

"This is Staff Colonel Cumpston of the UNSN. What
has been happening here?"

"You may speak in the Heroes' Tongue," said the
stocky human. "I understand it."

"The Jocelyn-human demanded I hand over the Jorg-
human to her. I refused. She brought up the cannon
and said she would destroy us if I did not comply. I
therefore acted to disable the cannon."

"I see."

"I thought it might be something like that," said the
stocky human. "A pity we didn't get here earlier."

"Pity?" The kzin did not understand the word.

"I mean, it is unfortunate. In any event," he went
on, "all Wunderland humans have now been placed
under the jurisdiction of the Free Wunderland Forces.
Captain Jocelyn van der Stratt anticipated her authority
slightly, but it is now a lawful request."

"And we? The kzinti of Ka'ashi . . . the . . . the
Wunderkzin?"

"You will not be mistreated. You are under joint
UNSN-Free Wunderland jurisdiction."

The abbot had been very near the car when the
beams hit it. He was pale and shaking and bleeding
around the head and mouth, he had lost his shoes and
showed bare monkey feet at the ends of thin pale legs
and his garment was scorched, but he was still capable
of speech. "I have also made a request that there be
proper treatment," he said. His voice shook as much
as his hands.

"Hroarh-Captain? I obey your orders!"

"I am no longer in a position to give orders here,
Raargh-Sergeant. It appears the Patriarch's armed forces
here are dissolved. As one individual kzintosh to another,

you are the stronger male now, or the less disabled, so perhaps if anything I am under your dominance.

"We have accepted terms of unconditional surrender," he continued, "in return for a monkey promise that all surviving members of our kind in this system will be spared. The alternative was to see us exterminated to the last kzinrett and the last kitten. The Patriarch's Forces are officially dissolved on this planet. I am now nothing."

Raargh-Sergeant slipped into the imperative tense as he replied. Humans would recognize that. What they perhaps would not recognize was the other constructions which he was inserting, in the rarely-heard ultimate imperative tense, generally used only by Royalty or in a situation where the Honor of the whole kzin species was at stake.

"We have Chuut-Riit's urine. May we keep it?"

Hroarh-Captain looked startled at the tense, but having virtually conceded dominance, he was slow to protest. Then, it seemed, the Sergeant's motive occurred to him.

"It is not valuable to humans," he replied. The concealed meaning was: "Animals have no conception of its value/sacredness."

"And Chuut-Riit's blood? That is there also." He gave a grooming lick to the air. To another kzin that could indicate a kitten.

"It is not valuable to humans," Hroarh-Captain repeated in the same tense. "We may prevent dishonor coming to Chuut-Riit's blood."

"I bid you speak in the tense of equals," said Staff Colonel Cumpston in an approximation of the dominant tense of the Heroes' Tongue. "I do not mean to humiliate you, but it is my duty to understand what you say."

Jocelyn strode forward, cradling a strakakker. Raargh-

Sergeant was suddenly aware that he still held two beam rifles. Her face was white and there was red human blood on her costume. The heady smell of it took his memory back for a moment.

"This ratcat has killed *another* four of my people and injured eight more! After the cease-fire!" She raised the strakakker. Raargh-Sergeant raised his beam rifles. It was hard to steady his prosthetic arm but a steady aim would hardly be needed. Staff Colonel Cumpston stepped quickly forward and raised a hand. Hroarh-Captain leaned forward into the path of the strakakker. The abbot also stepped forward. "No," he said. "I gave my protection. It must stand even now or it is nothing."

"It appears there was a factor of provocation," the UNSN colonel said. "I see that kzinti have died too." Raargh-Sergeant saw that though his face was impassive, Hroarh-Captain was trembling almost as much as the abbot. Lights flashed on the control panel of the thing that took the place of his legs as it sought to compensate for the movements.

"There are major considerations of policy here," the colonel went on. "It has been decided for various reasons that those of the kzinti who wish to remain on Wunderland may do so. In any case, we can hardly repatriate them. The war goes on."

"It is not repatriation that I was thinking of."

"I can assure you, Captain van der Stratt, that this was decided for a number of carefully considered reasons."

"So you want hostages. You can do without this one. How many of the *Teufels* do you think you need?"

"It is not only that. The Wunderkzin who have grown up with humans are an important asset to us!"

"Grown up with humans! As tyrants and predators! Not a family on Wunderland is not maimed by what they have done! Not one of us does not mourn dead! Apart from those who fought and died, two kinds of humans have lived on Wunderland for the last two generations: slaves and unassigned slaves! Not one of us, not even the human traitors in the house of Chuut-Riit himself, had an hour's security for our lives or our family's lives. Can you comprehend that, Staff Colonel!

"Have you lived and grown old knowing there was nothing—*nothing*—to prevent you, *your* wife, *your* parents, *your* children, *your* lover, *your* closest friend, from dying in the Public Hunt, or conscripted to die manning kzinti auxiliaries in space battles? To know that whatever day's life you gained, the only future for you and yours was as kzinti slaves? And you ask us to have mercy on these monsters?

"You know the new Munchen Space Port? We call it the *Himmelfarte,* the Heaven Way, not because it leads to the Heavens, but because so many of us died in the building of it, under the lashes and fangs of their 'Supervisors-of-animals' when fleet facilities had to be expanded quickly. Children, old ones, sick! A child would take food to its parent conscripted to slave there in the morning, and itself be dead under the lash by the time the First Sun had set!

"Orphanages raided, humans taken from the streets, casually, to provide specimens for neurological dissection when the Great Chuut-Riit, the Enlightened Chuut-Riit, the kindly planetary governor the collaborators flattered as a 'good master,' decided we should be studied! Humans taken to Kzin and its other colony worlds who are there still, lost souls in Hell. And we police, who licked the boots of our chief Montferrat-Palme in terror even as he prostrated himself before his Master, who might be a kzin trainer-of-humans too lowly to have a kzin name! Shall we forgive and forget those things?"

"You have had revenge on Chuut-Riit," said Hroarh-Captain. "He died terribly. And your vengeance is widespread. Few of full or partial name survive, and none of the best save Hroth who was Staff Officer. Where is Traat-Admiral who tried to be a benign master to you humans? Where are all those I knew? Indeed, even few of the nameless survive. I have sought to save a few kzinretts, and kits and wounded . . . You seek further vengeance on kzinti? Look at me, *man*. Would you be as I am?"

Jocelyn stared at the wreck of the kzin officer in its hovering craft as though seeing it for the first time.

"No," she said at last.

"Or Raargh-Sergeant? Is it a crime for a soldier to abide by his duty?"

"We never denied your strength and courage. Hell seeks always the worst ways to torment us, and it was one of the cruellest tricks of Hell that demons should be so magnificent. We could not—we cannot—afford to think of your suffering."

"I would not expect you to. We enjoy the smell of a prey's terror, but humans might as well have no noses. I remember in the Hohe Kalkstein, I smelt a group of ferals lying in ambush. I kept downwind and they never smelled *me* till I was a dozen bounds from them . . . Then one jumped up and leaped to heft his *strakakker* . . . too late. And underground . . ." Hroarh-Captain's ragged ears folded and unfolded in a kzinti laugh. Some memories were still good.

"Our fathers tried to negotiate with you when your ships first appeared in our system," she replied. "Some of us tried to empathize with you. Your answer was beams and bombs and enslavement. We were a peaceful culture then and nightmare fell upon us. Well, we have learnt better now, half-ratcat!"

"Let us all put down our weapons," said the colonel. "There is no need for more to die here, human or kzin. Enough have died in this war. And I see the guns in the monastery are still trained upon us. We have won, Captain van der Stratt, we do not need heroic rhetoric."

"But we *have* needed heroic rhetoric, Earthman. Flatlander! We who lived and died under the ratcats needed to rediscover heroism! And we did!"

"So did we," the colonel replied. "It was we who built the Space Navy."

"I can no longer order you to *sssurindir*, Raargh-Sergeant," said Hroarh-Captain. It was a difficult word to pronounce, a new word that had crept into the Kzinti vocabulary on Wunderland over the last few months, and until very recently, on the occasions it had been used, it had been prefixed by the modifier "*nevirr.*" He went on: "I can no longer take the burden from you. Who is in the Mess?"

"Wounded. A kzinrett. A very old Conservor. A few others . . . a suckling infant." He paused. "And a/the kit." He wondered if the humans would catch the blurring of the article. "And the Jorg. The human who has been under my protection."

"If they die, they will die uselessly, and there will be fewer of us left on Wunderland. We had better go to them."

"I shall come," said Staff Colonel Cumpston.

"A UNSN human enter a den of armed kzintosh?"

"I have not always been a staff officer. Jocelyn, you should perhaps wait here."

"Why? Do you think I fear a few shot-up ratcats, Flatlander? When we Wunderlanders have fought them face-to-face these years?"

"I am thinking of Jorg. I wish to negotiate with him."

"He is mine lawfully! As are all the human traitors

lawfully in the power of the Free Wunderland Forces to deal with! You have agreed to that!"

"Nevertheless, I think it would be best."

"No."

"Please do not forget our respective ranks."

How strange! thought Raargh-Sergeant. To the kzin, human discipline seemed both soft with its feeble punishments and unyielding in its hierarchy. Kzinti discipline was ferocious but admitted a streak of anarchy as well. He who gave an order was expected to be able to enforce it physically at once. *It is almost a parody of kzin dominance establishment, without death-duels. How much did they learn from us?*

"You may answer to Markham!"

"I answer to the UNSN alone."

"And do you think I do not know who the UNSN's real masters are? You have revealed more of yourselves than you think these last few days! This is our planet, our system!"

"Which we have just liberated for you! A few days ago you were still weeping at the wonder and glory of the Hyperdrive Armada. . . . Let the dust of this last battle at least settle before we quarrel among ourselves. Jocelyn, I ask you, let me handle this my way . . . and let us not be shamed—before Heroes. Very well. Come."

"Do you *sssurindir*, Raargh-Sergeant?"

"Hroarh-Captain, it seems there is no choice. H'rr."

"Let the monkeys settle with the monkeys then. I will tell our Heroes to fire no more. Our task is to save what we can of our own."

Chapter 4

The two kzin and eight humans, six of the latter armed troopers, crossed the compound, past the smouldering wreck of the gun car. Raargh-Sergeant still carried his guns, for no human had seemed disposed to take them from him, but their barrels pointed to the ground.

"It is finished," he said, as he entered the Mess—Hroarh-Captain could no longer negotiate the steps. "I shall report that you have accomplished your duties satisfactorily," he added in the old formula, though he did not know whom he would report to. The Fanged God, perhaps? He saw that the Staff Colonel removed his headdress as he entered. Jocelyn-Captain did not.

The remnants of his "garrison" fell back from the weapons. The head-wounded Hero was in a twitching coma; the kzinrett, thankfully, now seemed engrossed in the suckling kitten and needed no restraints. The great drum was broken, he saw. They must have struck it too hard in their efforts. *It hardly matters. We have no more Sergeants' Mess.*

"So you hand me over," said Jorg. He spoke not to Raargh-Sergeant but to the human male.

"I will make diplomatic representations," Staff Colonel Cumpston replied. "A fair trial, at least. I want to see no more undeserving dead. No more human dead, even no more kzinti dead."

"Hear the Flatlander," muttered one of the human troopers. "Merciful to ratcats he never fought against or suffered under."

Jocelyn said no word of rebuke. The colonel turned to the trooper and began to raise a hand, then dropped it. It might have been simply an aborted gesture, but it might have served the purpose of calling attention to the row of decorations that he wore.

"A fair trial! What farce is this!"

"What trial did you give the humans in your power?" flared Jocelyn. "A one-way ticket to the Public Hunt! 'Our masters tell us there is a continuing demand for monkeymeat, a quota to be met!' Do you think I have forgotten those words?"

"A quota *you* helped supply. And if we had not, things would have been worse. We had a civilization. We lost it. Do you think by these methods you will build it again?"

"Yes, plead for your life! You should do it well. You have heard plenty of your victims' pleadings. Take all their best phrases!"

"What is happening?" asked Bursar. "If there is a crisis, we must be calm. What is this monkey chatter?"

The kit ran to Raargh-Sergeant. "Yes, what is happening? May we fight now? The shooting was over very quickly."

"Not now," said the colonel. The soft syllables of the Female Tongue which the kit was used to were relatively easy for a human to pronounce, yet he could place in it a churr of authority as well: "Your Raargh-Sergeant Hero will tell you no more fighting." He strode around the room, nodding at what he saw. At the block encasing Peter Brennan, he made a peculiar gesture. Raargh-Sergeant realized he was beckoning to him.

"More should see this," he said.

"I do not think more will. There will be no more Sergeants' Mess."

"No. Tell me, Raargh-Sergeant, have you ever been on furlough in the hills?"

"A few times, when things were quiet. And I have hunted ferals there."

"I see. Captain Jocelyn wants you dead."

"I would like that tree-swinger dead too."

"She has reasons. Her family . . . H'rr."

"I have reasons too. She lied to us, and because of her, Lesser-Sergeant and the others are dead and my Honor is in the mud with monkey dung."

"Let us be calm. It would be too easy for a war of extermination to flare up again, and it is your kind that would perish on this planet. I and some others have tried hard to prevent that. So has Hroarh-Captain and Hroth-Staff Officer, and he is the last of Traat-Admiral's own Pride to survive."

"And when our Patriarchal Navy returns in force? What of you monkeys then?"

"They will find it hard to fight a space war against the hyperdrive, I think. But we look to a cease-fire not on Wunderland only, but between the planets. Perhaps you will go home to Kzin."

The concepts were largely too alien to take in. He grasped what he could.

"Home to Kzin? I was born here, as was my Honored Sire. Somewhere here lie my kit's bones. And why should Kzinhome receive us, who are defeated and

disgraced and should have died if we could not con-
quer? *Ka'ashi* is my home."

"Yes. Have you seen much of this home of yours,
Raargh-Sergeant?"

"I have been in the Patriarch's Forces since I was
a youngster. I have gone where I was sent."

"The mountains?"

"Yes, of course, as I said. I was made Sergeant and
Raargh-Sergeant in campaigning."

"There could be good hunting there, for man or
kzin."

"Yes."

"There still can be."

"I do not understand."

"No place for you here now. No place for you on
Kzinhome. The hills are wide."

"And what of Hroarh-Captain?"

"The UNSN will need him, and all the very few kzin
officers who have survived, to administer the kzin population. Montferrat-Palme has made arrangements."

"As the Jorg-human was needed by us?" So the humans'
highest controller had been a secret feral too.

"No. Come a proper peace settlement, the kzin will
not be enslaved. In any event, they could not be . . .
That kitten, is he your son?"

"No. A war orphan."

"So he will die?"

"Male kits who lose their fathers too soon usually die,
unless a kzintosh without get of his own adopts them."

"There must be many orphans on this planet now."

"Many indeed."

"I suppose the UNSN will be sitting up orphanages
for kittens as well as children. It will be interesting
to see the results in a generation or so."

"You would turn our children into monkeys?"

"No. Take your hand from your *wtsai*. It would be

futile to even try. But you asked of Hroarh-Captain. I
see a place for him."

"And the Jorg?"

"A traitor. He goes to the Free Wunderlanders."

"He dies."

"I will not kill him. But I will shed no tears for him.
How would you feel about a kzin who did what he
has done?"

"I do not know tears. But you monkeys are hard to
understand. No Hero would do what he has done."

"Raargh-Sergeant . . ."

"Raargh-Sergeant no more. There is no force for me
to be Sergeant."

"Raargh, then."

The single, rankless Name hung for a moment in the
air as the kzin tasted it.

"Raargh, I cannot allow you to spill more human
blood. You understand that."

Jocelyn strode to them.

"Raargh-Sergeant! There can be no further delay. It
is time for your kzin to hand over their weapons now!
We have two gun cars outside now. And there are more
humans all round the monastery, armed. If you refuse
I will take it as an act of war, and one UNSN officer
and one geriatric priest will not interfere."

Think quickly, he told himself.

Then: "Very well."

He spoke to the others in the Heroes' Tongue, using
the ordinary dominant tense in which military orders
were given.

"Step back from the weapons."

"And your own, Raargh-Sergeant!"

He set down the beam rifles.

"I suppose you had better stay here for the time
being. I have no facilities for these wounded. You may
be moved to a holding camp later."

"Jocelyn-Captain . . . the *Ptrr-Brunurn*. He is a trophy of the Sergeants' Mess."

"I said he could remain. I will abide by my word."

"But there is no Sergeants' Mess now, only a few wounded kzinti who will soon be gone I know not where. We can no longer toast him with ritual and honor him and Kzarl-Sergeant. I give him back to you, so humans at least may honor him as he deserves. He is at risk of being dishonored otherwise."

"Very well."

"There is another matter. Chuut-Riit's urine." He indicated the ceremonial jar.

"What do I want with cat piss? We will clear that stink away from this world."

"It was a great gift to the Mess, presented in token of our Honor and Valor. Again there is no Mess. You are the conqueror. Do with it what you will, but it is a great trophy and thing of pride for us. A great night it was." *Of feasting, too, though I should not say that, lest she think upon that feast. But, oh, my Sire, and O Honored Chuut-Riit, it tears my liver and shaves my mane to do this thing! Know that I pick my way as best I can along trails of Honor that have grown twisted.* "A gift from an old *rratcat* who tried to fight with Honor."

"Very well." She passed her beam rifle to a trooper and took the jar, noting, perhaps, its intricate carvings and inlays. She gestured at Jorg von Thoma. "Come."

The human party turned and walked towards the car. Staff Colonel Cumpston lingered, looking back at the collection of wounded kzinti.

"I will carry the *Ptrr-Brunurn*" said Raargh. He beckoned to the kit. "Vaemar," he said, "give me good help to move this honored human. For you see my arm and legs are little use." To the colonel he said, "There is a debt."

The human nodded just perceptibly. "I know that Heroes are honorable in their debts," he said, "for good or ill. I may collect this debt one day . . . In the meantime, your Name as your word that you will harm no more humans?"

"My Name as my word. Save in defense."

"I have been a sergeant myself. If I may say so, perhaps old sergeants of all kinds tend to understand one another. It is a thankless job."

"Thankless? We of the Patriarch's forces do not serve for thanks but for knowledge of Honor upheld."

"I know."

"And sometimes for the loot, of course . . . *Centurion*."

"You know that word? Yes. I see the jar is heavy."

They followed the other humans to the cars. The rear part of the second was already filled with the human and kzin remains that had been retrieved from the aerial combat, scorched, smoking, smelling like . . . a smell that Raargh realized he had had too much of, in the last few weeks and the last few years. *I have had enough,* he realized with amazement. He and Vaemar-Riit worked Peter Brennan's block into the small area that was left. He turned to the colonel.

"I ask you, one more thing. Not for myself, but for him: he has no colored ribbons for bravery like you but see that he is not buried as you bury humans under white stones."

"I will speak to the abbot. He will be reopening the monastery as it was. It will be up to him, I think. You know that you kzinti made us religious again."

"*Farewell.*"

His *wtsai* was out in a blur of light. He flung it with inhuman accuracy into the small intake port of the car. He seized the kit in one arm, Jorg in the other. A standing leap took him into the cockpit of the other car. He slammed the canopy closed, struck at the switches with claws and prosthetic hand that moved too fast for a human eye to follow. The glass and Teflon needles of a strakakker sizzled into the car, turning half the canopy behind him opaque.

From the corner of his eye, he saw Jocelyn drop the precious jar and snatch for a beam rifle. But the second's delay was enough. The car was already airborne, accelerating away at full thrust.

He dived, pulling out centimeters above the roofs of the human shanties. A couple of bolts came after him, but the buildings and then the smoke blinded the shooters. He banked away from an approaching human ground vehicle with red crosses on its sides and, hugging the ground, zoomed towards Grossgeister Swamp, swerving to left and right as they passed the first surviving trees. The car buffeted and boomed into supersonic, reached full acceleration.

The monastery left behind, he climbed fast, eye flickering to the fuel gauge. They could travel a long way yet. The landscape opening up below was pockmarked with craters, and there were scattered fires and drifting smoke, but the smoke was lit by the passage of no lasers and there were no new explosions. Across Wunderland the cease-fire seemed to be holding.

The UNSN would be sending radio warnings about him, but as long as he headed away from militarily sensitive areas, they would probably not shoot him down. They would have much else to do and a crippled sergeant and a human would hardly be worth the effort. Still, he stealthed the car.

The silver water and dark vegetation of the swamp flashed below, then open park-like land again, in the Wunderland multicolor of plants, the local red, the green of Earth and the orange of Kzin. A purplish tinge of night was beginning to appear in the sky and Alpha Centauri B stood forth in its glory.

He turned to his passengers.

"By the time they have got the other car airworthy, we will be well away," he told them. "I do not think we need fear pursuit."

"There is nowhere for me to hide on this planet," said Jorg, "I am a dead man. But I thank you for your efforts."

"I find I cannot protect you forever, as I was charged," the kzin replied. "And I see that to die defending you would not save your life. But I can give you a chance, and be as faithful to my Honor as I may. I will put you down in wooded country. You can hide there for a time and perhaps with time the monkeys will hate you less. You will have monkey justice but perhaps not given to you while their livers are still burning."

"And is monkey justice right, do you think? You with your Honor may have some power to ease my mind if you think I am not wholly traitor to my kind. What do you think?"

"I am not a monkey. It is not for me to say."

"And you? You cannot go back now?"

"I could not hand over Vaemar, Vaemar-*Riit*, could I? Not to a monkey orphanage or perhaps to the *Arrum*. A hostage of the Patriarch's blood and last kit of Chuut-Riit's line? . . .

"And I am Sergeant no more . . .

"He and I are heading for the hills beyond the Hohe Kalkstein. The country is open and empty but for game, and we will see how the Fanged God meant kzintosh to live!"

WINDOWS OF THE SOUL

Paul Chafe

For Christian, with love

Transport tunnel nineteen is one of thirty-two that run the fifty-kilometer length of Tiamat's axis to link the docking hubs. Normally it's full of twenty-meter cargo containers, gliding in virtual weightlessness. Last night a roller jammed in section A near the down-axis hub. The Port Authority shut the tunnel down and sent in a tech. The problem was a body. That's when I got involved. Pathology said it had been there nine days and the Scene Team had all the evidence. There was no reason to go down there myself, but I did. You can't get a handle on a crime if you don't get on the scene. I wished I hadn't.

The body was M18JSK98—Miranda Holtzman, nineteen standard years old, engineering student at the Centaurus Center for Advanced Studies. Her dossier holo showed sparkling blue eyes and brown-gold hair. She was a Wunderlander, just arrived in the Swarm on a work-study deal with a spun metal fabricator called Trist Materials. Good looking, smart and last seen alive at

179

a bounce-bar called the Inferno. She'd arrived with friends and left with a stranger. The witnesses agreed on dark hair and a Wunderlander build but little else. A movement trace came up blank. After she left the Inferno, she hadn't thumbed a single scanner—and on Tiamat that takes some effort. That was nine days ago. Pathology had it right on the money.

We identified her through her on-file gene scans so her next of kin didn't have to. That was a good thing. She'd been badly mauled in jamming the track rollers, but that wasn't the worst of it. She was slashed open from throat to groin and eviscerated, her skin was flayed off and her limbs were missing. Her empty eye sockets stared at nothing. The coroner listed cause of death as "unknown." There wasn't enough left to tell.

Now you know why I wished I hadn't looked.

I tubed over to Trist Materials. They were closing down early, hampered by a swarm of Goldskin investigators. I grabbed the top cop. "Captain Allson, ARM."

"How can I help you?" He looked harried.

"I'm looking for the primary witnesses."

He pointed out the couple to me. They were sitting on a couch in the reception area holding each other. Tanya's face was drawn and pale, she'd been crying recently. Jayce looked sombre.

"You got somewhere I can hold an interview?"

"We have their statements."

"That's not what I asked." He looked sour. ARM outranks the Goldskins, but they don't like it. He beckoned over a uniform to set me up with some cubic. I called up their dossiers on my beltcomp. It helps to know who you're talking to.

PCL9C3N4—Koffman, Tanya C., 24. Born Tiamat Station. Graduate Serpent Swarm Technical Institute. Physical engineer for Trist. Unmarried. Holder of a non-current belt navigation certificate rated for polarizers and fusion. No outstanding warrants, no criminal record.

BG309003—Vorden, Jayce I. F., 23. Born Tiamat Station. Also an SSTI graduate and Trist's Compsys specialist. Unmarried. No warrants but he had a record, two hits, public mischief. I tabbed the entry for the details. University pranks. He'd hacked in to the scoreboard during a championship skyball game and displayed insults for the rival team. Acquitted with a warning. Another time he'd gained access to the transit system and given himself priority routing and children's fare. Charged double back payments on his fares and five hundred hours community service. That was three years ago—he'd been clean ever since.

On a hunch, I punched up my desk from the beltcomp and did quick movement trace. Multiple hits—the pattern was clear. Jayce and Tanya traveled as a couple, starting three months ago. I scanned forward and found trouble in paradise—ten days with no visits. I called up the comm logs for the period. A few calls, all very short, then a long one. Right after that, the visits started again. They'd fought and made up. The fight started a week after Miranda arrived and she'd gone missing the day they got together again. I called up her comm logs and found long calls to both of them, starting her first day on station.

The facts suggested a scenario. Jayce and Tanya have a good thing going, then pretty Miranda shows up and gets in the middle. A week later they sort out the triangle and go out for a no-hard-feelings party, which goes bad. Someone kills Miranda and the other gets involved. They make up the dark Wunderlander as cover. It wasn't a perfect theory, but it was a start.

I stuck my head out the door and called Jayce over. He was tall and slender with dark hair and eyes and a Flatlander's blended facial features. I tapped RECORD on my beltcomp and began.

"What can you tell me about the night Miranda disappeared?"

He shrugged. "There just isn't that much to tell. We went to the Inferno after work like we always did. She was dancing with this Wunderlander. After a while they left together."

"By 'we' you mean Miranda and you?"

"Miranda, Tay and I." He was perfectly comfortable with his answer.

"You and Miss Koffman have been seeing each other for some time, is that correct?"

"Yes."

"I understand you and she had a serious argument a couple of weeks ago." I stated it as a fact.

He was taken aback. "What do you mean?

I kept pushing. "I mean that Miranda Holtzman precipitated a rift in your relationship. That gives you a motive for murder."

The shock he displayed was genuine. I just didn't know if it was due to hidden guilt or injured innocence.

"What was your relationship with her?"

"She was our friend, that's all."

"You didn't have an affair with Miranda which brought on a fight with Tay?"

"No."

"Why did you go to the Inferno that night?"

"We just did. It wasn't unusual, we went fairly often."

"The three of you."

"Yes."

"Did anyone else go with you?"

"There's a bunch of us who sometimes go out, friends of ours, but they didn't come that night."

"Why not?"

"I don't know, just busy I guess." He looked stricken as he said it. He felt he was digging himself in deeper with every word.

"So there's no one who can corroborate your story that she left before you."

"Tanya can."

I waved a hand dismissively. "Anyone else?"

"Maybe the bartender."

"But you don't know for sure."

He put his head in his hands. "No."

I changed tack. "What about this man she left with?"

He seized the question like a drowning man grabbing a straw. If I was asking it, I must believe his story. "He was a Wunderlander, thick dark hair. He had a glowflow bodysuit, set to rainbow smears."

"Had you seen him before?"

"Not that I recall."

"Do you think he knew Miranda or that she knew him?"

He was anguished. "I don't know, I wish I did. We just didn't know what was happening." Then, almost to himself, he repeated, "We just didn't know."

He was devastated by the sudden loss. Perhaps he hadn't known Miranda that well but he'd been with her the night she was killed. It wasn't his fault but he felt responsible anyway. Survivor's guilt—or simple guilt. Either way, I wasn't going to learn anything more. The Goldskins would go over his statement and cross-check for inconsistencies. I just wanted a read on the first-pass prime suspects.

"You can go now, Mr. Vorden."

"What?" He'd sunken into a reverie while I pondered.

"You're done. Thank you for your help."

"Oh." He seemed bemused for a couple of seconds, then gathered himself. "Good luck, Captain."

"Thanks," I said, and I meant it. I hoped he did too.

After he left, I punched my beltcomp's audio log through to my desk. I've got a program that analyzes voice microtremors—sometimes it even works. My system told me that Jayce was telling the truth—mostly. He was hiding something about his relationship with Miranda. That concurred with my theory. There had been infidelity, a fight, a murder. I just needed the link.

I had Tanya sent in. She was petite for a Belter—my height. Her eyes were red and she dabbed at them with a handkerchief. In other circumstances she would be pretty.

"Come in, Miss Koffman. Please sit down," I said in my best good-cop manner.

She sat, giving me a forced, trembling smile. She was barely holding herself together. If I pushed her, she'd go over the edge. At times like this it's a judgement call. Sometimes a little nudge brings an easy confession, sometimes it catalyzes uncrackable resolve.

And sometimes you're just adding pressure to a bystander already under emotional overload. *Maintien le droit*, the ARM motto cuts both ways. Tanya was a prime suspect. I would step softly, but I would find out what I needed to know.

"Look, I know you're upset. I just have a couple of questions for you, and then you can go." I said it gently, coaxing. She nodded in response.

"Were you jealous of Miranda and Jayce?"

She didn't answer; she just shook her head, biting her lip.

"But they did . . . did sleep together?" I couldn't think of a more delicate way to put it."

She nodded. Paydirt.

"That didn't make you jealous?"

She shook her head. "We had a . . . you know . . . all three of us . . ." She collapsed into tears.

I hadn't been expecting that. I sat back, implications

running through my brain while Tanya wept. No use questioning her further now, my theory was shot. I needed to reassess.

I sent her out and pulled up the transit logs again and cross-matched all three of them for Miranda's tube station. They'd both been spending nights in her apt. Far from causing a breakup, she'd been the hingepoint of a menage. Tanya and Jayce's transit pattern changed because they'd been spending their time at Miranda's. That didn't clear them but it reopened the question of motive. Miranda's file yielded another link. This was her second time on Tiamat. At sixteen she'd been on a six-month school exchange with FRCK1798—Koffman, Bris, Tanya's younger sister. That explained why Tanya was more upset than Jayce and where the spark for the expansion of their relationship had come from. And it told me what Jayce had been covering up about his relationship with Miranda. At least part of what he'd been covering up. The information also offered some good motive possibilities—jealousy now for Jayce instead of Tanya or an old grudge rekindled for her. Even so, my instincts were telling me that they weren't the culprits. I needed another angle.

After a while I got up and grabbed the tube back to my office. On the way, I thought about dossiers.

C137PUDV—Allson, Joel K., ARM Captain. 33 standard years old. Born: Constantinople, Earth. Current assignment: Chief of Investigation—Tiamat Station, Alpha Centauri. Fingerprints, retina prints, gene scan. A holo of a man with a Flatlander face, Arab, African, Slav, Balt and Mongol—boringly nondescript on Earth, noticeably different on Wunderland. Date of birth, date of marriage, date of divorce. Medical history, educational records, details of promotion. Case reports from Bangkok, New Delhi and Berlin. Commendations for service and commendations for bravery. Date of transfer outsystem.

A good record, I was proud of it. What's the measure of a man? Nowadays it's his data file. Dossiers are the tools of my trade. They give me a skeleton—my job is putting flesh on the bones.

The best cops are just one step this side of the law—that's how you get into a criminal's mind. I was one of the best. In deep-cover work, the line gets blurry. You make so many sacrifices you start to feel entitled to fringe benefits your cover requires you to take anyway. The Brandywine case cost me my marriage. When it blew up, my position was—confused.

The Conduct Review Board said, "Captain Allson's actions were directly related to his assignment and he did not act with criminal intent." They must have known more than I did. Prakit believed them because he believed in me but when the slot on Wunderland came up, he offered it, firmly. After Brandywine I'd never be safe undercover again, not on the Organization cases I'd made into my life. He never mentioned Holly, but it wasn't my cover that worried him. I took the assignment. What else was I going to do?

Wunderland—the name says it all. The colonists found a virgin paradise of mountains and forests, clear air and low gravity. They turned it into the jewel of Known Space, but the world they'd built was gone now. First the kzinti had invaded taking the land and turning the citizens into slaves—or dinner. Some fought, some fled, some tried to save what they could. Most just survived and carried on in a grimmer world.

Forty years later, Earth attacked with lightspeed missiles, twelve thousand gigatonne impacts that punched to the planet's core and blotted the suns from the sky. The UN wrecked the kzinti industrial base and much of Wunderland in the process. The survivors cheered anyway, and dreamed of liberation. And it came, faster than anyone could imagine, in an Earth armada with We Made It hyperdrives. The Provisional Government was formed and the Wunderlanders began to heal the scars of conquest. The rebels came out of the mountains and the pirates came in from the Swarm. The few kzinti left insystem adapted, disappeared into the forest, or died.

But liberation didn't end the war. Alpha Centauri became the UN advance base. The Provo Government was controlled by UN advisors and the Serpent Swarm made a UN territory outright. The economy went to full war production. The liberators quartered thousands of troops in Munchen in case the kzinti came back— and in case the Wunderlanders objected to the UN plan. Maybe the breakdown was inevitable. The kzinti were no harsher than the Provos and a lot less corrupt. A political party called the Isolationists emerged with a simple solution—Wunderland for Wunderlanders. The kzinti were gone, the Flatlanders could go too. By the time I arrived in Munchen, they were no longer a political party, they were a terrorist group. The Provisional Government's anti-collaborator campaign had become a random witch hunt. The whole infrastructure was falling apart—transportation, medical support, civil services, even basic maintenance stripped to feed the UN war machine. The black market thrived on everything from pleasure drugs to biochips and a dozen crime webs warred over the spoils. Whole outland regions rejected the Provos and UN troops were used to impose control.

I should have thrived in that environment—it was my kind of work, but the rot had spread to the ARM. Certain individuals, certain groups had immunity. Investigations that got too close were closed down. Critical evidence simply disappeared. I fought a losing battle to clean up the agency and made a lot of high-powered enemies. When they discovered they couldn't shut me up, they kicked me upstairs, big time. I wound up with the top job on Tiamat, half a billion kilometers skyward.

It was better on station. There was smuggling, theft, even murder—but no bombings, no assassinations, no gang wars. More importantly, the taint of corruption was gone. I needed that change most of all. It didn't tempt me, but it disturbed too many sleeping ghosts for comfort.

The tube stopped and I climbed out and hurried back to my office. I wanted to catch up to Hunter-of-Outlaws. One of the few wise decisions the UN made was to let the kzinti left in-system run their internal affairs as long as they toed the UN line when dealing with humans. Tiamat has a lot of kzinti, most in the Tigertown high-G section. They were surprisingly good citizens, considering, but keeping relations smooth was a balancing act. Hunter was my high-wire partner.

He was on his way out when I got back. I grabbed him before he could leave and outlined my findings.

"What do you think?" I asked when I was done.

"Hrrr . . . If Koffman and Vorden are to be believed the prime suspect must be the human she left with, on evidence of contacts. Since she left no transit log, it is probable she traveled on her companion's ident to the transport tunnel where she was killed. However . . ." he trailed off.

"Go on," I prompted.

He continued reluctantly. "The body was found near the kzinti sector. The corpse looks like a butchered prey animal. On the basis of these facts I would suspect a kzin."

I nearly laughed but he was dead serious. "You don't think a human would do that?"

"I have seen humans kill each other but I have never seen them strip a carcass so. It is the act of a carnivore."

"Never underestimate humanity, my friend." I grinned, but didn't let my teeth show.

He ignored the barb. "If it is possible, then we must consider it. It is conceivable the culprit was cutting the body up into manageable pieces and was disturbed before the task could be completed. Perhaps Miranda Holtzman held dangerous information and was killed to preserve its secrecy."

"I hadn't considered that, but you're right." I didn't go on.

Hunter considered, pupils narrowing. "Your manner tells me you have another thought." He knew humans well.

"Perhaps she was killed by a schitz." It was a wild idea, but it fit.

The kzin looked baffled. Maybe he didn't know humans so well after all. "What is a *schitz*?"

"It's a blanket term for someone who isn't wired properly. They respond to hallucinations, become paranoid or megalomaniacal. Specifics vary but they can be homicidal."

He knew what hallucinations were but—"What is paranoid and megalomaniacal?" He pronounced the words awkwardly.

"Paranoia is when you feel that the entire world is plotting against you. Megalomania is when you have delusions of grandeur." His expression continued quizzical. "As if a telepath was convinced he was destined to be Patriarch."

"A kzin so defective would not survive. I have never heard of these conditions."

"It's rare, the genes are being weeded out. There are drugs to control it too—but—med support is hard to get nowadays. On Wunderland people are dying for lack

of it. It isn't so bad up here . . ." I trailed off, thinking. Getting treatment was easy in the Swarm, but what
if someone didn't *want* treatment?

"Why do you suspect a schitz if they are rare? Prob-
ability would suggest another scenario."

"Yah, it would. But Miranda was a pretty young
woman last seen with an unknown male. Schitz crimes
sometimes involve violent sexual motives."

He gave me another quizzical look. "Violent sex is
a contradiction in terms. How can genes for this behavior propagate?"

"Schitzies aren't rational, I don't know how they
think. Dammit, I've only even *heard* of one schitz; this
is just what I learned in training." I thought about the
case I knew. An autodoc misread a med card and a
quiet sculptor murdered his roommates in a blind rage.
The error wasn't his fault but . . .

Hunter interrupted my reverie. "We have a wealth
of possibilities—a kzin with a lost temper, a human
with a definite motive and a connection to the victim, a schitz engaged in random murder. We lack
information. I suggest we gain some."

I smiled. "Let's do that." Hunter could be relied on
to cut to the heart of the matter. He gave me the kzin
gesture that meant concurrence-between-equals and left.
I watched him go and pondered. There was another
possibility.

Hunter's dossier told me he'd once been Kurz-
Commander, in control of the kzin base on Tiamat. During the occupation he'd gained a reputation as a hard
but fair governor and a ruthless, efficient rebel hunter.
He'd earned respect and even affection from his human
charges but he was their prime target on the day Tiamat
revolted. He survived because he was off station, organ-
izing a ragtag group of tugs and mining ships into a
last-ditch defense against the Terran fleet. He survived

the battle and the labour camps and eventually wound up back on Tiamat—this time to maintain order among the stranded kzin. He was the logical choice, he knew more about the asteroid's workings than anyone of either species. I relied heavily on his experience and judgment.

That gave him a lot of power, and made me vulnerable.

I called in Tamara Johansen, head of Criminal Investigation with Tiamat's Goldskin police. She'd served on Tiamat since before the liberation and would have had my job if the UN hadn't dumped me on top of her. It was a credit to her professionalism that she didn't let her resentment show—much. When she arrived I filled her in.

"Where do I fit?" she asked.

"There's a fourth scenario. Maybe Miranda was killed by a kzin with some connection to her. What if she knew something she wasn't supposed to?"

"What are you getting at?" She was intrigued.

"Look, we've got fifty thousand kzinti on-station. They're the ones smart enough to adapt to human rule. They know they have to work with us. That doesn't mean they've changed allegiance. Hunter-of-Outlaws doesn't mind suggesting that a kzin might have killed Miranda in a rage. What if a kzin killed Miranda because she knew too much about kzin underground activity?"

She didn't look impressed by my suspicions. "We know they run an intelligence net, but it isn't much. I'd be surprised if they've got a secret worth the trouble a murder investigation will bring. They can't even get information back to Kzin."

"What's your theory then?"

She held up an imaginary magnifying glass. "It is a cardinal error to speculate in advance of the facts." She gave me an exaggerated scowl.

I laughed and the ice broke a little. "Speculate any-way, Holmes, I won't hold you to it."

She became serious again. "I'd suspect a Kdaptist."

"What's a Kdaptist?"

"They're a kzin cult. They've only surfaced once in the swarm, but the case was a lot like this one. Right after the liberation, a fighter jock named Detoine dis-appeared. He was a real war hero, very famous. Had every decoration you could get, most of them twice. There was a huge search."

"So what happened?"

"We got nothing. Then three years later a kzin got caught with a human skin—the DNA was Detoine's. Turns out the kzin was a high priest in this breakaway cult. They believed their god abandoned them and they used Detoine's skin in their rituals to try and get him back."

"And the rest of Detoine?"

"They *ate* him. To absorb his heroic warrior spirit."

I shuddered involuntarily. "That's a close enough pat-tern to be worth investigating. That's your angle. Keep me posted."

She gave me a thumbs-up and turned to go. I stopped her before she got to the door.

"Why do you think Hunter is covering this up?"

She shrugged. "We don't know that he is. He was still in a security camp down on Wunderland when all that happened, he probably doesn't even know about it. Remember, Hunter-of-Outlaws is a kzin. His personal honour is the core of his identity."

"Meaning?"

"Getting involved in a cover-up is risking his honour, so he probably isn't. But if he is, it'll be something big. Very big."

She went off to start her inquiries and I sat at my desk and pulled up the files on the Kdapt cult. Service number K78131965—Squadron Leader Jean-Marc Detoine. Valour Cross, UN Cross, UN Medal and bar, Flight Medal and two bars and a dozen lesser awards. He had forty kills in atmosphere and eighteen in space. UNF Command put a lot of pressure on when he went missing and the Goldskins turned Tiamat upside down. They found nothing. Three years later, a kzin named Trras-Squadron-Battle-Planner forgot his shoulder pack in a tube car. The Transit lost-and-found opened it and discovered Detoine's skin, but Trras had scoured his quarters of evidence and committed suicide by the time the pack was traced. The search team got nothing but a paw-written Kdaptist creed. That dead-ended the case until a smart investigator connected the Kdapt view with the fact that Trras still carried his Fifth Fleet name. Seven kzin were found with similar names. All seven were involved with the cult. All seven were shot. I skipped the details and called up all unsolved murder files since the liberation. None came close to the Kdaptist's flay-eviscerate-devour pattern.

I pondered. If any Kdaptists were left, they weren't very energetic. Anyway, Miranda hadn't been eaten— at least not all of her. Perhaps Hunter simply didn't consider the cult a possibility worth mentioning. So, what else was big enough for the kzin underground to risk a murder investigation, big enough for Hunter-of-Outlaws to put his personal honour on the line?

Hyperdrive was the obvious answer. The UN's ongoing campaign against kzinti interstellar trade was strangling their empire. That strategy depended entirely on their lack of FTL travel. Hyperdrive ships aren't even allowed to dock at Tiamat because of the kzin population. The secret of hyperdrive was the only information they could get back to Kzin faster than a laser.

Was that what was going on? Was Hunter involved? I forced the question out of my mind. If he was on the level, there was no problem. If he wasn't, then Johansen and I would catch him—sooner or later. In the meantime, the angle was worth following. Trist Materials had nothing to do with hyperdrives, so Miranda wasn't a primary-source spy. I did a movement trace for the last two weeks of her life, then cross-referenced to anyone connected to the hyperdrive project. I got about a hundred thousand possible contacts, including myself. Hunter was right, I needed more data. Without it, I'd drive myself paranoid.

Thinking of paranoia brought me back to the schitz angle. I hoped it was wrong. I didn't want to think about a human depraved enough to do what had been done to Miranda.

Tiamat is a potato-shaped asteroid, 20 kilometers by 50 kilometers. The Swarm Belters formed it into a rough tube, spun it for gravity and honeycombed it with tunnels. It rotates every ten hours, creating a 1G pull around the circumference. Ships dock at the axis, low gravity industries take up the center of the tube, farms and parks take up the periphery. The Inferno was on a commercial arcade on the .4G level. After work, I tubed up to see how Miranda spent her last hours.

It was packed when I got there. Sound dampers kept the pulsating music out of the pedmall but inside it was deafening. The dance floor was a mass of gyrating bodies in simulated free fall down a holographic bottomless chasm. Dante-esque demons circled above them before plunging past into the depths. The dancers took full advantage of the low G to leap and twirl in fantastic combinations. Artificial pheremones filled the air with sex and danger.

I sat down at the bar. A local sound damper gave some relief from the thunderous beat. The usual selection of alcohol was on offer, as well as an array of pleasure drugs ranging from mild to mind bending. I ordered vodka and turned to survey the crowd. It was a mixed group, about half Swarm Belters and the rest an even mixture of Wunderlanders and Flatlanders. They were young and well off—the engineers and technicians who formed the backbone of Tiamat's industry, engaged in the species' oldest rituals.

I didn't have a specific goal in mind, I just wanted to circulate and see what I learned. Putting together a dossier is easy nowadays. An ARM ident and a few keystrokes make a thousand databanks divulge your secrets—bank statements, travel logs, medical records and more. Your life is laid out for me to read like entrails before a soothsayer. I have a window into your soul and through it I can know more about you than your closest friends. And yet the bare facts never describe the real person behind them. That was my real purpose for being at the Inferno. I wanted to put flesh on Miranda Holtzman's bones.

A huge dragon with burning eyes and golden scales swooped over the dancers and immolated them in holographic flames. They obligingly shrieked and writhed to the floor as the beast roared in triumph, drowning out the music as the controller changed tracks. It flew off in forced perspective, flapping heavily as the dancers picked up the new beat. A tall, elfin blonde caught my eye. I smiled back but made no move to go over. A short conversation in body language. "You look like fun, come join me." "Tempting ma'am, but no thanks." I beckoned to the bartender to refill my drink. As he did I showed him Miranda's holo. His manner stiffened ever so slightly. "I've already told the Goldskins everything I know."

"I'm not a Goldskin, I'm just doing a little unofficial inquiry."

He relaxed a bit. "Well, I've seen her of course. Her crowd were all regulars in here."

"Are they here tonight?" I didn't look around.

"They haven't shown up yet. I don't expect they will, since the news broke about her." Miranda was on all the 'casts.

"Yah, I understand. Listen did anything unusual happen the night she disappeared?"

"I really couldn't tell you; it was a week ago and I wasn't paying attention. I didn't know anything was wrong." He looked anguished, as if her death was his fault.

"No, of course not." Reassuring. "Listen do me a favor and keep your ears open. If you hear anything, let me know." I handed him my callcard and he assured me he would call with almost comical solemnity. My work is high drama for the citizens.

On the dance floor, another woman was looking at me, this one was a red-haired Wunderlander. She held my gaze for five intense seconds before whirling away, sensuous as a cat. Not an invitation but a challenge. "Bet you can't keep up."

I looked for the blonde. She was on her way out, arm in arm with a UNF captain. Maybe she liked Flatlanders. She was a Belter and I watched her long legs with frank appreciation. She caught me looking and gave me a look. "See what you're missing."

I shrugged and went to the edge of the dance floor. The holoshow had become a stormscape, thickened with real fog from a hidden nozzle. The clouds twisted in the virtual wind, forming wraiths for an instant before collapsing back into mist. At the height of the transformation, bolts of lightning formed eyes in the dark folds of their cowls. When the redhead came by, I caught her hand and she pulled me into the maelstrom. Her dancing was precise but uninhibited. I fell into rhythm with the bouncebeat, catching my partner and spinning her back into the crowd. Drowning myself in the deep blue pools of her eyes. I forgot about Miranda—and Holly.

As the music climaxed, she pulled me to her, pressing herself hard against me in the crush. She gave me the merest whisper of a kiss when the drumbeat crescendoed. Then thunder drowned out the music and strobes split the clouds with artificial lightning. She spun away as the new rhythm came up. By the time the spots cleared from my eyes, she was gone.

I was disappointed but intrigued. We hadn't spoken a word but her message was clear. "Catch me if you can."

She'd chosen the right man for the job.

The next day I got down to business. Identification had put together a composite holo of our suspect. Interview reports were trickling in as well. I also did a little personal work on UN time. I called up the Inferno's sales files for the previous night, cross-referenced for sex and description and found three women who might be my mysterious redhead. I screened their holos and found a match.

TLU5A169—Suze Vanreuter, 32, unmarried, no dependants, no record. She was a mining engineer, just arrived on Tiamat as a consultant to Corona Exploration. That's confidential information. A lot of speculators would pay high to learn that a prospecting operation has hired a mining engineer.

I wasn't interested in the stock market. The file didn't mention her catlike grace. The holo didn't show the sparkle in her eyes. No matter, I knew where I could find the real thing. I closed my eyes and remembered her taut body pressed against me. And the kiss. She put more erotic energy into that barely-there kiss than most women put into an orgasm.

That thought gave me pause and I thought back to

my life with Holly. She'd been more than an enthusiastic bed partner, she'd been my lifemate, my friend.
Losing her left an aching void in my soul. Was I now
replacing her with Suze? Surely I was too experienced,
too jaded to confuse love and lust.

I decided not. Suze wasn't better, she was different.
I didn't love her, I didn't even know her, but I *desired*
her more than I'd ever desired a woman before. Even
more than Holly.

Hunter came in and looked over my shoulder. I
should have closed my door. He gestured to Suze's holo
on my screen. "What is this one's role in the crime?"

I blanked the screen. "She isn't a suspect, she's just
a woman I saw at the Inferno while I was gathering
information. I called up her file for . . ." I hesitated " . . .
personal reasons."

The kzin nodded knowingly, rippling his ears in
amusement. He had dealt with humans, he understood
the subtext of the conversation. "You have mated with
her."

I was taken aback. "No, I haven't, I am . . ." I groped
for words " . . . interested in learning if I want to mate
with her."

The big cat sniffed the air, looking baffled. "How can
you not know if you are attracted to a female? Certainly your pheremones speak of desire."

Did he have any idea how personal he was being?
"I do know I'm attracted to her."

"Then you have already learned what you need to
know."

"Well . . . It's not so simple, she also has to . . . want
to mate with me."

"And this information is available in her dossier?"

"No no no. She's made it clear she's interested in me.
I'm looking at her file to get to know her better."

"Would it not be easier to ask questions directly? And

if you both desire sex with each other, why have you not already mated?"

Curiosity might not be killing the cat but it was certainly embarrassing the human. I groped for words, then inspiration struck. "Among humans, sexual negotiations are often like a hunt. The goal is hopefully achieved, but the real attraction is the excitement and challenge of the chase. The harder the pursuit, the more satisfying the feast is."

He nodded sagely. "I understand. This is the violent sex you spoke of earlier."

"No!" He was making *me* look like a schitz. "There is no violence involved."

"How then do you secure sexual relations with a resisting female?"

"She *isn't* resisting, damnit! She wants to be caught. More than that, she's actively seeking me as well."

"This sounds more like a duel than a hunt."

"Yah, maybe that's a better word." I was relieved that some understanding had been conveyed. Now maybe we could move on to less personal topics.

My relief had come too soon. Hunter had another question. "How do you determine the victor in this duel then?"

I wondered if he knew how disconcerting his persistence was. I watched him for signs of amusement but his face showed only curiosity.

I answered carefully. "There isn't a winner or a loser. If we manage to establish a . . . relationship . . . on mutually acceptable terms, we both win, insofar as we have gained something pleasant and desirable."

The kzin just looked baffled. "A hunt with no hunting, where neither side knows if it is predator or prey. A chase that ends not with feasting but with procreation. A duel with no winner. Why go through these convolutions? If the scent is right, mate."

It occurred to me that battle might be a better analogy. I started to sort out how to explain it in those terms but quickly gave it up.

Hunter was shaking his head dolefully. "I will never understand humans."

I was content to let him wonder. My concept of kzinti had been formed by holocubes on Earth. I'd learned they were remorseless alien killing machines intent on turning humanity into slaves and game animals. If anyone had told me then that one day I'd be trying to explain the dynamics of bounce bar dating to one, I would have died laughing.

I didn't laugh now. I didn't want Hunter to feel I was making fun of his lack of understanding. Even so, it was hard to keep my teeth from showing through my smile. I cleared Suze's file from the screen and brought up my investigation records in its place. I spent some time filling him in on my suspicions and intentions. He listened carefully before speaking.

"Have you further evidence that a schitz is involved?"

"None yet, it's still just a hunch."

"I would not dissuade you from your line of inquiry but I now have concrete reasons to suspect a kzin."

"What evidence?"

"My liver councils my head but my head councils my tongue."

It took a couple of moments before I figured out that the saying meant he wasn't going to tell me. I tried another tack. "How long before you know?"

"Soon enough, today or perhaps tomorrow. Even now First Tracker is stalking our quarry. I will inform you when I have more information."

He left to help First Tracker set his snares. Tracker was Hunter-of-Outlaw's right-hand man—or rather right paw kzin. I find it incredible that a population of fifty thousand can be policed by just two individuals—

particularly when the population is made up of fiercely individualistic carnivores with hair-trigger killer instincts. The contradiction underscored the curious nature of the kzinti social structure. At first glance, it's barely a step above anarchy. Kzinti are always fighting amongst themselves for wealth, status and honor. They fight individually and in groups, usually violently, often lethally. The only leaven of law is the Hero's code of honor, a rough-and-ready standard enforced with rough-and-ready justice. Yet despite this, they possess a cultural unity and stability that defies humanity. They had a single language and world government when human culture was nothing more than cave art. What's more, they have maintained their cohesiveness throughout the formation by colonization and conquest of an interstellar empire. Humanity's world government is already miserably failing in its attempt to make the transition to space.

Humans are more civilized than kzinti—any human can tell you that. But Hunter-of-Outlaws and First Tracker had no difficulty maintaining order in their bailiwick. Mostly they investigated the facts in disputes brought before the Conservors. They had lots of time left over to lend me a hand with human crimes.

Of course their caseload was helped by the fact that the kzin community required little "policing" in the human sense of the word. The Conservors offered guidance on the application of the honor code to new situations based on tradition and common sense. Individuals who violated the code were chastised, ostracized or killed depending on the severity of their transgression. Any other problem was a matter for the involved parties to settle by compromise, duel or Conservor arbitration according to their wishes. Most kzinti crimes were crimes against humans. It had taken a while after the liberation before kzin realized they couldn't simply kill a human for breaking a verbal contract or failing to show the proper respect. Finally, the Conservors had decreed that loyalty to the Patriarch required survival which required that humans be dealt with under human law. Eventually the majority had come around to that view. Those who didn't got weeded out sooner or later. Then the problem became humans who cheated kzinti knowing they hadn't the resources to secure redress. This issue was a much smaller problem for the UN, partly because it still took a brave human to cheat a kzin, but mostly because they just didn't care.

They cared a lot about violence against humans though. I had been hoping that a kzin had killed Miranda because I didn't want to think about a human so depraved. Now I worried that I might get my wish along with the explosive can of political worms it would open. Even ten years after the war, there were those who called for the extermination of the kzinti survivors of the Liberation. This incident would only fan those flames. If my fears about a kzin ring intent on hijacking a hyperdrive proved correct, the whole damn asteroid would go to war.

Alpha Centauri already had enough problems. I decided to keep working on the schitzies until Hunter gave me something solid. Before I'd hoped to find a kzin because I feared I'd find a schitz. Now I hoped to find a schitz because I feared finding a kzin.

Niggling at the back of my mind was another fear— the fear that the killer might not be a schitz either. Faced with a crime like this, one's natural instinct is to push it as far away as possible, to an outsider, to a deviant, to an alien. Easy to do when the victim is innocent and the crime abhorrent. Harder when the crime is clean and abstract. Hardest when you see yourself reflected in the criminal.

The more unhuman you can make the criminal, the

easier it is to deny the common threads that bind our experience together. To feel empathy for a criminal is to admit that it is circumstance as much as virtue that separates the outlaw and the community. Most important, it is to deny ourselves the only socially sanctioned target for the anger and frustration obeisance to the communal laws brings. If we didn't vilify outlaws, we might envy them for their freedom—the freedom we have traded for property, social position and stability.

I'd learned during Brandywine what true freedom is. Entering crime is like entering cold water. However daunting the prospect is at first, the exhilaration once you're immersed in it is indescribable. To make decisions with no pretense at morality grants immense personal power. Ironically, only when you have rendered society's laws irrelevant can you be truly honest with yourself. Your thoughts become incisive, unfettered by external entanglements. Your mind is free, you can do anything you like, be anything you want. Ultimately, freedom is about power. Ultimately, society has only the power we give it. Refuse the demand to submit to the social norm and, if you are smart enough and fast enough, you can walk like a god on earth. Such freedom is a heady drug indeed.

That drug comes with a high price. It means sacrificing home, career, family, every anchor and reward society offers us. I wasn't ready to make that sacrifice when Holly was my home. I thought I'd found a compromise in ARM undercover work—a challenging career, exciting work, unbridled license and a happy family too. I even got paid to do it, it was like living a dream. What I didn't realize is that freedom really is a drug—a little is never enough and too much is always disastrous. How far I'd slipped didn't register until I'd lost Holly and then it was too late. I nearly lost my career in the bargain and at the time I wouldn't have cared. I felt burnt out and directionless. I was an addict forced to confront my addiction. I made a decision and my career became the anchor that held me back from the abyss.

So far I'd managed to hold on.

I forced my mind back to the job at hand. Detective work is a matter of sorting through hunches. I glanced over the interview reports from Trist Materials and other sources. They were pretty sparse—Miranda had no family here and she hadn't been on station long enough for people to get to know her too deeply. I wasn't really as interested in what the interviewees had said as in the impression they'd made on the interviewer. Even more, I wanted to see if any of them had anything to do with hyperdrive production. None did, nor had any of my investigators red-flagged any as a potential suspect. With no way to narrow down my search for a hyperdrive connection, I concentrated on the schitz angle. There were about five dozen people with severe schitz tendencies on their medical records in the Swarm. I cut that in half by looking only at males on the theory that the killing was a sex crime. By midafternoon I'd eliminated all but eight of them for having the wrong physical description, for not being on Tiamat when the crime was committed or some other disqualification. I ran a detailed movement analysis on the remainder, tying up my hardware for over an hour. Three were eliminated, none were implicated outright. What to do?

I considered having the remaining five hauled in so I could ask a few questions. I didn't have to haul them in, my desk performs voice stress analysis perfectly well over the screen, but I prefer to talk to a suspect one on one. It makes the interview more personal, raising the stress level and giving the software something to work on. Besides, I like to see the reactions for myself and come to my own conclusions. The computer isn't infallible and neither am I. Using both techniques cuts the error rate.

If it worked I could wrap the case up that afternoon, if it didn't at least I could eliminate those five and get to work finding a new line of investigation. The risk was tipping off the murderer. If one of the suspects bolted, we'd have our man. Then we'd just have to find him. My instincts warned me that we never would. He'd disappear into the Swarm or the mountains down on Wunderland. Maybe in a year or ten the Provopolizei would catch him sniping politicians in Munchen for the Isolationists. The Isolationists would suit a schitz just fine.

My instincts were wrong, of course. I was used to Earth with its swarming crowds that could swallow a runner forever. Even on lightly settled Wunderland a fugitive who made it to the outskirts of Munchen could disappear into a thousand kilometres of virgin wilderness. In Tiamat's sealed environment there was nowhere to run and very few places to hide. Every time the suspect keyed a phone, the call would be monitored. Every time he thumbed a door or bought something, the computers would log it. Every time he walked a pedestrian mall, the vidscanners would be looking for him. If he were so foolish as to board a tube car, he'd be delivered right to the Goldskin headquarters' tube station and left locked in until I felt like coming to collect him. Tiamat was a law enforcement dream and a privacy nightmare. I punched the front desk and had my schitzies rounded up.

All five came in voluntarily, concerned about the murder, eager to do what they could to help. Ian Vanhoff was the one I had the most hope for. He ran a power loader in the container bays of the down-axis hub, giving him direct access to tunnel nineteen. I was sure I had the case locked up when I read that in his file. He gave me an ironclad alibi. The night Miranda disappeared he'd been working an extra shift in a storage bay on the other side of the asteroid. It hadn't been run through his personnel card yet because of union rules but his foreman and the rest of the loader crew could verify the times down to the minute. His wife could vouch for his arrival at home.

Thank you, citizen, you've been very helpful.

Dieter Lorz was at his girlfriend's apt that evening. She could corroborate that, as could another couple who'd visited with them.

Thank you, citizen.

Myro Havchek was upgrading his single-ship license. He'd been at the library studying. Yes, there were people who could testify they'd seen him there.

Get out of here, citizen. I've got a case to solve.

Two lacked alibis. Keve McCallum claimed to be asleep in his apt. Why hadn't the computer logged his entry? He didn't like the computer watching his every move, he had a mechanical lock on his door. Darren Sioban had been relaxing alone in a park on the 1G level. Why didn't he show as having taken the tube there? He'd walked, he needed the exercise.

Thank you, citizens.

The stress analyzer hadn't twitched, neither had my internal lie detector. I mulled it over. Could a schitz lie well enough to fool the computer and me? In our different ways we both responded to changes in stress. Getting past that would require nerves of ice.

So would taking Miranda apart.

Did not wanting the computer to know when you were home constitute paranoia? Knowing what I knew about information retrieval, it even made sense. What did Keve know about it? What did I expect from a registered schitz anyway? The drugs weren't perfect.

Were they?

Could a schitz off drugs construct a fantasy so powerful it became an internal reality? If the subject believed he was telling the truth, no lie detector would say anything else.

Was a schitz truly responsible for crimes committed while off drugs? I didn't even want to think about that one.

I had too many questions and not enough answers. I called up Johansen but she'd already gone. I dumped my interrogation files to her desk and tasked her to verify the alibis. I didn't expect them to be anything but solid. She wouldn't be thrilled with the job but she'd do it right.

I called up Dr. Morrow and found he'd gone home too. I hadn't realized how late it was getting. I asked the night intern a question. No, the drugs weren't perfect. Readjusting a schitz problem was a tightrope act. Too little and the patient destabilized. Too much and you had a walking zombie. Once upon a time any deviation from the social norm was drugged until it went away—totally. Now the doctors tried to intervene as little as possible. Around Alpha Centauri there wasn't even a law to enforce dosage. Minor personality quirks were not unusual.

I asked some more questions. Yes, a schitz off drugs might suppress a memory, or move in and out of an alternate reality. Yes, a schitz off drugs might have the cold control required to beat a lie detector.

What would happen when a criminal schitz had his drugs reinstated? Would his memory remain? How would he respond to the knowledge of his crimes? Anything was possible, it depended on the case.

Back to square zero.

Almost square zero. I left Johansen another message, asking her to collect blood samples from the group as well. Morrow could tell me if they were up to date on medication or not. If one of them wasn't, it would close the case up in a big hurry.

I put an ARM tag on their idents. That would stop them from boarding the next ship to never-never land. If any tried it, he'd be back in the hot seat as suspect number one.

Would a schitz off drugs choose to go back on them voluntarily? Another unanswerable question.

I screened their psych reports. McCallum was manic depressive and paranoid. That explained his mechanical lock. Sioban was borderline schizophrenic and highly antisocial, hence his habit of walking alone in the park. They were both intelligent and well educated: McCallum was an electronics engineer and Sioban was a process control specialist. Neither had any history of sexual deviance or aggression, neither had a criminal record. Despite their minor quirks both were productive, stable members of the community.

While they were on their drugs.

Without treatment they were question marks. They'd been diagnosed early and treated all their lives. Nobody knew what they were capable of, them least of all.

Even if one or the other was untreated, it wouldn't prove anything—none of the witnesses had chosen them. It *would* give me probable cause for a search warrant, which might turn up some physical evidence—the better part of Miranda had yet to surface. Until then I lacked a single link between the killing and—anything.

I mulled my hyperdrive suspicions over again. I had even less to go on there than I did with the schitzies. I thought about Tanya and Jayce. They lacked motive for starters and they were just too upset by Miranda's death, genuinely upset. Maybe my instincts were wrong on that point. Maybe if I hauled them in and grilled them with the stress analyzer listening in, they'd crack.

Maybe I was grasping at straws. I needed another angle, but first I needed a break. If nothing better suggested itself tomorrow, I'd run a detailed movement trace on every ident that went through the Inferno's accounting system the night Miranda disappeared and if that failed, I'd do it for every ident that even came within a kilometer of the place. If I split the compute task, I could get the results in a day or two, spend two weeks analyzing them and then maybe I'd have something to go on. Maybe. I was the last one to leave the office. Time flies when you're having fun.

I didn't go home after work, though I needed the rest. Instead I went down to the Inferno, eager for the second round of the developing game I was playing with Suze Vanreuter. On the way down I wondered what it was about her that appealed to me so strongly. She was attractive enough but there was more to it than that. Her energy and spontaneity had touched a long-buried chord—a part of me that I'd lost contact with.

When I got to the Inferno, I waited just inside the entry for a few moments to let my eyes adjust to the lower light levels. The holoshow was a burning pool of lava and the dancers were individually encased in a dynamic, digital flame that clung and followed their movements. Periodically the lava would form into a diabolic face that laughed maniacally, swallowed the dancers whole and spit them out again. The music was darker and heavier than the night before but the insistent, pulsating beat was the same.

I went in, expecting to find her in the middle of the show. Instead she was sitting at the bar. I sat down beside her.

"Good evening, Ms. Vanreuter," I said formally.

If my knowledge of her name surprised her she gave no sign. "Good evening, Captain Allson."

It was my turn to be startled. Perhaps I shouldn't have been. She probably knew the bartender. It would have been easy enough for her to discover my name. I hoped the surprise didn't show.

"Would you care to dance?"

"Enchanted." She favoured me with a megavolt smile and took my offered arm.

We danced as the holoshow engulfed us in living fire. The flames highlighted the blazing halo of her hair as she insinuated herself into the rhythm. Her concentration was complete, but she kept her eyes locked on mine. At first we connected only long enough to begin another energetic maneuver. As the night went on and the fatigue and endorphins built up, we stayed together longer and longer, building our own bubble of intimacy in the swirling throng.

It became hard to think straight, I wanted her so much.

After a while we left, half exhausted from the energetic dancing. We walked arm in arm along the pedestrian mall, recovering. The absence of the lights, music, pheremones and people was like a dash of cold water after a hot shower, shocking but invigorating. We talked about inconsequential things. Eventually we found a restaurant that boasted authentic Earth cuisine. The menu was a mishmash of Tandoor, Canton and Milan. The food was good in its own right but only a loose approximation of the originals it claimed to duplicate. It didn't matter. The atmosphere was cozy and the company delightful. I already knew her dossier, but I asked her about herself.

She shrugged. "There's not much to tell. I'm thirty-two. I'm a geologist. I used to do engineering work

for the UN mining consortium. Now I'm an indepen-
dent. That means I charge lots of money and I'm
usually unemployed. No children. What else is there?"
   "Parents?"
   "Killed in the kinetic missile raid."
   "I'm sorry."
   "Why?" She shrugged again but her eyes became icy
and distant, belying her studied nonchalance. "Everyone dies sooner or later."
   Talking about the past was risky. Alpha Centauri was
heavy with ghosts. I changed tack. "Plans for the future?"
   "I'm on a contract now. It's a good company. If things
pan out I'll go permanent with them. If not, I'll find
something else up here. I like it in the Swarm."
   "It's more relaxing than Wunderland. No gangs. No
assassinations."
   "Is that why you came up here?" She seemed surprised.
   "No, I came because of the corruption in the Provo
government . . ." I hesitated, doubtless out of some resid-
ual loyalty to my organization " . . . and in the UN."
   She nodded, far away for a moment. I didn't elabo-
rate. She'd seen more of it than I had. "So you're an
honest cop."
   "I am now."
   That sparked her interest. She raised an eyebrow and
licked her lips. "You weren't always?"
   "I used to work undercover. I spent most of my time
breaking the law in order to enforce it."
   "And?"
   "I crossed the line."
   "And you came back?"
   "I couldn't go back, it was too late. I came out here."
   She smiled. "And what are you doing here?"
   "You mean what's a nice guy like me doing in a place
like this?"

She just smiled and raised a querying eyebrow. I answered the unstated question.

"Investigating the Holtzman murder."

"I sort of suspected as much." Miranda was big news all over the asteroid. "How's it going?"

I hesitated, a police reflex. Investigative work-in-progress isn't classified, but neither do you want it to be common knowledge. Most importantly you never want the criminals to know where you are in the investigation. If they know you're on to them, they'll flee. If they know you're not, they'll just sit tight. What you want is to leave them uncertain, unwilling to commit to flight, unable to hold their ground with confidence. That way they're more liable to make mistakes. Once in a while they just can't stand the strain and voluntarily surrender.

On the other hand Suze wasn't with the press. She wasn't even a Swarm native plugged into the local gossip net. The odds of the information getting back through her were vanishingly low. She was a reasonable person who would hold anything I said in confidence. I was walking the road to paranoia again.

"It's going, that's about it. We're still looking for connections."

"Do you have a suspect?" Her eyes were burning blue electric arcs. The thrill of the chase.

"I thought it might be a schitz, but it doesn't look like it now. My partner thinks it's a kzin."

"What do you think?"

"I think it's a different kzin."

She laughed. "There's hope for you yet."

"Why?"

"Most Flatlanders can't tell kzinti apart."

"I couldn't when I first arrived, I've learned since," I said, a trifle affronted.

She held up a hand in apology. "I'm sorry. It just reminded of an old joke."

"Which old joke?"

"Promise you won't be offended?" She was smiling, impish dimples appeared, as if she were already laughing at the punchline.

"Go ahead."

She waited a second to get her expression under control. "How can you tell a Flatlander?"

"How?" I played along.

"You can't, they won't listen."

We laughed together and went on to other topics. Later I told her about Brandywine—and about Holly. After that I told her about tracking criminals and what it was like to crack a major case. She told me about hunting minerals in the Jotuns and how she felt when she made the strike that became the Wind Pass Complex. Her eyes were full of the wild, unbounded sky when she talked about the absolute freedom of hiking the high Jotuns alone and the power of total self-reliance. I suddenly understood what drew me to her. I recognized the look. I'd seen it on Earth, in the mirror.

We didn't talk about how we planned to spend the rest of the night but when we left we shared a tube car and she didn't punch in her address. By the time we got to the door of my apt the tension was thick enough to cut with a knife.

We went in and I offered her a seat. I have a miniature wine rack that holds six bottles. I went to get the glasses and asked, "Would you like a drink?"

"I didn't come here to drink." I turned around, surprised. She ran a finger down the front of her jumpsuit, unsealing the fabric. Her gaze was steady, half mocking, half inviting. It was the same challenge she'd offered the other night. "Bet you can't keep up."

I put the glasses down and went over and kissed her gently. She returned it with enthusiasm. A while later she pulled me down to the carpet. I didn't resist.

Afterwards we cuddled and talked in bed, making love languidly in sharp contrast to the almost desperate intensity of the first time. There was all the delight of exploring and discovering a new lover but little of the awkwardness. There had been other women since Holly. Asheya Ramal, sometime partner and longtime friend had pulled me into bed and away from the brink after Brandywine. Kerry Smythe, whom I'd known since childhood, had given me a last-minute going-away present before I'd left Earth. On Wunderland I'd lost a weekend with a blonde Valkyrie named Hanse who taught at the university. Asheya had been for solace and Keri for remembrance. Hanse was to forget. Suze was something more.

Was I falling in love this fast? A week ago I would have said I wasn't capable of it at all. Did I *want* to get involved? The wounds of my divorce were still too fresh. On the other hand, the sooner I started getting over Holly the sooner they would heal.

Don't think too much. Enjoy it for what it is and worry about tomorrow tomorrow. I traced patterns on her skin with my finger.

She had a fine scar that ran from her nipple to her cleavage before it faded out. It was thinner than a hair, barely noticeable. I traced it with my forefinger.

"What happened here?" I asked.

She hesitated before answering. "You know I worked for the mining consortium. They sent me up to sub-survey a new site. We were doing test blasts and a booster went off in my face." She shuddered. "It should have been no problem but the UN had all the hospitals tied up with the attack on W'kkai. By the time I got med-aid it was too late to prevent scarring. They told me I was lucky to live." She sounded bitter. "That's why I quit."

"They're barely there at all." I reassured her although I knew it wasn't the scars she was bitter about. I kissed the uphill end of the line.

"Flattery will get you nowhere," she growled, then pulled me up and kissed me hard. I would have begged to differ, but I was otherwise occupied.

Later I found other scars on her thighs, arms, chest and belly. One ran from her forehead to the side of her nose and across her cheek. They were all nearly invisible, just tiny misalignments in the texture of her skin. My detective's eye couldn't help reconstructing the accident. From the pattern of the tracery she'd been kneeling and bent forward slightly—likely setting the time dial on top of the charge. That saved her life. Boosters are shaped to explode downwards and the main detonation cone would have killed her on the spot. Instead she'd taken the backblast in the chest with spillover onto her belly and face. The scars came from agonized weeks spent bathed in Nutrol and breathing through a tube in an autodoc because real treatment wasn't available—proper clonal reconstructive surgery would have left no marks. I felt a cold wind brush against my back. Such a near thing. A little more pressure on the lever of fate and I would never have known what I missed. I didn't say anything more, I just held her tighter.

I arrived late the next morning. Hunter was on his way out. He rippled his ears knowingly but mercifully didn't ask any questions. Johansen was logged out checking alibis. First Tracker was doing something with the Conservors, probably playing poetry games. The usual backlog was waiting for me when I got to my desk. I scanned my messages first, prioritizing—coroner first. Johansen had delivered five blood samples. All five showed my schitzies had the right dosages.

Well, it had been a good hunch anyway.

I scanned down. There was the usual assortment from 'casters, looking for information on the killing. I forwarded them to the PR desk for the official brush-off. The rest were routine, half an hour of dull but essential paperwork. I buckled down to it; I wanted my desk clear when I started setting up the movement trace.

I was almost done when Hunter came in without knocking. "We have captured the kzin who killed the human Miranda Holtzman." His voice had more than the usual snarl to it. He turned on his heel and strode out again.

I sighed, picturing riots in the tunnels when the news broke. Be careful what you wish for, it might come true. I followed him out.

Work in the outer office was stopped dead with everyone staring at First Tracker. The big kzin was standing with his foot in the small of another kzin's back. The prisoner was lying spreadeagled and bleeding from numerous minor cuts. Hunter stooped over, grabbed the hapless captive by the scruff of the neck and turned his face to the gaping office staff. "This sthondat," he snarled "is known as Slave-of-Kdapt!" He screamed something into the prisoner's ear and dragged him into his office, nearly overbalancing First Tracker in the process.

Tracker spoke little English. He gestured towards the door as Hunter slammed it and said "Dominance." He looked around the room, lips twitching over razor teeth. Everyone was suddenly diligently at work again. When he was satisfied that he'd quelled the gawkers, the kzin picked up a box, handed it to me and said, "Evidence." Then he curled up on a visitors' couch, cozy as a kitten. He fixed his golden eyes on the door to Hunter's office, ears up and swivelled forward. For the first time I saw that he too was suffering from various cuts and contusions. The first scream came through and his mouth relaxed into a fanged smile.

I opened the box. Inside was a large, misshapen hunk of fine leather, crudely tanned. I didn't need DNA analysis to tell me it was Miranda Holtzman's skin.

A crash and another scream came through the door. First Tracker licked his chops. I took refuge in my office.

It wasn't much of a refuge. My office is right next door to Hunter's. Goldskin headquarters was once a factory process floor. It was converted to offices by installing inch thick sprayfoam walls. They were adequately sound-proof for normal conversation, but that wasn't what was going on now. The modulated snarls came through almost unimpeded by the barrier, punctuated by crashes, thuds and shrieks of rage and pain. At least I was away from Tracker and his intent satisfaction at the mayhem.

Sprayfoam is a mass-saving necessity on ships and a handy convenience on Tiamat. Its strength-to-mass ratio is very high but you can put your foot through it with a solid kick. I expected half a tonne of clawing, raging carnivores to land in my lap at any moment. Someday I'll have the budget to install privacy fields. I've seen a lot of violence, but brutalizing a prisoner like this ran against my grain. Slave-of-Kdapt, or whatever he'd been before Hunter renamed him, was a killer but he was still a human being.

No, I corrected myself, he wasn't a human being, he was a kzin, an alien carnivore whose species was dedicated to the enslavement of mine. Did that make a difference? Perhaps it did. After all, it was his own species working him over. Why did it disturb *me* then?

Because I'm a cop and so was Hunter-of-Outlaws and cops don't beat up prisoners to extract confessions— not where I come from.

Not on Earth, but they did on Wunderland and kzinti still weren't human. It wasn't for me to tell them how to run their internal affairs. I didn't even know if a kzin would respond to a nonviolent interrogation; maybe this was the only way that worked.

I still didn't like it.

I pushed the unease away. We had the evidence, we had the murderer, soon we would have the confession.

Except . . . The hyperdrive question kept buzzing around in the back of my head. If Miranda's death was connected with a spy ring that Hunter was covering for, how better than to hand me a culprit and dump the blame on a defunct cult? It wouldn't be hard for them to find a volunteer amid the despairing, honour-starved kzin of Tiamat.

That thought decided me. I wasn't going to accept confessions at face value. After Hunter was through with his interrogation, I'd pass the suspect up to the frightening efficiencies of UN Intelligence. I'd have an answer I could trust by shift-end tomorrow.

Case closed.

I opened the next file, someone was reprogging stolen keycards and draining citizens' bank accounts. It would take a lot of specialized knowledge, electronics, crypto and bank procedures at least. I set up some search keys and began screening dossiers, trying to tune out the sounds coming through the wall.

After an hour I'd made some good progress, narrowing down the field to about two hundred possibles. I picked the dozen who seemed most likely and set up a movement trace to link them with fraudulent withdrawals. While the trace ran in the background, I worked the opposite angle, starting with those who had access and linking that data back to the required skills. Hopefully I would get cross-matches and a start point for my investigation. I stopped noticing the violence next door until it ended.

I was trying to put my finger on the absence when Hunter strode in. He had a nasty slash on his chest and his expression was even less pleased than before. He didn't waste time. "We have a confession."

I wasn't surprised. "Good, put him in confinement and I'll get the proceedings drawn up." Hunter was in no mood for paperwork. That was a help. I'd have the suspect shipped up to UNF Intel quickly and quietly and he wouldn't even know I'd done it.

"Slave-of-Kdapt has confessed to no crime against human law."

"*What?*" I was dumbfounded.

"He is not the criminal we seek."

I gestured mutely at the box containing Miranda's remains.

"He tried to imply that he had slain the human Miranda Holtzman himself. He has now admitted that he bought the skin from a human. Not only did he accept carrion from . . ." he paused, substituting words " . . . another species and claim it as hunt-prey, he *lied* to hide his shame. That even the lowest coward could sink to such!" He paced and spat curses in the Heros' Tongue.

"Let me get this straight. He pretended that he did kill Miranda, but he didn't really? Why would he do that? He must know the penalties he's playing with."

"He has the liver of a sthondat and less honor. We pitiful survivors of K'Shai are thrice cursed by the Fanged God." He snarled again, twitching his tail and raking the air with his claws.

I decided to let the point go. The complexities of kzinti honour weren't my concern. The fact was, Slave-of-Kdapt wasn't a fall guy for kzin intelligence, or at least if he was, Hunter-of-Outlaws wasn't involved in the coverup.

That was the good news. The bad news was the killer was still unknown, still at large, and human.

Case reopened.

I filed my account-fraud data and went over the interrogation with Hunter. Slave-of-Kdapt had been Machine Technician. He was known to be a Kdaptist. He'd been caught because he'd started bragging about "following the true Kdapt faith." Tracker was quick to pick up on this spoor and the pursuit had been easy. Kdapt rituals with human sacrifice had been forbidden by the Conservors as disruptive of the essential kzin/human relationship but the hapless Technician's real crime in kzin eyes was trying to gain status through lying.

Hunter and Tracker were both too wound up with bloodlust for my taste. It was another hour till shift end but I sent them off to catch a ztigor in the Tigertown park. I wanted to talk to Slave-of-Kdapt myself and see what I could learn. They left, snarling amicably to each other. I called their battered prisoner in, had him make himself comfortable and began. I started by pulling up the schitzies I'd culled from the databank. Slave-of-Kdapt didn't finger any as the one who'd sold him the skin but admitted he couldn't always tell humans apart. His own description was almost uselessly vague and it fit a Belter, not a Wunderlander. He was pathetically eager to please, as though he could save himself through cooperation. Hunter thought he'd committed no human crime, but I could think of a dozen charges to bring against him ranging from concealing evidence to accessory to murder. For a kzin the penalties ranged from a short life in a labour camp to quick death in front of a firing squad. Even that was better than the fate his fellows had in store for him. Slave-of-Kdapt had violated his honour code. He would be an outcast. Eventually he would starve or die of misery or fall afoul of another kzin and be torn to shreds.

I questioned him thoroughly and fruitlessly. I was used to dealing with kzin like Hunter, whose mind stalked problems like game and pounced on solutions with precision and clarity. Machine Technician wasn't dull exactly—just woefully naive and uncurious beyond his narrow specialty.

He knew of other Kdaptists but didn't think any of them had anything to do with the murder or any other crime. They all followed the Conservor's dictum that human laws be respected. He didn't know Miranda Holtzman or anyone who might want to kill her. He didn't have any enemies who might be trying to frame him for her murder. He'd lied about killing her because he wanted the honour it would bring. Evidently that didn't violate the Conservor's dictum because it broke no human law—so he'd thought. Of course he realized he'd broken his honour code but he didn't think he'd get caught at that. Obviously he hadn't thought out the consequences of his claim becoming well known. His only motivation was status—he wanted more space and a kzinrett. It was the human who sold him the skin who'd suggested that Miranda's skin and the false prey-claim could be the way to achieve that. What humans would know he was a Kdaptist? He didn't know, he'd made no particular secret of it. He was sure he didn't recognize the human involved? Absolutely.

There was one correlate. Machine Technician's job was servicing loading equipment in the down-axis hub. That put him just five hundred meters from the point Miranda's body was found. It might be coincidence, but it was the only link I had.

I didn't charge him, I bought him a ticket to Wunderland. There were thousands of miles of wilderness down there, where Machine Technician could become Trail Stalker or Chaser-of-Gagrumphs with all the space he wanted and his own kzinrett if he could find one. Slave-of-Kdapt and dishonour would be forgotten. Pity for criminals is something a cop can't afford. Those feelings are reserved for the victims, but Machine Technician was as much a victim as Miranda. He'd been set up to take the fall, and he would have played his part to the hilt and to the death if Hunter-of-Outlaws' thorough . . . interrogation . . . hadn't allowed the truth to come out.

Or, come to think of it, the interrogation I had planned for him with UN Intelligence. Their methods are much gentler, but they're a lot less pleasant on balance. Machine Technician was lucky he'd been caught by one of his own.

He left, thanking me with embarrassing profusion. The one thing worse than an arrogant, dominant kzin is a pathetically humble one.

When he was gone, I went over the data and summed up.

Item: A male Wunderlander had left the Inferno with Miranda—if our only two witnesses were to be believed.

Item: A male Belter had sold her skin to Machine Technician, someone who knew him well enough to know he was vulnerable to this particular frame-up, but not so well that the kzin had recognized him.

Item: Machine Technician's admittedly inadequate description of the suspect was at considerable odds with the couple's.

So if there were two people involved, that pointed to a conspiracy and away from a schitz. If not, it pointed back at Jayce and Tanya. I still lacked too many pieces of the puzzle. I didn't even have a motive.

Tammy stuck her head in the door. "I hear you got a Kdaptist confession."

"Sort of. What we didn't get was a culprit."

"I heard that too. What's up?"

"Hunter tracked down this kzin who claimed he'd killed Miranda. It turns out all he really did was buy her skin from a human and try to claim credit."

"So he's an accessory after the fact. Why did you send him to Wunderland?"

"You hear a lot."

She grinned. "I keep my ears open."

"He was set up and framed, pure and simple. Now that his honour is compromised he's an outcast up here. I thought I'd give him another chance."

"What about using him as a witness?"

"Wunderland is still the safest place for him. How long would he have on Tiamat?"

She winced. "Good point. Well, I have to say I'm glad to hear it wasn't a Kdaptist after all."

I cocked my head. "Why is that?"

She held up her beltcomp. "Here's all the data I've tracked down on the Kdapt cult *and* current Kzin intelligence operations." She held her other hand up, thumb and forefinger forming an empty circle. "Zero."

"Sorry for the goose chase."

She smiled. "Don't be." She waved the beltcomp. "I've got a new contact and some leverage for a couple more out of it anyway. So where are we now?"

"We know there are at least two people involved. They must have planned to frame Machine Technician in advance of the killing—that's not the sort of detail you work out while you're hiding in a transport tunnel with a corpse. So Miranda wasn't chosen at random. That puts us back to Vorden and Koffman the love-birds, unless someone—some *group*—wanted her dead for a specific reason."

"It can't be the couple." She waved at the composite holo on the screen. "This is a male."

"We only have their testimony to say there's a second male. Anyway, I think it would be pretty easy to

fool Machine Technician on that aspect. Loose cloth-
ing would be all it would take."

"Visually, yah, but he could *smell* the difference. But
you're right about the testimony."

"Suppose it's a group for the sake of argument. They
must have had a specific reason they wanted her dead."

"So what's the reason?"

"That's what we need to know. Something she knew
or something she'd done. She just wasn't up here long
enough to have become involved in anything serious.
Trist Materials doesn't handle anything worth killing
for and if they did the target wouldn't be their brand-
new exchange student."

"So it must have been something she was already
involved with down on Wunderland."

"Right. Especially since a Wunderlander is a major
suspect."

"What groups operate both groundside and in the
Belt?"

I considered. "Anyone could send up an assassin. Any
of the crime rings, the Isolationists, Kzin intelligence,
collabo underground, collabo hunters. Even a few
branches of the Provisional Government if she crossed
the wrong people."

She shook her head. "We know it's not the tabbies
at least. The killers are human."

"But they could be working for the kzinti."

"Get serious. They tried to frame a kzin for the crime
and ruined his honour in the process. If they were
working for the kzinti, their bosses would *eat* them
when they found out. Alive."

"Good point."

"We've got a lead, though. If she was killed by
Wunderland assassins, they must have come up between
her arrival and her death. That's a narrow window.
Cross-check the Inferno's attendance list with the

passenger manifests for every ship that arrived during that time period."

I entered the search request and we watched the screen while it collected the data and compared it. It came up NO MATCHES.

"Maybe they knew she was coming. Try the previous six weeks."

I tapped in the query. It took a little longer this time because there was more data to retrieve and sort. The result was the same. NO MATCHES.

"Damn!" I cleared the screen.

"Not damn. Now we know the killer was already here. That means we've got to be dealing with an organization that's already in the Swarm. Smugglers for one of the crime rings probably."

"We'll have to get the Provopolizei involved. Get them to dig out a contact list for us."

"Attack it from both sides. Run a movement trace on every person who went through the Inferno that night too."

"I already thought of that. It'll take hours to run and weeks to analyze."

"So what have you got to lose? Run it overnight and we'll start the Goldskins on it in the morning. If we get a match, we'll refocus. At least you won't be totally reliant on the Provos."

She was right, of course. I wrote a cable to the ARM on Wunderland instead of the Provopolizei. It was adding another bureaucratic step, since they'd have to go to the Provos anyway, but I knew people I could trust in the ARM—people who could smell an evolving coverup. Then I set up my board to run the trace and let it go. Somewhere in the mass of data that it would generate would be the critical clue. I'd just had to find it—*if* the murderer was in fact the man she left with and *if* he didn't have a false ident. It would be hours before the trace was done. I screened Suze and made a date for dinner.

We met at the same Earth cuisine restaurant as before. Why not? The atmosphere was intimate and the menu inviting. Suze was already waiting when I got there. She greeted me with a kiss and asked, "How's the case going?"

"Well, we got a kzin who confessed to the crime."

"So you're done?"

"Well, not exactly. It seems he was confessing because he thought he'd gain status by it. He didn't actually do it."

"I don't understand."

"I don't think he understood himself."

"So where do you go from here?"

"Good question. Right now I'm running a movement trace on everyone who went through the Inferno that night. The murderer has got to be in there somewhere, unless he used a false ID."

"How do you know the man she left with is the killer?"

"Miranda wasn't just a random victim; someone wanted her dead for a reason. They watched her, figured out her movements and set her up."

"She was just a kid! Why would anyone want to kill her?" Her eyes showed worry.

"We don't know yet. Someone she was involved with on Wunderland, a criminal group."

"Do you know which group?"

"I haven't got a clue right now."

"I think that's your problem alright." The concern went away and her smile developed those mischievous dimples.

I missed the joke and riposted with a brilliant, "What?"

"You haven't got a clue."

I threw a miniature shrimp from my stir fry at her. I didn't throw it hard but I grossly misjudged the gravity field and the morsel went flying past her on a high, slow trajectory that eventually intersected the back of a balding patron's head. He looked around in irritated surprise while I tried to look oblivious and Suze suppressed giggles with difficulty.

It became a game after that. We took turns picking targets and launching shrimp at them. The low light level helped conceal our nefarious intent but the fifth time the maitre d' caught us and we were asked firmly to leave. Suze asked him if he'd call the ARM if we refused at which we both collapsed into gales of laughter. He turned red and looked ready to burst but she got ahold of herself and apologized, then smoothed over his feelings by insisting on being allowed to buy two liters of their crumbleberry cream pudding before going because it was so incomparably good. On the way down to the tube station she poked me in the ribs.

"Maybe you shouldn't have picked the maitre d' as a target."

"You're the one who threw the shrimp while he was looking."

"I had to. He was already watching us to see if we were the ones doing the throwing."

"No need to confirm his suspicions."

"He wasn't suspicious, he knew. He was just waiting to catch us."

"All the more reason not to hit him with a shrimp."

"He was a witness. I couldn't let him live," she said with mock ferocity.

"The shrimp or the maitre d'?" I asked innocently.

She laughed and poked me again. I caught her around the waist and held her and we walked arm in arm to the tube car, giggling and kissing. It wasn't in the best traditions of the ARM for Tiamat Station's Chief of Investigation to go around in public acting like a giddy teenager. Well, hopefully nobody knew who I was. Anyway, I felt better than I had since I'd arrived at Alpha Centauri and if anyone did notice me I didn't care.

Back at her apt she called, "Dessert!", opened the pudding container and sampled some with her fingers, then gave me a crumbleberry-flavored kiss. In the process some of the pudding spilled on her jumpsuit. That was an invitation if I ever saw one so I unsealed it and spilled some more pudding, then kissed it off. We fell to the floor into a sticky tangle of clothes and pudding, and passion. That led to the shower and steam and more passion which in turn led to the bed, cuddling, contentment and . . . love?

Maybe love.

I fell asleep with her in my arms, serene for the first time since I'd left Earth.

I was late again the next morning. Tammy winked at Hunter, who rippled his ears and double twitched his tail in a manner I could only assume was meant to be suggestive. I glared at them both and got another tail twitch from Hunter and a look of "Who? Me?" innocence from Tammy. Tracker snarled something at Hunter, then rippled his own ears as he was let in on the joke.

I was feeling too good to let it bother me. If my lovelife boosted morale I'd just chalk it up to my doubtless outstanding leadership skills. In the meantime, I gathered what was left of my dignity and went into my office.

On my desk display the exhaustive movement trace was done and waiting for attention. I went over my mail first. There was a message from Wunderland and I screened it, expecting a response to my ARM query. It was from a Provo named Loreli Novostet. She was working to penetrate a smuggling operation that supplied UN weapons to the Isolationists. An informant had given her a tranship code that had turned out to belong to a twenty-meter cargo container arriving from Tiamat. The cargo carrier's crew knew nothing, of course, and both the shipping and receiving companies were fronts. Perhaps I had some information that might help?

She'd attached the crew's idents and an inventory of what they'd seized. I called up the idents and dumped the dossiers for hardcopy, then scanned the inventory list. My eyebrows went up as I read—cases of pulse rifles with ammunition and battery packs, hiveloc launchers, sniper sights, infantry battle armor, combat drugs, hundreds of kilos of Tridex, boosters, a field hospital's worth of medical equipment, flash grenades, surveillance gear and more than enough comps and comms to run a regiment.

And something bizarre. A nitrogen freezer jam packed with somebody's limbs and organs. She'd attached the DNA pattern.

My hands flew over the keyboard. I knew the scans would match even before the computer screened Miranda Holtzman's gene record.

Organlegger. The word felt strange. A long time ago failure of a vital organ meant death. Transplant technology changed that. With a little luck you could live as long as your central nervous system lasted—as long as you could find donors to keep you going. Everybody wants to live forever but the organ banks couldn't always supply what you needed when you needed it. Organleggers took up the slack through kidnap and murder. It wasn't a nice profession but it was very lucrative.

Nowadays medical technology is more advanced. Autocloning has eliminated the need to scavenge for donors. Organlegging is yesterday's crime, like cattle rustling.

But medtech is in short supply around Alpha Centauri and the UN forces have first call. People were dying because they couldn't get treatment. The Isolationists had bigger medical problems. A suspected terrorist can't just show up at a hospital with blast trauma or laser burns and get treatment. Organlegging was a natural for them. They already had an effective and ruthless organization in place. It would take only a few donors to meet their own needs and what they didn't use themselves they could sell on the black market to finance their operations. Once news of their new side-line broke, they'd probably start using it as a terror weapon. For some reason, people dread being broken down for parts much more than simple death. A few prominent kidnappings would apply a lot of fear in high places.

Not a pleasant scenario but it gave me an edge. Miranda hadn't been chosen at random. Somewhere out there a terrorist was in need of spare parts. His tissue rejection profile would match hers. I called up Dr. Morrow. Rejection profiles weren't part of a person's file anymore, could he derive one from Miranda's gene scan? He could. While I waited I started a report to send down to the Provopolizei.

He was back on the screen an hour later. Miranda Holtzman was a rare universal donor. There were only a few thousand in system who couldn't accept her tissues.

I cursed myself. Of course she'd been chosen for exactly that reason. Another blind alley. I shelved the report and ran a trace on the container's tranship code. The shipping and receiving companies were fake but the container itself was real. Maybe its movements would give me a clue.

Container 19C01FD4 had arrived aboard the freighter *Achilles* at the up-axis docking hub, customs' sealed and coded for transport from MUN42104K to TMU19J234C. The manifest said "Machine Tools." I called up the operations manual for the cargo system and figured out the codes. "TMU" is the up-axis hub's destination code. "19" indicates the nineteenth of the asteroid's thirty-two axial transport tunnels. "J2" is the second container bay in the tenth two-kilometer section of the twenty-five that make up the length of the transport tunnels. "34C" is the third level of the thirty-fourth container rack in that bay. Once unloaded from *Achilles,* the automated routing system would have sent the container down tunnel nineteen to its destination and the receiver would have been notified of its arrival and shown up in due course to sign off with the Port Authority and take charge of its contents.

So far so good, but nobody had signed it off as received. The computer didn't even log it as arriving at 19J2. The next time there was a record was thirty-seven hours later as the container was being loaded aboard the freighter *Canexco Wayfarer* at the down-axis hub, still customs' sealed and manifested as "Machine Tools." Point of origin TMU19J234C, destination MUN42104K—Munchen Spaceport, Wunderland.

A neat trick. The container had been shipped from Wunderland and arrived on Tiamat, traveled straight through the core of the asteroid, come neatly out the other end and gone back where it came from. Somewhere along the line whatever was inside it had been taken out and Miranda Holtzman and an arsenal of UN weapons had been put in. So far as the computer was concerned nobody had touched the container so there was no way to trace the smugglers through it. The chips containing the tranship codes are crypted and self-verifying to prevent containers from being electronically hijacked en route. You need a Port Authority ident to originate or receive a shipment and of course that gets logged in the shipping control net. Somehow the smugglers had managed to swap origin and destination without the ident.

The trick got neater when I called up the information on container bay 19J2. It didn't exist. Somewhere in tunnel nineteen a 2000 cubic meter tranship box had disappeared for thirty-seven hours. I screened the history file for container 19C01FD4. It had traveled from MUN42104K to TMU19J234C and back twelve times. The tranship net had never logged it as delivered to anyone anywhere since it entered the system three years ago.

A picture was coming together and it wasn't nice. The Isolationists needed medical support and had decided to get into organlegging. They'd made a list of universal donors and Miranda was on it. Her departure for Tiamat put only a minor crimp in their plans. They already had a sophisticated smuggling operation set up in the Swarm to ship stolen UN weapons to Wunderland. She'd been targeted, abducted and packed into a freezer to ship down to Wunderland in a weapons consignment already set to go. The freezer wasn't big enough for all of her so they'd left her torso in the tranship tunnel and sold her skin to the Kdaptist Machine Technician to blur the trail.

I would rather have found a schitz. This was carefully calculated murder for profit. The people responsible for it couldn't be treated for some neurochemical imbalance. They were cold-blooded killers, plain and simple.

The most frightening thing was the organization. The killers had some major resources behind them. They were probably already long gone. Even if I caught them it wouldn't stop more innocents from being snatched and killed to fill the Isolationist organ banks. I could only pray they confined themselves to organlegging. If they decided to escalate, things would get a lot worse—and I would be one of their first targets.

It was time to take a better look at tunnel nineteen.

Johansen wasn't around so I collared Hunter. As an afterthought I belted on my patrol pack as well and we went down to the Port Authority at the up-axis hub. Jocelyn Merral was Port Chief, a handsome woman in her fifties—iron-gray hair and a penetrating gaze. We asked her to shut down the tunnel so we could go over it with a fine-tooth comb. She didn't get upset, she just refused. It would be too disruptive to her operations. Tunnel nineteen had been shut down for maintenance and investigation already. The backlog had kept a ship overtime at the down-axis hub. Did I have any idea how much that cost? It wasn't going to happen again.

I couldn't just order it done. The Port Authority is its own police within its jurisdiction. I tried to reason with her. "Ma'am, we are investigating a murder that involves the Isolationists and the smuggling of UN weapons to Wunderland. Surely the Port Authority is as interested in resolving this as we are."

She spoke slowly and firmly. "The Port Authority is not at all interested in shutting down transport tunnels at the casual whim of the ARM."

"Casual whim" was the key phrase. What she meant was that if we wanted her cooperation we were going to have to supply more information. I didn't want to do that. The odds were long someone in the Port Authority was involved with the smugglers, and as one of a handful with command access to the tranship net Merral was high on the suspect list.

Instead, I tried bargaining. "Look, we just need to inspect tunnel nineteen. Can that be done without shutting it down?"

"Certainly, I have just the thing." I was startled by her ready agreement. Information is currency to me, dealing for it is second nature. Merral had just been concerned about the efficiency of her operation. I wasn't used to taking people at face value.

She ushered us out of her office. The gravity was about a twentieth of a G and the corridors had static fields in the floor to aid traction. Merral walked in effortless forty-foot strides. Hunter moved with easy feline grace. I kept unsticking myself and hitting my head on the ceiling before settling awkwardly back to the ground. They had the manners not to laugh too much.

We left the corridor and entered the hub itself, a vast space full of container racks. I'd been in tunnel nineteen myself but there were no containers in it then. The files on the shipping system contained diagrams of the containers and the hubs but they gave no concept of the scale.

Shipping containers are ten meters square and twenty long. The down-axis hub is a hollow cylinder, a klick across and half that deep. Eight rows of storage racks line the hub—twenty-four thousand containers in hundred-meter piles. From any given point inside the cylinder the floor slopes upwards at an impossible angle and the looming racks seem about to topple over. Eventually the floor becomes what common sense dictates is a wall with the rows of racks marching up it with no respect for the gentle but insistent one-twentieth G tug beneath your feet. Farther still the wall becomes a ceiling with the racks dangling from it like massive swords of Damocles. Containers are moved simply by launching them from the rack sorters on gentle trajectories either to the docking hub at the center of the cylinder or one of the tunnel entrances around its edge. The empty space in the middle of the cylinder was full of containers in free fall and I had to consciously keep myself from cringing as they flew overhead with quiet rushes of air. I felt like a mouse in a warehouse, scampering to avoid being crushed by the frenetic, incomprehensible activity going on overhead.

Merral was watching me. "Impressive, ay?" she asked.

"Impressive isn't the word. I can't believe you let those things go in free fall."

She laughed. "It looks like disaster in motion, doesn't it? Actually it's very safe. There are eight hundred sixty-one trajectories. Whenever one is in use, all the intersecting flight paths are locked out until the container is down and clear of its destination."

I looked up at the graceful, ponderous, hundred-thousand-tonne aerial ballet. It wasn't that I doubted her, but it was hard to shake the feeling all those containers were going to fall on me as soon as God cut the strings.

Our destination was a cargo box, but this one had doors and large windows cut in the sides. Powerful lights were mounted flush with the walls. Jocelyn thumbed a door open and waved us in. "We use this for troubleshooting and inspections. It carries everything we need, and we don't have to shut down a tunnel to use it."

Inside the container was mostly empty space. There were doors and windows in the floor and ceiling as well as the walls and all the surfaces were padded and well equipped with handholds. Strapdown chairs with mounts that locked into the handholds were set up beside the forward windows. A quarter of the bottom rear was given over to a series of cabinets that housed batteries, switches and various tool chests. Beneath the forward window there was a spartan control board with a compact data terminal as well as various buttons, gauges and comm gear. Beside it was a small keypad.

I recognized it at once from the tranship operations manual. It was the container's shipping control panel, a duplicate of the one mounted on the outside.

I walked over and examined the panel. When Jocelyn joined me, I asked, "This contains the tranship codes?"

"Not just the codes, everything about the shipment. The freight manifest, maximum and minimum allowable temperatures, power requirements, loading parameters, whether the container is pressure sealed, center of mass, priority level, customs codes, COD status and charges. Everything." She tapped a few keys and cryptic data slid over the small screen inset on the panel. PRI, COD, KPA, BOT, and others along with numbers that didn't mean anything to me. I did recognize two codes. SRC and DST indicated the container's source and destination—both were rack addresses in the up-axis hub.

I tapped a few keys and managed to bring up the DST code. "Can you set this up to go anywhere?" I asked Merral.

"Anywhere on Tiamat. The lockouts don't allow us to be loaded for an offworld destination. This container isn't vacc sealed. I'll set it for the outbound receiving racks at the down-axis hub with a routing override so we get tunnel nineteen. That'll take us right through Tiamat."

It was better than I'd hoped for. "Can you try TMU19J234C?" I asked.

She looked at me with the half accusing "How do you know what that means?" look that's usually reserved for medical patients who show their doctor some basic piece of medical knowledge. Specialists hate it when you trespass on their specialty. It makes them less special. Nevertheless, she thumbed the pad to authorize the change and punched in the destination code. After a couple of seconds the screen displayed ACCEPTED, then reverted to DST: TMU19J234C.

"This transaction is now logged in the transport net, correct?" I asked.

Merral nodded, adjusting the restraining straps that held her in her seat. She motioned for me to do the same.

"Is there any way to circumvent that?" I asked, fumbling with the belts.

"How do you mean?"

"Can you enter destinations into this panel without having the system become aware of it."

"It could be done. You'd have to block the scan transceiver and trick the panel into thinking it had transmitted the change and received a valid authorization verification. It wouldn't be easy, we use dynamic encryption. Why would you want to?" She reached over and helped me get buckled in.

"A smuggler might change an onworld destination for an offworld destination, or perhaps just make a shipment the system isn't aware of."

"I see what you're getting at, but you misunderstand me. If you prevent the panel from talking to the net, the net will just ignore it. It won't get sent anywhere. There's a lot of ways to break the system, but once it's broken it won't work properly."

"I don't follow."

"Look, the system is vulnerable to tampering and there's no way to avoid that. Rather than try to make it tamper-proof we've made it fail-safe. Getting a container to move involves a series of steps, with our control procedures built into the chain. If any link is broken the system flashes us a trouble warning and won't move the container."

"And the data in the panel itself is all self-encrypted so you need a Port Authority ident to change it, correct?"

Merral warmed to her topic. She obviously enjoyed having someone show an interest in her work. It probably didn't happen too often. "Not quite. The source address is always locked so we can back-trace a shipment, nobody can change that. When the shipment arrives and is accepted, the destination address is copied to the source so the container can be sent out again. Manifest, COD charges and destination are set by the shipper and then locked when the PA verifies and seals the shipment. The user functions—like humidity, temperature and all that—can either be set and locked or left open at the shipper's discretion in case they need adjustment in transit."

"So you can't change the source or the destination in transit unless you have a Port Authority ident."

"Not even if you do have a PA ident. Once a setting is locked, it can't be changed until the receiver accepts the shipment and signs off with us. The system only lets that happen at the destination address."

"What if you hacked it, opened the box and modified the software?"

"All you'd do is cause a self-encryption verification failure. The system would halt the container at the next control point and drop a trouble flag."

"What if I supplied my own panel that allowed in-transit re-routing?"

"It still wouldn't work. Firstly, it would fail PA verification at the point of shipping. Second, the tranship net and the panel would disagree on the destination as soon as you modified it. The net would halt the container and you'd get another flag. It's fail-safe."

Fail-safe. It's a one-word lie. Nothing built by humans is fail-safe. I *knew* someone was playing games with the tranship net. What Merral was really telling me was that I needed to look for hackers in the net's high-level control software or corruption at the Port Authority itself. I didn't tell her that: she might be the one I was looking for.

Instead I offered a compliment. "Sounds like you're pretty secure. I've seen banks with looser systems." I meant it too. I didn't mention that I'd seen banks with looser systems because I'd gone in to investigate the frauds that had occurred at them.

"You've got to understand, there are better than two million containers in the system. Every day we move thirty thousand of them through Tiamat. The cargo value in just one of those can get into the tens of millions of crowns. We can't just lose track of one." There was pride in her voice. She was a hands-on technocrat and the tranship system was her baby.

The conversation was interrupted by the arrival of the conveyor crane. The rollers on the container rack slid us into the jaws of the waiting cradle. I felt like Captain Nemo being attacked by a giant squid. There was a clang as the locking dogs engaged and then we were on our way, swaying gently in the minuscule gravity field. The crane loaded us onto the roller rails at the end of our row of container racks. The cradle disconnected and the crane swung away. The rollers began spinning and our container moved off.

I watched out the windows like a kid on a train for the first time. There was a double jolt as we were loaded onto a sorter, then a gentle surge as we launched into free fall. I watched in fascination as we soared past the tops of the container racks. We spun slowly and I got a revolving view of the entire, bustling hub. To my surprise we didn't come within a hundred meters of another container. What looked like near misses from below were a trick of perspective. There was all sorts of room.

We reached the top of our parabola and began to descend. There was another surge as tunnel nineteen's container receiver pulled us in. We landed perfectly flat and I realized what the spin had been for—Maintain This

End Up at All Times. The whole experience was exciting but vertigo inducing. I got my stomach back under control and looked over at Hunter. He had eschewed the human-sized observation chairs, choosing instead to curl up on top of a large tool bin that afforded him a convenient view and loosely belting himself in with some cargo straps. He looked completely at home, curse him.

I was clearly going to have to get more zero-gravity time if I was going to fit in on Tiamat.

The conveyors hummed and with a gentle swaying we slid into the yawning entrance of tunnel nineteen. The swaying stopped as our container was grabbed by the roller tracks on all four sides of the tunnel. Darkness fell as we left the entrance behind. Merral hit a switch on her control panel and the floodlights came on, lighting the way ahead.

Vertigo jerked at my stomach as my inner ears fought to reconcile themselves with my eyes. The containers move down the tunnels at about fifty kilometers an hour. That's not very much in the scheme of things but with the tunnel walls rushing past just inches away it seems very fast indeed. The tiny pull of Tiamat's rotation is overwhelmed by the acceleration and deceleration forces along the container's axis as it's braked or speeded up to allow for other traffic in the tunnel.

My brain carefully weighed all this information and decided that I was falling headfirst down a bottomless elevator shaft. It was worse than the freefall in the hub. My knuckles were white on the arms of the chair and I found I couldn't make myself let go.

"How long will it take to get there?" I asked, trying to keep my voice calm. It came out sounding tense anyway.

"About forty minutes." It was clearly just routine to Merral.

Hunter yawned, curled up and went to sleep.

A track shunt appeared ahead of us. Luminous letters flashed by, too fast to actually read but I registered them as Y2. A black opening flashed by.

I closed my eyes and took three deep breaths and found I could relax my grip. I was just sitting in a chair in very low gravity. The seatbelt pulled gently as the container responded to the tracks and I could hear the whine of the rollers. I sat on my hands and opened my eyes.

Vertigo hit again, but I forced myself to keep sitting on my hands. Eventually I got used to the view. Another opening, another junction and W1 flashed by. Merral had brought up a tiny hologram on her board. I recognized it as a map of the shipping tunnels. Tiny white dots moved slowly along its tributaries. She pointed to one highlighted in red. "That's us."

I asked her some more questions about the tranship net and its security arrangements. She was happy to oblige me. I got detailed information on how data was stored, how transmissions were crypted and errors caught, how containers were sealed and how physical access was controlled. It really was an impressive system but she kept using the word "fail-safe." An engineer really ought to know better.

After a while the conversation lagged and I fell to watching the hypnotically repeating panorama of tracks, rollers and supports. P3 streaked past. I thought about Holly and Suze. P2, P1, O1, N4, N3. I stopped counting them and thought about Suze.

My reverie ended when the deceleration kicked in and pushed me against my safety belt. A scrabble of claws from behind told me that Hunter's nap had been interrupted and he'd nearly slid out of his improvised restraints. We slowed to a fraction of our former speed. A tunnel junction was coming up.

I looked in amazement at the luminous figures on

the tunnel wall. J2—the container bay that didn't exist. The floodlights illuminated a track shunt ahead, leading into a side tunnel identical to all the others we'd passed so far. I'd expected a complex trail of trapdoor computer programs and corrupt customs checkers. I'd imagined secret doors, illicit tunnels or a Slaver device that could move cargo containers into hyperspace pockets. I didn't know what I was looking for, but I certainly hadn't expected a perfectly normal tunnel junction, labelled with glowing letters four meters tall.

The rollers braked our container some more and we were switched onto the side track. We rocked slightly from side to side as we entered the container bay and lost the stability of being guided on all four sides. Automatic handling gear clanged as it coupled to the container's lifting lugs and slid us up a container rack. It was only four tiers high but otherwise identical to the one we'd started in at the up-axis hub. The locking dogs engaged with a solid thump and we were stopped.

Merral looked around from the side window. "Here we are," she said, as if there were nothing unusual about it. I looked out the window and I knew we'd hit paydirt. Jury-rigged spotlights lit the scene. Most of the immense bay was empty, with only a single row of empty racks, although the conveyer was built to service a dozen more. Another container was shunted onto the bay's only loading ramp. Its end doors were open and stacked around it were hundreds of white plastic crates stamped with UN code numbers. I had gambled on finding a lead. I'd found smuggler central.

Hunter and I piled out and jumped the thirty meters to the ground. He landed in a combat-ready crouch. I came down less gracefully but my nerves were just as taut. I drew my stunner from its holster on the belt of my patrol pack. I don't usually carry the pack but I was glad I'd brought it this time. Now I wished that

I'd worn my body armor too. For the first time I noticed Hunter's only weapon was his ceremonial dagger and I realized that it was all he ever carried.

Merral came down after us, cautiously. J2 was just the disused container bay she'd expected, but she was more than smart enough to make the connections. Without words she took up a position behind us, watching the tracks leading to the container tunnel and letting us concentrate on the bay itself.

Nothing moved. I was about to relax and tell Merral there was no danger when Hunter's sharp "Siisss!" warned me to silence. He was in a frozen crouch, his ears swivelled up and forward, twitching slightly back and forth. One paw was gesturing for quiet.

Suddenly he leapt, sailing across the vast chamber in seconds. His target was the entry to an access corridor in the opposite wall. He flew through the opening with unerring precision, landed on a handhold and took off again, down the corridor and out of sight. I followed him awkwardly. I knew I could never have the big cat's reflexes, but I fervently wished I had at least Jocelyn Merral's easy grace in microgravity. I missed my jump by better than twenty meters and floundered down while she waited patiently. The access corridor was half a klick long. I swallowed my ego and let Merral hold on to me. She pushed off into a long parabola. A couple of kicks en route brought us to the end of the corridor. The pressure door to the next section was closed and Hunter was examining it intently. He turned to us as we arrived.

"I heard a sound, which I now presume was this door being opened and then shut. There is fresh scent in this tunnel of a human male. He must have fled when our container's lights entered the trackway." The kzin showed his fangs and licked his chops with a deep-throated *mrrrowl*. "There is much fear in his sweat."

I went to thumb the door open but the plate had been ripped open and bypassed. Not even an ARM ident would work now. Closer inspection revealed the locking mechanism. A hole had been cut in the door's plasteel surface and a simple lever and pivot engaged the securing bolts inside. A metal pin attached to a chain could be inserted to hold the lever in the locked position. With the pin in place the door was proof against anything short of heavy energy weapons. The holes rendered the door useless in a depressurization emergency, but the smugglers wouldn't be worried about that.

I tried the handle reflexively. It didn't budge.

"I have already attempted that," said Hunter mildly.

"It's clear we're not going to get through. Let's seal this bay off and get the crime scene team down here."

I grabbed the comm unit from my patrol pack and called Dispatch. I didn't get anything but static. No repeaters in this unfinished section. Our runner had made a clean getaway.

Merral noticed the problem. "There's a Port Authority comm on the control board in the container." Hunter snarled in acknowledgement and launched himself back down the corridor, eager to be on with the chase.

I let him go, turning to Merral. "You know about this place?"

"Of course." She gestured at the door and the pirated wiring the smugglers had used to power their floodlights. "Although evidently I didn't know everything I thought I did."

"Tell me about it." We turned back down the corridor.

"This bay was supposed to serve a whole new industrial subsector they were going to put in right after the liberation. Turns out they overestimated the requirements and they never needed the space, so they just sealed it off and left it."

Her explanation made sense but there were other problems. "The tranship net doesn't even know it exists."

We turned the accessway corner into the main bay. Hunter jumped down from the container. "The crime scene team and a detachment of Goldskins are on their way. They will open the pressure door from the other side. I will meet them there." He leapt off again without waiting for an answer.

"Of course it does," Merral continued.

"It doesn't." I paused, decided to trust her. The smugglers already knew we were on to them anyway. "Miranda Holtzman's internal organs were found in a shipping container on Wunderland, along with a cache of stolen UN weapons. The container's point of origin was 19J2, but when I tried to punch up the data on it the system drew a blank."

"You did a shipping trace to get that data, right?"

"Yah."

She nodded. "When you do a trace, the net uses the billing system data because normally you're interested in who owns the shipment and who's paying for it. This bay isn't in the billing system because no customers are registered to it so it would never show up. But the routing software knows about every node around Alpha Centauri and that's the data set that gets used when a shipment is set up and verified."

The picture became clearer. "Is there any way someone could swap the source and destination addresses without a Port Authority ident, or at least without logging it in the computer?"

"Too easy." She laughed and tapped a few keys on a board at the base of the container racks. Its display came up with a duplicate of the inspection container's shipping panel. Another press brought up SRC and DST. She hit a final key and the readout flashed REJECTED for a moment and then, magically, TMU19J234C and TMUCA147A switched places from origin to destination. "You just refuse delivery."

"*What?*"

"You refuse delivery. If you accept the shipment, you need a PA ident to accept the COD, clear customs control, verify the manifest and all that. If you refuse delivery, the tranship box just gets bounced back to point of origin still sealed so none of that matters, so you don't need the ident. The shipper's delivery bond is forfeited to pay for shipping the container back and the transaction is cleared out of the net. It's a user function."

"A user function?" I couldn't believe my ears. "What happens if a refused shipment gets re-refused by the shipper?"

"Why would anyone do that?"

"What would happen?" I tried to keep my voice level.

She shrugged. "I don't know . . ." She paused, thinking. "Grounded at the originating port, I suppose. At worst it would go back to the recipient again. It couldn't get lost or redirected, only a PA ident can change the source or destination. Nobody could claim it unless they signed off with us." She paused again. "Unless . . ."

"Unless it got shipped here."

She nodded, understanding the problem. The tranship system had a couple of assumptions built into it — that the Port Authority was physically present at all the system endpoints, and that no shipper would refuse its own refused container. With dynamic encryption and multilayered security measures, the system was considered fail-safe. But a couple of reasonable assumptions made a security hole big enough to shove a twenty-meter container box through that wasn't defined as a failure. There were no hackers, no high-level corruption. The system just worked the way it was designed to. It was a brilliant setup, a sort of digital jujitsu. The smugglers were only caught because of human error. I wondered if they considered their system fail-safe too.

It would be a while before the crime scene team arrived. Merral scrambled up the container rack to call in her findings to her team. I took the opportunity to look into the cargo box on the loading ramp. I got a shock. The white crates were all clearly labelled. They contained high-tech drugs, each molecule assembled atom by atom in zero gravity. I recognized some of the names—Polyhalazone, Quadrol and Ricaline. Every case here was worth fifty thousand crowns at a minimum, at least treble that on the black market, and there were hundreds of cases. There was more in the container, stacked parcels of brown quickwrap a half meter on a side. I ripped one open. Brand new fifty krona wafers spilled onto the floor. I couldn't begin to guess how much was in the package. The next package yielded twenties. I ripped open a third. Hundreds. I picked one up and looked it over carefully. It gave away nothing to the naked eye although I knew it had to be counterfeit. I would have heard of a theft this big—the whole system would have. I was willing to bet it was a very good counterfeit. The Isolationists never did anything with half measures.

The scale wasn't half-measured either. I counted packages and did some quick mental arithmetic, then did it again because I didn't believe the results the first time. This container held a billion crowns at a conservative estimate. The krona isn't the rock solid currency it used to be. Its value has been steadily eroded since the start of the occupation and the slide has only accelerated since the liberation. Even so, a billion crowns was a staggering sum. A fraction of a percent of counterfeits in the cash supply will upset a currency's stability. With the Provo Government's grip already shaky, there was enough here to undermine the entire system's economy. If this container got through to Wunderland, Alpha Centauri would be in chaos within a month.

It wouldn't, though, because we'd gotten here first. I felt suddenly shaky. This was a *major* haul. I was well aware of what the Provos knew and did not know about the Isolationists. The scale of their smuggling system, their expansion into medical facilities and organlegging and their counterfeiting operation were all new pieces of information. We were going to get positive DNA idents from this site, and the Goldskin interrogators would get the names we didn't have from the ones we caught. This investigation was going to break the back of the Isolationists in the Swarm before they even got going and shut down a huge smuggling ring as well. The information we gained would let the Provopolizei put a major crimp in their operations on Wunderland too.

It was a good feeling—it was the way I used to feel when Prakit and I started to unravel one of our big cases back on Earth. And why not? This was just as big—maybe bigger. Tiamat might well wind up crowning my career and I'd only been here a month.

My enthusiasm damped itself. The whole Wunderland half of the project depended on the Provopolizei. They might well be "convinced" to close the case down by some pro-Isolationist politician.

I shook off the negative images. I was doing my job and doing it well. Wunderland was out of my control, but I'd already scored a major victory just by catching this shipment. No politician could take that away from me.

Merral came in, gasping when she saw the cash. "Impressive, eh?"

She just nodded.

"Don't get too excited, it's not real."

She looked at the stacked packages "There must be hundreds of millions of crowns here."

"A billion at the very least."

She whistled. "They could crash the market with this."

"I think that's the plan."

She tore her gaze away from the money and handed me a hardcopy. "Here, you're going to need this."

It was from the data terminal in the inspection container. It listed thirty-six tranship boxes that had passed through 19J2 at some point, along with their points of origin, shipper, receiver and supposed manifest. This bay was a hub for smuggling activities ranging from UN outposts at the edge of the system to remote monorail stations deep in the Jotuns on Wunderland. One container was even shuttling back and forth from Earth itself.

Hunter came in and reported. "The crime scene team has arrived and the access tunnel has been secured." He took in the container's contents and for the first time ever I saw him at a loss. "There is . . . considerable wealth here."

"Almost certainly counterfeit."

"Of course." He was back in control that quickly. "Shall I inform the UNF authorities that they can recover their pharmaceuticals as soon as the team has finished their sweep?"

"I'll do it; you take over here." His practicality reminded me that there was plenty of work to be done. The bay was secure and the sweepers would give me a report. I had to start coordinating the authorities whose jurisdictions were on Merral's destination list. It was a big criminal organization. Not everyone would get warned in time. A lot of crooks were about to get caught.

Johansen came in with First Tracker in tow. I took some time to fill them in on the findings and set them to tracing our runner. The sweepers were already at work in the bay by the time I left. I tubed back to the office and got the paperwork under way. I'd only been at my desk half an hour when the screen chimed. I punched the call through. It was Suze.

"Hi, am I interrupting anything?"

I smiled. "Big exciting things, but I'm glad you called anyway."

"Why don't you knock off early and tell me about them?" Her smile was rich in promises.

"I really shouldn't . . ." I looked at my long list of to-dos " . . . but what the hell." Any excuse to dodge paperwork. A twelve-hour delay wouldn't make much difference in the course of the investigation. I was just sending preliminary reports anyway. Most of the information I needed wouldn't be back from the field lab until tomorrow.

"Great, your apt, thirty minutes. I'll order dinner."

"Sold." She punched off and I stored my work in progress.

Suze was waiting at the door when I got to my apt. I thumbed the plate and kissed her. We went in and I unslung my patrol pack and hung it on a hook by the door. She looked at it with curiosity.

"You carry a gun?"

"It's just a stunner."

"Does that have anything to do with your big exciting happenings?"

"Not a whole lot as it turns out. We closed down an Isolationist smuggling operation in an abandoned container bay today. And we know who killed Miranda."

"Who?"

"The Isolationists." I paused, then shut up. I'd been

about to tell her about their organlegging operation,
but there was no need to upset her.

She didn't notice my hesitation. "Catch anyone?"

"Not yet, but we will. We got a big pile of stolen
drugs and about a billion in counterfeit krona as well."

She whistled. "That is big and exciting."

I grinned, still very pleased with the success. "I have
to convince the management that I'm earning my pay."

"You won't get fired this week anyway." She reached
past me and took my pack off the wall. "What else
do you carry?"

"Just what you'd expect. Comm unit, binders, medkit,
beltcomp, shockrod, that sort of thing."

She opened the pouch and examined the medkit. It
was ARM issue on Earth, more advanced than what
was given out here. "You're ready for anything, aren't
you?"

"As much as I can be."

She took out the binders, simple double circlets of
stainless steel—very low tech. She locked one cuff to
her right wrist.

"Anything at all?"

She held out her arms towards me, wrists together.
Her eyes were high voltage arcs. She wore a look of
invitation and defiance—"I dare you."

I walked over and gently took her hands. Her gaze
didn't waver. Without breaking eye contact, I lifted the
other cuff and closed it around her left wrist. The lock
is usually inaudible. This time the click sounded like
a gunshot.

She parted her lips. I pulled her arms over her head
and kissed her fervently, pulling her pliant body hard
against mine. Eventually, I picked her up and carried
her to the bedroom. My apt is on the .8G level and
she was as light as a feather in my arms.

✧   ✧   ✧

The screen chimed, though I had it set for privacy, dragging me out of a deep sleep. Priority call. I punched it through and got the Goldskin dispatcher. Emergency. Johansen had arrested a suspect and shots had been fired. She was hit—no word on her condition yet—and the suspect was fleeing. The Goldskins were in pursuit but weren't pressing their quarry. He had a strakakker and was moving along a pedestrian promenade. They didn't want to provoke a firefight.

I didn't blame them. I punched the dispatcher into audio only and patched in security surveillance. They'd be following him on the monitors. The screen showed a crowded arcade from halfway up one wall. A surging disturbance in the throng marked the escaper. He was a dark-haired Wunderlander, running awkwardly in the low G, brandishing his weapon and screaming. People were desperately scrambling out of his way. As I watched, a startled kzin leapt straight up and grabbed a light fixture on the ceiling fifty feet overhead. The fugitive jerked his gun up to cover the sudden motion but didn't fire. Between his panic and lack of coordination, it was a miracle he hadn't already emptied the strakakker into the crowd. One hint of pursuit and he'd do just that. The Goldskins had made the right choice. Let him run, exhaust himself and then hole up somewhere. Even if he took hostages and wound up killing them all it would be no worse than a shootout down on that floor. Hopefully, it would turn out much better.

Hopefully.

Suze came up behind me, rubbing sleep from her eyes and looking very fetching with her hair tousled into a fiery halo and wearing an oversized jump-shirt from my wardrobe.

"What's going on?"

I spoke quickly. "We've got a runner. Tammy

tagged a suspect from the container bay bust and got shot."

The dispatcher was still waiting for instructions. I split the screen and punched up Control's map. I got a floating 3D planview of the arcade and the levels around it. The fugitive was a tiny red ball on the .3G level, heading down-axis. Gold spheres marked the cops positioned around his route, moving to get ahead of him but staying out of the way. As long as he didn't open fire they'd stay there. Clusters of blue-marked med teams held in readiness. Control had sealed the pressure doors behind him but not ahead. Any route he chose was fine with them as long as it was off that arcade. I zoomed the map out and punched up a history trace. A red line showed his path. He was panicked but he wasn't running blindly. He was going straight down-axis, moving in every time he had a chance. He was heading for the low-G industrial zone near Tigertown.

Heading for the down-axis hub.

I told the dispatcher as much and blanked the screen. Suze was looking over my shoulder and I nearly knocked her over as I got up to grab my clothes. I threw them on in record time and grabbed my patrol pack. At the door I paused long enough to kiss her good-bye.

"Back soon."

She grabbed me with surprising strength, kissed me hard and whispered fiercely in my ear. "Don't let him live."

"What?" I said, taken aback, not understanding.

"Don't let him live. If he's caught, there'll be a trial. He's an Isolationist, they can buy the court or blackmail it or break him out. He'll get away. It's not right, after what they did to that girl." Her gaze was intense, burning blue. "If he's shot while escaping . . ." She let her voice trail off.

She didn't need to say more. I kissed her fiercely and left.

Control had a tube car ready and held on standby. I jumped in, thumbed the plate and the door slid shut. The route panel was already set for the down-axis hub. The dispatcher obligingly shunted everyone else out of my way and I made the thirty-kilometer trip in record time. On the way, I thought about Suze's plea. An armed and dangerous fugitive killed while fleeing arrest. There would be no questions if I ordered shoot to kill. We'd lose the chance to interrogate him of course, but he wouldn't evade justice—and it would be justice. Even if he wasn't an Isolationist with blood on his hands, he'd proved murderous intent by shooting Johansen.

Frontier justice. It wasn't the way the ARM did business on Earth, but this wasn't Earth. Maybe I should issue shoot to kill orders anyway. It was a reasonable response given the situation. I had to think of the danger to my troops as well. Stunners don't have a lot of range and if the runner got off a burst before going down it would be messy, even if we fired first. Pulse rifles would more than even the odds.

I decided to wait and see. Any risk of a firefight, I'd give the order, but not until. I'd played by the rules since I'd arrived and I wasn't going to go back now.

In the end it didn't matter. It was all over when I got there. The runner went straight for the down-axis hub. Control evacuated the accessways and when he got inside an empty corridor they sealed him in. His strakakker was loaded with armor-piercing explosive ammunition and he emptied it trying to blow open the plasteel pressure doors. When they failed to yield sufficiently, he reloaded and blew his head off instead.

Armor-piercing explosive. I felt sick as I remembered Johansen. I called the medical section and asked how she was, dreading the answer I knew I would get. Tammy took five rounds point-blank from her left hip to her right shoulder. Her body armor was blasted to ribbons absorbing the detonations. She might as well have been naked, she was dead on the scene. First Tracker took rounds in the thigh, belly and chest but his heavier kzin armor and built-for-battle physique saved his life—hopefully. The doctors would rebuild his devastated abdominal cavity and autoclone replacements for damaged organs and limbs, if he made it through the night.

He'd called in the shooting and the suspect, tourniqued his femoral artery and was giving CPR to Johansen when the crash team arrived. I'd pin his medal on myself.

If he made it through the night.

I screened Tam's journal for information. She'd done a search on the transit system logs for anyone who boarded a tube car in the access corridor to J2 up to five minutes after Hunter and I had chased our quarry from the container bay. One of the names on that list was a drive technician—HJ3U659A Wurzmann. Peter K. Wurzmann was suspected of smuggling but never charged through lack of evidence. Wurzmann took the tube to his apt, then another to the down-axis hub where he'd boarded the mining ship *Voidtrekker*. Johansen was on to him by then, but the police tag went on his ident seven seconds after he'd passed customs. *Voidtrekker* cleared docking control ten minutes after that and left on a prospecting trajectory that was bound to be a total fabrication. A comm check showed Wurzmann made four calls—*Voidtrekker*'s captain, a co-worker, a Wunderland tourist, and a Wunderland doctor named Joachim Weiss. The last call was marked NO ANSWER. Comm checks on the recipients expanded the list to sixteen names. Fifteen people had taken off with *Voidtrekker*—everyone on the comm list except Weiss. Weiss was the one with the strakakker.

So we'd flushed our quarry and they'd fled. I guessed the Wunderlanders were Isolationists and the Belters were contract smugglers. They were probably the entire control cell for 19J2—and they were all out of reach.

I screened Hunter and got him to take a search unit down to Weiss's apt. His lips were twitching back to expose his fangs, his speech laden with snarls and heavy with threats. He was barely under control. He took Johansen's death and Tracker's wounding as personal insults. After that, I called up the navy and asked them about intercepting *Voidtrekker*. A competent-looking commander told me the odds of an intercept were a little less than one in ten. *Voidtrekker* was polarizer driven, which meant she could put a lot of distance between herself and Tiamat in a very short time. A smuggler ship would have shielded monopoles in her drive, making tracking impossible. Once she cleared Tiamat's control sphere she'd be very difficult to pick up.

"Will the navy try anyway?" I asked.

"There's no question involved." The officer checked something off-screen for a second. "We'll have three ships boosting in the next two hours."

I gave my thanks and rang off.

After that, I went over Dr. Weiss's file again. The Provos had him tagged as Isolationist leaning—that was nothing, most Wunderlanders were. Everything else told me he was Miranda's killer. When the Goldskins had printed him for ID they'd gotten two files back. His retinas said he was Joachim Weiss, his fingertips said he was a bio-engineer named Cas Wentsel. Wentsel was on the Inferno's customer list for the night Miranda was killed and his movements for that night took him past the accessway to container bay J2. Weiss arrived on Tiamat just one day after Miranda, on the next available flight from Wunderland. He fit the physical description from the Inferno, such as it was. He was qualified to perform Class 3 surgery. I pulled up his library list. It was hopelessly technical but I gleaned all I needed to know from the titles—fifty-year-obsolete manuals about tissue preservation and rejection control. They amounted to a primer for organleggers.

Tamara was avenged. Miranda was avenged. I tagged her case file CLOSED.

I didn't feel the usual satisfaction I get when I close a case. Miranda and Tammy were still gone, Weiss's death wouldn't bring them back. His cohorts had escaped. The elation I'd felt when we'd shut down J2 was overshadowed by helpless frustration. On a hunch I pulled up his client files. Miranda Holtzman had been his patient since she was six. That was how he knew she was a universal donor, that was why she'd left the bounce-box with him. I felt ill.

It was late. In the morning I'd open a new case file on the flight of the *Voidtrekker*. I switched off the system and went home.

When I got back, Suze had gone out. I didn't blame her, but I did miss her. The events of the night and Johansen's death had left me totally drained. I fell into an exhausted slumber. Some time later I felt her slip into bed and snuggle against me, warm and soft. She gently kissed the back of my neck and I went back to sleep, feeling better.

The next morning Hunter was waiting for me.

"You are late. We have had developments."

"Why didn't you call me?"

He twitched his ears genially. "Your recreation had already been disturbed once."

I avoided the subject. "What happened?"

"There was an explosion in the down-axis docking hub."

"Serious?"

"Yes. The initiating explosive appears to have been thermite but the main blast and fire were caused by a volatile aerosol inside a tranship container. Damage was extensive."

I envisioned the havoc that a two-thousand-cubic-meter sealed vapor bomb would wreak and marvelled at the kzin's capacity for understatement. We were lucky the whole down-axis hub hadn't been blown into space.

"What action have you taken?"

"The area has been sealed and the crime scene team is going over it."

"Findings?"

"A human corpse has been found that appears to have been inside the transport container. The container itself was modified to support life."

"Support life? What do you mean?"

"We have found the remains of an oxygen recycler, food supplies and other items that indicate the container was designed to carry sentients in vacuum for extended periods."

I swore. The Isolationists had been moving people back and forth to Wunderland with perfect impunity, right under our noses. Finagle only knew how many. We'd missed a trick. Reception parties would be waiting for the thirty-six containers on Jocelyn Merral's list when they arrived at their destinations but I hadn't thought about intercepting them in transit. It hadn't even occurred to me that some might still be within my grasp on Tiamat.

"What about the guards and the security monitors. How come they didn't pick this up in progress?"

"The Port was running its normal night shift. The monitors didn't pick up anything out of the ordinary."

"So the perpetrator must have had access."

"Hrrrrr . . . Either that or a tampered ident."

"Granted. So once again we have someone operating in the down-axis hub. Someone who didn't flee on the *Voidtrekker*."

He raised a massive paw. "It would be foolish to assume that only one Isolationist cell was operating on Tiamat. I would presume we have flushed only those with a direct connection to 19J2."

"What other information do we have?"

"Little enough. Damage was extensive. We can assume that they were willing to kill this individual rather than risk his capture."

"Have they ID'd the body?"

"The coroner's report has not yet been released."

If I never spoke to Dr. Morrow again it would be too soon. I was tired of sifting through the details of dead lives. I screened his office and asked him what the delay was. He was having trouble determining if the body had been dead before the explosion or not. I told him to make the ID priority one. He asked me to wait and I watched his pleasant pastel hold patterns. Hunter grew impatient and left to pursue his own work. Fifteen minutes later Morrow was back on with the results.

I thanked him and screened the file. K8DH3N37—Klein, Maximillian H. Graphic designer, unmarried, thirty-four standard years old, fifth generation Swarm Belter. No previous arrests. He'd lived his whole life on Tiamat and worked for Canexco, a large shipping company. A bell rang in the back of my head. Miranda Holtzman's fatal cargo container had been shipped down to Wunderland aboard the *Canexco Wayfarer*. Perhaps there was a connection? I called up Max's employee file. He worked in corporate communications—nothing to do with the handling of tranship boxes but his company ident did include access to both hubs.

But what was a graphic designer doing in the container bays of the down-axis hub, with or without access? Was he involved or just caught in the wrong place at the wrong time? On a hunch I screened the composite holo created from Machine Technician's description. It was a rough match, not good but not bad considering the sketchiness of the source. Was he the one who'd sold Miranda's skin? Insufficient data. What was a graphic designer anyway? Presumably some sort of visual artist.

It occurred to me that I'd never seen a file listing "Artist" or "Musician" or "Gardener" as a profession on Tiamat. This airless rock was made fit for life with advanced technology and maintained by technologists. It exists solely to provide Alpha Centauri system with products of the very highest sophistication—products whose manufacture demands zero gravity or unlimited high vacuum or gigawatts of solar power. There's little room for someone not directly involved in survival—physical, economic or, since the kzinti came, military.

Of course the best engineers saw their work as art, even as the best artists refined their skills to a science. Maybe in this totally technical atmosphere, it wasn't surprising that people saw things through a technological lens. Idly, I punched up the work roster for the parks on the 1G level. Maybe I'd find at least a gardener.

The roster was full of eco-engineers and environmental control technicians.

I blanked the screen. It was a meaningless exercise. A rose was a rose, whether it was tended by gardeners or botanical techs. I had a feeling the difference was important, but it was too subtle to put my finger on. What's in a name? Maybe nothing. What does it mean when a society insists on calling an artist a graphic designer?

My mind was wandering. It was early morning and

already I needed a break. I gave up trying to work and let my thoughts drift to Suze. She was beautiful, intelligent, sensuous, exciting, graceful, uninhibited, warm. Adjectives did her poor service. If I'd been able to find the words, I might have written a poem. Instead I called up her file again. When the computer screened it, I blew up the ID holo and dumped it to the printer.

Dossier holos never do anyone justice but her radiance came through the bad image. She was wearing her characteristic high-energy smile. Her hair was longer when the holo was taken, a burnished auburn river flowing down over her shoulders. Her eyes were a dancing, sunny brown—lending just a hint of devilishness to her look.

I froze, cold horror seeping along my spine. Unnoticed facts clicked into place and my thoughts locked into a paralyzed frenzy of revelation and denial. I sat and stared for a long time. Then I commed her apt.

"Hi, what's up?"

I could hardly meet her gaze. I strove to keep my voice animated. "Care for brunch?"

"Sure, whenwhere?"

"Meet me at the office and we'll figure it out. Fifteen minutes?"

"Give me thirty and you've got a deal."

"See you then." She smiled her dazzling smile.

I rang off and waited as the minutes dragged by. I had the shakes under control by the time she arrived; even so I still couldn't bring myself to meet her gaze. Instead I tossed her the holoprint. She took it and stared at it uncomprehending for a moment. Then her face hardened. She dropped the holo and looked up. This time I forced myself to look her in the eyes. They were ice blue. Miranda Holtzman's eyes were ice blue.

Her voice was as cold as her gaze. "Now what?"

"You tell me."

"Name a price, you'll get it. I'll just walk away."

"In counterfeit?"

"In cash. Or credits if you like. You name it, you'll get it."

I didn't answer her directly. Instead I asked a question. "Why?"

She turned my words around. "You tell me."

"You're an Isolationist."

She nodded.

"You're a mining engineer. I'd guess that makes you their explosives expert. Something went off in your face. They can't put you in hospital so you wind up with scars, and of course they have to get you a new set of eyes somewhere or you're out of action."

"Wrong." The bitterness in her voice ran deep. "I got my scars from the UN mining consortium just like I told you. They hand out defective equipment and when there's an accident, it's just too bad. All they care about is the damn production goals for the damn war. I was one of the lucky ones. Luckier than my parents." I could see the rage cross her face at the memory. "That's why I'm an Isolationist."

"And your eyes?"

"I caught a laser bounce in a Provo raid."

"So you become the first beneficiary of the Isolationist transplant program."

"Not the first."

Of course not. "How did you expect to get past a retina scan?"

She laughed. "I think you'll find my file matches my prints. Someone forgot to update the holo—they'll pay for that."

"And that night in the Inferno?"

"I started going there as soon as I could see again. I knew you'd come after Weiss's stupidity. You or someone like you."

A vague unease tugged at the edges of my awareness. She was volunteering information too easily, too calmly. I forced it down. "Weiss messed up?"

"He couldn't get all of Miranda in the freezer. The dolt dumped her body in the transport tunnel instead of getting rid of it properly."

"And the hub last night, that's where you went from my apt."

She tipped an imaginary hat in reply, as if accepting a compliment. She was a professional. She took pride in her work.

"There was some evidence. It's not important now."

"And Klein?"

"Just a go-between. He got in the way."

I had one more question. "Why Miranda?"

"We needed a universal donor, and I've always wanted blue eyes." She smiled, briefly.

"Now what?"

Her voice was as hard and cold as steel. "How much do you want?"

My heart sank and I shook my head. "I can't let you go."

Suddenly there was a gun in her hand, a jetpistol. Designed for zero-G combat, it had virtually no recoil. It fired miniature rockets designed to mushroom on impact. They would turn a living body into hamburger. It was almost totally silent, small enough to conceal easily and had no power source or metal to trigger security alarms. She had chosen her weapon well.

"I don't think you have a choice." She smiled. She was right. The choice was hers and she'd already made it. Even so, I had to ask. "What about us?"

She laughed, a short, explosive sound. "I liked you, Joel. It was fun, but now it's time for me to leave." She raised the jetpistol. Her expression held regret and finality. I wouldn't beg, but my expression must have spoken for me. Perhaps she thought I was afraid of dying.

I glanced at the stunner hanging on my patrol pack— two impossible meters away.

She caught me looking and a smile played around the edges of her lips. I knew the expression. She was daring me to try.

I held her gaze but I didn't take the bait. "You can't kill everyone who knows you're here."

Her smile was as wide and predatory as any kzin's. "Watch me." The weapon's bore looked as big as a cannon's. Her finger tightened around the trigger.

There was a piercing scream and the wall behind her exploded around two hundred and fifty kilos of kzin. She fired reflexively but I was already on my way to the floor. Even so, she would have got me if Hunter's attack hadn't ruined her aim. The rocket slug went past my ear with a nasty *zzzwip*, leaving an acrid trail of burned propellant. Another slug slammed into my computer, spraying shards of plastic and glass over my head. A second later it was followed by Suze and the kzin in a tangle of limbs. They hit the wall and bounced to the floor. The jetpistol sailed into a corner. She lay on the floor beneath him, returning his fanged snarl in kind. I had to admire her courage.

I picked myself off the floor and shook off the ruins of my computer. The room was filling with startled clerks and cops from the outer office. As they disentangled Hunter and Suze, I retrieved the jetpistol and examined the thumbnail-sized hole it had left in the wall. On the other side was a crater the size of a serving platter. The outer office was showered in fragments of pulverized sprayfoam. Shattered remnants of my desk covered my office. I shuddered. It could have been the shattered remnants of me.

Hunter dusted himself off, scream-snarled and

bounded out to work out the fight juices. Someone hauled Suze off to the tender mercies of the UN Intel interrogation section. When they were through raping her mind, she'd have nothing left to tell. I'd have rather seen her face Hunter claw to claw.

When everyone was gone, I sat down at my desk. By reflex I pounded the switch, not registering its destruction. After that, I just sat; eventually I went home.

Suze was in interrogation three days. Her trial should have been in the Swarm but the UN moved it to Wunderland so she could be made an example of. By the time the Goldskins were done with her the extradition paperwork was finished. I didn't see her off. Instead, I asked a favor of Jocelyn Merral and watched from the hangar bay control deck as the guards escorted her to the ship that would take her to Wunderland and the ProvGov's version of justice. She caught sight of me as they led her onto the ramp and stopped, looking up. The guards yanked her along, and she was gone.

I kept watching out the window. I knew I wouldn't see her again. I just didn't want anyone to see my face.

That evening I sat at the bar in the Ratskellar, drinking beer and brooding. Earlier I'd sat in my room, drinking vodka and playing with the safety on a jetpistol that should have been sealed in an evidence bag on its way to Wunderland. I didn't decide life was worth living, I just couldn't live with myself if I took the coward's way out.

Of course, if I did I wouldn't have to. Alcohol doesn't make for logical decision-making. It was enough that I'd left the weapon behind.

The rockjack beside me suddenly left. His stool was taken by a huge orange hulk. Hunter-of-Outlaws ordered a liter of vodka and milk before speaking. "Humans have odd ways of celebrating victory."

I grunted. "Is it a victory I'm celebrating?"

"Hrrr. We have found the outlaw we sought and more besides. Several major criminal enterprises have been brought down and gutted. We have performed our duties well and with honor and our belts are heavy with trophies. It is a triumph worthy of our names."

I didn't answer directly; I asked a question. "How did you know to come through the wall like that?"

"How could I not know? My office echoes to your voice all day. I cannot close my ears tight enough to keep it out. For years I've been trying to get a privacy field." He growled deeply.

So much for soundproof sprayfoam.

"I owe you my life, you know."

He waved a paw dismissively. "You will repay that blood-debt when the situation arises. Now tell me why you choke on the meat of victory?"

"She offered me as much money as I cared to ask for. Of course, I couldn't take it."

"You are true to your honour."

"You don't understand. I loved her."

"I sympathize with your situation. Your species' reproductive arrangements are overcomplex. Such strong attachment to females can only lead to continuing tragedy."

"No, love is a continuing glory. She loved me too, she just loved . . . freedom . . . more. I would have gone with her in a second if she'd let me."

Hunter was staring at me, openly amazed. "You would have sacrificed your honour for the affections of this outlaw female?"

"It would have been a small price."

His ears flicked and his tail twitched as he tried to

make sense of that. He gave it up and quaffed his drink resignedly. "Truly, I will never understand humans."

I had to laugh. I clapped him on the back and gestured for another round. "Neither will I, my friend, neither will I."

FLY–BY–NIGHT

Larry Niven

The windows in *Odysseus* had been skylights. The doors had become hatches. I ran down the corridor looking at numbers. Seven days we'd been waiting for aliens to appear in the ship's lobby, and nothing!

Nothing until now. I felt good. Excited. I ran full tilt, not from urgency but because I *could*. I'd expected to reach Home as frozen meat in one of these Ice Class cargo modules.

I reached 36, stooped and punched the steward's bell. Just as the door swung down, I remembered not to grin.

A nightmare answered.

It looked like an octopus underwater, except for the vest. At the roots of five eel's-tail segments, each four feet long, eyes looked up at me. We never see Jotoki often enough to get used to them. The limbs clung to a ladder that would cross the cabin ceiling when the gravity generators were on.

I said, "Legal Entity Paradoxical, I have urgent business with Legal Entity Fly-By-Night."

The Jotok started to say, "Business with my master—" when its master appeared below it on the ladder.

This was the nightmare I'd been expecting: five to six hundred pounds of orange and sienna fur, sienna commas marking the face, needle teeth just showing points, looking up at me out of a pit. Fly-By-Night wore a kind of rope vest, pockets all over it, and buttons or corks on the points of all ten of its finger claws.

"—is easily conducted in virtual fashion," the Jotok concluded.

What I'd been about to say went clean out of my head. I asked, "Why the buttons?"

Lips pulled back over a forest of carnivore teeth, LE Fly-By-Night demanded, "Who are you to question me?"

"Martin Wallace Graynor," I said. Conditioned reflex.

The reading I'd done suggested that a killing snarl would leave a kzin mute, able to express himself only by violence. Indeed, his lips wanted to retract, and it turned his Interworld speech mushy. "LE Graynor, by what authority do *you* interrogate *me*?"

My antic humor ran away with me. I patted my pockets elaborately. "Got it somewhere—"

"Shall we look for it?"

"I—"

"Written on your liver?"

"I have an idea. I could stop asking impertinent questions?"

"A neat solution." Silently the door swung up.

Ring.

The Jotok may well have been posing himself between me and his enraged master, who was still wearing buttons on his claws, and *smiling*. I said, "Don't kill me. The Captain has dire need of you and wishes that you will come to the main workstation in all haste."

The kzin leapt straight up with a half turn to get

past the Jotok and pulled himself into the corridor. I did a pretty good backward jump myself.

Fly-By-Night asked, "Do you know why the Captain might make such a request?"

"I can guess. Haste *is* appropriate."

"Had you considered using the intercom, or virtual mail?"

"Captain Preiss may be afraid they can listen to our electronics."

"They?"

"Kzinti spacecraft. The Captain hopes you can identify them and help negotiate."

He stripped off the corks and dropped them in a pocket. His lips were all right now. "This main workstation, would it be a control room or bridge?"

"I'll guide you."

The Kzin was twisted over by some old injury. His balance was just a bit off. His furless pink tail lashed back and forth, for balance or for rage. The tip knocked both walls, *toc toc toc*. I'd be whipped bloody if I tried to walk beside him. I stayed ahead.

The Jotok trailed us well back from the tail. It wore a five-armhole vest with pockets. It used four limbs as legs. One it held stiff. I pictured a crippled Kzin buying a crippled Jotok . . . but Paradoxical had been agile enough climbing the ladder. I must have missed something.

The file on Jotoki said to call it *they*, but that just felt wrong.

"Piracy," the Kzin said, "would explain why everything is on its side."

"Yah. They burned out our thruster. The Captain had to spin us up with attitude jets."

"I don't know that weapon. Speak of the ship," he said. "One? Kzinti?"

"One ship popped up behind us and fired on us as it went past. It's a little smaller than *Odysseus*. Then a Kzin called us. Act of war, he said. Get the Captain to play that for you. He spoke Interworld . . . not as well as you." Fly-By-Night talked like he'd grown up around humans. Maybe he was from Fafnir. "The ship stopped twenty million miles distant and sent a boat. That's on its way here now. Our telescopes pick up markings in the Heroes' Tongue. We can't read them."

He said, "If we were traveling faster than light, we could not be intercepted. Did your Captain consider that?"

"Better you should ask, why are we *out* of hyperdrive? LE Fly-By-Night, there is an extensive starbuilding region between Fafnir and Home. Going through the Tao Gap in Einstein space is easier than going around and gives us a *wonderful* view, but we're *in* it now. Stuck. We can't send a hyperwave help call, we can't jump to hyperdrive, because there's too much mass around us."

"*Odysseus* has no weapons," the Kzin said.

"I don't have actual rank aboard *Odysseus*. I don't know what weapons we have." And I wouldn't tell a Kzin.

He said, "I learned that before I boarded. *Odysseus* is a modular cargo ship. Some of the modules are passenger cabins. Outbound Enterprises could mount weapons modules, but they never have. None of their other commuter ships are any better. The other ship, how is it armed?"

"Looks like an archaic Kzinti warship, *dis*armed. Gun ports slagged and polished flat. We haven't had a close look, but ships like that are all over known space since before I was born. Armed Kzinti wouldn't be allowed to land. Whatever took out our gravity motors isn't showing. It must be on the boat."

"Why is this corridor so long?"

Odysseus was a fat disk with motors and tanks in the center, a corridor around the rim, slots outboard to moor staterooms and cargo modules. That shape makes it easy to spin up if something goes wrong with the motors . . . which was still common enough a century ago, when *Odysseus* was built.

In the ship's map display I'd seen stateroom modules widely separated, so I'd hacked the passenger manifest. That led me to read up on Kzinti and Jotoki. The first secret to tourism is, *read everything*.

I said, "Some LE may have decided not to put a Kzin too close to human passengers. They put you two in a four-passenger suite and mounted it all the way around clockwise. My single and two doubles and the crew quarters and an autodoc are all widdershins." That put the aliens' module right next to the lobby, not far apart at all, but the same fool must have sealed off access from the aliens' suite. Despite the Covenants, some people *don't like* giving civil rights to Kzinti.

I'd best not say *that*. "We're the only other live passengers. The modules between are cargo, so these," I stamped on a door, "don't currently open on anything."

"If you are not a ship's officer," the Kzin asked, "what is your place on the bridge?"

I said, "Outbound Enterprises was getting ready to freeze me. Shashter cops pulled me out. They had questions regarding a murder."

"Have you killed?" His ears flicked out like little pink fans. I had his interest.

"I didn't kill Ander Smittarasheed. He took some cops down with him, and he'd killed an ARM agent. ARMs are—"

"United Nations police and war arm, Sol system, but their influence spreads throughout human space."

"Well, they couldn't question Smittarasheed, and I'd eaten dinner with him a few days earlier. I told them we met in Pacifica City at a water war game . . . anyway, I satisfied the law, they let me loose. I was just in time to board, and *way* too late to get myself frozen and into a cargo module. Outbound Enterprises upgraded me. Very generous.

"So Milcenta and Jenna—my mate and child are frozen in one of these," I stamped on a door, "and I'm up here, flying First Class at Ice Class expense. My cabin's a closet, so we must be expected to spend most of our time in the lobby. In here." I pushed through.

This trip there were two human crew, five human passengers and the aliens. The lobby would have been roomy for thrice that. Whorls of couches and tables covered a floor with considerable space above it for free fall dancing. That feature didn't generally get much use.

An observation dome exposed half the sky. It opened now on a tremendous view of the Nursery Nebula.

Under spin gravity, several booths and the workstations had rolled up a wall. There was a big airlock. The workstations were two desk-and-couch modules in the middle.

Hans and Hilde Van Zild were in one of the booths. Homers coming back from Fafnir, they held hands tightly and didn't talk. Recent events had them extremely twitchy. They were both over two hundred years old. I've known people in whom that didn't show, but in these it did.

Their kids were hovering around the workstations watching the Captain and First Officer at work, asking questions that weren't being answered.

We'd been given vac packs. More were distributed

around the lobby and along the corridor. Most ships carry them. You wear it as a bulky fanny pack. If you pull a tab, or if it's armed and pressure drops to zero, it blows up into a refuge. Then you hope you can get into it and zip it shut before your blood boils.

Heidi Van Zild looked around. "Oh, *good!* You brought them!" The little girl snatched up two more vac packs, ran two steps toward us and froze.

The listing said Heidi was near forty. Her brother Nicolaus was thirty; the trip was his birthday present. Their parents must have had their development arrested. They looked the same age, ten years old or younger, bright smiles and sparkling eyes, hair cut identically in a golden cockatoo crest.

It's an attitude, a lifestyle. You put off children until that second century is running out. Now they're precious. They'll live forever. Let them take their time growing up. Keep them awhile longer. Keep them *pure.* Give them a *real* education. Any mistake you make as a parent, there will be time to correct that too. When you reverse the procedure and allow them to reach puberty they'll be better at it.

I know people who do that to kittens.

Some of a child's rash courage is ignorance. By thirty it's gone. The little girl's smile was a rictus. Aliens were here for her entertainment; she would not willingly miss any part of the adventure, but she just couldn't make herself approach the Kzin or his octopus servant. The boy hadn't even tried.

First Officer Quickpony finished what she'd been doing. She stood in haste, took the vacuum packs from Heidi and handed them to the aliens. "Fly-By-Night, thank you for coming. Thank you, Mart. You'd be Paradoxical?"

The woman's body language invited a handshake, but

the Jotok didn't. "Yes, we are Paradoxical, greatly pleased to meet you."

The Kzin snarled a question in the Heroes' Tongue. Everybody's translators murmured in chorus, "Is *this* the bridge?"

Quickpony said, "Bridge and lobby, they're the same space. You didn't know? We wondered why you never came around."

"I was not told of this option. There is merit in the posture that one species should not see another eat or mate or use the recycle port. But, LE Quickpony, your security is a joke! Bridge and passengers and no barrier? When did you begin building ships this way?"

Captain Preiss looked up. He said, "Software flies us. I can override, but I can disable the override. Hijackers can't affect that."

"What of your current problem? Did you record the Kzin's demand?"

The Captain spoke a command.

A ghostly head and shoulders popped up on the holostage, pale orange but for two narrow, lofty black eyebrows. "I am *Mee-rowreet*. Call me Envoy. I speak for the Longest War."

My translator murmured, "*Mee-rowreet*, profession, manages livestock in a hunting park. *Longest War*, Kzin term for evolution."

The recording spoke Interworld, but with a strong accent and flat grammar. "We seek a fugitive. We have destroyed your gravity motors. We will board you following the Covenants sworn at Shasht at twenty-five naught five your dating. Obey, never interfere," the ghost head and voice grew blurred, "give us what we demand. You will all survive."

"The signal was fuzzed out by distance," Captain Preiss said. "The ship came up from behind and passed us at two hundred KPS relative, twenty minutes after we dropped out of hyperdrive. It's ahead of us by two light-minutes, decelerated to match our speed."

I said, speaking low, "Pleasemadam," alerting my pocket computer, "seek interstellar law, document Covenants of Shasht date twenty-five-oh-five. Run it."

Fly-By-Night looked up into the dome. "Your intruder?"

We were deep into the Nursery Nebula. All around were walls of tenuous interstellar dust lit from within. In murky secrecy, intersecting shock waves from old supernovae were collapsing the interstellar murk into hot whirlpools that would one day be stars and solar systems. Out of view below us, light pressure from something bright was blowing columns and streams of dust past us. It all took place in an environment tens of light-years across. Furious action seemed frozen in time.

We had played at viewing the red whorl overhead. In IR you saw only the suns, paired protostars lit by gravitational collapse and the tritium flash, that had barely begun to burn. UV and X-ray showed violent flashes and plumes where planetesimals impacted, building planets. Neutrino radar showed structure forming within the new solar system.

We could not yet make out the point mass that would bend our course into the Tao Gap and out into free space. Turnpoint Star was a neutron star a few miles across, the core left by a supernova. But stare long enough and you could make out an arc on the sky, the shock wave from that same stellar explosion, broken by dust clouds collapsing into stars.

My seek system chimed. I listened to my wrist computer:

At the end of the Fourth Man-Kzin War, the Human Space Trade Alliance annexed Shasht and renamed the planet Fafnir, though the long, rocky, barren continent kept its Heroes' Tongue name. The Covenants of Shasht were negotiated then. We were to refrain from booting Kzinti citizens off Fafnir. An easy choice: they prefer the continent, whereas humans prefer the coral islands. They were already expanding an interstellar seafood industry into Patriarchy space.

In return, and having little choice, the Patriarch barred himself, his clan and all habitats under his command, all others to be considered outlaw, from various acts. Eating of human meat . . . willful destruction of habitats . . . biological weapons of certain types . . . killing of Legal Entities, that word defined by a *long* list of exclusions, a narrower definition than in most human laws.

Futz, I wasn't a Legal Entity! Or I wouldn't be if they learned who I was.

Quickpony projected a virtual lens on the dome. I'd finish listening later. The Kzinti ship and its boat, vastly magnified, showed black with the red whorl behind them. There was enough incident light to pick out some detail.

For a bare instant we had seen the intruder coming up behind us, just as our drive juddered and died and left us floating. After it slowed to a relative stop, a boat had detached. The approaching boat blocked off part of the ship. Gamma rays impacting their magnetic shields made two arcs of soft white glow. Ship and boat bore the same glowing markings.

The ship was moving just as we were, its drive off, falling through luminous murk toward Turnpoint Star at a tenth of lightspeed.

First Officer Helm said, *"Odysseus'* security systems can deal with hijackers, but they're just not much use against an armed warship. Is that what we're seeing?"

"I see a small warship designed for espionage and

hunting. I don't know the make. My knowledge is too old. The name reads *Sraff-zisht*." My translator said, "Stealthy mating."

Fly-By-Night continued, "Captain, I can't see, are there magnetic moorings on *Sraff-zisht*?"

"No need. Those big magnets on the boat would lock to the ship's gamma ray shielding."

"The boat is armed, the ship is not? There is no bay for the boat? Understood. Leave the boat in hiding among asteroids. Land an unarmed converted cargo ship on any civilized world. Yes?"

"Speculative," Preiss said.

"Do you recognize the weapon?"

"No. I assume it's what burned out our thrusters . . . our gravity motors."

I sat and dialed a cappuccino. The Kzin joined me, dwarfing the booth. I dialed another with double milk, thinking he ought to try it.

The other passengers shrank back a little and waited. Any human being knows how to fear a Kzin.

I said, speaking low, "Pleasemadam, seek Heroes' Tongue references, stealthy mating, literal, no reference to rape." There had to be a way to narrow that further. I guessed: "Seek biological references only. Run it."

Fly-By-Night tasted the cappuccino.

Captain Preiss said, "Why would they be interested in *us*?"

"In me. The boat is close." Fly-By-Night sipped again. "Do you know of the *Angel's Pencil*?"

The Kzin was speaking Interworld as smoothly as if he'd grown up with the language. Some of us gaped. But his first words to me had been Interworld, after I startled and angered him . . . and he liked cappuccino.

Fly-By-Night said, "*Angel's Pencil* was a slowboat, one of Sol system's slower-than-light colony craft. Four hundred years ago, *Angel's Pencil* sent word of our coming. Sol system was given years to prepare. My ancestor Shadow contrived to board *Pencil* after allying himself with a human captive, Selena Guthlac. He and she joined their crew."

"That must have been one futz of a makeup job," Nicolaus Van Zild said.

"He had to stoop and keep his ears folded, and depilate! Whose story is this, boy?" Nicolaus grinned. The Kzin said, "*Angel's Pencil*'s crew had already destroyed *Tracker*. They later destroyed *Gutting Claw*, the first and second kills of the First War, not bad for a ship with no intended armaments.

"*Pencil* was forced to pass through Patriarchy space before they found a world to settle. None of those ramscoop ships were easy to turn, and none were built for more than one voyage. We were ninety light-years from Earth. One hundred and six years had passed on Earth."

I asked, "We?"

"*Gutting Claw*'s Telepath, later named Shadow, is our first sire. *Pencil* rescued six females from the Admiral's harem. Our species have lived together on Sheathclaws for three hundred years. We remained cut off. Any message laser aimed at human space would pass through the Patriarchy. We spoke with no sapient species, we did not even know of faster-than-light travel, until . . ." Fly-By-Night looked up.

Stealthy-Mating's boat had arrived. We were looking directly into an obtrusively large electromagnetic weapon.

Nicolaus asked, "Can you read minds?"

"No, child. Some of us are good at guessing, but we don't have the drug. Where was I?" Fly-By-Night said, "They told me in the hospital after my first failed name quest. The universe had opened up—" He cut himself off as a furry face popped into hologram space in the workstation.

"I am Envoy. I speak for the Longest War. Terminate your spin. Open the airlock."

Captain Preiss nodded to Quickpony. Reaction motors whispered, slowing us.

Fly-By-Night spoke more rapidly. "Boarding seems imminent. You cannot protect me. Give me to them. If you live long enough to speak to your people, tell them that three grown males left Sheathclaws on our name quests. Half our genes derive from Shadow, from a telepath. The Patriarch needs telepaths. Now he will learn of a world peopled by *Gutting Claw*'s telepath, none of whom has felt the addiction to sthondat lymph in three hundred years."

Gravity eased away until sideways thrust was all there was, and then that was gone too. *Odysseus'* outer airlock door opened.

The boat thumped into place against our hull. The older Van Zilds and I had our seat webs in place. The children floated, clinging to the arms of couches.

"They will have *my* genes. They will find Sheathclaws," Fly-By-Night concluded. "You will face my children in the next war, if they have their way."

Two big pressure-suit shapes left the boat on jet packs. One entered the lock. We heard it cycle. The other waited on the hull, to shoot the dome out if he saw resistance.

The inner door opened. The armored Kzin entered in a leap, up and into the dome where his companions could see him, a half turn to keep us in view. In his hand was a light that he aimed like a weapon. He was graceful as a fish.

I squinted to save my vision. The light played over every part of the lobby and workstation. What he saw must have been reassuring.

Envoy said, "We have demands. The Covenants will be followed where possible. All losses will be paid. Give us your passenger. He is in violation of our law. Fly-By-Night, is this Jotok your slave?"

"Yes."

"Fly-By-Night, Jotok, you must enter your vacuum packs. Fly-By-Night, give your w'tsai to Packer."

"W'tsai?" Fly-By-Night asked. "This? My *knife*?"

"Carefully."

Giving up his w'tsai was the ultimate surrender. If *I* knew that from my reading, surely a *Kzin* knew it. Three hundred years among humans . . . Had they lost the tradition?

But Fly-By-Night was offering a silver knife-prong-spoon ten inches long and dark with tarnish.

A spoony? We ate with those! They matched several shapes of digits and were oversized for human hands. *Odysseus'* kitchen melted the silver to kill bacteria, then squirted it into molds for the next meal.

Packer took it, stared at it, then showed it to Envoy's hologram. Envoy snarled in the Heroes' Tongue. He wasn't buying it.

Our passenger answered in Interworld. "Yes, mine! See, here is my symbol," the sign of Outbound Enterprises, a winged craft black against a crescent world. "Fly by night!"

A laugh would be bad. I looked at the children. They looked solemn.

Of Packer's weapon I saw only a glare of light. But he held it on Fly-By-Night as if it *had* to fire something deadly, and he snarled a command and lashed out with his tail. Under the minor impact Fly-By-Night spun slowly so that Packer could examine him for more weapons.

He snarled again. Fly-By-Night and Paradoxical pulled tabs on vacuum packs. The packs popped into double-walled spheres. Held open by higher pressure, the collar on each refuge inflated like a pair of fat lips.

Fly-By-Night had trouble wriggling through the collar. Once inside he had room. These vacuum refuges would have held the whole Van Zild family. Paradoxical looked quite lost in his.

Envoy spoke. "Captain, you carry human passengers frozen in three cargo modules. Release these modules."

The world went gray.

I began to breath deep and hard, to hyperoxygenate, because I dared not faint.

Captain Preiss' hands hadn't moved. That was brave, but it wouldn't save anyone.

The elder Van Zilds buried their faces in each other's shoulders. The children were horrified and fascinated. They watched everything. Once I caught them looking at their parents in utter contempt.

Like them, I had been half enjoying the situation.

This would have been my last interstellar flight. Chance had me riding not as frozen cargo, but as a passenger, aware and entertained.

Flying the ship would have been more fun, of course.

Quickpony had suggested joining our cabins, as we were the obvious unpaired pair. I showed Quickpony videos displayed by the circuitry in my ring. Our lockstep ceremony. Jenna/Jeena just a year old. Sharrol/Milcenta not yet pregnant again; I should have updated while I could. *We are lockstepped, see, here is our ring.* Quickpony admired and dropped the subject.

And that left *what* for entertainment?

Kzinti hijackers!

I'd treated it like a game until *Stealthy-Mating* claimed my family. Bound into my couch by a crash web, I let my hand rest on the release while I considered what weapons I might have at hand.

Lips drawn back, fangs showing, Envoy's speech was turning mushy. "Examine the Covenants, Captain Preiss. They were never altered. We take only hostages. They will be returned unharmed when our needs are satisfied. Compensation will be paid for every cost incurred."

"What crime do you claim against Fly-By-Night?" Quickpony asked.

"His ancestor committed treason against his officers and the Patriarch. Penalties hold against his blood line forever. We may claim his life, but we will not. We value his blood line."

"Has *Fly-By-Night* committed a crime?"

"False identity. Purchase of a Jotok without entitlement. Trivia."

Dumb and happy Mart Graynor wasn't the type to carry weapons aboard a spacecraft. The recorded Covenant of 2505 might be the only weapon I had. I let it play in one ear. The old diplomatic language was murky. . . .

Here it was. *Hostages are to be returned in health if all conditions met, conditions not to be altered . . . costs to be assessed in time of peace at earliest . . .*

Was I supposed to bet *lives* on *this*?

Heidi asked, "Do you eat human meat?"

Packer and the hologram both turned to the girl. Envoy said, "Hostages. I have *said*. The Covenants *say*. Kitten, we consider human meat to be . . . - *whasht-meery* . . . unsafe. Captain Preiss, the modules we want are all addressed to Outbound on Home, yes? We will deliver them. Else we would face all the navies of human space."

Preiss said, "I have no such confidence."

Packer kicked down from the dome. He set his huge hands on the girl's waist and looked into her face. He still hadn't spoken.

Nicolaus screamed and leapt. As he came at the

armored Kzin, Packer reached out and wrapped both
children against his armored chest. They looked up
through the bubble helmet into a Kzin's smile.

Nicolaus bared his teeth.

Envoy said, "Pause, Packer! Captain Preiss, think!
Without gravity generators you must still fall around
Turnpoint Star and into flat space. Hyperdrive will take
you to the edge of Home system. Call for help to tow
you the rest of the way. What other path have we?
We might smash your hyperdrive and hyperwave and
leave you to die here, silenced, but your absence at
Home will set the law seeking us.

"This is the better risk, to violate no law unless we
must. We take hostages. You must not call your authorities until you arrive near Home. We will transport our
prisoner, then deliver your passengers."

Packer's arms were full of children: hampered. Preiss
and Quickpony were on a hair trigger. I was unarmed,
but if they moved, I would.

"Wait," Envoy said. Preiss still hadn't moved. "You
carry stock from Shasht? Sea life?"

"Yes."

"I must speak with my leader. Lightspeed gap is two
minutes each way. Do nothing threatening."

We heard Envoy yowling into his communicator. Then
nothing.

My pocket computer dinged.

Everybody twitched, yeeped or looked around. Heidi
floated to the rim of my booth and listened over my
shoulder.

Sea lions around the Earth's poles live in large
communities built around one alpha male, many females
and their pups, and several beta males that live around
the edges of the herd. When the alpha male is otherwise occupied, an exile may rush in and mate hur-
riedly with a female and escape. Several species of

Earth's mammals have adapted such a breeding strategy, as have life forms on Kzin and even many Kzinti clans. Biologists, particularly reproductive biologists, call them *sneaky-fuckers*.

I said, "Maybe there's a more polite term for the journals. Anyway, good name for a spy ship. Pleasemadam, seek Longest War plus Kzinti plus piracy, run it."

We waited.

When Hans Van Hild couldn't stand the silence any more, he said, "Heidi, Nicolaus, I'm sorry. We should have let you grow up."

"Hans!"

"*Yes*, Hilde, there was all the time in the world. Hilde, there's *never* time. Never a way to know."

Envoy spoke. "Release one of the modules for Outbound Enterprises and two addressed to Neptune's Empire. The passengers will be returned. Neptune's Empire will be recompensed for their stock."

Fish?

Captain Preiss's fingertips danced. Three cargo modules slowly rose out of the rim. I felt utterly helpless.

Packer left the children floating. He pushed Fly-By-Night's balloon toward the airlock.

I said, "Wait."

The armored Kzin turned. I squinted against the glare of his weapon. "We do not permit slavery aboard *Odysseus*," I said. "*Odysseus* belongs to the Human Space Trade Alliance. The Jotok stays."

"Who are you? Where derives your authority?" Envoy demanded.

"Martin Wallace Graynor. No authority, but the law—"

"Fly-By-Night purchased a Jotok and holds him as property. We hold Fly-By-Night as property. Local law crawls before interspecies covenants. The Jotok comes. Are you concerned for the well-being of the Jotok?"

I said, "Yes."

"You shall observe if he is mistreated. Enter a vacuum refuge now."

I caught Quickpony's horror. She spun around to search her screen display of the Covenants for some way to stop this. Packer pulled Fly-By-Night toward the airlock. He wasn't waiting.

Neither did I. I launched myself gently toward the refuge that held the Jotok.

It would not have occurred to me to hug the only available little girl before I disappeared into the Nursery Nebula. I launched, Heidi launched, and she was in my path, arms spread, bawling. I hugged her, let our momentum turn us, whispered something reassuring and let go. She drifted toward a wall, I toward the Jotok's bubble.

She'd put something bulky in my zip pocket.

I crawled through the collar into the Jotok's vacuum refuge and zipped the lips closed.

Packer pushed Fly-By-Night into the airlock, closed it, cycled it. His armored companion on the hull pulled the bubble into space. Packer came back for us and cycled us through.

Two bubbles floated outside *Odysseus*, slowly rotating, slowly diverging. Packer was still in *Odysseus*.

The boat jerked into motion. We watched as it maneuvered above one of the brick-shaped cargo modules attached to *Odysseus*. A pressure-armored Kzin stood below, guiding.

Nobody was coming after us.

The Jotok asked, "Martin, was that sane? What were you thinking?"

I said, "Pleasemadam, seek interspecies diplomacy plus Kzinti plus Longest War. Run it. Paradoxical, I was thinking of a rescue. I tried to bust you loose. You know more about Fly-By-Night than I could ever learn. I need what you can tell me."

"You have no authority to question us," the Jotok said, "unless you hold ARM authority."

I laughed harder than he would have expected. "I'm not an ARM. No authority at all. Do you want Fly-By-Night freed? Do you want your own freedom?"

"We had that! LE Graynor, when Fly-By-Night bought us from the orange underground market on Shasht, he swore to free us. On Sheathclaws chains of lakes run from mountains to sea. We would have bred in their lakes. All of the Jotoki populace of Sheathclaws would be our descendants. We have been robbed of our destiny!"

I asked, "Did Fly-By-Night take more slaves than just you?"

"No."

"Then who did you expect to mate with?"

"We are five! Jotoki grow like your eels, not sapient. Reach first maturity, seek each other, cluster in fives. Brains grow links. Reach second maturity, seek a lake, divide, breed and die, like your salmon. LE Mart, you yourselves are two minds joined by a structure called *corpus callosum*. Join is denser in Kzinti, that species has less redundancy, but still brain is two lobes. We are five lobes, narrow joins. Almost individuals cooperate, *Par-Rad-Doc-Sic-Cal*, *Doc* talks, *Par* walks, *Cal* for fine-scale coordination. Almost five-lobe mind, sometimes lock in indecision. In trauma or in fresh water we may divide again. May join again to cluster differently, different person. You perceive?"

Futz, it was an interesting picture, but I'd never grasp what it was like to *be* Jotok. The point was that Paradoxical was a breeding population.

I asked, "Are you hungry? What do you eat?"

"Privately."

"Didn't Fly-By-Night see you eat?"

"Only once."

I'd put a handmeal in my pocket, but I wouldn't eat in front of Paradoxical after that. "Orange market?"

"An extensive market exists among the Shasht Kzinti. They trade intelligence, electronics, stolen goods and slaves. Shasht the continent is nearly lifeless. They seeded several lakes for our breeding and confinement, but without maintenance they die off. The trade could be stopped. Our lakes must show a different color from orbit. I surmise the law has no interest."

"You once held an interstellar empire—"

"My master tells me so. The slavers don't teach us. Properly speaking, they do not hold slaves at all. They hold fish ponds. When a purchaser wants a Jotok, five swimming forms are allowed to assemble. Our master is the first thing we see."

"Who chose your name?"

"My master. I am free and slave, many and one, land and sea dweller, a paradox."

"He really does think in Interworld, doesn't he? They must teach kzinti as a second language."

A magnetic grapple locked in place, and the first module came free.

My pocket computer *ding*ed. We listened:

Longest War, a political entity never named until after the Second War With Men, has since been claimed by many Kzinti groups. It may appear in connection with piracy, disappearing LEs or disappearing ships, but never an action against planets or a major offensive. Claim has been made, never proved, that Longest War are any Patriarch's servants whom the Patriarch must disclaim. We surmise also that the Longest War names any group who hope for the eye of the Patriarch. Events include 2399 Serpent Swarm, 2410 Kdat—

✧   ✧   ✧

Fly-By-Night had drifted so far that he was hard to find, just a twinkle of lensed light as starfog glow passed behind his vac refuge. Why didn't they retrieve him? Was it really Fly-By-Night they wanted, or something else?

I watched *Stealthy-Mating*'s boat retrieve a second cargo module. They weren't being careful. Two of those boxes held only Fafnir's thousand varieties of fish, but the other . . . was in a quantum state. It held and did not hold Sharrol/Milcenta and Jenna/Jeena, until some observer could open the module.

In all the years I'd flown for Nakamura Lines, I had never seen a vac pack used. Light-years from any world, miles from any ship, with nothing but clear plastic skin between me and the ravenous vacuum . . . it seemed a good time to look it over.

This wasn't the brand we'd carried. It was newer, or else a more expensive model.

Loops of tough ribbon hung everywhere: handholds. Air tank. A tube two liters in volume had popped out. Inner zip, outer zip: an airlock. We could be fed through that, or get rid of wastes . . . a matter I would not raise with Paradoxical just yet.

A light. A sleeve and glove taped against the wall, placed to reach the outer zip. Here was a valve . . . hmm . . . a valve ending in a little cone outside. Inside, a handle to aim it.

To any refugee there might come a moment when a jet is more important than breathing-air.

Not yet.

"Why would you want to rescue my master?" Paradoxical asked.

"They have my wife and daughter and unborn, one chance out of three. Two out of three they're still safe aboard *Odysseus*. Would you bet?"

"No Jotok knows his parent. Might you find another mate and generate more children?"

I didn't answer.

"How do you like your battle plan so far?"

I couldn't hear sarcasm, but I inferred it. I said, "I have a spare vac pack. So does Fly-By-Night. Did you see what he did? He triggered a pack on the wall. Kept his own. And Heidi passed me something."

"What did the girl give you?"

"Might be some kind of toy."

The Jotok said, "*Mee-rowreet* means make slaves and beasts go where can be killed. Not *Envoy*. *Whasht-meery* means infested or diseased, too rotted or parasitical for even a starving predator. Prey that dies too easily, opponent who exposes belly too soon, is suspect *whasht-meery*."

I waited for our spin to hide me from *Stealthy-Mating's* telescopes before I pulled Heidi's gift free.

It was foam plastic, light and bulky. A toy needle gun. If this was real, her parents . . . Wait, now, Heidi was almost forty years old!

They wouldn't think quite like human adults, these children, but their brains were as big as they were going to get. Their parents *might* want them able to protect themselves . . . and if not, she and her brother had spent decades learning how to manipulate their parents.

I couldn't test it.

"Needle gun. Anaesthetic crystals," I told Paradoxical. "They won't get through armor. One wouldn't knock out a Kzin anyway. Better than nothing, though. Where is Fly-By-Night's w'tsai?"

"You saw."

"Paradoxical, we are in too much trouble to be playing children's games."

Paradoxical said nothing.

Stealthy-Mating's boat locked on to the third cargo module.

I said, "That was fun to watch, though. Giving Packer silverware!"

Paradoxical rotated to show me his mouth.

I saw a star of tentacles around a circle of lip enclosing five circles of tiny teeth in a pentagon. Something emerged from one circle of teeth. Paradoxical vomited up a long, narrow, padded mailing bag. I pulled it free, unzipped it, and had a yard of blade and handle.

The blade looked like dark steel. The light caught a minute ripple effect . . . but it was all wrong. To my fingertip's touch the ripple was just a picture. The blade weighed almost nothing. The weight was all in the handle.

In the end of the hilt was a small black enamel bat. Bats exist only on Earth and in the zoo on Jinx, but that ancient *Batman* symbol has gone to every human world. *Fly by night.*

Futz, I had to try it on *something*.

My lockstep ring had a silver case. That's a soft metal, but the blade only scratched it. I tested my thumb on the edge, gingerly. Blunt.

Customs change. A weapon can be purely ceremonial . . . but why make the handle so heavy? Why was Paradoxical watching me?

Because it was a puzzle.

Push the enamel bat. Nothing.

Wiggle the blade. Push it in, risk my fingers, feel it give. A Kzin could push *harder*. Nothing? Pull *out*, and my fingertips felt a hum. The look of the blade didn't change. Carefully now, don't touch the edge—

It sliced neatly through my lockstep ring, with a moment's white sputter as circuitry burned out. The cut edges of the classic silver band shone like little mirrors. There should have been *some* resistance.

A variable-knife is violently illegal: hair-fine wire in a magnetic field, all edge and no blade, thin enough

to slice through walls and machinery. Often enough
it hurts the wielder. When it's off it's all handle, and
the handle is heavy: it holds the coiled wire and the
mag generator.

This toy was similar, but with a blade of fixed length,
harder to hide. More sporting. A groove around the edge
housed the wire until magnets raised it for action.

The onyx bat was recessed now. I pushed and it
popped out. The vibration stopped.

We had a weapon.

What was keeping Packer? They had the telepath,
they had hostages, they had two modules of Fafnir
seafood. What was left to do in there? Get on with
it. I had a weapon!

"Wait before you use it. I know my master," the Jotok
said. "He will take command of the boat. The larger
ship is weaponless against it."

"Paradoxical, he'd be fighting at least three warriors
trained in free fall. Don't forget the pilots. Four if we
get as far as the ship."

"*Whasht-meery* may currently be on autopilot or
remote. Possession of armor does not imply training.
Fly-By-Night was a champion wrestler before he was
injured. We fear you're right. But we must try!"

"Wrestler?"

"He tells me they fight with capped claws on
Sheathclaws."

Somehow I was not reassured.

Packer emerged.

He and his companion jetted toward Fly-By-Night's
bubble. They pulled Fly-By-Night toward the boat.
Clamshell doors opened around the snout of the
solenoid weapon. The three disappeared inside.

I safed and wrapped the w'tsai and gave it to the
Jotok. He swallowed it, and the needler after it. He

must have a straight gut . . . five straight guts, I thought, like fish or worms all merged at the head.

The two armored Kzinti came for us. They towed us toward the boat.

The boat was a thick lens, like *Odysseus* but smaller. The modules were anchored against one side. The other side was two transparent clamshell doors with the hollow solenoid sticking out between them.

The doors closed over us.

The interior had been arrayed around the solenoid weapon. There were lockers. Hatch in the floor, a smaller airlock. A kitchen wall big enough for a cruise ship, with a gaping intake hopper. A big box, detachable, with a door in it. I took that for a shower/washroom. I didn't see a hologram stage or a mass pointer.

Mechanisms fed into the base of the main weapon. A feed for projectiles? The thing didn't just burn out electronics, it was a linear accelerator too, a cannon.

Fly-By-Night's vacuum refuge had been wedged between the cannon and the wall. He watched us.

The doors came down and now our balloon was wedged next to his. Gravity came on. *Stealthy-Mating's* crew anchored us with a spray of glue, while a third Kzin watched from the horseshoe of a workstation. The two took their places beside him.

Four chairs; three Kzinti all in pressure suit armor. There was no separate cabin because they might have to work the cannon. It could have been worse.

They talked for a bit, mobile mouths snarling at each other inside fishbowl helmets. They fiddled with the controls. A sound of tigers fighting blasted from Paradoxical's backpack vest. My translator murmured, "So, Telepath! Welcome back to the Patriarch's service."

Two or three seconds of silence followed. In that moment *Odysseus* abruptly shrank to a toy and was gone. Disturbing eddies played through our bodies. The boat must be making twenty or thirty gravities, but it had good shielding. This was a warcraft.

Their prisoner decided to answer. "You honor me. You may call me LE Fly-By-Night."

"Honored you should be, Telepath, but your credit as a Legal Entity is forged, a telepath has no name, and Fly-By-Night is only a description, and in Interworld, too! Still you will command a harem before we do. We should envy you." That voice was Envoy's.

"Call me Fly-By-Night if I am expected to answer. Does the Patriarch still make addicts of any who show the talent?"

"You have hibernated for three centuries? We use advanced medical techniques in this age. Chemical mimic of sthondat lymph, six syllable name, more powerful, few side effects, diet additives to minimize those."

A second Kzin voice said, "You need not taste the drug yourself, Telepath, by my alpha officer's word."

"Only my poor kits, then. But how well do Kzinti keep each other's promises? I know that *Odysseus* was disabled despite all reassurance."

What? Fly-By-Night had *no way* to know that. *I* was only guessing, and his vac refuge had floated further from *Odysseus* than our own.

But Envoy said, "All follows the Covenants sworn with men at Shasht. That was my assurance, and it is good."

"Do those allow you to maroon a Legal Entity ship in deep space?"

"Summon them. Read them."

"My servant carries my computer and disk library."

The pilot tapped; we heard a *click*, then silence.

Paradoxical turned off his talker. "We can use this to speak to my master, but they may listen. What can you say that those oversized intestinal parasites may hear too?"

"Right now, nothing. Thrusters were yours first, weren't they? Called the *gravity planer*?"

"Jotoki created gravity planers, yes. Kzinti enslaved us and stole the design. Your folk stole it from Kzinti invaders."

"Is there anything you know about thrusters that they don't? Something that might help?"

"No. Idiot. What we learned of gravity motors, we learned from Kzinti!"

"Futz—"

"I had thought," Paradoxical said carefully, "that they would not keep their control room in vacuum."

"Their hostages are all frozen. Can't fight. Can't escape. Maybe they like that? Anything we try now would leave us dying in vacuum. How long can a Jotok stand vacuum?"

"A few seconds, then death."

"Humans can take a few minutes." Humans had, and survived. It was rare. "I might go blind first. Do you mind if I think out loud for a bit?"

"Do you talk to yourself to move messages across that narrow structure in your brain, the *corpus callosum*?"

"I have no idea." So I talked across my corpus callosum. "This is bad, but it could be worse. We might have been in a separate cargo hold, *still* in vacuum and locked out of a flight cabin."

"Rejoice."

"I thought I wouldn't have to worry about *Odysseus*. The ship's on a free fall course around Turnpoint Star, through the Gap and into free space. They still had hyperdrive and hyperwave and the attitude jets, last I saw. Attitude jets are just fusion reaction motors. That won't *take* them anywhere. Hyperdrive only works in flat space, so it won't get them *into* a solar system. They could still cross to Home system, call for help and get a tow. Two weeks?"

"Envoy said all of that to Captain Preiss. Wait—but—stop—didn't Envoy confess otherwise?"

"I heard. Futz." Fly-By-Night had done that very cleverly. But Envoy hadn't confessed; he had only insisted that he had not violated the Covenants.

"We'd better assume Packer shot up the control board. That would leave *Odysseus* as an inert box of hostages. Leave them falling. Retrieve them later."

Paradoxical said nothing.

"Next problem. Fly-By-Night can't get out of his refuge."

"Surely—"

"No, look, he can't *slash* his way out. He's got only his claws. He can *zip* it open. All the air spews out, and now he can try to get through the opening. He's too big. He'd die in vacuum while he was trying to wiggle free with those three laughing at him."

"Yes. Less than flexible, human and Kzinti. Are you small enough to get through the collar?"

"Yes." I was pretty sure. "Now, we can't warn Fly-By-Night. Any fighting, I'll have to start it. You're dead if I slash the refuge open, so I don't. I unzip it. Air pressure blows me out, *poof.* You zip it behind me *quick* so the refuge re-inflates. I'm in vacuum. I slash Fly-By-Night's refuge wide open and hand him the w'tsai. We're *both* fighting in vacuum against three Kzinti in pressure armor. How does it sound?"

"Beyond madness."

"There's no point anyway. If we could take the boat, we still couldn't break lightspeed, because the hyperdrive motor is on the ship. We'd die of old age here in the Nursery Nebula."

"You don't have a plan?"

I was still feeling it out. "The only way out has us waiting for these bandits to berth the boat to *Stealthy-Mating*. Maybe it's a good thing Fly-By-Night doesn't have his w'tsai. Kzinti self-control is . . . there's a word—"

"Oxymoron. But my master integrates selves well."

"They'll have to move the cargo modules inside the ship. Can't leave them where they are, they're blocking the magnets, the docking points. Where does that leave us? Whatever we do, we want the ship *and* the boat. After they birth the boat, likely enough they'll *still* leave the cabin in vacuum and us in these bubbles."

"My kind can survive six days without food. Two without water."

Two of the Kzinti crew might have been asleep. The third wasn't doing much.

One presently stirred—Envoy, by his suit markings—got up and disappeared into the big box with a door in it. Fifteen minutes later he was back.

Wouldn't a shower or a toilet *have* to be under pressure?

I watched my alien companions and my alien enemies. I watched the magnificent pageant of stars being born. I thought and I read.

Read everything.

Covenants of 2505. Commentary, then and recent. Kzinti sociology. Revisions: what constitutes torture . . . loss of limbs and organs . . . sensory deprivation. Violations. The right to a speedy trial, to speedy execution, not to be evaded. What is a Legal Entity. . . .

Male Kzinti were LEs. A computer program was not. Heidi and Nicolaus were not, poor kids, but Kzin kittens weren't either; it was a matter of maturity as an evolved being. Jotoki and Kdat were LEs unless legitimately enslaved. Entities with forged identities were not. Ice Class passengers were LEs. Good! Was there a rule against lying to hostages? Of course not, but I looked.

Paradoxical produced a computer from his backpack and went to work. I didn't ask what he might be learning.

I did *not* see Fly-By-Night tearing at his prison. When I caught his eye, I clawed at my own bubble. Our captors might be reassured if they saw some sign of hysterics, of despair.

He didn't take the hint.

Maybe I had him all wrong.

A telepath born among the Kzinti will be found as a kzitten, conscripted, and addicted to chemicals to bring out his ability. Telepaths detect spies and traitors; they assist in jurisprudence; they gradually go crazy. Alien minds drive them crazy much faster.

If a telepath feels an opponents' pain, he can't easily fight for mates. For generations the Patriarchy discouraged their telepaths from breeding. Then, battling an alien enemy during the Man-Kzin Wars, they burned them out.

Probably Envoy had spoken truth: what the Kzinti wanted from Fly-By-Night was more telepaths.

They'd get the location of Sheathclaws out of him. After they had what they wanted, they'd give him a harem. They'd imprison him in luxury. Envoy had said they wouldn't force the drug on him; it might be true.

A Kzin might settle for that.

I could come blasting out of my plastic bottle, screaming my air away, w'tsai swinging . . . cut him loose, and find myself fighting alone while he blew up another bubble for himself.

Fly-By-Night floated quite still, very relaxed, ears folded. He might have been asleep. He might have been watching his three captors guide the boat toward *Stealthy-Mating.*

I watched their ears. Ears must make it hard for a Kzin to lie. Lying to a hologram might be easier . . . and they wouldn't have called him *Envoy* for nothing.

Flick-flick of ears, bass meeping, a touch on the controls. We were flying through a lethal intensity of gamma rays.

The Jotok's armtips rippled over his keyboard. His computer was a narrow strip of something stiff; he'd glued or velcroed it to the bubble wall. The keyboard and holoscreen were projections. I knew the make— "Paradoxical? Isn't that a Gates Quintillian?"

"Yes. Human-built computers are superior to Patriarchy makes."

"Oh, that explains the corks! Fly-By-Night's fingers are too big for the keyboard, so he puts corks on his nails!"

The Jotok said, "You are Beowulf Shaeffer."

I spasmed like an electrocuted frog, then turned to gawk at him. "How can you possibly . . . ?"

How can you possibly think that a seven foot tall albino has lost fourteen inches of height and got himself curly black hair and a tan?

Hair dye and tannin secretion pills, and futz that, we had *real* trouble. I asked, "Have you spent three hours researching *me?*"

"You are the only ally at hand. I need to understand you better. You are wanted by the ARM for conspiracy abduction, four counts."

"Four?"

"Sharrol Janss, Carlos Wu, and two children. Feather Filip is your suspect co-conspirator. ARM interest seems to lie in the lost genes of Carlos Wu, but Sharrol Janss is alleged to be a flat phobe, hence would never have left Earth willingly."

"We all ran away together."

"My interest lies in your abilities, not your crimes. You were a civilian spacecraft pilot. Were you trained for agility in free fall?"

"Yes. Any emergency in a spacecraft, gravity is the first thing that goes."

"You're agile if you've escaped the ARM thus far. What has your reading gained you?"

"We have to live. We have to *win*."

"These would be good ideas—"

"No, you don't get it." The Jotok *had* to understand. "The Covenants of 2505 permit taking of hostages. They only put restrictions on their treatment. I've played those futzy documents three times through. *Odysseus* is hostages-in-a-box, live and frozen. They won't starve. Envoy can take Fly-By-Night anywhere he likes, however long it takes, then come back and release *Odysseus*. It's all in the Covenants."

"If anything goes wrong," Paradoxical said, "they would never come."

"No, it's worse than that! If everything goes *right* for them, there's *no good reason* to go back unless it's to fill the food lockers! The Covenants only apply when you're caught. My family is one hundred percent dead if we can't change that."

"Envoy's word may be good. No! Bad gamble. We should study the pot odds. Beowulf, have you evolved a plan?"

"I don't know enough."

The three crew were awake now, watching us as we watched them, though mostly they watched Fly-By-Night.

Paradoxical's talker burst to life. My translator said, "Tell us of the fight that injured you."

Fly-By-Night was slow to answer. "Sheathclaws folk are fond of hang gliding. We make much bigger hang gliders for Kzinti, and not so many of us fly. I was near grown, seeking a name. My intent was to fly from Blood Park to Touchdown, three hundred klicks along rocky shore and then inland, at night. Land in Offcentral Park. Startle humans into fits."

Packer snarled, "Startling humans is no fit way to earn a name!" and the unnamed Kzin asked, "Wouldn't the thermals be different at night?"

Fly-By-Night said, "Very different."

"Your second naming quest brought you here," Envoy stated.

"Yes. I hoped that a scarred Kzin might pass among other Kzinti. Challenge would be less likely. Any lapse in knowledge might be due to head injury. I might pass more easily on a world part Kzin and part human, like Shasht-Fafnir."

"You dance lightly over an important matter. Who lifted you from your world?"

"Where would be my honor if I told you that?"

"Smugglers? Bandits? What species? You will give us that too, Nameless." We heard the click: communication severed.

One of the Kzinti stood up. Another slashed the vacuum, a mere wrist gesture, but the first sat down again. The stars wheeled . . . and something that was not a star came into view, brilliant in pure laser colors: *Stealthy-Mating*'s riding lights.

I said, "We're about to dock. If anything happens, you keep the needle sprayer, I want the blade. Closing the zipper turns on the air, so don't lose *that*."

"No fear," said Paradoxical.

Gravity went away. We floated. The ships danced about each other. I would have docked less recklessly. I'm not a Kzin.

"*They* know too much about *us*," I said.

Paradoxical asked, "In what context?"

"They knew our manifest. They knew our position—"

"Finding another ship in interstellar space is not a thing they could plan, Beowulf."

"LE Graynor to you. Look at it this way," I said. "The only way to get here, falling through the Tao Gap in Einstein space, is to be going from Fafnir to Home. *Stealthy-Mating* got our route somehow. They started later with a faster ship. They might catch us approaching Home during deceleration . . . track our graviton wake . . . or snatch you and Fly-By-Night after you got through Customs. They *could not possibly* have expected to find *Odysseus* here. Catching us here was a fluke, an opportunity. They grabbed it."

"As you say."

"I *like* it."

Paradoxical stared. "Do you? Why?"

"Clients, overlords, allies, any kind of support would have to be told that *Stealthy-Mating* is en route to Home. Any rendezvous with *Stealthy-Mating* is *at Home*. When could they change that? They're still headed for Home!"

"Very speculative."

"I know."

Stealthy-Mating's cargo bay was bigger than the boat's, under doors that opened like wings.

The boat released the cargo modules. Two Kzinti went out and began moving them. Envoy stayed behind. He watched the action in space, ignoring us.

"Not yet," Paradoxical said. I nodded. Fly-By-Night floated half curled up. He seemed to be asleep, but his ears kept flicking open like little fans.

I ate my handmeal. Paradoxical averted its eyes.

Packer and the nameless third crewperson set the modules moving one by one, and juggled them as they approached *Stealthy-Mating*. Waldo arms reached up to pull them into the bay and lock them. It seemed to take forever, but I'd have moved those masses one at a time. They were in a hurry. Rounding a point mass would scatter this loose stuff all across the sky.

Turnpoint Star must be near.

The cargo doors closed. *Stealthy-Mating* rotated, and the boat was pulled down against the hull. Now we were all one mass.

The hatch in the floor opened. Three Kzinti came through in pressure suits to join Envoy. The newcomer's chest and back showed a Kzinti snarl done in gaudy orange dots-and-commas. He spared a glance for me and Paradoxical, then turned to Fly-By-Night.

My translator said, "I am Meebrlee-Ritt."

"Futz!" Fly-By-Night exclaimed in Interworld.

"Your concern is noted. Yes, I am of the Patriarch's line. Your First Sire was *Gutting Claw*'s Telepath, who betrayed the Patriarch Rrowrreet-Ritt and showed prey how to destroy his own ship!"

"And he never even went back for the ears. Then again, they were inside a hot plasma," Fly-By-Night said.

To Envoy Meebrlee-Ritt said, "This one was to be tamed."

Envoy cringed, ears flat. Even I could hear the change in his voice, the whine. "Dominant One, this fool crippled himself for a failed joke, and that joke was his name quest! A lesser male he must be, never mated. His arrogance is bluff or insanity, or else life among humans has made him quite alien! But let Tech give us air pressure, release the telepath, and the stench of your rage will cow him soon enough!"

"Let us expend less effort than that." Meebrlee-Ritt turned back to Fly-By-Night. "Telepath, your life may be taken by any who happen upon you."

"Did you need my consent for this?"

"No!"

"Or my First Sire's confession? *That* may be summoned by any Sheathclaws' school program. Then what shall we discuss? Tell us how you gained your name."

"I was born to it, of course. Let us discuss your future."

"I have a future?"

"Your blood line may be forgiven. You may keep your slaves, such as they are, and a harem of my choosing—"

"*Yours?* Dominant One, forgive my interruption, please continue."

Even if he was familiar with human sarcasm, it wasn't likely Meebrlee-Ritt had been getting it from Kzinti! I'd read that Kzinti telepaths were flighty, not terribly bright. Meebrlee-Ritt spoke more slowly. "Yes, *my* choosing! You may live your life in honor and luxury, or you may die shredded by my hands."

"Meebrlee-Ritt, you would not expect me to leap into so difficult a decision. Will you bargain for the lives of your hostages?"

"Submissive and unarmed Humans." Meebrlee-Ritt sneezed his contempt. "But what would you bargain *with?* Your world?"

"Only my genes. Consider," said Fly-By-Night. In the Heroes' Tongue his speech was a long snarl, but the translation sounded placid enough. "He who is obeyed, who fights best, who *mates* is the alpha, the dominant one. You command that I mate? How will you persuade me that I am dominant? Submit to this one easy demand. Rescue my erstwhile hosts. Release them at Home."

"Why would I want you in rut? There are no females aboard *Sraff-zisht*. Packer, Envoy, you remain. Leave the gravity off. Tech, with me. Turnpoint Star is near."

Two Kzinti went through the hatch. Two took their

seats. Their hands were idle. Now the boat rode *Stealthy-Mating* like a parasite.

I asked, "Can you see Turnpoint Star?"

"At point six kilometers across? You flatter me. I surmise it may be centered in that curdle," said Paradoxical.

Curdle? The tight little knot of glowing gas? I watched, watched . . . A red point blew up into a blue-white sun and I fell into it. The stars wheeled. The balloons that housed us rippled as if batted by invisible children. My body rippled too.

I'd been through this once, but much worse. I clutched the ribbon handholds in a death grip. I howled.

It only lasted seconds, but the terror remained. One of the Kzinti pointed at me and both laughed with their teeth showing.

Packer made his way to the shower/toilet. The other, Envoy, stayed at the board to look for tidal damage.

Fly-By-Night took handholds, subtly braced, ears spread wide. His eye caught mine. I said, "Paradoxical, *now.*"

Paradoxical splayed itself like a starfish across the wall of the refuge, just next to the opening. It disgorged the handle of the w'tsai.

I pulled the wrapped blade from its gullet and stripped off the casing. Clutched the blade against me, exhaled hard, opened the zipper all in one sweep, smooth as silk. Pressure popped me out into the cabin, straight toward Envoy's back, screaming to empty my lungs before they exploded.

Push the blade in, pull out, feel the vibration.

I had thought to recoil off a wall and slice Fly-By-Night free. That wasn't going to work. The Kzin diplomat saw my shadow and spun around. I slashed, aiming to behead him, and shifted the blade to catch the cat-quick sweep of his arm.

He swept his arm through the blade and whacked me under the jaw.

That was a powerful blow. I spun dizzily away. His arm spun too, cut along a diagonal plane, spraying blood. Attached, it would have ripped my head off.

I caught myself against a wall and leapt.

The seat web still held Envoy. His right arm and sleeve sprayed blood and air. Envoy smashed left-handed at the controls, then hit the seat web and leapt out of my path. I got his foot! The knife was hellishly sharp. My ears were roaring, my sight was going, but vacuum tore at him too as his arm and ankle jetted blood and air. His balance was all off as he recoiled from the dome and came at me. He kicked. My angle was wrong and he grazed me.

Spinning, spinning, I starfished out so that the wall caught my momentum and killed my spin. I tried to find him.

The roar continued. My sight was foggy . . . no. The *cabin* was thick with fog. Fly-By-Night clawed his refuge wall, which had gone slack. We had air!

I *still* didn't have time to free Fly-By-Night because— *there* he was! Envoy was back at the controls. I was braced to leap when a white glare blazed from his hand.

He had the gun.

I changed my jump. It took me behind the cannon. Two projectiles punched into the wall behind me. I swiped the w'tsai in a wide slash across Fly-By-Night's vacuum refuge, and continued falling toward the shower/toilet. Packer couldn't ignore Ragnarok forever.

The door opened in my face and I chopped vertically. Packer was naked. His left hand was on the doorlock so I changed the cut, right to catch his free hand, his claws and the iron w'tsai he'd been holding. He whacked me hard but the blow was blunt. I spun once and crashed into Envoy and slashed.

Glimpsed Paradoxical behind him, braced myself and slashed. Paradoxical was firing anaesthetic needles. The Kzin wasn't fighting back. I didn't see the implication so I kept slashing.

"Mart! LE Mart! *Beowulf!*"

I screamed, *"What?"* Disturbing me now could . . . what? Before me was a drifting cloud of blood and butchered meat. Paradoxical had stopped firing needles into it. Behind me, Fly-By-Night was on Packer's back, gnawing Packer's ear and fending off the hand that still had claws. Packer beat him with the blunted hand. They both looked trapped. Packer couldn't reach Fly-By-Night, but Fly-By-Night dared not let go.

I approached with care. Packer's arms were busy so he kicked to disembowel me. I chopped off what I could reach. Kick/slash, kick/slash. When he slowed down I killed him.

The air was thick with blood globules and red fog. We were *breathing* that futz. I got a cloth across my face. Fly-By-Night was snorting and sneezing. Paradoxical had placed meteor patches where Envoy had fired at me, but now he floated limp, maybe dying. I put him into the refuge and got him to zip it.

Fly-By-Night went to the controls. Minutes later we had gravity. All the scarlet goo settled to the floor and we could breathe.

I had gone berserk. Never happened before. My mind was slow coming back. Why was there air?

Air. Think now: I slashed Envoy's suit open. He pressurized the cabin to save his life. Paradoxical must have come out then. The Jotok's needles knocked Envoy out despite pressure armor . . . why?

Because Paradoxical was putting needles into flesh wherever I'd slashed away the Kzin's armor. And of course I hadn't got around to releasing Fly-By-Night until late—

I safed the blade. "Fly-By-Night? I believe this is yours."

He took it gingerly. "No witness would have guessed *that*," he said, and handed it back. "Clean it in the waterfall."

Kzinti custom: *never* borrow a w'tsai. If you do, return it clean. Waterfall?

He meant the big box. The word was a joke. I found a big blanket made of sponge, a tube attached. When I wrapped it around the w'tsai, it left the blade clean. I tried it on myself. The blanket flooded me with soapy water, then clean water, then sucked me dry. Weird sensation, but I came out clean.

The toilet looked like an oval box of sand with foot- and handholds around it, though the sand stayed put. *Later.*

A pressure suit was splayed like a pelt against the wall for easy access.

There was a status display. I couldn't read the glowing dots-and-commas, but the display must have told Packer there was air outside, and he'd come charging out—

I was starting to shake.

I emerged from the waterfall box into a howling gale. The blood was all gone. I couldn't even smell it. Fly-By-Night and Paradoxical were at the kitchen wall feeding butchered meat into the hopper.

"This kind of thing must be normal on Patriarchy spacecraft," Fly-By-Night said cheerfully. "Holes in walls and machinery, blood and corpses everywhere, no problem. This hopper would hold a Great Dane . . . a big dog, Mart. The cleanup subsystem is running smooth as a human's arse." He saw my shivering. "You have killed. You should feed. Must your meat be cooked? I don't know that we have a heat source."

"Don't worry about it."

"I must. I'm *hungry!*" Fly-By-Night smiled widely. "You wouldn't like me *hungry*, would you?"

"Futz, no!" A Sheathclaws local joke? I tried to laugh. Shivering.

Paradoxical was crawling over one of the control panels. "This kitchen was mounted separately. It is of Shashter manufacture, perhaps connected to the orange underground. It will feed slaves." It tapped at a surface, and foamy green stuff spilled into a plastic bag. Pond scum? It tapped again and the wall generated a joint of bloody meat. Again: it hummed and disgorged a layered brick.

A handmeal. While Paradoxical sucked at his bag of pond scum and Fly-By-Night devoured hot raw meat, I ate *three* handmeal bricks. They never tasted that good again.

Fly-By-Night had kept Packer's ears, one intact and one chewed to a nub, and Envoy's, both intact. These last he offered to me. "Your kill. Mart, I can dispose of—"

I took them. *My* kill.

We had taken the boat. Now what?

Fly-By-Night said, "The hard part will be persuading Meebrlee-Ritt that all is well here." His voice changed. *"Dominant One, all runs as planned but for the Telepath's behavior. Cowed by fear, he has soiled his refuge. Shall we clean him? It might be a trick—"*

Funny stuff. I was still shivering. "That's *very* good, *I* can't tell the difference, but Meebrlee-Ritt or Tech might."

"Guide me."

"I can't find the hologram stage."

Fly-By-Night touched something. This whole side of the main weapon became a window, floor to dome, a gaudy panorama across orange veldt into a city of massive towers. We'd been prisoned on the other side of it.

I said, "Tanj! He'll see every hair follicle. All right, I'm still thrashing around here. We've got Packer's pressure suit. The orders were to leave the, ah, prisoners in vacuum and falling. Try this—

"Whenever Meebrlee-Ritt calls, Packer is in the waterfall room." We hadn't heard enough of Packer's speech to imitate Packer. "LE Fly-By-Night, you're Envoy. You're in the pressure suit, we're in the vac refuges. We'll have to change the markings on the suit. I'd say Envoy's move is to wait patiently for his Alpha Officer to call." I didn't like the taste of this. "He could catch us by surprise."

"I should find an excuse to call *him*."

"Anything goes wrong, you give us air *instantly*. Paradoxical, have you found an emergency air switch?"

"Here, then here."

"Stet. Envoy, what's wrong with your voice?"

"Nothing," said Fly-By-Night.

"Well, there had better be."

"Stet," the Kzin said. "And we don't really want vacuum, do we? Let's try this instead. I'm calling because we're *not* in vacuum, and my voice—"

And his tale was better than mine, so we worked on that.

We spent some time looking those controls over, trying a few things. We found air pressure, air mix, emergency pressure, cabin gravity, thrust. Weapons would be harder to test. There were controls you could hit by accident without killing anyone, and that was done with virtual control panels. Weapons and defenses were hardwired buttons and switches, a few of them under locked cages, all stiff enough but big enough that I could turn them on or off by jabbing with the heel of my hand. Paradoxical couldn't move those at all.

The hologram wall was the telescope screen too. Paradoxical got us a magnificent view back into the Nursery Nebula, all curdles and whorls of colored light. It found *Odysseus* a light-hour behind us, under spin and falling free with no sign of motive power, only a chain of corridor lights and the brighter glow of the lobby. That didn't tell us if they still had hyperdrive. They couldn't use it yet.

Ahead was nothing but distant stars. We had to be approaching flat space, where *Stealthy-Mating* could jump to hyperdrive.

Fly-By-Night was wearing Envoy's pressure suit. The markings were right. He would keep the right sleeve hidden. We had cut off part of the helmet, raggedly, to obscure his features. Now Fly-By-Night tapped at the kitchen wall. It disgorged a soft, squishy, dark red organ that might have been a misshapen human liver. He smeared blood over his face and chest, then into the exposed ear.

My shivering became a violent shudder. Fly-By-Night looked at me in consternation. "LE Mart? What's wrong?"

"Too much killing."

"*Two* enemies is too much? Get out of camera view, then. Are we ready?"

"Go."

Meebrlee-Ritt snarled, "Envoy, this had best be of great interest. We prepare for hyperdrive."

"Dominant One, the timing was not of my choosing," Fly-By-Night bellowed into the oversized face. "The human attacked while Packer was visiting the waterfall. I have killed the telepath's slave—"

"The Jotok is dead?"

Fly-By-Night cringed. "No, Dominant One, no! Only the man. The Jotok lives. Telepath lives."

"The man is nothing. Telepath did not purchase the man! Is Packer functional, and are you?"

"Packer is well. I have nosebleeds, lost lung function, lost hearing. The man had a projectile weapon, a toy, but he damaged my helmet. I managed to put the cabin under pressure. Packer keeps watch on Telepath. Shall I return the cabin to vacuum? One of us would have to remain in the waterfall."

"Set Packer at the controls. What can he ruin while there is nothing to fly? Maintain free fall. You and Packer trained for free fall, our prisoner did not. You, Envoy, talk to Telepath. Learn what he desires, what he fears."

Cringe. "Dominant One, I shall."

Again we faced an electromagnetic cannon. I said, "Good. Really good."

Space around me winked like an eye. I caught it happening and looked at the floor. Fly-By-Night looked up, and blinked at the distortion. "Mart, I don't think . . . Mart? I'm blind."

Paradoxical was in a knot, his arms covering all of his eyes. I said, "Maybe you'd better take Paradoxical into the waterfall and stay there."

"Lost! Confused! Blind! How do you survive this?" the Jotok demanded. "How does any LE?"

"They'll close off the windows on *Stealthy-Mating*. I don't see how to do that in here. I guess they leave the boat empty if they can. Fly-By-Night, lower your head. Look at the floor. See the floor? Hold that pose."

"Stet."

I got under Paradoxical and he wrapped himself around me, sixty pounds of dry-skinned octopus. I eased him onto Fly-By-Night's shoulders until he clung. "Gravity's on, right? Just crawl on around to the waterfall. Don't look up."

In hyperdrive something unmeasurable happens to electromagnetic phenomena, or else to organs that perceive them: eyes, optic nerves, brains. A view of hyperspace is like being born sightless. The Blind Spot, we call it.

In the waterfall room we straightened up and stretched. Fly-By-Night said, "None of us can fly—"

"No. We're passengers. Stowaways. Relax and let them do the flying."

Paradoxical asked, "How can any mind guide a ship through this?"

I said, "There are species that can't tolerate it. Jotoki can't. Maybe puppeteers can't; most of them never leave their home system. Humans can use a mass pointer, a psionics device to find our way through hyperspace, as long as we don't look into the Blind Spot directly. But that's . . . well, part of a psionics device is the operator's mind. Computers don't see anything. Kzinti don't either. There are just a few freaky Kzinti who can steer through the Blind Spot directly."

"It is the Patriarch's blood line," Paradoxical said. "After the first War with Men, when Kzinti acquired hyperdrive, they learned that most cannot astrogate through hyperspace. Some few can. The Patriarch paid with names and worlds to add their sisters and daughters to his harem. Today the -Ritts can fly hyperspace."

Fly-By-Night said, "Really?"

"It happened long after your folk were cut off. LE Graynor, I did research on more than just you. Of course you see the implications? Meebrlee-Ritt must fly *Stealthy-Mating*. He will be under some strain, possibly at the edge of his sanity. Tech must see him in that embarrassing state. Envoy and Packer need not, and no prisoner should."

"He won't call?" I made it a question.

"He would not expect answer. Packer and Envoy would be hiding in the Waterfall," Paradoxical said.

That satisfied us. We were tired.

For three days we lived in the waterfall room.

One Kzin would have crowded the waterfall. With a man and a Jotok it was just that much more crowded. The smell of an angry Kzin made me jumpy. I couldn't sleep that way, so a high wind was kept blowing at all times.

We used the sandpatch in full view of each other. There were ribald comments. The Jotok was very neat. Fly-By-Night covered his dung using gloved feet and expected me to do the same, but it wasn't needed. The magnetized "sand" churned and swallowed it to the recycler.

Somebody had to come out for food. It developed that nobody could do that but me.

Our talk ranged widely.

Fly-By-Night never told us how he had reached Fafnir, nor even how he had passed through Customs. He did tell us something about the two who had come with him on their name quests. "I left Nazi Killer still collecting computer games and I set out to buy a Jotok—"

"What kind of name is 'Nazi Killer'?"

"It's an illicit game. Our First Sires' children found it among exercise programs in *Angel's Pencil*. Nazi Killer is very good at it. On Shasht he bought improved games and modern computers and waldo gloves for Kzinti hands, thinking these would earn his name."

"Go on."

"Maybe he's already home. Maybe the Longest War caught him. He would not have survived that. As for me, I wasted time searching out medical techniques to heal my broken bones. Such practice has only evolved for Humans! Kzinti still keep their scars. Customs differ.

"But Grass Burner got what *he* wanted. Kittens!"

"Kittens?"

"Yes, six unrelated, a breeding set. On Sheathclaws there are only photos and holos of cats, and a library of tales of fantasy cats, and children who offer a Kzin kit a ball of yarn just because it makes their parents angry, nobody remembers why. Cats will get Grass Burner his name. But we remember Jotoks too. Paradoxical, if two species are smarter than one, three should be smarter yet. You will earn my name, if we can reach Sheathclaws."

I snapped out of a nightmare calling, "What was its name? *Stealthy-Mating?*"

"We were asleep," Paradoxical complained. "We love sleeping in free fall. Back in the lake. But we wake and are still a self."

"Sorry." I almost remembered the dream. A lake of boiling blood, Kzinti patrolling the shores, wonderfully desirable human women in the shadows beyond. I was trying to swim. The pain was stunning, but I was afraid to come out.

Broken blood vessels were everywhere on my body. It hurt enough to ruin my sleep.

It was our fourth morning in hyperdrive.

"Sraff-zisht," said Paradoxical.

"Pleasemadam, seek interstellar spacecraft local to Fafnir, Kzinti crew, Heroes' Tongue name *Sraff-zisht.* Run it."

Fly-By-Night woke. He said, "Make a meat run, Mart."

When I went out for food, we detached the shower blanket so I could use it as a shield. Meebrlee-Ritt had ordered us to keep the boat in free fall. No way could we be *really* sure he wouldn't call. I had to use handholds. I'd made a net for the food.

My computer dinged while we were eating. We listened:

Sraff-zisht was known to the Shasht markets, and to Wunderland too. The ship carried red meat to Fafnir and lifted seafood. At Wunderland, the reverse. Crew turnover was high. They usually stayed awhile. This trip they'd lifted light and early.

"*Sraff-zisht* is not armed," I said. I'd hoped it was true, but now I knew it. "Wunderland customs is careful. If they never found weapons or mounts for weapons, they're not there. We have the only gun!"

"*Yes!*" Fly-By-Night's fully extended claws could stop a man's heart without touching him.

"I've been thinking," I said. "There *has* to be a way to close that window strip. A Kzinti crew couldn't hide out in here! They'd tear each other to pieces!"

"I knew that. It's too small," Fly-By-Night said. "I just didn't want to go out there. Must we?"

We three crawled out with the shower blanket over us, Paradoxical riding the Kzin's shoulders. We stayed under the blanket while we worked the controls. I felt like a child working my flatscreen under the covers after being sent to bed.

There was a physical switch under a little cage with a code lock. None of us had the code. The switch wasn't a self-destruct. We *knew* where *that* was. When we ran out of options I sliced the cage away with the w'tsai, and flipped the switch.

From under the blanket we saw the shadows changing. I peeked out. Lost my vision, lost even my

memory of vision . . . saw the edge of a shield crawling across the last edge of window.

If Meebrlee-Ritt had called earlier, he would have seen
us flying hyperspace with windows open. Some mistakes you don't pay for.

"I think you'd better spend a lot of time in disguise
and out here," I told Fly-By-Night. I saw his look: better
not push that. "The next few days should be safe, but
we should practice getting a disguise *on* you. Meebrlee-
Ritt *will* call when he drops us out, and he *will* expect
an answer, and he *will not* expect you to be still
covered with blood and half hidden in ripped-up armor.
Home is an eighteen- to twenty-day trip, they said. Ten
to go, call it three in hyperspace."

The Kzin was tearing into a joint of something big.
"Keep talking."

"We need to paint you. Envoy had a smooth face,
no markings except for what looked like black eyebrows
swept *way* up."

"What would you use for paint?"

"The kitchens on some of the Nakamura Lines ships
offered dyes for Easter eggs. Then again, they went
bankrupt. What have we got? Let's check out the
kitchen wall."

Choices aboard *Sraff-Zisht*'s boat were sparse. One
variety of handmeal. Paradoxical's green sludge. Twenty
settings for meat . . . "Fly-By-Night, what *are* these?"

"Ersatz prey from Kzin, I expect. Not bad, just
strange."

They weren't all meat. We had two flavors of blood,
and a milky fluid. "Artificial milk with diet supple-
ments," Fly-By-Night told us, "to treat injuries and
disease. Adults wouldn't normally use it."

Three kinds of fluids. Hot blood— "Is one of these
human?"

"I wouldn't know, and that's one damn rude question to ask someone you have to live with—"

"I'm sorry. What I—"

"—for the next nine to ten days. If I get through this they'll *have* to give me a name."

"I just want to know if it coagulates."

Silence. Then, "Intelligent question. I've been on edge, Mart."

I didn't say that Kzinti are born that way. "Ease up on the cappuccino."

"We should thicken this. Mix it with something floury. Mush up a handmeal?"

The handmeals would pull apart. We worked with the layers: a meatlike pâté, a vegetable pâté, something cheesy, shells of hard bread. The bread stayed too lumpy: no good. Cheese thickened the blood. One kind of blood did coagulate. We got a thick fluid that could be spread into a Kzin's fur, then would get thicker. Milk lightened it enough, but then it stayed too liquid. More cheese?

We covered Fly-By-Night in patches everywhere, except his face, which we didn't want to mess up yet. This latest batch looked good where we'd spread it on his belly. I gave him a crossed fingers sign and worked it into his face.

Not bad.

We tried undiluted blood for the eyebrows. Too pale. Work on that later. I stood back and asked, "Paradoxical?"

"The marks weren't symmetrical," Paradoxical said. "You tend to want him to look too human. They're not eyebrows. Trail that right one almost straight up—"

"You'd better do it."

He worked. Presently he asked, "Mart?"

"Good!"

That was all Fly-By-Night needed. He set us spinning as he jumped for the waterfall room. We gave him an hour to dry off, because the shower blanket didn't suck up all the water, and another to calm down. Then we started over.

We couldn't get the eyebrows dark enough.

Finally we opened up a heating element in the kitchen wall, hoping we wouldn't ruin anything, and used it to char one of Envoy's ears. We used the carbon black to darken Fly-By-Night's "eyebrows." We bandaged one ear ("exploded by vacuum.")

Then we made him wait, and talk.

"*Sraff-Zisht* drops back into Einstein space. There's an alarm. Do we get a few minutes? Does Meebrlee-Ritt clean himself up before he shows himself? Does he want a nap?"

"I was not raised among the children of the Patriarch."

"He's dropped us out in the inner comets. That's a huge volume. He's not worried about any stray ship that happens along, but he might want to check on *us*. He still has to worry that the big bad telepath has murdered his crew. Fly-By-Night? Massacres are routine?"

"Duels, I think, and riots. Mart, the cleanup routines are very simple. Any surviving crew with a surviving fingertip could set them going."

"Meebrlee-Ritt calls. Right away?"

"He will set a course into Home system. Then he will make himself gorgeous. Let the lesser Kzinti wait. Count on forty minutes after we enter Einstein space."

"Stet. He calls. Envoy's all cleaned up. Big bandage on his ear. What is Envoy's attitude?"

Fly-By-Night let his claws show. Kzinti do sweat, but we'd cooled the cabin. His makeup was holding. "Half mad from sensory deprivation, still he must cringe

before his alpha officer. Repress rage. Meebrlee-Ritt
might enjoy that. Change orders just to shake up
Envoy."

"Cringe," I said.

Fly-By-Night pulled himself lower in his chair. His
ear flattened, his lips were tight together.

"Good. Envoy wouldn't *eat* in front of Meebrlee-
Ritt—?"

"No!"

"Our makeup wouldn't stand up to that."

"No, and I promise not to eat the makeup!"

We kept him talking. I wanted to see how long the
makeup would last. I wanted to see if he'd go berserk. A little berserk wouldn't hurt, in a Kzin who had
been trapped in sensory deprivation for many days, but
he had to remember his lines.

Three hours later . . . *he* didn't crack, but the makeup
started to. We sent him off to get clean.

Morning of the ninth day. I couldn't stop chatter-
ing.

"We'll drop out of hyperspace at the edge of Home
system. We almost know when. There is only one speed
in hyperdrive—" though Quantum Two hyperdrive is
hugely faster and belongs to another species. "If *Sraff-
Zisht* has been traveling straight toward Home at three
days to the light-year, we'll drop out in . . ."

"Four hours and ten minutes," Paradoxical said.

"The jigger factor is, *where* does Meebrlee-Ritt drop
us out? Hyperdrive takes "flat" space. If there are
masses around to distort space, the ship's gone. Pilots
are *very* careful not to get too close to their target sun.
Really cautious types aim *past* a target system. Just what
kind of pilot is Meebrlee-Ritt?"

"Your pronunciation is terrible," said Fly-By-Night.

"Yah?"

"Crazy Kzin. Dive straight in. Cut the hyperdrive ten ce'meters short of death. Let our intrinsic velocity carry us straight into the system. Mart, that is the only decent bet."

"Where is Packer? *Still* in the waterfall?"

"I will think of something."

"I want you in makeup two hours early."

"No."

"H—"

"*Yes*, he might drop out short! But he might circle! He might enter Home system at an angle. Our window of opportunity has to slop over on either side." Fly-By-Night's speech was turning mushy again, lips pulling far back, *lots* of gleaming white teeth. Even Envoy didn't look like that. Sheathclaws must have good dental hygiene.

"We *know* that he will not show himself to Envoy and Packer after nine days of letting the Blind Spot drive him crazy and ruin his hairdo. You'll have forty minutes to make me beautiful."

"Stet. What next? Decelerate for a week. Drop the boat somewhere, maybe in the asteroids, without changing course. The Home asteroid belt is fairly narrow. Still plenty of room to hide."

"They'll bring you aboard ship just before they drop the boat. Because you're dangerous. Thanks." He'd dialed me up a handmeal. "You're dangerous, so they'll keep you in free fall until the last minute. If we're wrong about that, we could get caught by surprise."

"Bring me aboard? How does that work? Order Envoy and Packer to stun me and pull me through the small lock? We can't *do* that. They're dead!"

"Lure the technology officer in here."

"How?"

"Don't know. Make up a story. Let's just get through dropout without getting caught."

❖   ❖   ❖

A recording spoke. A computer whined, "Dominant Ones, we have returned to the universe. Be patient for star positions."

Paradoxical started the curtain retracting. Stars emerged. I went to the kitchen wall and dialed up what we needed.

The recording reeled off a location based on some easy-to-find stars and clusters. Paradoxical listened intently. "Home system," he said. "We will use the telescope to find better data. Can you do that alone?"

"Yah." We'd practiced. In free fall we were still a bit awkward, but I mixed the basic makeup, then added char to a smaller batch. A bit more? *All?* Ready. "You do the eyebrows, Doc."

"First I will finish this task."

Fly-By-Night held still while I rubbed the food mixture into his facial fur.

Paradoxical said, "Graviton wake indicates a second ship."

"Damn!" Fly-By-Night snarled. I flung myself backward; my seat web caught me.

Paradoxical said, "We find nothing in visible light."

"Don't move your mouth. Aw, Fly-By-Night!" He was in an all-out snarl, trying to talk and failing. Drool made a darker runnel. "If Meebrlee-Ritt saw *that* he wouldn't care *who* you are. Lose the teeth!"

Fly-By-Night relaxed his mouth. "Your extra week is down the toilet, Mart. They're making pickup here and now."

The makeup had stayed liquid. "Paradoxical, give him eyebrows." I brushed out the drool, then settled myself out of camera range. They'd given me the flight controls. Paradoxical on astrogation, Fly-By-Night on weapons.

Paradoxical finished his makeup work and moved out of camera range, fifteen minutes ahead of schedule. I asked, "Shall we talk? Is this second ship just an escort?"

"No. Why make *Sraff-Zisht* conspicuous? Transfer the telepath, then move on to Home. This new ship runs to some outer world, or to Kzin itself—"

Meebrlee-Ritt popped up bigger than life and fourteen minutes early. He demanded, "Envoy, is the telepath well?"

Fly-By-Night flinched, then cringed. "The telepath is healthy, Dominant One. I judge that he is not in his right mind."

"The Jotok? Yourself? Where is Packer?"

"The Jotok amuses themself with a computer. I will welcome medical attention. Packer . . . Dominant One . . . Packer looked on hyperspace."

"He knew better!"

"Envoy" recoiled, then visibly pulled himself together. "Soon or late, Dominant One, every Hero looks. Wealth and a name and the infinite future, if he has sisters and daughters, if he can stay sane. Packer did not. He hides in the waterfall when I let him. Set him in a hunting park soon or he will die."

"That will not be our task. *Leap For Life* will be here soon. Transfer the boat to *Leap For Life*. Haste! No need to take Telepath out of his vacuum refuge. You will be relieved aboard *Leap For Life*."

"Yes, Dominant One!"

"Packer must guard the telepath. The telepath will attack now if ever."

"Yes—"

Meebrlee-Ritt was gone.

"We have it!" Paradoxical projected what he was seeing against the cannon casing.

Still distant, backlit by Apollo, Home's sun, a sphere
nestled in a glowing arc of gamma ray shield, its black
skin broken by holes and projections and tiny windows.
Dots-and-commas script glowed brilliant orange. "We
find heavy graviton wake. That ship is decelerating
hard."

"Built in this century," Fly-By-Night said.

Sraff-Zisht dropped us free.

This was not much of a puzzle. I spun the boat,
aimed at *Leap For Life* and said, "Shoot."

My hair stirred. Fly-By-Night's fur stood up and
rippled. He said, "Done. Doc?"

"The graviton wake is gone. You burned out its
thrusters."

I boosted us to put *Sraff-Zisht* between us and *Leap
For Life*. *Leap For Life* had the weapons, after all. I
set our gun on *Sraff-Zisht* and said, "Again."

"Done. I burned out something."

"Graviton flare," Paradoxical said, just as *Sraff-Zisht*
vanished.

"Meebrlee-Ritt must have tried to return to hyperspace," Fly-By-Night said. "We burned out the hyperdrive. But he still has thrusters!"

I rotated the boat to focus the gun on the immobi-
lized *Leap For Life*. "Projectiles. Shoot it to bits."

Fly-By-Night punched something. We heard the
weapon adjusting, but he didn't shoot. "Why?"

I screamed, "They've got all the weapons, our *shield*
has flown away—"

"Stet." The boat's lone weapon roared. It was right
in the middle of the cabin/cargo hold. The noise was
amazing. The boat recoiled: cabin gravity lurched to
compensate. *Leap For Life* jittered and came apart in
shreds.

"—And *they* don't have the hostages! And now it's
one less tanj thing to worry about."

"Stet, stet, I understand!"

Paradoxical said, "We win."

We looked at the Jotok. He said, "We may report all that has happened, now, via laser broadcast to Home. We fly the boat to Home with our proofs. The law of Home can arrange to retrieve *Odysseus*. With his hyperdrive burned out, Meebrlee-Ritt is trapped in Home system. In the full glare of publicity he must follow the Covenants. He may trade his hostages for some other consideration such as amnesty, but they must be returned. Stet?"

"He's still got my family! But I think we can turn on the cabin futzy gravity now, *if* you don't mind—" I stopped because Meebrlee-Ritt, greatly magnified, was facing Fly-By-Night.

"Some such consideration," he mimicked us. "You look stupid, Telepath, covered with food. Only one consideration can capture my interest! Read my mind if you doubt me. Release my entourage and surrender! The hostages for yourself!"

Fly-By-Night's claw moved. No result showed except for Meebrlee-Ritt's widening eyes, but Fly-By-Night had given him a contracted view. He was seeing all of us.

"Lies! You killed my Heroes? Eeeeerg!" A hair-lifting snarl as Fly-By-Night lifted Packer's ear into view.

It seemed the right moment. I showed Envoy's surviving ear. "We had to use the other."

"Martin Wallace Graynor, you may buy back your hostages and your *life* by putting the telepath into my hands!"

It began to seem that Meebrlee-Ritt was mad. I asked, "Must I subdue him first?"

A killing gape was my answer. I asked, "And where would you take him then, with no hyperdrive?"

"Not your concern."

"We're going to call for help now. Over the next few

hours all of Home system is going to know you're here. A civilized solar system *seethes* with telescopes. If you have allies in the asteroids, you can't go to them. You'd only point them out to the Home Rule."

"What if you never make that broadcast, LE Graynor? And I can . . . thaw . . . sss." He'd had a notion. He stepped out of range. Ducked back and fisheyed the view to show his whole cabin. The other Kzin, Tech, was at his workstation, watching.

A wall slid away. Through an aperture ten yards wide I could see a much bigger cargo hold and all of *Odysseus'* cargo modules. Meebrlee-Ritt moved to one of them, opened a small panel and worked.

Back he came. "I can reset the temperature on these machines. I thought you might wonder, but soon I will show you thawed fish. You cannot do to me what you did to *Leap For Life* without killing my hostages too. If you broadcast any message at all, I will set the third module thawing, and then I will show you thawed dead hostages."

I was sweating.

The Kzin aristocrat said, "Telepath . . . Fly-By-Night. I will give you a better name. Your prowess has earned a name even as an enemy. What is it we ask of you? Take a harem. Raise your sons. See your daughters grow up in the Patriarch's household. A life in luxury buys survival for sixty-four Human citizens.

"Think, then. I can wait. A boat's life support is not the match for an interstellar spacecraft. Or else—"

The mass of an interstellar spacecraft jumped into our faces. Meebrlee-Ritt was tiny in its window, huge in the hologram stage. He threw his head back, a prolonged screech, mouth gaping as wide as my head. Forced his mouth to close so he could ask, "Graynor, have you ever flown a spacecraft? Do you think you have the skill to keep me from ramming you?"

I said, "Yes. Space is roomy, and the telepath is *our* hostage. Doc, can you give me a deep-radar view of yon privateer?"

Paradoxical guessed what I meant. The mass outside our dome went transparent.

I looked it over. Fuel . . . more fuel . . . a bulky hyperdrive design from the last century. Gravity and reaction motors were also big and bulky. Skimpy cargo space, smaller cabin, and that tiny box shape must be a waterfall room just like ours.

I spun the boat. "You say I can't shoot?"

Meebrlee-Ritt looked up. He must have been looking right into our gun. "Pitiful! Are all Humans natural liars?"

Fine-tuning my aim, I said, "There *is* a thing you should know about us. If you eat prey that is infested . . . *whasht-meery* . . . you may be very sick, but it doesn't kill off your whole blood line. Shoot," I said to Fly-By-Night.

The gun roared. Meebrlee-Ritt's image whirled around. The boat recoiled: gravity imbalances swirled through my belly. In our deep-radar view the waterfall room became a smudge.

Then *Sraff-Zisht* was gone.

"We track him," Paradoxical said. "Gravitons, heavily accelerating, *there.*"

A green circle on the sky marked nothing but stars, but I spun the boat to put cross hairs on it. "Electromagnetic," I shouted.

"Am I a fool?" The gun grumbled, shifting from projectile mode.

"Graviton wake has stopped."

Fly-By-Night cried, "I have not fired!"

I said, "He's got no hyperdrive—"

Paradoxical said, "Gravitons again. He will ram."

The room wobbled, my hair stood on end, Fly-By-

Night fluffed out into a great orange puffball. "Graviton wake is gone," Paradoxical said.

I moved us, thirty gee lateral, in case his aim was good.

Sraff-Zisht, falling free, shot past us by two miles. I chased it down. Whim made me zip in alongside the ship's main window. Grinning like a Kzin, I screamed, *"Now* wait us out!"

In the hologram stage Meebrlee-Ritt hugged a stack of meteor patches while he pulled on the waterfall door. Vacuum inside would be holding the door shut. We could see Tech working his way into a pressure suit, but Meebrlee-Ritt hadn't thought of that yet. He turned to look at the camera, at us.

He cringed. Down on his belly, face against the floor.

Paradoxical set our com laser on Home. The light-speed lag was several hours, so I just recorded a help call and sent it. Then, as we'd have to anyway, we three began recording the whole story. That too would arrive before we could—

Tech stood above Meebrlee-Ritt, watching us. When Fly-By-Night looked at him he cringed, a formal crouch. "Dominant One, what must we do?"

Fly-By-Night said, "Tend your cargo until you can be towed to Home. Meebrlee-Ritt also I place in your charge. Set your screamer and riding lights so you can be found. You may dream of betrayal but do not act on it. You know what I am. I know *who* you are. Your hostages' lives will buy back your blood line."

He'd said he couldn't read minds. I still think he was bluffing.

A century ago the new settlers had towed a moonlet from elsewhere into geosynchronous orbit around Home. Home Base was where incoming ships arrived, and where they thawed incoming Ice Class passengers.

The law had business with hijackers and kidnappers; we were their witnesses. We were the system's ongoing news item. Media and the law were waiting.

I rapidly judged that anchorpersons and lawyers were my fate. The only way to hide myself was to sign with Home Information Megacorp and talk my head off until my public grew bored.

If Carlos Wu tried to call me they'd be all over him too. I hoped he'd wait it out.

Sraff-Zisht we had left falling free through Home system. Home Rule had to round up ships to bring it back. It took two of their own, four Belters acting for the bounty, and one shared by a media consortium, all added to the several they sent after *Odysseus*. It took them ten days to fetch *Sraff-Zisht*.

For eight days I was questioned by Home and ARM law and by LE Wilyama Warbelow, the anchor from Home Information Megacorp. Wilyama was wired for multisensory recording. What she experienced became immortal.

They'd wanted to do that to me too.

The last two days were a lull: I was able to more or less relax, and even see a bit of the captured asteroid. Then *Sraff-Zisht* descended on tethers to Home Base, and everybody wanted Mart Graynor.

The Covenant against sensory deprivation as torture has long since been interpreted as the right to immediate trial, not just for Kzinti but throughout human space, a right not to be evaded. I was to submit to questioning by Meebrlee-Ritt and Tech, by their lawyer and everyone else's, while two hundred Ice Class passengers were being thawed elsewhere.

I screamed my head off. Cameras were on me. The law bent. When they thawed the hostages from *Sraff-Zisht*, I was there to watch.

My wife and child weren't there.

And we all trooped off to use the holo wall in the Outbound Enterprises Boardroom.

The prisoners watched us from an unknown site. It didn't seem likely they'd burst through the holo wall and rip us apart. Meebrlee-Ritt's eyes glittered. Tech only watched.

The court had restricted the factions to one advocate each. All I had for company were Sirhan, a police commissioner from Home Rule; Judge Anita Dee; Handel, an ARM lawyer; Barrister, a runty Kzin assigned as advocate to the prisoners; a hugely impressive peach-colored Kzin, Rasht-Myowr, representing the Patriarch; and anchorperson Wilyama Warbelow.

Judge Dee told the prisoners, "You are each and together accused of violations of local law in two systems, and of the Covenants of 2505 at Fafnir. A jury will observe and decide your fate."

LE Barrister spoke quickly. "You may not be compelled to speak nor to answer questions, and I advise against it. I am to speak for you. Your trial will take at least two days, as we must wait for other witnesses, but no more than four."

Meebrlee-Ritt spoke in Interworld. "We have followed the Covenants. Where are my accusers?"

They all looked at me. I said, "Gone."

"Gone?"

"Fly-By-Night and Paradoxical and I signed an exclusive contract with Home Information Megacorp for our stories. I got a room here at Home Base. They'll thaw my family here, after all." If they lived. "We gave LE Warbelow," I nodded; the anchor bowed, "an hour's interview, presumed to be the first of many. Fly-By-Night and Paradoxical transferred to a shuttle. The Patriarch's representative missed them by just under two hours. They disappeared on the way down."

I've never doubted their destination. Fly-By-Night had come to Home for a reason, and he never told anyone *who* had arranged their transport to Fafnir.

The law raised hell, as if it were my fault they were gone. Warbelow was more sensible. She paid for my room, a major expense that wasn't in our contract. With the aliens gone, I had become the only game in town.

They got their money's worth. Mart Graynor emerged as a braggart with a Fafnir accent I'd practiced for two years. I played the same tune while various lawyers and law programs questioned me. I hoped nobody would see a resemblance to documentaries once made by Beowulf Shaeffer.

Barrister reacted theatrically. "Gone! Then who is witness against my clients?"

"We have LE Graynor, Your Honor," Sirhan said, speaking for Home Rule, "and the crew and passengers of *Odysseus* will be called. *Odysseus* had to be chased down in the Kuiper belt, the inner comets, and towed in. They'll be arriving tomorrow. Any of the passengers might press claims against the defendants."

The judge said, "LE Handel?"

The ARM rep said, "The Longest War threatens all of human space. We need what these Kzinti can tell us. They've violated the Covenants. There was clear intent to store humans as reserves of meat—"

"This was a local act against Homer citizens!" Sirhan said.

Judge Dee gestured at the big peach-colored Kzin, who said, "The Patriarch's claim is that Meebrlee-Ritt is no relative of his and has no claim to his name. I am to take possession—"

Meebrlee-Ritt leapt at us, bounced back from the wall— or from a projection screen—and screamed something prolonged. "I flew outside the universe!" said my translator. "Who can do that? Only the -Ritt! In cowardice does the Patriarch disclaim my part in the Long War!" He changed to Interworld: "LE Graynor knows! Nine days through hyperspace, accurately to my rendezvous!"

"I am to take possession and return him for trial, and his Heroes too. I must have Envoy's ear, Graynor, unless you can establish a kill. Nameless One, Kzinti elsewhere can fly hyperspace. Females of your line may have reached the -Ritt harem. What of it?"

"My line descends from the Patriarch! I violated no Covenants!"

The runty Kzin who was his advocate caught the judge's eye. He too spoke Interworld. "To properly represent the prisoners I must speak with them alone and encrypted to learn their wishes. I expect we will fight extradition. Rasht-Myowr," a prolonged howl in the Heroes' Tongue. The Patriarch's designate was trying to loom over him. My translator buzzed static. The runty Kzin waited, staring him down, until the big one stepped back and sheathed his claws.

Barrister said, "Violation of the Covenants would hold my clients here in any case, but none of these claims has any force until we can interview the victims. *Odysseus'* crew and passengers will reach Home Base tomorrow. We have only LE Graynor's word for any of this."

"He's telling the truth, though," I said.

Meebrlee-Ritt barked his triumph. The ARM man said, "Futz, Graynor!"

Judge Dee asked, "LE Graynor, are you familiar with the Covenants of 2505?"

"As much as any law program. I've examined them half to death."

"Did you see violations?"

"No. I thought I had. I thought Packer must have

shot out *Odysseus'* hyperdrive and hyperwave, putting *Odysseus* at unacceptable risk, but it's clear he didn't. Hyperdrive got *Odysseus* into the Home comets, and they called ahead via hyperwave as soon as they were out of the Nursery Nebula."

Rasht-Myowr's tail slashed across and back. "Your other claims fail! The false lord is mine, and his remaining Hero too!"

I said, "Whatever these two learned about Fly-By-Night and his companions, taking them back to Kzin for trial gives that to the Patriarch. On that basis I'd keep them, if I was an ARM."

"But you're testifying," the ARM said bitterly, "that they didn't violate the Covenants."

"Yah."

"Mine! And Envoy's ear," Rasht-Myowr said. "His *one* ear. Did you kill him?"

"I killed them both. Do you need details? Fly-By-Night was trapped in his vac refuge. We'd just rounded Turnpoint Star and Envoy was flying the ship. Difficult work, took his full attention. Back turned, free fall, crash web holding him in his chair. I had Fly-By-Night's w'tsai." The police had already confiscated that. "He would have killed me if he'd released his crash web in time."

"He would have killed you anyway! Why would you keep only one ear?"

For an instant I couldn't speak at all. Then I barely remembered my accent. "I h-heated one for charcoal to paint Fly-By-Night. Packer was wrestling Fly-By-Night when I chopped *him* up, so Fly-By-Night got the ear. He chewed off the other one. They stole, *you* stole my wife and child and unborn, my *harem*, you *whasht-meery* son of a stray cat! I still haven't seen them alive. I memorized those *whasht-meery* Covenants. They only forbid my killing your relatives!"

"Duel me then!" Meebrlee-Ritt shouted. "Back turned, crash web locked, free fall, my claws only, *blunt* them if you like—"

"Barrister, you will silence your client or I will," the judge said.

"—And you armed! Prove you can do this!"

Meebrlee-Ritt, I decided, was trying to commit suicide. He didn't want to go with Rasht-Myowr. Let the Patriarch have him, I owed him nothing.

Almost nothing.

I said, "Judge Dee, if you'll let me ask a few questions, I may solve some problems here."

"You came to *be* questioned, LE Graynor. What did you have in mind?"

"Rasht-Myowr, if a violation of the Covenants can't be proved, then I take it these prisoners are yours—"

Judge Dee interposed. "They may be assessed for *substantial* property violations, Graynor. Rescue costs. A passenger ship turned to junk!"

"I will pay the costs," Rasht-Myowr said.

I asked, "You'll take them back to your Patriarch?"

"Yah."

"They'll be tried publicly, of course."

The peach-colored Kzin considered, then said, "Of course."

"The court will have a telepath to question him? They always do."

"Rrr. Your point?"

"Would you let a telepath find out what Meebrlee-Ritt saw of the telepaths of Sheathclaws? And learn how they live? *Really?*"

He didn't get it. I said, "Three hundred years living alongside Humans. Sharing their culture. Their schooling programs. Instead of theft and killing, hang gliding! Meebrlee-Ritt, tell him about Fly-By-Night."

The prisoner looked at the Patriarch's voice. He said, "I crawled on my belly for him."

Rasht-Myowr yowled. "With the -Ritt name on you? How dare you?"

"I meant it."

"Meant—?"

"Do you think I was born with no pride, to take and defend a name like mine? I found I could fly the Outsider hyperdrive! I knew that I must be a -Ritt. Then fortune favored me again. A telepath lost on Shasht, healthy and arrogant, the genetic line that will give us the Longest War!

"Even after questioning, crippled, Nazi Killer tore up one of my unwary Heroes so that we had to leave him. He *knew* things about me . . . but Nazi Killer was no threat. Frustrating that we had to kill him, but he'd told us how to retrieve another. It was Fly-By-Night and his slaves who stripped me of everything I am! He killed my Heroes. He *became* Envoy! Reduced my ship to a falling prison."

Rasht-Myowr demanded, "Technical Officer, is your alpha officer mad?"

Tech spoke simply; his dignity was still with him. "I followed the telepath's commands exactly. What he had done to us, to him I followed, how could *I* face him? With what weapons? But Fly-By-Night was not alone. Kzin and 'man and Jotok, *they* took our ears."

I hoped then that there were unseen defenses, that nobody would have set fragile humans undefended among these Kzinti. Rasht-Myowr turned on me a gaping grin that would not let him speak. His alien stench was not that of any creature of Earth, but I knew it was his rage.

"You can't take them back to the Patriarchy," I said to Rasht-Myowr. Because they had kept faith.

✧   ✧   ✧

Quickpony and the Van Zild children were with me when Outbound Enterprises thawed two modules of passengers taken from *Odysseus*. The way they were wrapped, I couldn't tell who was who until Jeena was wheeled out of the cooker. We clung to each other and waited. If Jeena was alive, so was her mother.

We waited, ice in our veins, and she came.